PRAISE FOR

RED, WHITE, AND BLOOD

"Christopher Farnsworth's premise—that the presidents of the United States have, starting with Andrew Johnson, had a vampire at their beck and call—is simply fun. And in Farnsworth's strongest book yet in the Nathaniel Cade series, Cade encounters an old enemy he's killed over and over in various guises . . . none other than the Boogeyman. The ingenious part of the book (using various notorious serial killers and their quotes to confirm the existence of such a creature) is—well, I'm envious. Cade continues to be one of modern literature's most frightening vampires, and this is an excellent read."

—Charlaine Harris, #1 *New York Times* bestselling author

"[A] high-octane . . . supernatural thriller . . . Farnsworth keeps the twists and explosive violence coming, keeping readers in suspense until the very last page."

—*Publishers Weekly*

"Farnsworth's universe of vampires and otherworldly creatures comes alive." —*Kirkus Reviews*

continued . . .

THE PRESIDENT'S VAMPIRE

"Thrilling . . . Events build to a cinematic showdown . . . The conclusion will leave the reader breathless and wondering what horrors the future holds." —*Publishers Weekly*

"There are plenty of chills and thrills . . . Readers who enjoy adventure with a compelling cast of characters will enjoy this clever, witty sequel to *Blood Oath.*" —*Library Journal*

"If you like your thrillers with a bit of bite, look no further than *The President's Vampire.*" —*Seattle Post-Intelligencer*

"A heady, fast-paced (albeit gory) read and a good second entry in Farnsworth's Nathaniel Cade series . . . Visually rich vignettes are packed with action and lead like a chain of violent beads along the threads of the story line. Humor and humanity flash briefly against the grim backdrop, providing breaks from the increasing tension and creating a thriller with dimension, texture and a sharp sense of reality."

—*Fresh Fiction*

"Fans will be hooked by this exhilarating thriller that makes a vampire and human and monstrous terrorists seem real. Fast-paced and loaded with action, the story line never allows a respite as even President Curtis needs two cigarettes. Urban fantasy fans will relish what is turning into one of the best series the sub-genre has to offer." —*Alternative Worlds*

"Once again political conspiracies and the supernatural meet in an explosive fashion in *The President's Vampire* . . . A hugely entertaining novel. It combines the best aspects of the action-driven thriller with the supernatural and gains enough substance to become greater than the sum of its parts . . . This fast-paced supernatural thriller is jam-packed with dangerous monsters and bloody violence and is a superior example of just how good this genre can be." —*Love Vampires*

BLOOD OATH

"This action-filled debut by scriptwriter Farnsworth reads like a cross between P. N. Elrod's historical vampire adventures and Thomas Greanias's conspiracy thrillers."

—*Publishers Weekly*

"Don't think of Mr. Farnsworth's debut thriller as the umpteenth vampire knockoff on the market. Think of it as the inventive one in which a brave young White House staff member asks, 'You really expect me to believe we've got a vampire on a leash, and we can just send him after terrorists and spies whenever we want?' Multibook series and $200 million movie franchises have been built on a lot less."

—*The New York Times*

"Christopher Farnsworth's taut thriller . . . is an irresistible page-turner . . . a complex and unnervingly realistic tale in which vampire Nathaniel Cade, a Secret Service agent sworn to protect the president, is far less of a monster than his human colleagues at the CIA and FBI . . . Dazzlingly clever."

—*The Washington Post*

"Farnsworth's series debut asks the reader to set aside disbelief and buy into this premise, among other more fantastic concepts, and it's almost easily done with his adept writing style."

—*Library Journal*

"The two key elements that make *Blood Oath* an entertaining espionage paranormal thriller are the clever intermingling of history with the supernatural . . . and [a] plot [that] never takes itself seriously." —*Alternative Worlds*

continued . . .

"*Blood Oath* is exactly how I like my presidential thrillers. With vampires." —Brad Meltzer, author of *The Inner Circle*

"The vampire novel that finally gets it right. Christopher Farnsworth has done his homework in places where most writers wouldn't even know to look—and the result is a rollicking tale of the supernatural grounded in some of the true oddities of American history. If Dan Brown wrote a vampire thriller, this would be it." —Mitch Horowitz, author of *Occult America*

"As someone who thinks Stoker's *Dracula* has never been bettered, and who would happily stick a stake through the heart of most modern vampire fiction, it almost pains me to say how much I enjoyed *Blood Oath.* Witty, exciting and compulsively readable, with a central character who seems destined to become a favorite of both skeptics and true blood believers, this may just be the best debut vampire novel in many years."
—John Connolly, *New York Times* bestselling author of *The Wrath of Angels*

TITLES BY CHRISTOPHER FARNSWORTH

Blood Oath

The President's Vampire

Red, White, and Blood

RED, WHITE, AND BLOOD

CHRISTOPHER FARNSWORTH

JOVE BOOKS, NEW YORK

THE BERKLEY PUBLISHING GROUP
Published by the Penguin Group
Penguin Group (USA) Inc.
375 Hudson Street, New York, New York 10014, USA
Penguin Group (Canada), 90 Eglinton Avenue East, Suite 700, Toronto, Ontario M4P 2Y3, Canada (a division of Pearson Penguin Canada Inc.) • Penguin Books Ltd., 80 Strand, London WC2R 0RL, England • Penguin Group Ireland, 25 St. Stephen's Green, Dublin 2, Ireland (a division of Penguin Books Ltd.) • Penguin Group (Australia), 250 Camberwell Road, Camberwell, Victoria 3124, Australia (a division of Pearson Australia Group Pty. Ltd.) • Penguin Books India Pvt. Ltd., 11 Community Centre, Panchsheel Park, New Delhi—110 017, India • Penguin Group (NZ), 67 Apollo Drive, Rosedale, Auckland 0632, New Zealand (a division of Pearson New Zealand Ltd.) • Penguin Books (South Africa) (Pty.) Ltd., 24 Sturdee Avenue, Rosebank, Johannesburg 2196, South Africa

Penguin Books Ltd., Registered Offices: 80 Strand, London WC2R 0RL, England

This is a work of fiction. Names, characters, places, and incidents either are the product of the author's imagination or are used fictitiously, and any resemblance to actual persons, living or dead, business establishments, events, or locales is entirely coincidental. The publisher does not have control over and does not have any responsibility for author or third-party websites or their content.

RED, WHITE, AND BLOOD

A Jove Book / published by arrangement with the author

PUBLISHING HISTORY
G. P. Putnam's Sons hardcover edition / April 2012
Jove premium edition / December 2012

Copyright © 2012 by Christopher Farnsworth
Cover photos: (STCA-0817) Man Walking © Stephen Carroll/Arcangel-images; (RB-2151) Gate © Roy Bishop/Arcangel-images; Capitol Building © Konstantin L/Shutterstock.
Cover design by Richard Hasselberger.
Text design by Kristine del Rosario.

All rights reserved.
No part of this book may be reproduced, scanned, or distributed in any printed or electronic form without permission. Please do not participate in or encourage piracy of copyrighted materials in violation of the author's rights. Purchase only authorized editions.
For information, address: The Berkley Publishing Group,
a division of Penguin Group (USA) Inc.,
375 Hudson Street, New York, New York 10014.

ISBN: 978-0-515-15303-3

JOVE®
Jove Books are published by The Berkley Publishing Group,
a division of Penguin Group (USA) Inc.,
375 Hudson Street, New York, New York 10014.
JOVE® is a registered trademark of Penguin Group (USA) Inc.
The "J" design is a trademark of Penguin Group (USA) Inc.

PRINTED IN THE UNITED STATES OF AMERICA

10 9 8 7 6 5 4 3 2 1

If you purchased this book without a cover, you should be aware that this book is stolen property. It was reported as "unsold and destroyed" to the publisher, and neither the author nor the publisher has received any payment for this "stripped book."

To Marv,

who started being my dad long before he married my mom.

Thanks.

An election is a moral horror, as bad as a battle except for the blood.

—George Bernard Shaw

RED,
WHITE,
AND
BLOOD

PROLOGUE

June 23, 1975, Ojai, California

Jenny straddled Tom's lap in the backseat, her tongue deep in his mouth. The Eagles wailed on the radio. He lifted his hands under her blouse to her breasts. She ground herself into his crotch and he let out a groan. Tom's erection threatened to tear through the zipper of his pants. They'd been here so many times before. He knew he'd have to stop soon.

Tom and Jenny came to the overlook near the creek bridge every night now. They didn't even make a pretense of going to the movies or out for a burger. Just hours of dry humping and kissing before curfew. Then Jenny, as if an alarm clock went off in her head, would pull back and rearrange her clothes, put her bra back on, and tell him to start driving home.

Tom thought he'd explode if this kept up much longer,

but he forced himself to stay patient. As frustrated as he got, Jenny was the hottest chick he'd ever seen, let alone touched. Unlike most seventeen-year-old guys, he could be a little patient. Tom wasn't about to blow this chance.

She moaned and ground harder. Tom's eyes crossed under his closed lids. She broke away for a moment, both of them gasping for air.

"We should stop," he managed to choke out.

She reared back from him. Her mouth spread into a grin. "Fuck that," she said, and laughed. With one swift move, her blouse was off and over her head. "Fuck *me*," she said to Tom.

He didn't have to be told twice. His pants became a ball on the floor of the Buick. She shimmied out of her own tight jeans and underwear, and then pulled him on top of her again. God, they were both naked, this was really going to happen, they were really about to *do it* . . .

Tom hesitated.

"What?" Jenny said. "I swear to God, if you tell me you don't have a rubber—"

Tom tried to look out the window. It was totally steamed over by their breathing.

"I thought I heard something."

She smiled at him. She thought he was stalling. "You don't have to be nervous. I want to do this. Really."

"So do I," he said. He thought he heard the sound again. Like something swishing through the tall grass at the side of the road.

"You didn't hear that?"

She shook her head. "You're not scared of the Char-Man, are you?"

They both laughed. The Char-Man was an old story, passed along from senior to freshman at Nordhoff High. Supposedly some guy was caught in a big fire back in the '40s, and had gone insane from his hideous burns. Now he lurked in the woods near the bridge and attacked anyone foolish enough to be caught out after dark. It was a joke. Nothing more.

Sure, bodies had turned up over the years. A couple kids from school went missing. And yes, a few weeks ago, there was that story in the paper about the dead hitchhiker by the bridge. But bad stuff happened. Everyone said the same thing—"The Char-Man got them." But they smirked when they said it.

Tom looked at her. This was what he'd wanted for so long. What was he waiting for?

"I'm not scared," he said.

She smiled and leaned back a little. He could see everything. Jesus, she was beautiful.

All Tom could think was, Oh man oh man oh man oh man.

Then there was the terrible scraping noise of metal on metal.

Tom and Jenny both turned toward the sound in time to see the door of Tom's Buick peeled away like the pop-top of a beer can.

A huge man stood framed in the weak glow of the dome light. He only stood there a split second, but Tom knew he would never be able to erase the image from his mind. A full-sized ax looked like a toy hatchet in one of his hands. His clothes were ragged leather, sewn together in irregular patches. And the smell—the smell was like a sewer below a slaughterhouse. It hit them like a physical slap.

Worst of all was his face: skin hanging on the skull in long yellowish drips, like wax melted and left to cool in place, crisscrossed with blackened scabs that oozed fresh blood.

The Char-Man. He was real.

Tom had no time to recover from the shock. The Char-Man's hand darted into the car, impossibly quick, and yanked Jenny from the backseat. She fell on the ground.

Tom could hear her screaming. His own mouth was open and his throat was raw. He realized he'd been screaming the whole time too. He scuttled back as far as he could into the corner of the seat.

The Char-Man roared with frustration and reared out of the open door. A second later, the blade of the ax bit through the roof of the car directly above Tom's head. It began to move, drawn back through the metal and upholstery like a knife. The Char-Man was literally slicing the roof open to get to Tom.

His eyes darted out the open door. He saw Jenny, frozen with shock.

He managed to form a single word. "Run!" he screamed.

That broke her from her daze. She got to her feet, tripped, fell, and got up again.

Tom heard the tortured metal of the car give way. The roof was suddenly open to the night sky, distant stars completely oblivious to what was going on beneath them. A shadow blotted them out as the hideous shape loomed above him. Tom's eyes darted involuntarily back to Jenny, who barely seemed to be moving at all. She had just made the edge of the road when Tom heard the grunt from above.

The Char-Man had seen her, too. If it was possible to read that melted nightmare of a face, Tom saw frustration. The Char-Man was not about to lose one of his victims.

Tom saw the Char-Man lift the ax and cock it back over his shoulder. He knew what was coming next. He tried to yell, but the blade flew before Tom could draw a breath.

It spun end-over-end in a perfect spiral toward the back of Jenny's head.

As if she could sense it coming, Jenny turned and looked. Tom saw tears streaming from her eyes as the ax whirled like a rotor through the dark.

Then, out of nowhere, a hand snatched it from midair.

For a moment, everything stopped. Tom and Jenny went silent. The Char-Man stood like a statue. They all looked at the man who had not been there only a second earlier.

He didn't seem much older than Tom. He was just a guy in a cheap suit. He certainly didn't seem anywhere near as powerful as the Char-Man. But he wasn't afraid.

Tom could see one unusual thing about him: he wore, under the open throat of his shirt collar, a metal cross that glinted in the moonlight. It was so at odds with the rest of his outfit and his square haircut.

The young man looked at the ax, then at the Char-Man, and finally broke the awful silence.

"You dropped this," he said. "By all means, have it back."

He hurled the ax. It spun through the air even faster than before, a pinwheeling blur that ruffled Tom's hair.

He seemed to hear the impact seconds after it must have happened. A deep, hollow *thunk*—as if the ax hit wood rather than bone and meat.

The Char-Man stared at the ax lodged deep into the space between his eyes. Then he toppled over.

Hands grabbed Tom. He was being hustled from the car by someone else—another man, not so young, wearing a suit as well. Clearly a plainclothes cop, Tom thought, despite the shaggy sideburns. The guy pulled a gun from a shoulder rig, and that was all the confirmation Tom needed.

"Come on, kid, move," the cop said. "We've got to get out of here."

Tom realized they were jogging toward the young man and Jenny. The man had given Jenny his coat.

"But—wait, what's going on?" Tom wanted to know what was happening. Why were they running? "What about my car?"

They reached Jenny. The cop was still hustling them toward the road. A car waited there, exhaust puffing from the tailpipe.

The young man gave Tom a look that chilled him as deeply as the sight of the Char-Man. "Answers later," he said. "Move now."

"Who are you?" Tom asked.

"Shut up and get in the damn car," the cop ordered, and Tom and Jenny complied. They piled into the backseat. The young man stood by the passenger side while the cop got behind the wheel.

Just as he put the car into drive, the engine died. The sudden quiet lay over them like a shroud.

"Ah, damn," the cop said. He jerked at the shifter and tried to restart the car.

The young man stood by the door, watching the spot where the Char-Man lay. "Too late now," he said. "I'll handle this."

"I can get it," the cop said as he turned the key. He put his whole arm into the motion, as if he could hand-crank the engine back to life.

"No, you can't," the young man said. "It always works like this. The engine always stops. The phone is always dead. The police always go to the wrong address. It's just the way the world is around him."

"What are you talking about?" Tom demanded. "He's dead. We're safe now, right?"

A bellow of rage answered him. Tom looked over at the body by his ruined car.

Slowly, the Char-Man rose, the ax still deep in his skull.

"God damn it," the cop said.

"Don't blaspheme," the young man said.

Tom was speechless. Jenny just kept saying, "No, no, no, no, no," over and over.

With one hand, the Char-Man gripped the handle of the

ax. A firm yank, and it came loose. His face was now split in half. Tom could see the wound filling with blood, the skin dripping over it already. In a moment, it would be one more scar among many.

The cop had his gun up. He turned to the young man, who stood waiting. "You sure about this, Cade?"

The Char-Man advanced on them one slow, confident step at a time.

The young man—Cade, the older guy called him—smiled. "Looking forward to it."

Tom turned to face him. He was about to ask if the guy was out of his fucking mind. You'd need a tank— Hell, you'd need an army to kill that thing.

But he stopped before any of that could leave his mouth.

He saw teeth. Not teeth. Fangs.

Cade wasn't human, any more than the Char-Man. They were both something other.

Cade moved. Tom blinked, and he was gone—there was a puff of dust on the ground, and then he was on the Char-Man. Together, they hit Tom's car hard enough to crumple the frame.

The cop stepped out of the driver's seat and opened the back door. He waved impatiently to Jenny and Tom. "We need to run," he said.

Tom and Jenny were still moving like molasses. Their bare feet hit asphalt. It was like they couldn't get their bodies to respond. They couldn't stop looking at the Char-Man. Tom didn't know why everything seemed so goddamn slow.

The cop tried to pull them along. Jenny wouldn't

budge. "We can't just leave him," Jenny said. There were more sounds from the fight—awful, inhuman sounds.

Tom looked back. Cade didn't look like he was winning. The Char-Man swung the ax at his head, driving him back toward Tom's car and the edge of the overlook. A few more steps and he'd be backed up against empty air.

Cade stepped toward Tom's car rather than closer to the ravine. The move cost him. The Char-Man took a big chunk of flesh from the side of Cade's ribs.

Cade curled in pain. His back was exposed to the Char-Man, his arms against the car for support.

The Char-Man lifted his ax with both hands and prepared to deliver the final blow.

"We really should have run," the cop said.

The ax fell like a meteor from the sky.

Tom heard something. He realized what it was later. But he saw the fanged smile again and he knew that the Char-Man had been fooled just as they had.

Cade spun, impossibly fast again, and got under the hulk of the Char-Man. Unbalanced, falling forward, the Char-Man was helpless as Cade lifted him up into the air.

Right over the door post of the car, jagged and exposed from where the Char-Man had torn back the roof.

The Char-Man landed with a sickening noise. The door post tore through his abdomen, pinning him like an insect in a shoe-box diorama.

It didn't kill him.

He wriggled and struggled. Tom realized the Char-Man was trying to get a handhold or foothold so he could push himself up and off the metal that impaled him.

But Cade would not give him the time or the chance.

Cade was already at the front of Tom's car, pushing as hard as he could. The car moved. Tom had set the emergency brake. It snapped under the strain.

The wheels rolled freely after that. Driven by nothing more than Cade, Tom's car began rolling toward the edge of the overlook.

The Char-Man seemed to realize what was happening. He doubled his efforts. He began to turn, to try to tear the door post through his side rather than pull himself off it.

He almost made it.

Then Cade sent the car over the edge and down into the ravine.

Tom didn't know why, but he had to see what happened next. Without thinking, he ran to the edge of the overlook.

The car bounced once on the rocks and crumpled. Then it rolled over, crushing the Char-Man before it slipped into the water and vanished.

Cade stood there for a long moment. Tom realized Jenny and the cop were both right next to him. They all watched the surface of the water.

Nothing. Not so much as a bubble.

"Is he dead?" Jenny asked.

Cade seemed to ignore her. "Try the car," he told the cop.

The cop walked back to the road. Tom heard the engine start like it was still on a showroom floor.

"Dead enough," Cade said to Jenny. "For now."

They all drove back to town together. Jenny kept Cade's

coat, and the cop—he said his name was Griff—found a dusty blanket in the trunk for Tom.

They dropped the teenagers off at the local hospital with a good-enough cover story: Tom and Jenny had parked on the overlook without setting the brake. They got out just before the car went over, taking their clothes with it. People would laugh at them and their parents would be furious. But that all seemed very small to Tom now. They were alive. His perspective had just grown much wider, if a little darker.

The cop, Griff, whatever he was, warned them never to tell anyone the truth. People would think they were crazy. This was better left forgotten.

Jenny looked at Tom like he should say something. But Tom only watched as the cop left them behind.

Jenny never really forgave him for staying quiet, even if they did end up having sex—indoors only—all summer long. That small betrayal, that tiny bit of cowardice, was enough to drive a wedge between them that would lead to Jenny dumping him before she went to college.

Tom didn't care.

Cade, for his part, didn't say another word to them. And Tom was grateful.

Tom married someone other than Jenny, did well in real estate, had two kids, divorced, and married again. He grew into a prosperous middle age, gained twenty more pounds and learned to golf.

Most days he could almost believe it was something that happened to someone else, like a ghost story or a UFO sighting.

But he could never forget the sound he heard when he saw Cade's smile, right after he'd impaled the Char-Man.

Cade was laughing. He sounded happy.

The Char-Man had nearly killed Tom. But it was that laughter that echoed in Tom's nightmares for the rest of his life.

ONE

Bogeyman. The word comes from the Russian, *bog*, meaning "god."

—Peter Levenda, *Sinister Forces*

SEPTEMBER 20, 2012, THE OVAL OFFICE, WHITE HOUSE, WASHINGTON, D.C.

The President of the United States was afraid.

Zach Barrows had worked personally with President Samuel Curtis for eight years, starting as a campaign volunteer in high school. He'd seen Curtis at the end of twenty-four-hour campaign marathons, in the small hours of the morning weighing a missile strike, playing ball with his son, and dealing with dangers that staggered the imagination. It was safe to say Zach knew the president as well as anyone in the White House, with the possible exception of his wife. Curtis regarded an emotional display the same way he'd look at grime on the cuff of one of his immaculately cut suits: he didn't put up with it. But Zach could see the fear.

And when the man who commanded a nuclear arsenal and the greatest military in history was frightened, it meant that something other than human intervention was required.

That, unfortunately, was part of Zach's job every day now. That was where Nathaniel Cade came in.

Cade stood next to Zach on the Oval Office carpet. Cade was a vampire.

Zach remembered how he'd laughed when he first heard that.

Then he actually met Cade. Although Cade looked like a fairly normal guy in his twenties—maybe a little pale—he exuded an aura of menace. People had been known to start gibbering uncontrollably just by standing near him. Zach figured this was an inborn survival mechanism in humans; the fight-or-flight response telling the brain to get the hell away from this thing before it turns you into lunch. In response, Zach had wet his pants.

The laughs were few and far between after that.

Zach once thought he'd be the president's chief of staff—the youngest in history—but instead found himself shanghaied into a world that, for most people, simply didn't exist. The conspiracy theorists had it all wrong, he'd been told. Werewolves, zombies, demons, witches, and various other creatures had all been on this planet for a long time, waiting in the dark for their chances to feast on human blood and souls. The United States had been fighting a holding action against these horrors almost since it was founded. The entire secret history of America was a record of this war. Like an infectious disease, every time there was an outbreak, the government did its best to contain it quietly and quickly.

In 1867, the country found the right weapon for the fight. Cade was discovered on a ship that ran aground outside Boston Harbor. At some point in the long journey, he killed and fed on the other members of the crew. He had chewed through their flesh and sucked the meat dry of all blood. A half-dozen soldiers shot him at point-blank range without killing him when he was found.

For the first time in its history, the United States government had captured a vampire.

But rather than destroy him, then-President Andrew Johnson bound him to serve the United States with a blood oath administered by the voodoo queen Marie Laveau. Cade was sworn to follow all lawful orders of the president and his appointed representatives, then turned against the other creatures of the night.

Cade was stronger, faster and tougher than anything human. And in almost one hundred fifty years, there wasn't a monster in the world he hadn't killed at one time or another.

President Curtis selected Zach to serve as a liaison to Cade when Cade's previous handler, William H. Griffin, was due to retire. Zach was the first political operative to fill a job that ordinarily went to ex-FBI, ex-CIA, and ex–Special Ops. Zach still wondered occasionally if he was being punished for a onetime fling with the First Daughter in the Lincoln Bedroom.

After three years, Zach had to admit the job was interesting. At the very least, Cade hadn't tried to eat him yet

"We have a problem," the president said. "Earlier tonight, Brent Kirkman—one of the advance staffers on my campaign—was killed along with a local volunteer."

"Jesus Christ," Zach said.

Cade gave Zach a look. The vampire wore a cross around his neck, using the pain as a tool to combat his thirst. He was still a believer, even if he knew he'd never get to Heaven himself. "Someone has to protect the meek until they can inherit the earth" was his only explanation. Zach still didn't understand how that worked, but he usually knew not to take the name of the Lord in vain. Cade hated that.

But Brent—Brent had been a friend.

"You knew him?" Curtis asked.

Zach nodded. "We were both on the Illinois staff when we started."

The president nodded. "You may not want to look at this, then."

He lifted a folder and handed it to Cade. Cade flipped through it in seconds, his face never changing expression.

Zach took it. He swallowed hard to keep his lunch. Despite all he'd seen on the job—and it was a lot—he never got accustomed to all the ways a human body could be degraded and ruined in death.

It was hard to tell where one corpse ended and the other began. They were carved up, skin and organs and bones sheared clean through, the torsos laid open like a biology experiment. Muscle and fat were sliced cleanly off their frames. Blood stained the walls of the tight, confined space around the bodies.

Zach figured out why he was having such a hard time understanding the pictures. Suddenly, the images made sense, like a vase resolving itself out of the silhouette of two faces. The woman had been on the man's lap when they were killed. They were intertwined with each other when someone had hacked them to bits.

"What did that to them?" he asked.

"We had the FBI do a rush analysis. Fortunately, it was a very distinctive weapon," the president said. "Blade was too thin to be a standard ax or hatchet, but too thick to be a machete. The blade got stuck in the bone at one point. He was able to match the metal traces with a military survival ax. Used to clear brush from World War Two to Vietnam. Also slices through people pretty good, as you can see."

A picture was helpfully included in the folder. The tool had a handle like a pirate sword's grip and ended in a wicked hook at the end of a curved blade. It looked mean.

"I didn't see anything about this on the news," Zach said.

"And you won't," the president said. "We've got the crime scene locked down and we're invoking the Patriot Act to keep the murder of Mr. Kirkman and the volunteer out of the public record. You should understand better than anyone, Zach."

He did, all too well; Zach still watched the polls between zombie outbreaks. The president's reelection campaign was in trouble.

Curtis had been riding a wave of high ratings after the attempt on his life in the White House three years earlier. For an all-too-brief time, insulting him was like burning the American flag. Even the commentators at Fox had to smile when they said his name. At that point, reelection looked like a walk.

Unfortunately, the president and his advisers underestimated the rage. People wanted to blame someone—anyone—for the economy's ongoing death march, and Curtis was the man behind the big desk. People wanted to see some return on the billions of dollars funneled to the banks and financial giants in the bailouts, and all they got were foreclosure notices and pink slips. The end result was record profits for the people who'd blown a hole beneath the waterline of the U.S. economy. As far as the electorate was concerned, Curtis might as well have signed the multimillion-dollar bonus checks to the bankers personally.

Still, it was more than just the issues. The fury running across America was almost visible, a red mist that burned like tear gas in the eyes, sending regular people into frothing, teeth-gnashing tantrums on TV every night. It didn't matter what the topic was; there was always someone ready to howl with outrage over it.

Curtis had the massive advantages of incumbency, not to mention an unprecedented billion-dollar campaign war chest, in his favor. But his party got stomped hard in the midterms—"a real pasting" is how Curtis put it the morning after the results—and he'd been playing a defensive game ever since.

He was battered daily by attacks that shouldn't have made the back page of the supermarket tabloids: he was secretly a Satan worshipper; no, worse, he was an atheist; he'd sold the national park system to Saudi Arabia; he had given the codes to the nuclear arsenal to the United Nations; and the old reliable from the 2008 election, that Samuel Curtis was the Antichrist himself. Zach sometimes wondered how an admittedly rather half-assed attempt to give health care to poor people ignited such raw hatred, but hey, that was politics.

Campaigns were stories more than anything else, and Zach could feel the narrative thickening like quicksand around Curtis's feet: Jimmy Carter. High gas prices, the economy flatlining, wars and tension in the Middle East—it all added up to the same ending: loser.

If the media heard about Kirkman getting murdered while screwing a volunteer, that would become the whole story: a president so unpopular anyone connected to him was actually in danger. It had just the right elements to appeal to the 24/7 noise machine: plenty of sex and danger, with zero issues to get in the way. The pundits could regurgitate something like this for months. Curtis's chances of winning in November would go subterranean.

Zach realized now why President Curtis was afraid. He was scared to lose.

Cade turned to the president. The slight movement made Zach twitch involuntarily. As a rule, Cade didn't move much. But when he did, things usually died. They'd been working together almost three years, but that didn't mean Zach was done being afraid of him.

Zach once visited an exotic animal sanctuary where the owner kept big cats—lions and tigers—he'd raised from cubs. Zach watched as he tossed a steak to one tiger for a snack. The tiger began eating. The owner took a step in its direction. The tiger gave a murmur and flicked its tail—barely a sign of annoyance. But the guy who had literally fed this animal by hand for its entire life backed away like he had touched a hot stove. "It's still a wild animal," he said when he saw the look on Zach's face. "You can't change nature."

Zach always tried to keep that in mind about Cade.

"Why am I here?" Cade asked the president.

Vampires are not big on social graces, Zach reminded himself.

But Cade had a point. This was a murder. Awful, yes, and ugly, no question. But hardly in the same league as the things he and Cade dealt with on a daily basis. Only a week ago, they had dealt with a squad of men who'd learned to use Spontaneous Human Combustion to make themselves into living bombs; they could walk through any kind of security and simply will themselves to explode. Like all of the threats Cade dealt with, they had tapped into the occult to make themselves into something inhuman that required an inhuman response.

Only two of the SHCide bombers managed to reach their targets; the other four were easy prey for Cade.

Curtis didn't mind Cade's question, or didn't show it if he did.

"This is why," he said. He passed a single photo across the desk to Cade. "I'd like you and Zach there in person before sunrise."

Cade scanned it. His mouth curled in a frown.

Zach felt his stomach sink again, and it wasn't the pictures in the folder now. Cade never showed emotion. A slight frown from him was like a scream from a human. Zach was instantly on alert.

Cade spoke directly to the president. "This is not good."

Oh shit, man the lifeboats, Zach thought. Cade says it's bad.

Regretting it even as it came out of his mouth, Zach asked, "Somebody mind telling me exactly what we're talking about here?"

Cade handed the photo to him.

The killer had used his victim's blood to draw and write all over the walls. Zach had seen that already in the other crime-scene photos. But this was a close-up of one line in particular, written directly above the bodies.

It said, IT'S NICE TO BE BACK.

Zach couldn't see why it made Cade react the way he did.

"All right," Zach said. "I hate to admit it, but I'm lost. What makes this so terrible?"

The president looked to Cade to answer. Cade said, "Because I've seen it before."

"You know who this is? Great. So we'll pick him up—"

"As I said, it's not that simple," Cade said. "It's the Boogeyman."

Zach waited a full five seconds. Nobody laughed. If anything, the tension in the room only increased.

"The Boogeyman," he said, just to be sure. "The *Boogeyman* killed an employee of the President of the United States."

The president nodded.

Some days, Zach thought, I really hate this job.

TWO

> Hello from the gutters of N.Y.C. which are filled with dog manure, vomit, stale wine, urine and blood. Hello from the sewers of N.Y.C. which swallow up these delicacies when they are washed away by the sweeper trucks. Hello from the cracks in the sidewalks of N.Y.C. and from the ants that dwell in these cracks and feed in the dried blood of the dead that has settled into the cracks. . . . You can forget about me if you like because I don't care for publicity. However you must not forget Donna Lauria and you cannot let the people forget her either. She was a very, very sweet girl but Sam's a thirsty lad and he won't let me stop killing until he gets his fill of blood. Mr. Breslin, sir, don't think that because you haven't heard from me for a while that I went to sleep. No, rather, I am still here. Like a spirit roaming the night. Thirsty, hungry, seldom stopping to rest; anxious to please Sam. I love my work.
>
> —"Son of Sam" letter to Jimmy Breslin, May 30, 1977

September 20, 2012, Mansfield, Ohio

The crime scene was a mess. Like everyone else, patrol officer Fred Baker stood around, unsure of what to do. Nobody on the force was used to this sort of thing. They were a small-town department. They didn't get many homicides. Baker had only been close to dead bodies once before in his three years on the force. He'd been the first to respond when a couple cars met in a head-on near the interstate. One driver wasn't wearing a seat belt and had been splattered all over the road. Baker took one look at the man's skull and tossed his cookies.

Surprisingly, he didn't throw up when he saw the carnage in the utility closet. Maybe it was because it didn't look like anything human, at least not from the waist up. Waist down, it was easy to see what had been going on—and he wasn't sure how they were going to handle that, either—but above, it just looked like something from a slaughterhouse.

It was too surreal for him to be sick. Like everyone else, he stood around, waiting for the state police. It wasn't even a close call. Let them handle it. This was a nightmare.

Baker realized someone was talking to him. Her voice snapped him out of his daze. He remembered he was supposed to be keeping a perimeter.

"Move along, ma'am," he said automatically to the woman. "This is a crime scene."

Only then did he really see whom he was talking to. She was a gorgeous blonde—she looked like someone he'd see in a magazine. But when she spoke again, he saw what was wrong with her, as half her face turned down in an ugly sneer.

"I know it's a crime scene, dipshit," she snapped. "That's why we're here."

Baker didn't reply. He was staring. He knew it was rude, but he couldn't stop himself. Half of the beautiful face simply didn't move. It was frozen perfectly in place, as if preserved under a thick coat of shellac. The other side looked tired and angry, but the frozen part was fresh and perfectly calm.

Then she brought her creds right up to his nose, breaking his stare. He managed to read the letters "FBI" before his eyes crossed and blurred.

She pulled the badge and ID away and half-glared at him again. He felt mortified and stupid. His uncle had had a stroke, and half of his face didn't work, either. She probably hated it when people stared, too.

"Sorry, ma'am," he said. "I didn't, uh, I didn't know we'd called in any federal assistance yet."

She was already moving past him, pulling one leg along with her in a kind of shuffle, on the same side as her immobile face. An older Latino man moved with her, lifting the crime-scene tape to allow her to get under it without stooping.

Baker's sergeant noticed the intruders and stepped in front of them. "Hey, this is a crime scene," he said. "What the hell are you doing?"

The blond woman sighed heavily and brought out her shield again. The Latino man did the same.

"Agent Courtney," she said. "And this is Agent Vincent. We're with VICAP."

The FBI's famous serial killers apprehension unit. The sergeant tried not to look impressed and failed.

"We didn't call anyone," he said. "And I don't see how this is a federal case." But he didn't sound sure, so at the end his voice curled up in a kind of question mark.

"Your case might have bearing on an ongoing federal

investigation," Courtney said. Baker wondered how someone so pretty could sound so mean in just a few words. "It's important we get a look."

The sergeant hesitated. Baker knew he was wondering how the feebs got here before the state police. But Courtney didn't seem interested in waiting around.

"Sergeant? You going to show us the crime scene now? Or do we have to wander around until we find it ourselves?"

Her tone got the sergeant moving again. "Baker," he snapped. "Show the agents to the scene. Don't disturb anything."

Agent Courtney snorted. "Believe me, it's not my first murder scene," she said.

She shuffled away, and Baker scurried after her.

She and Vincent were both perfectly respectful of the scene, however. They put on gloves and booties, and Courtney put her hair under a shower cap. That was more than Baker had done, and he'd been walking around the area for almost an hour.

Courtney gently opened the door of the closet. She peered in at the wreckage.

Baker tried not to look at it, but it was simply impossible.

The man and woman had been in the act of coitus—that was how Baker would write it up in his report—with the woman against the sink in the closet, the man pressed up against her. His pants were around his ankles and her skirt was hiked up to her waist. That much was obvious.

Everything else looked like a bomb hit a slaughterhouse.

Their torsos were sliced and hacked into bits. The man's arm had been cleanly sliced away and sat on the tile floor, still wearing its watch. The woman's mouth was open, but only the jawline remained. From the nose up, there was nothing but broken bone and blood.

Courtney barely even noticed the bodies. Her attention was focused on the symbols and writing scrawled in blood.

She looked at Vincent. "It's him."

Vincent nodded.

"Who?" Baker said. He couldn't help asking.

"Sorry," Courtney said, using her teeth to strip off her gloves. She tossed them on the floor, already stomping away. "That's privileged information."

They were out the door. Baker jogged after them.

"Wait," he said. "Aren't you going to stay? The state police will be here soon. I'm sure they could use—"

"Not our case," Vincent said without looking back. They moved under the crime-scene tape again, headed for an anonymous black sedan.

"But you know who this is. I heard you. Don't you want to catch him?"

Courtney paused at the passenger door of the car. She seemed to take pity on Baker. Half her face quirked in a smile. "Don't worry about it," she said. "We know just what we're going to do with him."

She slammed the door and they drove away.

An hour later, the head of the regional FBI office showed up. He looked like he'd been rousted out of bed. He had a whole SWAT team of other federal guys and they locked down the scene. The head FBI guy simply ignored the sergeant and ordered them all around like they were fast-food jockeys.

"Did the other agents call you?" Baker asked him, trying to get a little professional respect.

Baker got nothing but a blank stare in return.

"You know. From VICAP? The serial killer guys?"

"VICAP hasn't been anywhere near this case," the fed said coldly. "What the hell are you talking about?"

Baker might not have been a federal agent, but he was not stupid, either. He realized he'd let unauthorized people into a crime scene; he'd be lucky if the photos didn't show up on someone's Facebook page.

He shut his mouth and followed orders after that. He didn't have a clue what was going on, and he decided he preferred it that way.

THREE

> There is an ancient America that lurks beneath the threshold of our collective, corn-fed consciousness. We see it all the time. It surrounds us with its feral glow; we have learned to fear it in the dark without learning what it is, what it means. It's not just the woods out back, the lonely desert trails, the virgin mountains where we lose our Boy Scouts or survivalists in the winter snows. It's also in the Laundromats, the gas stations, the drug stores and diners.
>
> —Peter Levenda, *Sinister Forces*

THE RELIQUARY, WASHINGTON, D.C.

Zach followed Cade through the dank tunnel and into the hidden chamber underneath the Smithsonian Castle. Urban legends and paranoids on the Internet talked about the hidden network of tunnels below the White House and other parts of D.C. None of them mentioned anything about a vampire using them to get between meetings during the day.

The lights in the chamber flickered to life—fluorescents, of course; even the most secret parts of the government had to obey energy-saving guidelines—and revealed secrets that would confirm a hundred more urban legends and horror stories. The leg of a cockroach roughly the same size as a human arm hung on the wall with a plaque reading, OPERATIVE SAMSA, W. BERLIN, 1948. A gallon jar filled with formaldehyde held an insect claw labeled DELAMBRE REMAINS, 1958. This was dwarfed by another glass case that held the dried-out husk of a six-foot-tall praying mantis marked JUDAS BREED, ADULT STAGE, NEW YORK, 1997.

Zach barely saw these things anymore. This was the Reliquary: where Cade slept and kept his trophies from previous attempts by the Other Side to break into the world of the living. Like other hunters, it was in his nature to keep bits and pieces of his kills. But the Reliquary was also the closest thing Zach had to an office, and with enough time, even things like the stuffed and mounted pterodactyl (TOMBSTONE, ARIZONA, 1886) started to look as dull as the copy machine in the corner.

"Fine," Zach said. "The Boogeyman is real. Why am I even surprised?"

The president had dismissed them after giving a terse set of orders: "Maybe you'll have better luck this time, Cade," he said. "I want you in Ohio ASAP. I want this thing truly finished."

That was all. Cade had been silent all the way back through the tunnel to the Reliquary. Zach had been patient as long as he could. It wasn't unusual for him to be kept in the dark until a new threat popped up. The shadows behind the White House hid a lot of secrets. Zach was subject to information containment: he learned only what he needed to do the job at hand in case he ever ended up being captured and tortured. It had already happened once in Zach's brief time on the job and, he had to admit, he broke immediately. He would have spilled any secret he was asked, but his captors actually knew more about the dark history of the nation than he did.

But just because Zach understood the reasons behind information containment didn't make it any less of a pain in the ass. "Don't mind me," Zach muttered. "I'll be right here if anyone wants to let me know what's going on."

Cade pretended not to hear as he walked to the far side of the Reliquary. Zach knew this was an act, because he could hear Zach's heartbeat if he listened.

"We've reached a need-to-know moment," he said.

Cade kept records of his previous century-plus of cases in the basement, stored in files that ranged from antique wooden drawers to 1940s-era steel cabinets to a series of hard drives attached to a government-issue PC. Zach was supposed to be given access to the files as needed. Most of the time he was too busy to do much more than skim his briefing book.

Not this time, however. Cade went to one of the oldest wooden cabinets lining the walls and opened a drawer.

Zach walked over. "This is all about him?"

"It."

"What?" Cade's propensity for using an absolute minimum of words when speaking could make him incomprehensible sometimes.

"It," Cade said again. "Not 'him.' It's not human. Stop thinking like it is. The Boogeyman is real. It is out there. It could be anyone. And its body count is among the highest of anything I've faced."

Zach swiped his pad to life and began tapping away at the virtual keyboard. The pad was basically an early adopter's wet dream: a high-powered, ruggedized touch-screen computer with GPS, satellite, Wi-Fi and cell phone access all built in. Zach had used a phone with many of the same features until recently, but he couldn't resist an upgrade. It was one of the only pieces of super-spy tech he got to play with, so he wanted to have the very best.

Sometimes Zach saw people complaining about the deficit on the news and ached to tell them: *You think that was caused by spending on NPR? Guess again. Fighting monsters isn't cheap, kids.*

He only noticed the silence when he finished calling for transport to Ohio on the pad's encrypted channels. Cade waited for him to pay attention.

"All right," Zach said, closing the pad. "I'm listening."

"The Boogeyman is, essentially, the patron saint of serial killers," Cade said. "It has appeared in various places over the past century, slaughtering innocents. It leaves what you call urban legends in its wake: stories of escaped mental patients with hooks for hands and so on. Those are only the host bodies. It is a spiritual parasite. It moves into a human shell and slowly turns its host into an unstoppable killer. It is inhumanly strong. It heals from most wounds as fast as I do, if not faster. And it has an uncanny knack for turning up at the worst possible moments. Luck always runs in its direction—and always in a bad way. Phones stop working. Cars will not start, or they run out of gas, or they break down unexpectedly. The batteries in the flashlight or the oil in the lantern runs out."

"Human hosts? This is like demon possession?"

"Similar," Cade said. "But not exactly. I've managed to kill the host several times. But the entity itself has always come back. It always comes back."

Suddenly, Zach figured it out. That was why Cade was so annoyed. He hated leaving anything unfinished.

"Something you killed didn't stay dead? Wow. That must really have put some termites in your coffin."

Cade didn't laugh. Not that Zach expected it. He only said things like that to make himself feel better.

"Read these," he said, pointing to the files, then walked away.

Zach knew it was useless to ask for any more detail. It was all in the file or Cade would have said more. That might have been the scariest thought all day. Zach was actually starting to understand Cade.

He pulled the first folder out and opened it. The top sheet was a copy of an old letter. It was printed in all caps, the pen strokes jagged and crabbed, like something scratched into the paper rather than written on top of it.

IT'S NICE TO BE BACK, it began.

Zach sat down and began to read.

October 29, 1919
The White House, Washington, D.C.

Cade entered the sitting room outside the president's bedroom and waited. He could hear voices inside the bedroom. Mrs. Wilson spoke in her usual clear, strident tones to the chief usher. When he tried to interrupt, she cut him off.

"I know what the president wants. I've been listening to him far longer than you."

There was a long pause. Then the usher simply responded, "Yes, ma'am."

Even with his enhanced hearing, Cade could hear nothing from the president except labored breathing.

He exited a moment later, his eyes never leaving the floor as he headed for the stairs.

Mrs. Wilson closed the door behind her quickly when she came out to meet Cade. Cade didn't say anything. She shushed him anyway.

The president had just completed a grueling twenty-two-day tour of the western states in an attempt to drum up support for his League of Nations. Then, just after his final stop in Colorado, he collapsed. He was delivered back to the White House, exhausted, but still coherent enough to send for Cade, who was out of the city on other business.

When he returned, Cade found the White House turned into a hospital. The president had suffered another, more severe stroke. Mrs. Wilson informed the president's top deputies that the doctors had instructed her to act as his sole intermediary, to reduce any further exertion on him.

That was four days ago. No one, aside from her and the medical personnel, had seen the president since.

"The president is resting," Mrs. Wilson said. She nodded to him and he followed her down the hall, away from the door. They entered the First Lady's sitting room, which now looked more like an office. Charts and maps covered the tables, and telegrams sat in a stack a foot high on Mrs. Wilson's chair.

"He'll recover soon enough," Mrs. Wilson said, again without any prompting from Cade. The line felt rehearsed. "He has to deal with this navy matter right now, so he sends his regrets at not being able to meet with you personally. But he gave me his instructions for you."

Cade waited. Mrs. Wilson was polite enough to him. She'd known of his existence since the day the president had taken office. She spoke to him without revealing much of her distaste for what he was. And she never appeared particularly afraid of him, either.

Mrs. Wilson was a great deal more formidable than most people knew. She found a clipping on her sewing table and brought it to him.

"While the president was out campaigning, he heard

several disturbing rumors. There were reports in the yellow rags about a murderer. Someone in New Orleans. Ordinarily, this is something for the local sheriff. But then, he saw this."

The clipping was a reproduction of a letter sent to the newspaper, according to the caption.

And the letter was, according to the first line, sent from Hell.

Hell, March 13, 1919

Esteemed Mortal:

They have never caught me and they never will. They have never seen me, for I am invisible, even as the ether that surrounds your earth. I am not a human being, but a spirit and a demon from the hottest hell. I am what you Orleanians and your foolish police call the Axman.

When I see fit, I shall come and claim other victims. I alone know who they shall be. I shall leave no clue except my bloody ax, besmeared with blood and brains of he whom I have sent below to keep me company.

"AT LEAST NINE have been attacked so far. Seven are dead," Mrs. Wilson said.

"What makes this something for me?" Cade asked.

"The local policemen are helpless. He apparently appears and disappears at will. He enters houses through locked doors that are never unlocked."

Mrs. Wilson's iron determination wavered for a moment. "He says he is collecting souls."

She collected herself and the stern look was back. "If he is not something like you, then he is something of your world, at the very least."

Cade took the clipping. "I will deal with it."

She nodded. "I'll inform the president."

Cade's lip curled in a kind of half-smile.

Mrs. Wilson noticed. Her eyes went cold. "Do you find this amusing, Mr. Cade? Does our simple human suffering warm your dead heart?"

Cade's lip curled again. Not many people who knew what he was would dare speak to him like that, even with the protection of the oath.

"I meant no offense," he said.

"My husband—the president—expects your obedience, Mr. Cade."

"And he has it. As do you, Mrs. Wilson."

That stopped her.

"What do you mean?"

"Only that with me, at least, you do not have to pretend."

She nodded again, and for a moment her face softened.

Then she stood up again. "There is a cabinet meeting in an hour. The president has information to relay to them. I'm sure you can see yourself out. Good day, Mr. Cade."

"Good day, Mrs. Wilson."

She left the room before Cade, her back ramrod-straight, mind already on other things. Cade imagined the weight of the burden she was now carrying, completely alone.

A formidable woman, indeed.

Cade went to the tunnel in the basement and left the White House, his first step on the long journey to New Orleans to find this "demon."

He didn't think it would take long.

FOUR

OPERATOR: 911 operator, what is your emergency?

CALLER: [SILENCE]

OPERATOR: [AUDIBLE SIGH] 911, what is your emergency? Hello? Is anyone there?

CALLER: I'm here.

OPERATOR: This line is for emergencies only.

CALLER: It's a [inaudible].

OPERATOR: Does your mother know you're calling 911?

CALLER: It's a emergency. Mommy said. Press the button.

OPERATOR: She did? Well, you could get into a lot of trouble for calling me, sweetie. So could your mommy.

CALLER: It's a emergency. Mommy's—[MUFFLED SOBBING]

OPERATOR: Honey, what is it? You can tell me. What's wrong?

CALLER: Mommy's got a bad owie. Mommy's broken.

OPERATOR: Your mommy is broken? Honey, do you need help?

CALLER: Yes. Please help my mommy.

—Transcript of 911 call to Fort Collins (Colorado) Dispatch Center, 7:33 A.M., November 11, 2010

NOVEMBER 11, 2010, OMAHA, NEBRASKA

He sat at the stoplight, waiting for it to turn green. Ridiculous. Useless. Nobody was ever out at this hour. He waited five to ten minutes every damn time, despite the fact that he was the only car on the road.

Out of the corner of his eye, he thought he saw another one of the black things, scuttling like a crab toward him. He jumped a little and turned. Nothing there but the empty road and the gray predawn light.

Still, he couldn't help brushing his left ear and shoulder. He kept seeing the black things, and every time it felt like an earwig looking for a way to burrow into his skin.

He thought about getting his eyes checked, but if that ever got out, he'd be taken right off the job and that would be it. Besides, he was just tired. He knew it. He'd been working triple shifts. Cutbacks had reduced the ranks and everyone had to pitch in and work harder. That's what they said. Nobody complained. There was always another round of cutbacks coming, and whiners were the first ones out the door.

He sighed and adjusted his collar. It itched. He barely had time to get his uniforms dry-cleaned anymore. This thing was supposed to bring him respect, money and women. Now he didn't even get an allowance to buy new shirts. That was all out-of-pocket these days. Cutbacks. And as everyone kept telling him, he was lucky just to have the job. He'd need to hang on to it for a good long time, too. Social Security and Medicare were so deep in the red he'd never retire.

It probably didn't help that he spent so much time on the Internet once he was home. But he felt like it was his duty to stay informed. And then he'd get so furious, reading about all the crap the government kept pulling these days. One outrage after the next. Total surveillance of all cell phone traffic, with key words like "terrorist" ensuring a visit from FBI goons. Kids kicked off school lunch programs while the president dropped two million bucks a day to go on vacation. Illegal immigrants flooding across the border to sign up for welfare benefits. United Nations troops stationed in the United States like an occupying army.

Before he knew it, it was almost dawn again, his eyes bleary and red from staring at the computer monitor all night. His few hours of sleep were filled with more of the black bugs, crawling all over his skin, into his eyes and ears. He woke up twitching.

Every time he opened his eyes, slapping at the insects that weren't there, the feeling kept growing inside him. He was more certain of it every day: this wasn't supposed to be his life.

He was pissed off all the time. He was supposed to get

respect. “Captain.” Even the title sounded like a joke to him now. Spread his annual salary across the hours he was working, deduct taxes—Jesus Christ, *taxes*—and all the other ways he got screwed out of every little penny, and he was making less than minimum wage.

And he still had to wait at this goddamned light every morning.

He was sick of it. Sick of it all. Looking at the red light, he felt his rage build, and build, and build. The black bugs seemed to dance at the edge of his vision, crawling all over him, swarming, itching, pricking.

Let go, a voice told him. *Just give in. Give yourself over to the rage.*

And why the hell not? Why should he be the one who got screwed when everyone else did whatever the hell they wanted? What was he hanging on for? Why should he follow the rules?

Enough. He’d had enough. Something tore loose deep inside him. Some piece of him gave up its hold and fell away forever.

He closed his eyes, and the black bugs swarmed in. They poured in through his ears, his mouth, his nose. They filled him up and the itching finally stopped, replaced with a dark certainty. He didn’t have to play by their rules anymore. He could do whatever he wanted.

His skin stopped itching for the first time in months.

At the same moment, eyes still closed, he stood on the gas pedal and his car peeled through the intersection under the taunting red light.

He heard the screech of brakes and a crumpling noise as two cars collided behind him, but he didn't even slow down.

He opened his eyes and everything felt better.

He felt like a new man.

FIVE

At approximately 0805 hrs my partner OFFICER R. RESSLER and myself received a call from dispatch regarding a possible injury or disturbance and an unattended child in an apartment in the Hilltop area. Upon arrival, we knocked and asked for entry. With no response, we called upon the apartment manager, ALFREDO GUTIERREZ, to open the door for us. Once inside, we found the 911 caller, CASSIE REYNOLDS, age 6, still on the phone with DISPATCH. Officer Ressler sought to calm her while I cleared the apartment. Inside the master bedroom, signs and obscenities had been painted in the walls with what appeared to be human blood and feces. On the bed, I discovered the body of the occupant of the apartment and mother to Cassie, CHARLENE REYNOLDS. Her head had been severed from her body at the neck and placed so that it balanced on the chest of her body. At that point, I called for backup.

—Fort Collins (Colorado) Police Department Report,
November 11, 2010

Zach put the file down. He was done. Not with the file's contents, which contained many hundreds more pages. But he was done enduring it. He often had to witness inhuman horror. It never got easier, but at least he knew never to expect mercy or compassion from creatures that fed on human blood and misery.

But the scale the Boogeyman worked on was simply too small, too human. It somehow inversely magnified the tragedy of each life lost. He—or it, as Cade insisted—worked on an extremely personal level.

There were photos from crime scenes included. But it wasn't the gory ones that turned Zach's stomach. It was the ones with the seemingly inconsequential details: a framed family picture knocked askew; a laundry basket left on a couch in front of a TV; a child's stuffed bunny tossed upside down in a corner.

The Boogeyman extinguished people in the places where they most expected safety. He tainted the concepts of security and comfort. It was the skull beneath the skin. And it never stopped grinning.

They were flying in a military transport, riding on benches in the back of a C-130 cargo plane next to the specially modified government sedan they used. Cade could function during the day, though at about half strength, as long as he was indoors and out of direct sunlight. So the car had windows tinted to block the UVA and UVB radiation that would cook Cade in his own skin. Even with that protection, the daylight would hurt him like hell. Just not enough to incapacitate him.

"Questions?" Cade asked, pointing at the file where Zach had stuffed it into his messenger bag.

"Yeah," Zach said. "Any chance I can go back to D.C.?"

"Any useful questions?"

"Do you think it's really the Boogeyman that killed Brent? You think it's back?"

"I sincerely hope not."

"When you say things like that, I start to cry a little on the inside. If you can't kill him—"

"It. Not him."

"Right. It. So how do we stop *it* if it just keeps coming back?"

Cade gave him the nanosecond smile. "I just keep killing it."

Ask a stupid question . . . "Have you ever tried putting him—sorry, it—in prison?"

"Yes. Nineteen seventy-one. The results were disappointing."

"Define 'disappointing.'"

"Thirty-nine dead. We had to engineer a riot to cover the casualties."

"Solitary confinement?"

"Suicide. Every time. It will restart the cycle itself if necessary."

"Insane asylum? Or do I not want to know how that ended up?"

"You probably do not."

"There's got to be some way to stop him."

"It," Cade said. "I've been trying for some time. If I've missed anything, I would appreciate you letting me know."

"But in the meantime, people die."

"People die all the time," Cade said. "It won't stop until people stop killing one another."

"Yeah, yeah. The world's a cruel place, man is inhumane to man, we should all be united in peace and harmony and all that. Surprised to hear it from you, though."

"You misunderstand me. People kill for the Boogeyman. That's how it exists, how it's summoned."

"I have a bad feeling you're going to explain that."

"Blood sacrifice. The oldest and most powerful of rituals. There is a group that continually makes offerings. The Boogeyman is a creature of fear and pain. Before it can manifest in a human host, it needs to be fed. It requires sacrifices to gain strength between appearances. Breaching this world from the Other Side is not easy. It costs. There are people willing to pay the price for the Boogeyman's passage."

"Jesus Christ." It slipped out before Zach thought about it.

"Don't blaspheme," Cade said. The cross was not just an affectation or a hedge against his thirst. Cade was a believer. He took his faith seriously.

"I think this time it qualifies as a prayer." Zach wasn't joking. Some of the killings in the file had been gruesome but seemed unrelated to the Boogeyman. Some were well-known, even famous, victims of serial killers. Now he understood. Another conspiracy. Only, this one was truly occult: dedicated to the care and feeding of an inhuman entity that did nothing but slaughter people.

"You're afraid," Cade said.

Can't hide a thing from someone who can smell fear, Zach was reminded. He'd admit it to Cade, if no one else.

"Yes. This scares me," he said. "It seems to go deeper

than just another monster, you know? Monsters I'm beginning to understand. I mean, you don't expect a werewolf to have table manners when he's chewing on human flesh."

"Some do," Cade reminded him.

Zach ignored that. "But how can people go to the store, go to a family picnic, and then carve up their kids and neighbors in the name of a patron saint of serial killers?"

"Not all humans side with the human race. You know this."

"Makes me wonder sometimes who we're saving."

"Ours is not to reason why. Ours is but to do and die."

"Once again, you are a huge comfort. It's like being wrapped in a warm, fuzzy blanket."

"You want comfort? All I can offer you is this: I know all this entity's patterns. If this really is the Boogeyman, this is an old fight. It will follow a predictable pattern. We go out there and put the kibosh on this and we're done."

"The kibosh?"

"You know what I mean."

Zach did; he was quite used to Cade's weird habit of occasionally allowing slang from a previous decade to seep into his current vocabulary. It was an inevitable side effect of Cade's perfect memory and the effort required to slow down his thinking to the speed of a normal conversation. However, among the few small joys Zach had in this life were the moments he could feel a bit superior to the ruthlessly competent, human-shaped killing machine.

"Does that help?" Cade asked.

Actually, it did. "We're cool," Zach said.

"Straight from the fridge, Dad," Cade replied.

SIX

The Minot Police Department addressed rumors of a Satanic cult connection to the homicide of a young hitchhiker in an interview with the News on Monday.

"We've seen no evidence of any conspiracy or any kind of occult motivation for this crime," Detective Lee Newton said.

Newton did confirm rumors that the deceased, found near an overpass on State Highway 83, had the number "666" carved into one hand. However, Newton said this wound was self-inflicted and probably unrelated to the multiple stab wounds that were the cause of death.

In occult lore and Hollywood horror films, 666 is allegedly the number of the Beast of the Apocalypse or Satan.

Newton said the victim, who remains unidentified, appears to have scratched the number into his own hand for reasons unknown.

Police have not yet named any suspects or motives in the murder.

—"Police Dismiss 'Satanic' Motive in Recent Killing," *Minot Daily News*, January 19, 2011

JANUARY 19, 2011, OMAHA, NEBRASKA

The blackouts were getting worse. It wasn't just the lack of sleep. He had to admit that, if only to himself. He couldn't account for whole nights now. Once, it had even happened on the job. He felt like he was waking up but realized he'd been functioning for hours without any memory of what he'd been doing.

It should have troubled him more than it did.

But there were benefits. The rage that coiled in his gut seemed to subside, as if it was going someplace when his body walked around without his conscious thought. The little black things at the edge of his vision—the ones that seemed to crowd inside him—weren't as frightening. They felt almost friendly and sympathetic.

And physically? Physically he'd never felt better in his life. Despite no sleep and his constant junk-food diet, he was getting stronger every day. He could feel it. He rarely looked at himself in the mirror anymore, but he caught a glimpse one morning on his way out of the shower: his body was covered with new, sharply defined muscle, as if he'd put on a suit of armor under his skin. He stared at himself, fascinated, until he noticed again how his eyes didn't move the way he thought they should anymore, how his own face seemed unfamiliar. Then he looked away and got dressed quickly.

His online activities seemed to decline as the blackouts got more frequent. When he checked his accounts, he found he hadn't posted anything in weeks. Nobody missed him.

The high-pitched chatter of the message boards just went on and on. There was still plenty to be outraged about, of course. But it felt more distant.

His real-life friends were already on their way out of his life. He had a buddy from work over for a beer on a rare night that he felt social. It did not go well. The man left early with an excuse about going to the gym in the morning. Later, he realized that he'd scared the man away. He remembered how the man had looked at his house, with its piles of laundry and garbage scattered in random heaps. He'd been too quiet, he knew. He spent most of the evening staring at a blood vessel that pulsed just under the skin at the man's temple. He found himself thinking of hammers, saws and other tools in the garage.

And the really weird part? None of this scared him.

In fact, down deep, he knew he should be scared. But he wasn't.

Whatever he was becoming, he liked it.

SEVEN

You don't understand these things because you're not under the influence of Factor X. The same thing that made Son of Sam, Jack the Ripper, Harvey Glatman, Boston Strangler, Dr. H. H. Holmes, Panty Hose Strangler of Florida, Hillside Strangler, Ted of the West Coast and many more infamous characters kill. Which seems senseless, but we cannot help it. There is no help, no cure, except death or being caught and put away. It is a terrible nightmare but, you see, I don't lose any sleep over it. After a thing like Fox I come home and go about life like anyone else. And I will be like that until the urge hits me again.

—Letter from the BTK Killer to TV station KAKE, February 10, 1978

MANSFIELD, OHIO

It was just before dawn when they arrived at Mansfield-Lahm Regional Airport. They decided they had enough time. Cade drove to the crime scene, a surprisingly modern glass-and-stone building in the middle of the small town, where a young cop from the local PD waited.

"I'm Agent Barnes and that's Agent Rogers," Zach said, flipping his phony creds. "FBI."

The cop, a kid named Baker, walked them back to the

janitor's closet near the auditorium. It had been sealed and guarded since the bodies were discovered. He kept telling them nobody had been in there but police. Nobody, he insisted.

He unlocked the door and stepped back behind it, as if afraid of what was inside.

Zach didn't blame him.

The blood had gone brown, but it was somehow worse that way. There was a stink of decay and metal. Zach stepped back involuntarily.

Cade stepped forward.

Without bothering to put on gloves, he clicked on the light.

The drawings came out in sharp relief.

A circle with a cross through it, like a rifle sight. 666. A pentagram. DEVIL. KILL. And at the center of it all, in the biggest letters, IT'S NICE TO BE BACK.

Cade took a deep breath, scenting the air. Underneath the blood, the gas and shit of ruptured bowels and the small bits of flesh left in the grooves of the tiles, but above the chemical tang of cleaning products and ammonia, he detected a note of corruption. It was unique in this world.

Like all members of his kind, Cade's memory was perfect, the neurons of his brain adapted to maximize storage and recall where humans favored narrative and association. From this perfect hard drive, he matched the odor immediately.

The scent was like a scream from tortured cells forced to accommodate the demands of a new and wholly inhuman metabolism. It was a human body's cellular engines running too fast, forced to rebuild itself even while running at top capacity.

Cade had smelled it before, several times. The Boogeyman, making its host into a home.

October 31, 1919
New Orleans, Louisiana

The sounds of jazz played from every window in every building, merging into an indistinct yowl that rose over the French Quarter like an audible fog.

Cade paid little attention to it as he ducked under the long blade of the ax. The madman spun past him, carried by the weight of his swing.

No one was on the streets tonight. The Axman, as he was called, had just claimed another victim two nights before. Now everyone in the city was playing music as loudly as they could. It was supposedly the only way to ward off his attacks. Locked doors didn't stop him. He seemed to glide right through them, leaving them undisturbed and only dead bodies as evidence he'd ever been inside.

The Axman came up again, too fast, pivoting directly into Cade's path. Cade barely dodged the ax's blade this time.

The Axman looked human. He was unremarkable, physically. A brown-haired, brown-eyed, white-skinned man wearing clothes that were disheveled but clean. On his head was a crude hood made of burlap with two holes for eyes. He'd bathed recently, was well-fed and appeared free of disease or injury. Cade had thought he was just another lunatic—a waste of his time and talents.

But now he wondered.

There was something too smooth in his movements. He'd already lasted far too long with Cade. And he was quiet.

It had been Cade's experience, since becoming a vampire, that humans were rarely ever quiet.

They continued to dance in the back alley near Bourbon Street. Aside from the occasional grunt and the sound of his feet scuffing in mud, the Axman didn't make a sound. If he was surprised that Cade had found him, he didn't say anything. If he wondered how Cade was able to avoid his ax with supernatural ease, he didn't show it.

Instead, he simply fixed on Cade and began swinging, as if this were nothing more than a regular part of his job.

Cade decided to end it. He stepped inside the swing of the ax, blocked it with one arm, and punched the man in the chest with the other.

It should have caved in his ribs. At the very least, it should have put him flat on his back, gasping for air.

But the Axman barely moved.

Cade was flabbergasted. "What—?" he started to ask.

Then he was knocked backward by the Axman's fist, sent tumbling head over heels into a pile of garbage.

Cade had definitely never been hit like that by anything human.

He was forced to reconsider his assumptions. He thought back to the Axman's taunting letter to the press and police—at the same time he barely avoided another swing, planted firmly in the ground where his head had just been.

The Axman had said he was a demon from Hell collecting souls to keep him company and feed himself.

Cade had to consider that a real possibility now.

He stopped fighting like his opponent was mortal.

He scaled the wall above him and launched himself into the air. The Axman looked up and turned around. Cade was already on the ground, his leg slicing out, knocking the Axman's feet from under him.

The Axman went down, the ax still clutched in one hand. Cade didn't give him a chance to get up.

He fought with more brute force than skill. He pounded on the Axman's skull with both fists. He felt something give under the hood. He heard bone crack.

The Axman stopped moving.

Cade leaned back. He felt no breath in the body under him. He listened carefully for a heartbeat.

Nothing. Cade got to his feet and stood back from the corpse.

Cade looked down the alley to check for witnesses. He wondered what he would do with the body.

He barely heard the ax cutting through the air in time. He ducked. The blade opened a deep gash along his face but failed to remove his head from his neck.

Cade staggered back. He rolled and tumbled, doing his best to open up distance.

Back on his feet, Cade saw the Axman charging him again. His eyes burned through the holes in the hood, now wet with blood. The ax was drawn back, ready to chop clean through Cade if given the chance.

Cade did not succumb to panic or shock. It was not in his nature. And so, where a human might have frozen at seeing a clearly dead man rise up again, Cade accepted it without hesitation.

He simply looked for the best way to make the man dead again.

Cade reached up and grabbed the ax as it came down toward him. He used the momentum and all his own strength to flip the Axman into an arc over his head.

The ax flew away and landed in a pile of garbage. The Axman hit the ground hard. Cade didn't let him get back up. He spun and grabbed the Axman's head, one hand on his chin, the other dug into a knot of the burlap hood at the base of his neck.

He twisted, using all his strength. There was a slick, popping sound. He kept twisting. He heard the unmistakable sound of flesh ripping apart.

With a final yank, the Axman's head came off. Cade nearly spun around with the effort.

The Axman's body fell to the ground.

Blood puddled on the dirt of the alley. Cade smelled something rank there; he was not in the least tempted to drink.

He looked at the bundle in his hands and unwrapped the hood. Underneath the cloth, he'd seen the features of a man. Just one more face in the crowd. There was nothing to distinguish him. He was nobody special.

But even in death, something was off about him. His

mouth was yanked slightly askew by some last nervous twitch or by the violence of Cade's hands. Either way, if Cade didn't know better, he'd swear the Axman was smirking at him.

Cade dropped the head. He found the ax and went to work.

When he was done, all the Axman's parts could be neatly gathered into a bundle and placed inside the burlap hood, which Cade used as a sack.

He tied it shut and walked to the river. Just before sunrise, he dumped his burden into the water and began heading back for his coffin, waiting at the train station.

He wondered where and how the Axman gained such power. But in a moment, the question ceased to matter. After all, Cade would never have to face him again.

EIGHT

I can only liken it to—and I don't want to overdramatize it—being possessed by something so awful and alien, and the next morning waking up and remembering what happened and realizing that in the eyes of the law, and certainly in the eyes of God, you're responsible. To wake up in the morning and realize what I had done with a clear mind, with all my essential moral and ethical feelings intact, absolutely horrified me.

—Ted Bundy, interviewed on death row January 24, 1999, the night before his execution

Zach's voice dragged him back to the present.

"You recognize the work?" he asked.

"It's him," Cade said.

"Don't you mean *it*?" Zach asked, his voice slightly mocking.

Cade didn't rise to the bait. "Yes. Thank you. Will you make the call? I'd like to take a little more time with this."

If Zach was surprised by Cade's polite tone, he didn't say anything. He walked away from Baker to make the call to the White House. This was just what Cade had wanted. There was another scent, also familiar, but it was slightly different than his memory. It could not be a coincidence.

It would be like someone having two sets of fingerprints. And unlike fingerprints, human odors could change over time.

Still, he had to be sure.

"Who else was here?" he asked Baker.

Baker gulped audibly. "What?"

"You let someone else into this area."

"What?"

Cade turned his full attention on Baker. The young cop started sweating. Right now, his brain was telling him two completely different things. The civilized portion was concerned with his career and keeping the truth from the slightly odd but still very polite FBI agent in the suit. The primal, survival-oriented portion was screaming at him to run as fast and as far as he could.

"Who was it?" Cade asked again.

Baker hesitated. "Nobody. I swear."

Cade simply kept staring at him.

Baker whimpered without knowing why. "I didn't know, all right? I thought they were FBI like you. They had badges and everything. I thought they were legit."

Cade took a step closer to the young cop.

"Tell me about them," he said. It was not a request.

NINE

Questioning of the apartment manager indicated the victim was involved with ERIC STEWART PALMER, 29. Neighbors complained frequently about fights between the couple. My partner ran an outstanding warrants check on Palmer and discovered he was currently on probation for aggravated assault and drunk and disorderly conduct. Palmer was also reported to be a member of Satan's Service motorcycle gang and had prior arrests for narcotics possession with intent to distribute. With backup and detectives en route, we proceeded to Palmer's last known address from the file. When we arrived, we discovered Palmer, identified from his most recent mug shot, about to depart in a white van. Palmer did not resist arrest and gave us permission to search his person and the van. We discovered the bloodied clothes and read Palmer his Miranda rights. As we placed him into custody, he said the following, which I include because it seems indicative of a confession. Palmer stated, "You don't understand. It wasn't for me. It was for him." When queried as to what this meant, Palmer said, "You'll see. He's coming back. He's almost here."

—Fort Collins (Colorado) Police Department Report,
November 11, 2010

September 20, 2012, Canton, Ohio

Agent Courtney locked herself into the hotel suite and pulled the blackout blinds on the window. Sometimes she wondered why hotels bothered with windows. Hotel rooms were supposed to be the last bastion of privacy; an anonymous little cave where you can shut out all natural light, walk around with your gut and your ass hanging out and order pay-per-view porn without feeling too guilty. Nobody really wanted to be seen inside a hotel room.

Least of all Agent Courtney. Formerly Helen Holt of the CIA, DHS, and above and beneath all of those, the Shadow Company.

Helen—as she still thought of herself in the privacy of her own mind, at least—was now unofficially retired from all of her former aliases, mainly because her former bosses supposed her to be dead.

They were half right.

Helen rolled her neck as best she could and began the long process of disrobing and preparing for the night.

With her right hand, she removed the scarf that covered the tight bandage on the left side of her neck. She examined the wound. It had started only as a needle prick, but it never healed. It was the only thing on her left side that looked vaguely alive. It was still fresh with blood. She kept the bandage on to keep it from spreading or becoming infected.

She used her right hand to undo her shoulder holster, a specially designed double rig with a SIG Sauer and a .44 Colt lined up one under the other. Her left hand was useless for reloading. She carried the SIG for the number of shots it carried, the .44 as backup in case the SIG jammed.

She struggled from her clothes next. That was getting easier all the time. It had taken her months to do anything more than drag her left side around like a slab of frozen meat on a hook. Now it responded to her commands, but as if it were receiving them across a great distance.

Other people might take her for a stroke victim, as the young cop had earlier that night. Or they might assume some disease or accident or birth defect had left her partially paralyzed.

Only when Helen was naked, examining herself in the full-length mirror, was the split running down her body starkly and readily apparent.

It was as if her left side were petrified, turned into flesh-colored stone. Her eye did not blink, did not tear up. It was clear as glass. Her skin had become flawless and cold, smooth and unblemished. The muscle underneath was several times heavier now; if she swung her arm against a man's neck he'd go down like he'd been clubbed with a tree branch. And any damage to her left side simply went away after a while. A bullet wound she'd suffered on her upper biceps hadn't healed; it had filled in, like someone patched it with cement. That spot was number and deader than the rest of her.

At the middle of her body, there was a border marking the change back to human flesh. Her right side moved and breathed. Her pulse jumped under skin that freckled in the sun. She had a slight cut scabbing on her knee from where she'd shaved that morning; hair still grew on her right leg, and she only ever had to cut one side of the hair on her head. She was stuck between immobile perfection and flexible but flawed humanity.

She began her nightly ritual of exercises. She levered herself into a sitting position on the motel bed, her legs straight out in front of her.

Helen had found that she did not really sleep anymore. She could drop into a kind of dull trance at night, but her open eye kept seeing, and half of her body would never really rest. Part of her brain could doze and dream. The other part would keep puttering along, a constant low murmur of thoughts and plans.

However, if she didn't work her left side and work it hard every night, then it grew more frozen and stony. So instead of sleeping, Helen planned and schemed while she forced her tombstone-silent limbs to respond. She started with the toes, mentally screaming at them to wiggle, dammit, wiggle. After she'd gotten a slight twitch from each one, she moved on to her ankle, her knee, and so on.

Sweat poured from her right side as her muscles shook with the effort. She never considered stopping or giving up. Helen hated both sides of herself. But not nearly as much as she hated the people who did this to her.

First, she blamed Dr. Johann Konrad—an asset she'd

been assigned to protect several years before. A mad scientist of the very old school, he'd promised her a way to eternal youth if she betrayed her country. She'd thought she was playing him, but it turned out he'd never trusted her. Instead of his Elixir of Life, he gave her an altered version that slowed her biological processes to geological time scales. If it had not been for a last-minute, reflexive second of mistrust when she slapped away his syringe, he would have given her a full dose. She would have been frozen inside her own body for God only knows how many years, unable to do anything but think. As it was, he'd managed to cut her in two.

The second entity she blamed for this was the Shadow Company itself. They had promised her power and they delivered. They'd recruited her from the CIA for her ruthlessness, for her total lack of a moral compass. But they knew her weakness, her fear of aging and death, and they dangled Konrad and his Elixir in front of her. As it turned out, they'd seen her intentions before she even formed them. When she thought she was betraying them by giving Konrad the ability to carry out his attack on the White House, she was actually doing what they wanted. Then she was sacrificed like any other pawn.

Konrad had left her, half paralyzed, half dead, without looking back. The Company had abandoned her, assuming Konrad had killed her. But neither had banked on the sheer power of Helen's hatred.

She would live if only to spite them and to get her revenge.

Konrad was still out there in the world. She knew she

had plenty of time to deal with him. Nothing would kill him before she did. So he became the bottom of her list of priorities.

The Shadow Company was powerful and vast and mysterious. It was a much more difficult target, as she knew from her years inside it. Agents worked in cells and information was sequestered. There was no hierarchy or chain of command that anyone at Helen's level could see. It would take extraordinary effort to break open the Company's inner structure. It would take years just to find out how to begin.

That was all right. She had years. And, thanks to the skills and knowledge she'd amassed inside the Company, she had the funding and intel to be patient. She'd used passwords no one had bothered to change to empty several offshore accounts that no one had bothered to close. She set up back doors and secret log-in codes deep in the information structure of the Pentagon, the NSA and the DHS. She had everything she could want to run a one-woman insurrection.

All of those tools and all of her preparation went into the hunt for her primary target, the center of her purest hate. She thought of him almost as a beloved doll she would take out in the middle of the night and hold and stroke with the fingers of her mind. She imagined all the lovely, lovely ways to hurt him.

It wouldn't be easy. He was smart, he was tough and he wasn't human.

Nathaniel Cade. He'd insulted her more than anyone

else. He'd ignored her and belittled her. He hadn't even considered her a threat.

And for that, he was going to die.

She recruited—or kidnapped, take your pick—Reyes, who was the only surviving member of her cell back in Los Angeles. Reyes was more scared of her than he was of an ancient conspiracy that worked to topple the U.S. government from within. And for good reason. She was always closer than the Company, and he'd seen her work on people who crossed her.

With Reyes at her side, Helen sought to find a weapon that might finally destroy Cade. Once Cade was truly dead, she could move on. Find a little peace. A little closure. And start working on killing everyone inside the Shadow Company.

A girl had to do something to fill her days, and she suspected she had a lot of them ahead of her. Her left side had not aged at all since Konrad's injection. She could go days without food, water or sleep. Her right side might die, but she wasn't sure that would mean anything at all.

That was the other reason Helen wanted to save Konrad for last. He could either restore her or deliver what she'd originally been promised. She was sure of it. But it would take time to figure out how to get enough leverage on him to make him do it right this time.

Helen finally finished her routine. Her right side was soaked in sweat and rank and feverish. Her left was still as cool and unscented as poured concrete.

On her shaky right leg, she stumbled to the shower. She

tripped and didn't have the strength to put out an arm to stop herself. She plowed facedown into the carpet.

For a moment, she just lay there, damp and stinking and exhausted.

She hated this. She hated every single second of this weird half-life.

But she hated Cade more.

After a moment, she shoved herself up and dragged her body toward the bathroom once again.

After her shower and a quick, impersonal use of Reyes's body, Helen Holt sat down in the hotel room's faux-leather armchair. She'd thrown operational guidelines into the trash and asked for a room on a high floor. She felt the need to be above things for a little while.

With her good hand, she lifted a tumbler of minibar vodka and drank while she stared at the dead TV screen.

Reyes had wasted no time getting dressed and leaving the room. He was probably already in one of the nearby restaurants—a TGIChiliMcAppleBarrel's or whatever—to order his usual variation on a burger and too many drinks.

This life was killing him slowly. He was running to fat, his reflexes had slowed, and he struggled through a fog of hatred for her every day. She could see it. Her sexual needs—she thought of it as her physical therapy—seemed to leave him more drained every time. He was essentially in prison, dying inside the cell she'd built around him. Not that she cared much. But it meant she'd have to replace him eventually.

Right now, she had more pressing concerns. She had to find the Boogeyman. She had to interrupt the cycle.

Helen still had access to the Shadow Company's extensive computer archives—she'd installed a back door in the intranet when she was still among the living—so she had a basic outline of how the conflicts between Cade and the killer worked. The Boogeyman would kill, his actions written off as unrelated disappearances, mass hysteria or random violence until he amassed a body count high enough to draw the attention of the press and the people in the federal government trained to look out for these patterns. Then Cade would travel to his latest hunting ground, find him and kill him. The Boogeyman would return to the Other Side until his cultists could slaughter enough innocents in ritual fashion and bring him back. And the cycle would start again.

Not even the cultists knew where or who the Boogeyman would become. Looking at the scattered, loosely affiliated network of Satanists, drug addicts, social rejects and sexual sadists, Helen found it hard to believe they'd been spawned from the same Order that once employed her. They were mostly amateurs, funded sporadically by wealthy burnouts who believed their money had elevated them above mere mortals or by criminals who believed they owed something to Satan. Helen found them all more than a little bit pathetic. If your master plan depends on a group of stoned teenagers chanting Led Zeppelin lyrics backward, she thought, then you seriously fucked up somewhere in the process.

Still, she couldn't deny their ability to inspire fear—or turn regular citizens into corpses. What they lacked in skill or intelligence or strategy, they made up in enthusiasm. Sure, they almost all got caught or ended up sacrificed on their own altars. But there was never any shortage of fresh recruits to take their place. Someone always believed he could get the best of a deal with the Devil.

Helen put herself in the mind of a psychopathic killer (done) and mentally assembled what she knew from the archives. She tried to think illogically. Rather than killing for the most direct benefit, the Boogeyman killed to fulfill some obligation to whatever spawned him on the Other Side. When Helen had been with the Company, they used occult tech—as they called it—as a tool, a means to an end. They didn't think of it as a duty or a contract with whatever made it work. It was a means to an end.

But the Boogeyman was invested with power as an end in itself. He had to use it in a certain way. He had to follow a pattern—

She sat up in the chair.

Of course. It wouldn't make sense. Not to anyone else. But it would to him.

She opened her laptop and pulled up a map. She had the first two killings marked on the green expanse of the United States. She dragged the cursor between them, measuring the distance. A little junior high geometry to extrapolate the other distances and angles and she could draw the rest.

It looked so obvious now.

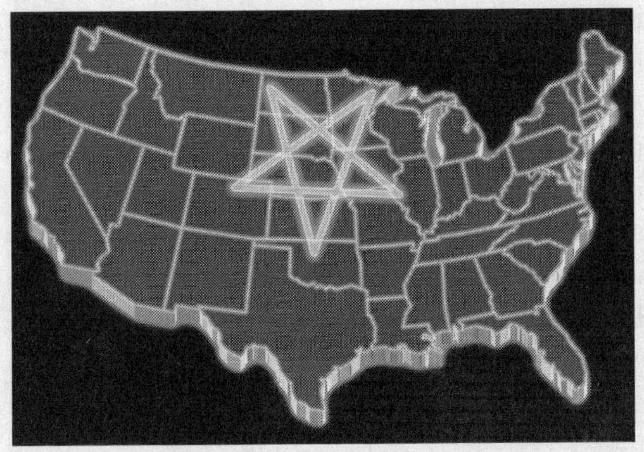

A PENTAGRAM.

Inverted, as it was in the old rituals meant to pervert the magic Solomon used to command demons and protect his people from their evil. Most modern-day wannabes got all their info from the Internet and heavy-metal bands, so they all got the orientation wrong.

But right at the center. Right where you'd put a demon if you wanted to summon it.

Omaha, Nebraska.

She grabbed her phone. Reyes answered instantly. "Get out your credit card," she told him. "We need to charter a jet."

She hung up without waiting for his reply. Half of Helen's face smiled. This might be easier than she thought.

She knew she had no chance against Cade in a head-on confrontation. She'd tried that before. The bastard had walked away from a C-4 explosion and just kept on moving. She knew vampires were tough to kill, but Cade had to be part cockroach as well.

However, her time with the Company taught her that there were other things that bumped in the night. And this one, in particular, was literally made to fight Cade.

She'd like to believe the Boogeyman stood a chance against Cade. But experience had taught her otherwise. The Boogeyman simply wasn't going to beat him.

Not without a little help.

TEN

This is the Zodiac speaking. I wish you a happy Christmas. The one thing I ask of you is this, please help me. I cannot reach out because of this thing in me won't let me. I am finding it extremely difficult to keep in check I am afraid I will lose control again and take my ninth & possibly tenth victim. Please help me I am drowning. . . . Please help me I can not remain in control for much longer.

—Letter from the Zodiac Killer, December 20, 1969

AUGUST 24, 2012, OKLAHOMA CITY, OKLAHOMA

It was so easy. The part of him that was still human didn't know it was going to be that easy.

He'd picked his victim without much thought at all—probably because he kept telling himself she wouldn't really be his victim. Right up to the point where he took out the blade, he kept telling himself it was nothing more than a dry run, to see how far he could go before backing away.

But the part of him that was drowning in blackness knew that was just an excuse. A necessary excuse, so it let him believe it.

He saw her at the hotel bar. She was in her early thirties, reasonably attractive but worn down by a day of airports and layovers. Still, she gave him a slight smile when he approached.

The uniform helped. His mother had once told him that women love a man in uniform. It was true. Despite all that talk of feminism, they still wanted a big strong man to tell them what to do. They would trust anyone who gave them an order in the right tone of voice.

They had a few more drinks. The alcohol hit her hard. He didn't even feel it. It was like drinking water. His eyes remained sharp and clear while hers grew unfocused.

He suggested returning to his room—he wasn't actually staying at the hotel, but she didn't know that. She nodded and slipped off the bar stool, nearly toppling when her heels hit the floor.

He helped her along, and she didn't object to his arm around her.

On the second floor, they stopped at a door. It wasn't his room. It wasn't anyone's; it led to a corridor that led to a laundry room. But it looked like a hotel room, made to blend into the upscale decor. More important, it was out of the view of any of the security cameras—he'd checked the angles a few days earlier, when he was scouting this place, again telling himself it was just an exercise, just a little harmless playacting. Every man needed a hobby. Some guys played at Civil War reenactments. Others went on fishing trips. He just wanted to see if he could do it. It didn't mean he really would do it.

He shoved her roughly against the door and kissed her hard. She kissed him back, maybe a little hesitantly—maybe she began to sense something was off about this. About him.

He knew he could walk away right now. She'd be confused, but alive. And no one would ever know.

Standing there, he knew the time had come to make the choice. Then it happened so fast, it barely seemed like a choice at all.

His fist came up and punched her in the temple like a piston had fired somewhere in his arm. The woman's eyes rolled up into her skull, and he caught her as she fell. His body felt like it was moving automatically, his arms and legs working as if running through some prewritten software program.

He moved quickly down the corridor, out the stairwell door, and down the stairs, carrying her as if she was still only drunk and stumbling. He kept up the charade for anyone who might step out of their rooms unexpectedly rather than any concern for the security cameras. The cameras were blacked out with spray paint. He didn't expect the hotel's security to notice until they ran the recordings.

Something in his head promised him this was the only time he'd have to take measures like this. He didn't know how he knew that. But he knew. After this, things would just work out on their own.

His car waited by the stairwell exit on the back side of the hotel. There was no light in this corner of the parking lot—someone had smashed the overhead security lamp with a rock, and the other guests had avoided parking nearby.

He tossed her into the backseat and drove away calmly. The human part of him was amazed at how calm he was, how relaxed. It was like he'd done this a thousand times before.

The dark part of him just eased into the old familiar rhythms.

He went to the spot he'd picked by the river. His breath fogged, but he didn't feel the cold.

She began to stir as he carried her roughly over the uneven ground. That was fine. He wanted her to be awake. He wanted her to see this coming.

If he'd been honest with himself, he would have known there was no turning back now. He was looking at prison. Disgrace. Shame.

But he wasn't being honest with himself. That time was long gone. He kept telling himself this was only a test even as the dark heart in him quickened.

If he'd been honest with himself, he would have admitted he was not even a little worried about prison.

The woman was crying and gibbering in fear as he yanked her to her feet. She'd lost her shoes somewhere along the way. He noticed only because her feet were not touching the ground. He wasn't sure when it had happened, but he'd dragged her up and now was holding her, one-handed, her coat and blouse bundled in his fist, dangling just a few inches off the ground.

He knew he'd gotten stronger, but this was still a surprise. It was like she weighed nothing. He felt proud.

He looked at her crying face, the snot and tears flowing down across her mouth like a toddler throwing a tantrum.

It occurred to him that he couldn't hear her. There was a buzzing in his ears that drowned out everything but a few words here and there. It made her look like a badly dubbed foreign film.

He laughed at the thought.

He had the blade in his other hand now. He'd concealed it in a special pocket in his coat, with a slit so he could simply reach inside and draw it out whenever he wanted.

She screamed. At least he assumed she did, because her mouth was wide open and her head was pitched back.

He didn't care. There was no one around for miles. He'd picked the spot carefully. Back when this was only a game.

Now he knew. Now he knew this was real. He was going to do it.

And then it was done.

The blade was still in his hand, but the fear was gone from her eyes. Everything was gone from her eyes. Warm blood flowed down his glove from the ugly gash in her throat. Her head lolled back at a steep angle, and he realized what he'd done.

He had done it. It all happened so fast. She was dead.

He had a brief moment of clarity as he realized this was the last step in a long process. Everything he had been before slipped away; inside himself, the last tethers to his humanity slipped and snapped, leaving him dangling over the edge of a great chasm.

Just behind him, he could feel it. The new him. The one ready to take over now, to take full possession.

But he knew it had been him, and no one else, who had taken the last step up to the cliff. He could have stopped himself from ever going this far. He could have stopped the other as well.

Now it was too late. He felt a great sadness. Then there was a pressure behind him, propelling him down, down, down, into the dark, and he fell away forever. And with that, he was dead too. The black thing in his heart welled up and filled his veins and soaked into every fiber of his being.

A moment later, he looked around with new eyes. He blinked away something and gazed at the fresh kill still in his hand.

He dropped the corpse to the ground. The changes were already under way. Physically, he would start to get much, much stronger. He could already hear the life in the meadow by the river. The tiny movements of birds and animals waiting, hiding in fear. Fear of him.

There was still something blurring his vision. He wiped his eyes and looked at the moisture. It took him a moment to recognize it.

Tears.

He would have laughed if he was capable of that anymore. But, like crying, that was something gone forever now.

He realized he'd smeared blood on his face. It seemed fitting. A baptism. A new beginning.

"It's nice to be back," he said out loud.

THE NEXT MORNING, safe at home, four hundred miles from the crime scene, he woke and looked at the ceiling. He knew it should look familiar—on an intellectual level, he realized it must have been the sight he'd been waking to for years now. But there was nothing familiar about it. It simply existed, like the body that served him as a shell.

Memory was always a problem for him. There were remnants of conflicting histories lurking all through his skull: images of life as a boy at a summer camp, or as a janitor at an elementary school, or wrapped in a straitjacket in an institution somewhere. None of those past lives were particularly significant to him, however. He'd nested in too many places to count, finding a new one every time he came back. Their experiences sometimes got tangled with his own, surfacing at odd moments. But none of them made any difference in who he really was. At best, they were scenes on a decaying screen at an abandoned drive-in, fuzzy and filled with gaps, played by unknown actors who died and never returned for any sequels.

He was born, not made. He was becoming. Rising up, like maggots through a corpse, chewing little pathways to the surface and breaking through the skin. And every time he was reborn, he woke up with the same need. It was simple, inarguable and always present. No matter where he was—or who he was—he needed to kill. And that was all he needed.

But for the first time, he wanted something else. It scratched at the back of his mind with an almost physical insistence.

He rose from the bed and walked to the kitchen. He needed food.

Soon, he wouldn't. Already he was stronger. Last night, he'd gripped the bathroom doorknob and crumpled it like a soda can. His tolerance for pain was increasing, too. He didn't notice the cuts on his palm and fingers until he saw the trail of blood droplets following him around the house.

In the kitchen, the pressure at the back of his skull increased. Some memory from all his previous incarnations nagged at him. There was an obstacle. Something that would keep him from his task. Something—someone—who wouldn't let him do his job.

Cade.

With the name came the memories, and with the memories, the rage.

Too many times, Cade had stopped him too soon. (It was always too soon. In truth, he never wanted to stop on his own.)

He could start again, he knew, but Cade would come after him eventually. No matter how often they fought, it always ended the same way. Strong as he was, he'd never managed to kill the vampire. He had to face the truth: he probably never would.

That grated on him for a long time. He realized he'd been standing with the fridge open. He took out milk and poured it on a bowl of cereal.

He began to want something even more than he wanted to kill.

Well, maybe not more. But just as much, certainly. This time, he wanted to hurt as well as to kill.

He was tired of Cade's interference. He used to see the vampire as nothing more than an obstacle. Now he wanted revenge. It was a novel sensation. He'd been driven after certain targets before, certain people, but this was different.

He wanted Cade to pay. And he knew just how he would do it.

It was right there on the front page of the newspaper his host had read only the day before. The President of the United States. The one thing in the world Cade was forced to care about.

Just another weak bag of flesh. It was almost going to be too easy.

He realized he'd been clutching the spoon so tightly he'd reopened the cuts on his hand. Blood dripped into his cereal bowl. The milk was bright red now.

He kept eating.

December 21, 1890
Mystery Hill, New Hampshire

Francis Tumblety's eyes stung. Sweat rolled down his brow. He'd dressed in thick wool for the New Hampshire winter, and now his clothes were soaked. He was not accustomed to this type of physical effort. Walking up the hill in the dying light had been hard enough. But killing the whore was far more work than he'd anticipated.

To be honest, none of this was going as planned.

He tried, once again, to wipe his hands clean of the blood. The knife had almost slipped from his fat fingers while he was wearing gloves, so he'd removed them before he stepped behind the woman and put the blade to her throat.

It had all seemed much simpler in his mind. He was surprised when the blade encountered resistance, and then shocked when the whore turned and fought him despite the wound. He realized he'd never actually cut into a living human being, despite all the years he'd called himself "doctor." She smacked a fist into his eye and he nearly fell over.

He'd been forced to stab the woman again and again until she finally fell to the dirt floor of the cave. He didn't mind that part. She was a disagreeable creature. They'd ridden in a warm, comfortable coach all the way here, him gagging on her unwashed scent while she complained ceaselessly. He'd left the details of procuring the whore to his brothers in the Order, but apparently he should have specified they find one who'd bathed recently. As far as she knew, she was being taken to a rich man's party to be used and abused by his guests. She drank an entire bottle of brandy by herself and swore like a sailor when Tumblety informed her they'd have to walk up the hill from the road.

But the location was crucial. Crowley had been very specific. "It must be a place of power," the English magician had told him. "Otherwise, your ritual will fail."

Tumblety looked in his books of Indian lore and potions and found references to what was now called the Whateley Farm. The locals, however, called it Mystery Hill. Strange lights, eerie sounds, and a giant carved stone table, located in a room quarried from the rock. The Indians took no responsibility for it. They said it belonged to the "ones who came before" and shunned the place.

To Tumblety, it sounded perfect. When they had arrived, however, the whore balked. "A rich man is having a party in there?" she said, pointing at the cave. She laughed and turned back to the carriage. Tumblety looked around nervously, but there was no one to hear her except the driver and he was of the Order. The only sign of human life was an empty, moldering farmhouse. Otherwise, the area would have looked just as it did before settlers ever touched the shores.

Tumblety had given her more money on the spot, and

that was enough to salve any suspicions she might have. "I always get the strange ones," she muttered, but she'd gone with him into the chamber willingly.

Now he nudged the woman with his boot. She made another sucking, strangling sound. Her hand scrabbled out as if clutching at her rapidly departing life. Tumblety stepped away quickly.

Her blood was pooling on the ground and congealing. He couldn't have that. He needed it.

While she desperately gasped for air, Tumblety briskly set about removing her garments. She was heavily layered against the cold and seemed to carry everything she owned on her person. The smell did not improve. Tumblety choked and gagged several more times.

But he got the clothing off and managed, heaving and straining, to get the woman onto the flat ceremonial table. In the dim lantern light, he saw old red stains on the stone before her fresh blood covered them.

His ineptitude at the actual killing turned out to be a benefit. Her heart continued to pump for a long time. He needed every minute to draw the symbols on the walls and floor. Actual blood was much harder to use than the paints he'd practiced with, and the dry rock seemed to drink the red liquid faster than he could move the brush.

After what seemed like hours, it was done.

Tumblety was still drenched. His long handlebar mustache, usually waxed and curled, drooped below his fleshy neck. He wiped the sweat from his eyes. He wished he'd been able to use the driver for the hard work—the man was loyal, and well-paid for it. And aside from him, Tumblety had his confederates in the Order. But Crowley had been specific about this, as well. "The work must be done by your hand, and your hand alone," he'd intoned, doing his best to sound like an Old Testament prophet. Still, Tumblety was in no position to argue. Crowley had conjured a moonchild—a living being from nothingness. The proof was all over London's Whitechapel district. Along with great buckets of blood, but that was to be expected.

Tumblety adjusted the lantern so he could see the paper and read the words Crowley had scrawled for him there.

He began to chant. Nothing happened at first. He'd done similar incantations as part of the show he delivered to the people who paid top dollar for his medicines. But with those, he was sure none of his treatments really worked. True, he would shout down any man who challenged his results or his credentials. But there was always that nugget of doubt, like a stone caught in a horse's hoof, that worried him. For some reason, he always managed to forget some crucial detail or get some important step wrong. He'd seen others work seeming miracles and create abominations, but he wondered if they were fooling him or if he was fooling himself.

To stiffen his resolve, Tumblety thought of the reasons for doing this. He'd been imprisoned, unlawfully detained by the federal government on suspicion of involvement in that tyrant Lincoln's death. Grant, that inebriate, had ordered a massive sweep of arrests in the wake of the assassination. It had been widespread, indiscriminate and wholly illegal. It had also managed to scoop up many of the members of the Order.

A judge forced the release of all the prisoners—freedom was not completely dead in the country, despite how the war ended—but Tumblety never forgot the humiliation. More than ever, he was convinced of the rightness of his cause, of the need to abort this bastard child called America.

However, the brush with extinction—never before had so many of them faced exposure—caused a split in the Order. The majority of the members wanted to continue with the current plan, to overthrow the government from within. They saw the rituals of the Order as tradition or superstition, nothing more. They no longer believed in the powers that gave birth to the Order. But others, like Tumblety, were tired of waiting for success from earthly means. He and his sect broke away to find methods beyond the merely human to accomplish their goals.

Tumblety was more convinced than ever when he heard about the vampire. Through his connections in New Orleans, he learned the pretender to the throne had enlisted Marie Laveau to create a supernatural protector for the White House. He knew the members of the old Order would fail. They could not hope to defeat something that was not of this world. Only Tumblety could create a counter to the creature now serving the president.

Tumblety found the records of the witch cult of Salem; paid an exorbitant price for the journal hidden in the home of the bloody Bender family; and finally, made his trip to England to consult with Crowley.

If he didn't want to waste all those years, he knew he

could not falter now. He chanted louder, calling to nameless things that had fed at this trough centuries before. He knew they were there. He knew it.

The air grew even colder. Steam rose from the woman's blood. He kept chanting.

The light grew dimmer.

Tumblety felt a small excitement. A wind picked up in the chamber. The lantern dimmed as if swallowed in a dark fog. Tumblety didn't care. He closed his eyes, the words spilling from his lips as if he'd learned them since birth. He no longer needed the paper. He no longer needed light. The smell of blood filled his nostrils. The room was saturated, drowning in blood. It didn't make him ill this time. It thrilled him to his very core.

For some reason, in his mind's eye, Tumblety thought of a massive sea creature, like the Bible's Leviathan, like the Midgard Serpent, rising to the surface of the ocean. It was enormous, its back breaking the waters, and it just kept rising, rolling back the waves like a newborn continent—

And then it turned and noticed him.

Tumblety was flung across the room. He hit the stone wall hard. Spots danced in his eyes, and for a moment, he passed out.

He wasn't sure how long he was unconscious. It was probably only a few minutes. His mouth tasted of copper, and his body was wrung out. He imagined this was how Ben Franklin must have felt after the lightning struck.

Tumblety rose unsteadily to his feet and looked around the chamber. There was no new presence there. The lantern burned steadily. It was as if nothing had happened.

He'd failed.

Then, with a start that nearly took him to his knees again, he realized what was missing.

The body of the whore was gone. The table was as clean as a plate licked by a hungry dog.

Tumblety staggered back. His heart skipped. In future years, he'd trace the chest pains that would eventually end his life back to this night. In that moment, he realized, he'd entered into a compact with something far older and more primal than even Crowley could understand. That creature he'd seen in his mind, that feeling of something huge, whatever it was, sat beneath the whole of the American landscape, raising its snout only to guzzle blood and death. It slept for centuries. It was here long before anything human.

And Tumblety had woken it.

In return, perhaps, it had given him something back. But it would require more blood.

Fortunately, he and the other members of the Order were prepared to supply all it needed.

Tumblety hurried back to the coach. He would never come to Mystery Hill again. He wouldn't have to.

The thing he'd done here would follow him all the way to the grave.

ELEVEN

WICHITA, Kan.—Confessed BTK serial killer Dennis Rader made his first public apology for the murders that horrified a community for a quarter-century, blaming a "demon" that got inside him at a young age.

Rader, who pleaded guilty last week to 10 first-degree murders in the Wichita area from 1974 to 1991, nicknamed himself BTK, for "Bind, Torture, Kill," as he taunted media and police with cryptic messages about the crimes. He faces sentencing Aug. 17.

"I just know it's a dark side of me. It kind of controls me. I personally think it's a—and I know it is not very Christian—but I actually think it's a demon that's within me. . . . At some point and time it entered me when I was very young," said Rader, who was once president of his Lutheran church.

—"BTK Sorry for Murders, Blames 'Demon,'"
Associated Press, Thursday, July 7, 2005

SEPTEMBER 21, 2012, OMAHA, NEBRASKA

The Boogeyman got home just before 3 A.M. The kill of Curtis's flunky and the whore with him had gone incredibly well. He wore his uniform and jumped the security line and was able to bring his tools home.

No one else had been inside this house since long before his host's final step into the abyss. No one ever joined him for a beer or to watch the game anymore. His neighbors had stopped looking his way when he emerged from his place. Despite his appearance, which was still normal enough to pass for human, he radiated a strangeness that caused discomfort in anyone who got too close. His coworkers had learned to tolerate it, but nobody would spend more time with him than absolutely necessary.

So he was surprised to see the blond woman standing in his living room as he entered.

He reached his conclusions quickly and ruthlessly. No one came to visit him now; any intruder meant discovery; he wasn't finished with his work; therefore the woman had to die.

It took him a fraction of a second to add this all up, the same amount of time it took his muscles to launch himself at her.

But she had more than one surprise of her own.

With huge effort she swung her left arm in an arc to meet him. He expected to brush it away like dust. Instead, it was a solid oak beam colliding with his skull, sending him straight to the floor.

He prepared to spring at her again but froze. Another man was behind him. He was so intent on the blonde he hadn't noticed the other intruder until the man's gun was placed against the back of his head.

For an instant, he was filled with the familiar, adolescent rage. He wasn't done with his work. He wasn't finished, God damn it.

Then he realized these two were not here to kill him or stop him. If they were, the man would have pulled the trigger at once. Even if he had, though, it wouldn't kill the Boogeyman. He could take several bullets without slowing. He could have torn them both apart before they would have recovered from their shock.

But he was intrigued. His eyes met the blonde's.

He saw now. He could even smell it a little. She had a touch of the Other Side in her. It had taken part of her body and remade it. Half of her was as inhuman as he was now.

"Are you going to behave?" she asked from the side of her mouth.

He nodded.

She made an impatient gesture. The Boogeyman felt strong steel manacles lock around his wrists and ankles.

"You'll forgive me if I don't trust you entirely," she said. But the man withdrew his gun and crossed to stand beside the woman. He was a thick Hispanic man with once-handsome features gone blunt and cruel.

"I know what you are," she said. "More important, I know what you want to do. And I know you're going to fail. Again."

That irritated him a little. She was still mainly human. Who was she to judge him?

She seemed to sense this. "It's not your fault," she said. "You've got someone in your way. He's been an obstacle to me as well. I haven't done any better against him. You know who I'm talking about, right? You do remember why you've failed every time before?"

He nodded again. The look on his face was murderous.

"Cade," she said with a smile. "Believe me, I feel the same way. I know what you were planning. Kill Curtis's people. Draw Cade out. And while he's looking for you in one place, you circle around and go after the president. Not a bad plan. But if I can figure it out, so can Cade. In fact, the only reason I'm here before him is because I was waiting for you. I've been waiting for you for a long time. I've been tracking the killings that made you."

The Boogeyman looked at her with new respect. He wasn't sure who—or what—she was, but she was clearly not fully human.

"You haven't realized yet that Cade will race back to protect the president before you ever get within a hundred miles. Believe me on this one. I've tried. He and that little shit Barrows are already on their way to D.C., I bet. A frontal assault is only going to end the same way it always does for you. You want to hurt Cade? You need to keep him off balance. You have to change your methods."

He flinched. Changing his methods was like dying. What he did was what he was.

"Don't worry. You'll only have to adjust a little. It will be like aiming a gun instead of throwing a grenade. You'll still get your recommended daily allowance of blood and death. But you do it my way and you'll get Cade, too."

He hesitated. There was no way to trust this blond creature. But she made a compelling case.

"Tell you what," she said, reaching inside her bag with her good hand. "I have a little item here that should seal the deal. Consider it a free gift. No obligation to buy."

She tossed it on the floor in front of him. It was a Halloween mask, a rubber hood designed to cover the whole head. The latex was a bright, hideous yellow with black markings over the places where the wearer's eyes and mouth would peek out of tiny slits.

It was supposed to be a smiley face.

It was beautiful. He loved it instantly.

The Boogeyman thought it over. He stood and snapped the manacles. He gave her his answer with a question.

"Who do I have to kill?"

Half of her face lit up with a grin. "That's the best part. Trust me, you're going to love this."

TWELVE

If it is true that the gods of one religion become the demons of the one that replaces it, then we in America must deal with the generations of demons once worshipped here who now wander the countryside, the city streets, the interstate highways and dead end roads, the theme parks and fast food restaurants, the shopping malls and parking lots, the peepshow parlors and cathedral aisles like hungry ghosts on a mission from Hell. We gaze with horror on their crimes, and don't understand. We stare into the eyes of their hideous creatures, and don't understand. We clean up the crime scenes and mop up the blood, and don't understand. We imprison, institutionalize, execute to make it all go away . . . and don't understand.

—Peter Levenda, *Sinister Forces*

September 21, 2012, The Reliquary, Washington, D.C.

Cade turned on his computer. Zach had gone home to sleep. They were to meet with the president in less than four hours. He intended to write down the details of the crime scene for the archives.

Instead, he found an e-mail waiting for him.

This was unusual. There were only two people with his

e-mail address. Zach and the president. Neither used it. Mostly, Cade received random advertisements for something called Cialis.

But the return address on this caught his attention.

From: ASmileIsYourUmbrella@gmail.com
To: Cade@WhiteHouse.gov
Subject: Miss me?

This was new. The last time, the Boogeyman had still been using the U.S. Postal Service.

Times change, he thought, and his microsecond smile crossed his face. Then he opened the message, and his expression went cold and dead again.

It's been a while, hasn't it? I'm sure you thought I was gone for good. But you know me. The proverbial bad penny. I always turn up.

It occurs to me that you're one of the few people who actually knows what that expression means. Kids these days, right? Ignorant and in love with their ignorance.

You know you can never beat me. Not as long as they keep feeding me. And they're never going to stop. They're all over the country. It makes me wonder, Cade. Why do you keep trying? How long do you think you can stop me from doing what I want? You're not really immortal. Not like me. Eventually, that corpse you're wearing is going to fail. Then you're dust.

Think about it, Cade. There have to be better uses of your time. Even if you left me alone, even if I killed a thousand people a year, it wouldn't make a dent in their numbers. They're everywhere. Packed in their houses, squatting on top of one another. The country is filled to bursting, like fat grubs squirming in a dead log. And they keep making more. Even the ones who don't squeeze out a clutch of larvae can't stop gobbling down food, making themselves even bigger, taking up more space. You can't tell me you don't find them as disgusting as I do.

Maybe you're just jealous. I have a ticket to an all-you-can-eat buffet while you're perpetually starving. You must hate me for that alone.

I always come back. One of these days, you won't be here.

Cade took the bait. His fingers danced on the keyboard.

From: Cade@WhiteHouse.gov
To: ASmileIsYourUmbrella@gmail.com

Then I suppose I'll have to find a way to kill you permanently this time.

He didn't have to wait more than a minute for the response.

From: ASmileIsYourUmbrella@gmail.com
To: Cade@WhiteHouse.gov

That's the spirit.

I'm warning you right now, Cade. This was just the beginning. I'm going to tear the president's heart out and make him watch. I'm going to destroy him utterly.

And you won't be able to do a thing to stop me.

But I sure hope you'll try.

Your lighthearted friend.

CADE KNEW BETTER THAN to attempt another message. Besides, there was nothing more to say.

He reached for his phone and called Zach.

"Wake up," he said.

"What? What's going on?"

Cade looked at the message again.

"Apparently, the rules of the game have just changed."

THIRTEEN

An ideal form of government is democracy tempered with assassination.

—Voltaire

The Oval Office, Washington, D.C.

"With all due respect, sir, are you out of your mind?"

The president raised an eyebrow. This would ordinarily be enough to shut Zach up, but not today.

However, Dan Lanning, the president's campaign manager, was more vocal in his displeasure.

"Barrows, I've got no idea what you're doing back," Lanning snapped, "but I'm sure as shit not going to take advice from a snot-nose who was fired from his last job at the White House."

That stung a bit, even if it was true as far as the world knew. His cover story had him resigning under pressure from his former post as deputy director of political affairs.

"Zach is going to be consulting on the campaign," Curtis said.

"Oh, well, now we're saved," Lanning said, voice dripping with sarcasm. "You know, it's not unusual for the opposition to send in a spy. They usually pick someone who was fired. Who might have a grudge. Somebody who needs the money."

"Dan," Curtis said, a warning tone in his voice. "Zach's loyalty is not a question."

Lanning frowned and turned to Cade. "And I don't even know who the fuck you are, let alone what you're doing in this meeting."

Cade didn't respond. Lanning seemed to realize something was off about him and looked away. Zach was impressed he'd been able to hold eye contact with Cade for as long as he did.

But then, Lanning was a throwback to a tougher time. He'd been friends with the president since Curtis's days in the Illinois state legislature. He ran Curtis's first campaigns for the Senate and the White House, then left for the private sector just before Zach started working with Cade. For a while, Lanning made insane amounts of money as a regular guest on the cable shoutfests. Now he was back, and everyone knew why. Every pundit in Washington wondered if he still had the ability to claw four more years out of the voters for Curtis.

The two men could not have been more opposite. President Curtis was always impeccably dressed; Lanning rumpled a suit ten minutes after he put it on. In private, the president was cerebral, reserved, and cool to the point of being cold. Lanning was given to shouting even when he was in a good mood. Zach had been on the receiving end of a few of Lanning's ass-chewings back in the day. They were epic sagas of righteous fury and perfectly applied touches of profanity. It was like being verbally disemboweled. And they were all the worse because Lanning was rarely ever wrong.

But Zach wasn't about to be intimidated by Lanning now. After three years working with a vampire, someone yelling at him just didn't carry the same jolt of fear anymore.

And given what they were planning forty minutes earlier, Zach was pretty sure Lanning was going to get Curtis killed.

FORTY MINUTES EARLIER:

Zach and Cade had arrived and been escorted into a campaign meeting in the Oval. (Every president walked a fine line when it was time to start campaigning. There were laws and regulations prohibiting the use of government facilities for campaign purposes, but exceptions for White House political appointees. The president couldn't really just pick up and leave the White House every time he wanted to talk politics. But as hypersensitive as voters were to even a hint of corruption, Curtis and his team had to be very careful. In light of that, the Curtis campaign reimbursed the White House kitchen $75 for coffee and muffins. God forbid the media find out the taxpayers bought muffins again.)

Zach wanted to tell the president immediately what they'd found and about the e-mail. (He had some concerns about why Cade was apparently Facebook friends with the patron saint of serial killers, but he'd put those aside.)

However, they had entered the room just in time to hear Lanning start talking.

"All our polling has us dead even with Seabrook," he said. "The prick has been hammering us as elitist and out of touch. We retreat into the White House and he'll tell everyone we're scared of the voters. As if he's the great voice of the common man. The guy was born with a silver dick in his mouth."

Everyone laughed. Lanning's foul mouth always managed to cheer people up.

"So we are going to take that stick away and beat him with it."

Then Lanning unveiled a five-state bus tour into the Heartland. Most of these states were deep red on the electoral map—considered locks for Seabrook and the Republicans.

That was the point, Lanning said. Curtis would arrive, do the grip-and-grin with voters who were unfriendly at best and openly hostile at worst. In public, Curtis was a charismatic figure. In person, he was one of the best retail politicians ever—up there with Clinton, maybe almost as good as Reagan. This would prove the president could still win votes out in "Real America."

And while he was doing that, his campaign would be working like hell in what Lanning called "the real target—Ohio."

Ohio was a swing state right in the middle of the Red Zone. "This election is going to come down to one or two precincts," Lanning said. "We make Seabrook fight for his base and we win over the undecideds in a crucial state. And most important, we show the world that President Curtis is still a regular guy who can walk around Main Street, U.S.A."

Everyone had loved the idea.

Zach thought it was suicide.

WHICH BROUGHT THEM TO THIS closed-door meeting with Curtis and Lanning.

"Look," Zach said, trying to keep his temper. "You may not be aware of everything that's been going on—"

The president gave Zach a curt shake of his head. Zach got the message instantly. Lanning was not "inside the knowledge," as they said of anyone who knew about Cade. Only a select few on what was called the Special Security Council and a handful of trusted Secret Service agents were allowed that privilege. Zach was glad to see Curtis was keeping the list short; too many people knew about the president's vampire for his comfort as it was.

That did make explaining things difficult, however. "There's been a death threat" was what Zach had to settle for.

"So what else is new?" Lanning said. "There are more mouth-breathers and whack jobs than ever out there. They get bored with Internet porn and watch *Taxi Driver* too many times and they think they can take out the president. It's part of the job."

"That's pretty easy for you to say, Dan. It's not your ass."

Lanning's face darkened. "You're not on the first team

anymore," he told Zach. "You haven't seen the latest numbers. Seabrook has the momentum. We're trending downward in the battleground states. If the president doesn't get out there and rally the troops, he's dead."

A sudden silence.

"Sorry," Lanning said. "Bad choice of words. But you know what I mean."

"Zach," the president said. "This is a crucial time. If I want to be in the White House in January, then I can't hide here now."

Without waiting for another protest from Zach, he turned to Lanning. "Dan, didn't you want to go over the logistics on the buses with Agent Butler?"

Lanning knew when he was being shoved out the door. "Yeah," he said. "I can do that."

He went to the door. "For what it's worth, Barrows, I'm glad you're back." It was as close to an apology as Lanning would ever get.

"Yeah, Lanning. You're lucky I'm here to bail you out again."

Lanning flipped Zach the finger before leaving.

Curtis looked at Zach and then Cade. "This is about Ohio, I assume."

Cade finally spoke up. "It's worse than we thought."

"It's him?"

Cade nodded. (The president didn't get corrected on the whole "it-him" thing, Zach noticed.) "Do you still intend to go through with this plan?"

"I do," Curtis said.

"Do you want to live to be inaugurated?" Cade asked.

The president's face set into a hard mask. He was not used to being questioned anymore. It came with the job. People did not disagree with the president. It was a handicap, because it reinforced the illusion of infallibility that most politicians have anyway. Zach had once heard the president described as "the most dangerous narcissist alive, because the world really does revolve around him."

The person who'd said that had been Samuel Curtis, back when he was just a United States senator.

But Cade couldn't be fired or demoted. This gave him a certain amount of ability to speak his mind to the president. And since his loyalty was unquestionable, the president couldn't simply dismiss his concern.

"I'm aware of the risks," Curtis said.

"I don't believe you are," Cade said. "This incarnation of the Boogeyman could literally be anyone. He has targeted you directly. You will not be safe until I can deal with this. I suggest you stay in the White House," he said.

The president actually laughed at that. "You do remember there's an election in a couple months, right?"

"Your life is in danger."

The president smiled a little. "It's not always safe here, either, as I'm sure I don't need to remind either of you."

Zach thought of his first assignment with Cade, which ended in a full-scale assault on the White House. There had been two bodies in the Oval Office alone, one of them belonging to his predecessor, Griff.

"The fact is, I want to keep this job," Curtis said. "I have things I still want to do. I am unconvinced my opponent will understand the real nature of the threats we face. I've made my decision. I trust you to handle it. That's why you will accompany me on this excursion."

Cade could not refuse a direct order from the president. It was built into him by his oath. He simply nodded.

Zach, however, needed a little more clarification.

"Whoa, whoa, whoa. You want to take Cade on the campaign trail? It's hard enough for civilians when they meet him, and that's usually after something from Hell has chewed up the local sheriff and spat him out. Bring him to a fund-raiser where the scariest thing people expect is a mention of Sarah Palin and your supporters will mess their silk undies. Humans do not mix well with vampires," he said to Curtis. He turned to Cade. "No offense," he said.

Cade's face was as stony as ever. "None taken."

"You've dealt with this reaction before, Zach. And Cade will still need someone to act for him in the daylight. That's why you've been officially rehired as a campaign consultant. Cade, you will work the night shift as a part of my Secret Service protection team."

Zach tried one last time. "Sir. That means increasing the number of people who know about Cade. You're talking about bringing an entire Secret Service detail inside the knowledge. I've been with you on the trail. There's no way to avoid them knowing. Cade will have to be fed. Placed in the coffin and shipped during the day. That means they will have to be briefed on all of this. The Boogeyman. The Other Side. Everything."

"You need to make it work. I trust you to deliver

as much information as necessary to the agents. After all, they're sworn to protect me, too. And none of them drink blood."

"Even so, sir, you're talking about a massive risk—"

President Curtis slapped one hand down on the table like a judge gaveling court to a close. "I am going to campaign. That is nonnegotiable," he said. He looked at Zach until the younger man looked away.

"Yes, sir," Zach said.

The president stood. Once he'd made a decision, he moved forward. The meeting was over. "Just one other thing," he said. "You'll need someone who can go between you and the campaign."

Zach didn't like the sound of that. "I thought we weren't going to play that game again."

The president knew what he meant. Curtis had tried to delegate the responsibility for Cade and Zach to his chief of staff about nine months earlier. Then it turned out that the man had betrayed the president to a shadowy conspiracy dedicated to overthrowing the government by occult means. When it all fell apart, he committed suicide rather than face Cade's wrath. The press chalked it up to the pressure of the midterm elections.

"We're not," the president said firmly. "But you do need someone with official status in the campaign who's already inside the knowledge about Cade. Someone who can get you access and information whenever you need it. Someone you can trust."

Zach couldn't think of anyone who filled that wish list.

Then Curtis pressed a button on the intercom. "You can come in now, sweetheart," he said.

Sweetheart? Zach's brain froze up. That couldn't mean—

The door opened.

A very attractive young woman walked in. Despite her efforts to dress conservatively in a suit jacket and skirt, she would still draw stares anywhere she went. She was twenty-one years old. Zach had sent a card on her last birthday. She hadn't replied.

The president sounded just a little amused when he said, "I believe you remember my daughter, Zach."

FOURTEEN

Oh, Candace. We see how you're trying, honey. You don't want to be the Paris Hilton of the political world anymore. You want to put that whole party-girl image behind you. You've even taken time off from that third-rate safety school to campaign for your daddy. (BTW, WTF? UCLA? Really? The President of the United States can't even get his daughter into Brown?) And really, we'd love to stop picking on you. But, sweetie, you are not making it easy for us. I mean, you cannot show up at an Iowa fund-raiser—Iowa! Farmers! The Heartland! Family values!—wearing a blouse that goes transparent under the TV lights. We even heard one of the people there say, "If I'd known there were going to be strippers at this thing, I'd have left the wife at home." We're sure you mean well, Candace. But you're not helping.

—Mudslinger, a political blog

The president left his own office. "I'll let you work out the details," he said to Candace and Zach.

Zach would have sworn he was smirking.

"This is how it's going to work," Candace told them. "He"—pointing at Cade—"does not go anywhere near the press or the public unless absolutely necessary. I still wake up from nightmares about what he did at the White House."

Cade said nothing.

"You mean where he saved your life?" Zach said.

She went on as if she hadn't heard him. "Zach, before he does anything, you will coordinate with me. I want to be consulted about every possible threat. Then the Secret Service will assist you and Cade in whatever action is approved by the president. I've written it up as this plan of action—"

"No," Cade said flatly.

"Excuse me?" Candace said.

"You heard me. You are frightened and you're trying to impose order on a fundamentally irrational situation. I can understand that. But I will not allow it. This is not a political problem. And you have no idea what you are dealing with. You do not know what's at stake."

"I know what's at stake," Candace said sharply. "I was there."

"Then don't interfere with me," Cade said.

"You think you can just run around a campaign killing people at random and no one will notice?" Candace said, her voice tight with anger. "You have got to have some kind of plan."

"Humans plan," Cade said. "God laughs."

"That's really deep. But like it or not, the president told you to cooperate with me."

"Yes," Cade said. "But you do not give me orders. You're his daughter, not a government official. My job is to protect you, not obey you."

"You keep talking to me like I'm a teenage bimbo and I'm going to find a stake," she shot back.

"Enough," Zach said. "Candace, stop it. I know you and I didn't leave things on the best of terms—"

"Really? You want to have that talk right now?"

"No," he said. "I want to solve the problem. You're right. We can't let anyone know about Cade. But I have been doing this for a while now. And if you want your father to live, you're going to have to listen to me."

"I suppose you've got a better idea?"

"Yes. As a matter of fact, I do."

Candace fumed for a moment, then gave him a smirk a lot like her dad's.

"So you've grown a pair, huh? All right, Zach. Tell me how it's going to work."

FIFTEEN

Remember all those photographs of Kennedy that adorned the apartments, shops and homes of people from North America to South America, from Europe to Asia, in the years after the assassination; usually placed next to a picture of Jesus or the Pope, it had a place of honor tantamount to a Last Supper painting. Without being able to articulate why, in many cases, the average person—particularly the average Catholic person—saw something divine, something terrible and sacred, in the idea of the murdered President.

—Peter Levenda, *Sinister Forces*

SEPTEMBER 23, 2012, PRESIDENTIAL EMERGENCY OPERATIONS CENTER, WHITE HOUSE, WASHINGTON, D.C.

The small conference room wouldn't have looked out of place in a business-class hotel. Only its location made it unique. Dug into the bedrock beneath the White House, the Presidential Emergency Operations Center had been built during the Kennedy administration as a bomb shelter and then seriously upgraded since 9/11. The room was usually reserved for the president for occasions like terrorist attacks or wars. It also linked to a tunnel leading back to the Reliquary. Deep under the ground and out of the light, it was Cade's main entry point to the White House.

The two dozen Secret Service agents squirmed uncomfortably. Some of them hesitated before sitting at the big conference table, as if they expected someone more important to take their chairs.

But as far as Zach was concerned, these men and women had just become more important than almost everyone in the United States government. They were about to be brought inside the knowledge.

Camden Butler, head of the president's personal detail, already knew about Cade. A couple of his most trusted agents were in on the secret as well. It would have made all their jobs impossible otherwise. But even these agents looked nervous. Not even the head of the Treasury Department or the director of the Secret Service knew what they were about to reveal.

Butler cleared his throat and began speaking.

"Let's get started," he said. "I'm only going to say this once. This is no joke. Your job just got significantly more difficult today. Your supervisors and I chose you because we believe you can handle it. This is above classified. What you're going to hear is a national security secret far bigger than anything you've ever dealt with before."

None of the agents spoke, but a few of them smirked quietly. They were responsible for protecting the most powerful people in the world day and night. That meant they got to see things the public never would; they knew everything from the location of nuclear codes to how long it took for the president and the First Lady to reach orgasm. It was not easy to impress them.

"I mean it," Butler said. "Anyone who thinks they're going to have a great new chapter in their memoirs or something to tell the grandkids, you need to realize we are talking about charges of treason, a military tribunal and execution."

Now there were a few scowls from the agents. They were the gatekeepers. They were never supposed to be on the wrong side of a secret.

One agent raised his hand. "If this is so secret, why do we have so many people here? Basic operational security: the fewer people who know, the better. So why tell us?"

Butler opened his mouth to reply, but he was cut off.

"Because I don't expect most of you to live through this," Cade said.

He simply appeared at the head of the table, moving quietly from the hidden entrance. Irrational panic seized the agents' hearts. Some jumped. One or two swept their jackets back to reach for their guns.

They were feeling the fear that Cade evoked. The fact that the man triggering this response was dressed just like them, in dark suit and white shirt, only made it worse.

"Easy," Butler said. "This is special operative Nathaniel Cade. He might be familiar to a few of you."

Zach saw some slow nods around the room. Cade was often at the edges of the Secret Service's professional turf.

Butler looked at Cade and nodded. His part was done.

Cade spoke again. "The President of the United States is under a threat that none of you are capable of handling."

There was some more murmuring and scoffing at that. Zach distinctly heard someone cough out the word "Bullshit." Cade zeroed in on the man. The agent shrank in his chair and silence filled the room again.

"This is not a reflection on your abilities. It is simply because the threat is not human."

Now there was open snickering. The cougher got his courage back. "What, is this where you tell us about the aliens?" he said. Nervous laughter.

Cade glanced at Zach, his eyebrow rising only a tiny fraction of an inch, as if to say, *They always need to see it for themselves . . .*

"The threat is not human. Neither am I."

Cade opened his mouth. His jaw seemed to hang far too low as his fangs jutted out, gleaming white in the light from the overhead lamps.

The laughter stopped. The agents froze in place. For a moment, Zach thought he could hear them sweating.

Cade closed his mouth.

There was a long moment of silence. Finally, a male agent stood. "This isn't funny."

Cade cocked his head slightly at the agent.

"Sit down, Thomason," Butler said.

The agent called Thomason wheeled on him. "Fire me if you want, but fuck this. It's too late for April Fools' and too early for Halloween. I don't know why you're doing this, but I can think of a lot better ways to spend my evening. If you need me, I'll be back in the real world."

Thomason turned to go.

And nearly bumped into Cade.

Thomason stumbled backward, eyes wild. He looked at the head of the table where Cade had been a second before. The space was empty. The other agents were now completely spooked. The room erupted in competing voices and noise.

"You're not in the real world anymore," Cade said. "You're in mine. If you want to survive the experience, you'll sit down and listen."

Just like that, he was back where he started as if he'd never moved at all. His voice didn't seem any louder than the agents', but somehow it cut through their babble like a knife. They all complied—even Thomason.

Cade looked over every one of them, met all of their eyes without blinking.

"I am a vampire," he said. "Whatever you've believed in the daylight, I exist. I protect the president and this country. I have done so for over a hundred and forty years. When this is done, if you are lucky, you can go back to not believing in me. Until then, we don't have time to waste on pointless denial."

One young female agent raised her hand timidly. Cade nodded to her.

"Why?" she asked. "Why would you protect us?"

"That's classified," Cade said. "And it's not why you're here."

Zach lit up the conference room video screen: a newspaper clipping from New Orleans about the Axman; a bloody hook stuck in the door handle of a late-1970s Camaro; a discarded clown costume behind crime-scene tape.

"Code name: BOOGEYMAN," Cade said. Nobody laughed. Zach figured they were afraid to see Cade's fangs again.

"This is an entity that emerges periodically to slaughter innocents. It has also shown a remarkable adaptability and a wide variety of physical and preternatural abilities."

Zach flipped to the e-mail he and Cade had shown Curtis.

"And now it wants to kill the president."

Zach sensed something then. The agents sat up a little straighter. They focused. A monster had crossed the threshold into their world, but it was still their world. As strange as their lives had just become, they understood now what they were being asked. They would do their best to be ready.

Zach moved on to the next slide, a list of confirmed and suspected encounters with the Boogeyman: FAIRVALE, CA; CAMP CRYSTAL LAKE, NJ; OJAI, CA; SPRINGWOOD, IL; SAN FRANCISCO BAY AREA, CA; NEW ORLEANS, LA; ASHLAND, KY; WICHITA, KS; LAKE HAVASU, AZ; TEXARKANA, TX.

"These are some of the known encounters with the Boogeyman. Sometimes I was able to stop him. Other times, I wasn't."

"Can we get any of this material?" the female agent asked.

Butler answered for Cade. "No, Dunn, you cannot. No paper. No notes. Everything is memorization only. We will not have any leaks. Period."

The agents stared harder at the list and its accompanying map, trying to burn it into their brains.

The cougher raised his hand now. Butler called on him. "Yeah. Latham."

"It's been around for almost a hundred years," Latham said. He looked at Cade. "Is it like you? A vampire?"

"No," Cade said. "It's worse."

"Awesome," Latham muttered.

"The best term for it might be a psychic parasite. It generally manifests in a human host until it consumes all traces of the original personality."

Cade got nothing but blank looks. "It takes over a human body," he explained. "It will drive that body until it breaks. Then it will find a new host and begin in a new incarnation."

"Do we know who he—I mean, who it—becomes?" Agent Dunn asked. "I'm not sure how to say this, but what kind of person does it—?"

Cade cut her off. "It could be anyone. It generally prefers white males; loners, alienated from society and lacking in ties to family or community. It looks for a weak spirit who wants to be more powerful, someone enraged at the world, nursing a grudge."

"Well, we got no shortage of guys like that in our files," Latham said. A few people even laughed.

Zach could see the microscopic shifts in Cade's demeanor that signaled anger. He clicked the remote and a new scene came up. The laughter stopped.

"This is what it does," Zach said. "It's claimed victims

across the United States, sometimes within twenty-four hours of one another."

Many of the agents grew pale in the reflected light of the images on the screen. Zach couldn't blame them. Some of the victims' bodies would not have looked out of place in a surrealist painting.

"How the hell can anything do that?" Dunn asked, her voice almost a whisper.

"Each time it's different," Cade said. "Different weapons, different methods. But two things are always the same. It makes its host body inhumanly strong and resistant to damage. And it creates a kind of reality-distortion field whenever it is on the hunt."

"A what?" Dunn asked.

"Phones stop working. Cars won't start. Locked doors open," Cade said. "Even the weather changes. Rain- and snowstorms appear in midsummer. Then it vanishes into thin air."

"You sure there's only one of them?" Thomason asked, pointing at the screen. "I see some overlap with established serial killers. BTK. Zodiac."

"Not all humans side with the human race," Cade said.

Zach saw the looks of confusion at that. He jumped in.

"Uh, what Cade is trying to say is that there are people who basically worship the things that go bump in the night. Some of these *Jeopardy!* champs think it's their job to feed the Boogeyman blood and victims while he's between manifestations."

"Then why aren't we starting with them?" Thomason said. He found it easier to challenge Zach.

"Not really how it works," Zach said. "Even the higher-ups in the cult don't know who it will become, any more than we do. All we'd get from them are some chants that sound like bad heavy-metal lyrics."

Zach clicked through another series of crime-scene photos. Some were famous—HEALTER SKELTER in blood on a refrigerator door in Los Feliz—and others sealed forever from public view by federal mandate.

Thomason didn't back down. "I don't buy it," he said. "For all we know, this guy is working with them. One man couldn't pull off that kind of carnage and—"

Cade growled slightly in frustration. It had the effect of causing the five agents nearest him to push their chairs farther away. Thomason immediately shut up.

"This is *not a man*," Cade said, his voice like a crypt door slamming. "In almost a hundred years, I have seen it shot, stabbed, drowned, burned, decapitated, dismembered and buried. And in almost a hundred years, there's only been one thing that's ever been able to kill it."

"What?" Latham asked, his voice squeaking.

Cade's eyes speared every agent in the room as he answered:

"Me."

IT DIDN'T TAKE someone with Zach's experience to see Cade wasn't thrilled.

"I don't need instructions," Cade said. "I think a hundred forty-five years of experience should be enough."

Butler looked at Zach, who shrugged. He'd promised

to bring Cade in for a briefing on how to prepare to act like a Secret Service agent. He hadn't offered anything more.

They were in the West Wing of the White House in the Secret Service's offices a floor below the Oval. It was past 3 A.M. and the place was clear of people. Even the most devout members of Curtis's staff had to sleep sometime.

Cade stood rigid, his usual air of menace sharpened even further by irritation.

But Agent Dunn seemed to take his attitude as a challenge.

"Really? You think we all wear heavy metal jewelry around our necks?"

She pointed at Cade's cross. Dark-haired and dark-eyed, Dunn radiated a contained energy from her compact, athletic frame. She no longer seemed at all scared of Cade. Maybe that's why Butler brought her.

Cade touched the cross lightly. "This is necessary," he said.

"Then at least wear a tie and keep it under your shirt."

"I have," Cade said. "It's too often become a noose."

Dunn rolled her eyes. She reached over to Butler and popped his tie from his collar with a quick jerk. "Yeah. That's why we wear clip-ons. A hundred and forty-five years and you never heard of one?"

She threw it over to Cade.

"Thank you," Cade said flatly. "That's a great help."

Zach had to hide a smirk as Cade buttoned his collar and attached the tie.

"Better," Dunn said. "Now these."

She reached into a pocket and withdrew a pair of cheap imitation Wayfarers.

Cade put them on.

They looked at him. Something still wasn't right. Butler saw it first.

"Wristwatch," he said. "Yours is way too expensive."

Cade's watch was atomic-clock synched to sunrise and sunset in whatever time zone he was in. It was also as tough as a tank and cost more than a small car. He hadn't always worn it. Zach figured out, from the way Cade studiously failed to mention it, that it was a gift from Tania.

Tania was Cade's—well, the term "girlfriend" didn't really apply to a sixty-six-year-old vampire who regularly murdered people and ate them. When she was human, Cade had once promised to save her from being turned into a vampire. He'd failed. And she was, frankly, overjoyed. She'd flitted in and out of Cade's life ever since. Zach had tried to rope her into working for the U.S. government on an occasional basis. She'd saved Cade several times. They also had ear-shattering vampire sex in the Reliquary, as Zach had witnessed firsthand, despite his best efforts to avoid it. Unlike Cade, however, Tania was not bound by any oath—or any sense of morality, for that matter. She killed when she wanted and drank human blood. Perhaps out of guilt or loneliness, Cade hadn't yet destroyed her. Tania, for her part, seemed to view Cade as her property. And she refused to allow anyone or anything else to kill him, if only because it would be trespassing on her turf.

However, Cade took the watch off and dropped it to the floor without a word. Dunn rummaged in a desk and found a cheap but sturdy Timex.

Cade took the Secret Service's standard-issue radio and equipment as they were handed to him. He might have smirked for an instant when Butler handed him the SIG Sauer pistol in its holster, but he added that as well.

"So why doesn't the Boogeyman just use a rifle in broad daylight?" Dunn asked. "Seems like a much easier way to kill someone. And you certainly couldn't stop him then."

"What it does is what it is," Cade said.

Dunn waited. Cade didn't elaborate. "I'm going to need a little more than that," she said.

"The Boogeyman can't change its nature any more than I can," Cade said. "It's a thing like me. It needs to kill by hand or with a blade, up close and personal. It cannot get any sustenance without personally experiencing the pain and terror as a human being dies. It has to see the light of the soul wink out, to see the utter humiliation as a human spirit is reduced to nothing more than bloody meat."

"And he can't do that during the day?"

"As I said, it's a thing like me. We all hate the daylight. We work at night. Your world fades a little in the dark. My world starts to intrude. During the day, it will be weakened as well. Its host will appear almost human again. At night, the Boogeyman comes out."

"So there really are monsters in the dark," Dunn said. "I feel sort of like calling my mom and saying she shouldn't have given me so much crap about the night-light."

Cade had a question for her now. "Why aren't you as frightened as the others?"

"Would it do any good?" she asked. "Fear's just an alarm clock. It wakes you up to the danger. Then you turn off the alarm, get out of bed and get to work."

"That's a rare attitude," Cade said.

Zach looked offended. "Is that a dig at me? I'm standing right here, you know."

"I know."

Cade finished strapping on his holster, his belt, his tactical baton, his radio, and his spare ammo clips. He stood there, on display again. This time, he looked the part.

Dunn had one last touch, however.

She went to her own desk and opened a drawer. She took out a half-dozen aerosol spray cans.

"Strip," she said to Cade. "Down to your boxers or whatever."

Cade didn't ask why. He was out of his suit in a moment.

Dunn had two of the cans, one in each hand, then caught her breath when she looked up.

Butler and Zach were both looking elsewhere. Cade was an elegantly carved statue of pale skin and muscle.

"I don't wear boxers," he said.

Dunn blinked. "Right. Hold still."

Within a few moments, the tanning spray had covered most of Cade's body. Dunn emptied one can after another, applying multiple coats, working without haste, covering every square inch.

She looked Cade over with a critical eye and nodded.

Zach and Butler finally looked directly at Cade again. The bright orange of the tanning spray was muted somewhat by Cade's bloodless pallor. He still looked a little like a fresh Cheeto. But in a lineup of agents, especially at night, he wouldn't stand out.

Dunn looked Cade up and down one more time.

"Good enough," she said. "Welcome to the Secret Service, Cade."

He stood there, coat of paint still wet, arms away from his sides. "I wonder if you couldn't have done this first," he said.

Dunn flashed him a sudden, radiant smile. "Now, where's the fun in that?"

March 18, 2003
Lake Havasu, Arizona

"God damn it, God damn it, shut it down. I said, shut it down. That's enough!" Kevin Lane hit the cameraman on the back of the head to get him to stop recording. The girl on the deck of the boat stretched the frat boy's penis like Silly Putty—with about the same response. Lane yelled at her again, and she shrugged and quit.

The frat boy gave him a halfhearted protest but couldn't keep the look of relief from his face. It was no big surprise. Guys always jumped up when he asked for volunteers, but maybe one in ten of the horny college pukes could actually get it up for sex on camera.

The trouble with amateur porn, Lane thought, not for the first time, is all the goddamn amateurs.

Thank God he always had plenty of drunken skanks to fill the tapes. That's why he was on Lake Havasu, better known as the "amateur porn capital of the world." He'd started out here when he was at ASU, amazed at the acres of exposed, tanned flesh on display. You could practically step from houseboat to houseboat across the entire lake without ever seeing a woman wearing clothes.

"All right, let's do the girl-on-girl," he said with a sigh.

"We're losing the light," his cameraman said, pointing out the obvious. The sun was almost down behind the mountain range surrounding the reservoir.

Lane ground his teeth before replying. "Hey, what's that thing on your camera, Nick?"

The cameraman looked at him blankly for a full second. Then he looked at the light on the camera as if seeing it for the first time and broke into an idiot grin. "Oh, yeah," he said. "Right."

He gave Lane a thumbs-up. Lane ground his teeth some more and hoped to Christ there would be some usable footage. He'd have to talk to Nick about the bong hits. He wasn't going to lose a girl-girl orgy just because the nimrod forgot to take the lens cap off.

Once everything was rolling properly—he checked the viewfinder himself, just to make sure—he picked five girls from the group on the houseboat and arranged them on the deck.

Then another boat pulled up with the flag of a different fraternity flapping over the side. Two more guys on Jet Skis raced up, nearly colliding with the houseboat. Together they kicked up enough water to douse all the girls on deck—instant cold shower.

"Delta rules, douche bags!" a blond giant in the pilot's seat of the other boat shouted. A rain of empty beer cans followed. The girls ducked for cover. The frat boys on Lane's boat began throwing stuff back.

"Motherfucker!" he screamed. He opened the tackle box near his feet and took out the gun he kept there.

"Whoa, dude, relax—" the blond guy at the wheel said, suddenly sober.

"Fuck you! Get the fuck away from my fucking shoot!" Lane bellowed. He waved the gun in the air.

The Deltas didn't have to be told twice. They spun about so fast their boat nearly capsized. The Jet Skis were already a half-mile away.

Nick blinked at Lane. "I didn't know you had a gun."

Lane scowled at him and showed him the gun in the light. It was made mostly of plastic. "It's a flare pistol, you asshole. Come on. Let's find someplace a little more private."

THE SKY WAS pitch black by the time they anchored in a cove far away from the main crowds. The parties were still going on the other side of the lake, but they were dim lights and distant echoes.

It had taken a lot more booze and some of his own stash of drugs to get the girls back in the mood. He'd been patient, letting them get dry and warm in the main cabin under the deck of the boat, which was fitted with couches and overstuffed chairs. Lane worried he'd doped them up too much, but then they started touching and rubbing each other despite their glazed eyes.

The first soft moans rose from the girls like tiny butterflies. There was something real here, something spontaneous despite all the obvious and cheap tricks Lane always used to engineer these scenes. Everyone in gonzo porn lived for this, but rarely ever saw it—a genuine, unguarded moment; unrehearsed and irreproducible, as if the cameras really were not there.

Until the heavy thump from on deck broke the spell. The girls blinked and the moment burst like a soap bubble.

"Son of a bitch," Lane shouted. He was going to motherfucking kill whoever did that. The frat boys crowded into the cabin got out of his way fast once they saw the look in his eye.

He stormed up the stairs to the houseboat's deck, screaming at every step, "All right, you limp-dick closet cases, who did that? Because I am going to cut off your fucking head and—"

Lane wasn't able to get out any more of his plans. In a split second, he realized everything had changed. It took his THC-saturated neurons a moment to absorb this new reality.

Sheets of water drenched the boat and lightning struck the lake from boiling black clouds. Lane wondered when it had started raining. The day had been clear and blistering.

The boat had been untied from its mooring in the cove at some point. They were now floating out in the middle of the lake. With the rain and the darkness, he couldn't find the shore.

That was all bad news. But the worst part was right at his feet. Lane gagged.

Even in the darkness, he could see the deck was covered in blood.

His eyes followed the river of gore right to the headless corpse of one of the Kappas where it lay on the hardwood planks.

Only then did he notice the man looming over the corpse: a very large man wearing a rain slicker and holding an obscene, bloody machete. The machete swung right for his head.

"Oh Christ," Lane said in a very small voice and closed his eyes.

"Don't blaspheme," a cold voice said from behind his right ear, and Lane realized he wasn't dead. He opened his eyes again.

There was another man, his arms locked with the killer's, keeping the machete at bay.

Lane didn't know what to do. They struggled without making a sound.

The man who'd saved him—wearing black, his skin pale as talcum powder—spared him a glance. "This is not as easy as it looks," he snapped.

"What?" Lane still couldn't believe he wasn't dead.

"*Run*," the man snarled, and Lane moved just as the stalemate broke. The killer shoved downward. The machete sunk into the doorjamb of the cabin, right above Lane's head.

Lane fell down the stairs.

Nick met him at the bottom. "Dude, what's going on? We're ready to go again—"

Lane screamed incomprehensibly. But Nick and the others got the message when the two men tumbled down the stairs a moment later, still struggling for the blade.

Running. Screaming. Chaos.

Nick got to his feet just in time to be impaled. The machete punched through him with an audible scraping of bone. The camera dropped from his shoulder and bounced into a chair.

Nick's death was an afterthought for the killer, Lane could see. He kicked the man in black away and whirled his blade through the remaining frat boys.

He was headed for one girl who had not made the stairs, terrified beyond all movement. She huddled in the corner as if pinned there.

Oh, she's dead, Lane thought.

But the man in black leaped up and rode the killer to the floor again. He pounded his fists against the bloody rain slicker and tried to get purchase under the hood. His fingers scrabbled for a grip and yanked. Lane thought he should have heard the head snap off at that angle.

But whoever—whatever—was under there wasn't cooperating. He rolled with the force of the twist, throwing the man in black to the floor again.

The distraction had given the girl a moment to run upstairs. The killer bounded up after her, his slicker flowing like a cape, leaving everyone else as afterthoughts.

The man in black ran after him.

And Lane, not knowing what the hell he was doing, grabbed the camera and followed them both.

THE KILLER WAS GONE. So was the girl.

The rain kept pouring down, but the camera was a sport model and almost totally waterproof. He'd wanted to do some fancy underwater shoots with the girls, maybe call it "Going Down Below" or something—gotta keep those perverts interested, give them something new—but now he focused on the man in black, who stood in the hissing rain like a statue.

He flipped on the lights.

Before he knew what was happening, he was pinned against the wall of the houseboat by his throat, the camera on the deck.

"What are you doing?" the man asked, not loosening his grip in the slightest.

Lane said something like, "Frgxl."

The man in black dropped him. Lane gasped for air.

"Stay out of my way," he said.

"Wait," Lane croaked. "Who the hell are you? Who's that guy? What's going on?"

"My name is Nathaniel Cade," he said. "Ordinarily, there would be someone here to explain things to you. Someone more—"

Lane tried to help him out. "Someone less scary?"

"Someone more human," Cade said. Lane made a mental note to stay quiet.

"He could tell you how this works. But he's not here. So listen closely. Find someplace to hide. Do not come out until you see daylight. This will all be over by then. One way or another."

He turned to go, but Lane grabbed his arm. Another mistake. Cade shrugged, but the tiny movement knocked Lane back like he'd been hit with a baseball bat.

"What?" Cade said, facing Lane again, eyes darting in every other direction.

"It's not a big boat, but—but—"

Cade leaned in closer. This didn't help Lane concentrate. His words came out in one explosive burst of verbal diarrhea: "There's a small elevator shaft for dishes and bottles and stuff between the upper and lower cabins they use it when they have parties on the boat you can get up there that way you don't have to use the stairs that should help right?"

Cade nodded. "Useful," he said.

Then something hit Cade from out of the dark. The sudden impact slammed them both down the stairs again.

Lane hit his head at the bottom. He must have blacked out. When he opened his eyes, the rain was still lashing at the boat. Cade was still, one more body among the other pieces of bodies on the floor.

Carefully, Lane crawled over to him and shook him. "Hey. Hey, man. Hey. What happened?"

He realized Cade's eyes were open and glaring at him. Cade's head moved, but the rest of his body did not.

"While you were talking, he severed my spine just above the T7 vertebrae."

"Oh. Shit. Sorry."

"It's going to take me at least five minutes to regain full use of my legs."

"Wow. Really?"

"That's more than enough time for him to kill every one of you on this boat."

"You didn't come out here alone, did you? I mean, aren't there cops or something just waiting to come on board?"

"No."

"You can't be serious. Wait. Didn't you say something about another guy?"

"He's on medical leave."

"Awesome."

Lane slumped to the floor again. He heard screams from above. Lane found a bottle of vodka that was, miraculously, unbroken and mostly full. He took a deep swig.

Cade looked at him.

"Are you going to try to help them?"

Lane belched a ball of vodka fumes. "No way, *hombre*. You said he's going to kill us anyway. No sense rushing things."

Cade hoisted himself up on his arms. "He can kill *you*. I can stop him. But I need you to do something."

Lane took another hit off the bottle. The warm, liquid feeling of well-being cushioned everything around him, especially the chopping noises coming from the upper decks of the boat. "Pass," he said.

With surprising speed and power for someone dragging himself by his hands, Cade gripped Lane by the arm and squeezed. Lane dropped the bottle and gasped in pain.

"I wasn't asking," Cade said.

LANE FOUND HIMSELF on the upper deck of the boat, walking as quietly as he could.

It looked like a slaughterhouse's trash bins had been emptied over every available surface.

Rain hit the canopy covering the upper deck. There was no sign of the killer or anyone else left alive. He was about ready to say screw it and jump over the balcony into the lake when he heard something behind him. He spun and pointed his only weapon, the flare pistol.

It was the girl; now the only girl, the final girl. Everyone else was dead. She uncurled herself from the place she'd hidden, an empty compartment under the seats that should have held life preservers.

"Ah shit," he said.

"Quiet," she whispered at him. "He could be back any moment. We've got to swim for it."

"Which direction?" Lane hissed. "I can't see dick out there. You could swim in circles for hours until you drown."

"You got any better ideas?"

"Maybe he's gone."

Of course, that was when the roof above them tore open.

The killer used his blade to slice open the canopy, pouring inside with all the rain and pooled water. He stood, dripping.

The girl screamed and ducked behind him. The killer took an unhurried step toward them both.

Lane shoved the girl and they ran.

They slid down the stairs, past the main deck, into the cabin, where Cade said to lead him—

The room was empty again, except for the bodies. Cade was nowhere to be seen.

The killer appeared at the other side of the room, walking down the opposite stairs. Taking his time. Inside the gloom of his hood, Lane could see gleaming teeth set in a feral grin.

They were so completely fucked.

The killer took another step. Then another.

He was less than four feet from Lane and the girl.

Then the hull of the boat behind him seemed to burst open, a panel knocking free of the wall and slamming into the killer.

He turned, and there was Cade, crammed into the small dumbwaiter compartment, a length of hose in his hands. He sprayed something all over the killer.

Lane smelled it. Gasoline. Crawling around under the deck, Cade had found the fuel lines. He drenched the killer in diesel.

Lane realized Cade was shouting at him. "Any time now would be good," Cade said.

Lane looked dumbly at the flare pistol and finally figured it out. He aimed and pulled the trigger.

A white-hot flower bloomed at the end of the barrel. It grew until it reached the killer, who blossomed into a thousand more tiny, dancing flames.

Cade pulled Lane and the girl away. He limped, but his legs moved. He carried them over his shoulders, up the narrow stairs and out onto the deck.

It felt like a rocket launching behind them as they flew out over the water.

When Lane made the surface again, debris was still coming down from what was left of the boat. All his equipment, all his footage, all his drugs—all gone.

At least the rain had stopped. The sky was clear and the moon and stars lit up the lake in shades of purple and deep blue. The shore was closer than he'd guessed.

He saw the girl—he realized he'd never learned her name—floating nearby, arms wrapped around a life preserver.

"You all right?" he felt compelled to ask.

"The fuck do you care?"

Fair point, Lane thought. He kept treading water, looking around for something to hold on to. "Hey, I don't suppose you'd want to share that—"

"I'm going to sue the shit out of you," the girl said.

So no, then. Something funny occurred to him. He smiled. "You know," he said, "if this were a movie, this would be the part where the killer jumped out."

The water between them exploded. A horrifically burned body, pieces of rubber rain slicker melted into its flesh, thrashed and dove at them like a shark in a feeding frenzy.

It raised its machete, still in one badly charred hand, over the head of the girl.

Then Cade erupted from the water as well, moving like a torpedo. He slammed into the killer and took them both down into the depths of the lake.

Lane and the girl treaded water amid the wreckage for a short while.

"I don't think they're coming back," he finally said.

Something bumped his arm. His camera bobbed near him. Amazing. Watertight as well as waterproof. He was glad he'd spent the extra money on the rental.

The girl let him hold the life preserver as they kicked their way to the shore. He dragged the camera along with his other hand. She walked past his prone form, headed for the road.

"I'm still going to sue your ass," she said.

"Good luck with that," Lane said. "You signed a release."

"Asshole." She kept walking.

Lane was too out of breath to respond. After a little while, he figured she must have made the road. She'd be fine. There were hundreds of boats that would be overjoyed to have a hot, naked chick join the crew.

As for him, Lane planned to lie here until the sun came up and then maybe for a while after that. But not too long. He had a golden ticket right next to him in the shape of a video camera. Some of the footage would be blurry, sure, but he knew that some of the good stuff survived. His instincts for a good scene hadn't completely failed him when he was scared shitless. What he had on this footage was deeply weird, but it was authentic. It was going to vault him right into the big time. He saw the tabloid news shows bidding for it. Then maybe his own reality-TV deal, something like *Kevin Lane Presents: The Unexplained: Uncensored*. Mix up sex and the supernatural. That could be a big hit.

Lane lifted his head at the sound of something breaking the surface of the lake.

From out of the water, first his head, then his shoulders. Cade. Walking. Not swimming, but walking, as if he'd hiked to shore all the way from the bottom of Havasu.

Lane discovered he was not too tired to be terrified. He was just too tired to do anything about it.

Cade, without breaking stride, picked up the camera and kept on walking.

"Hey," Lane said. "Hey! That's mine!"

Cade ignored him.

"Ah, come on, man! That's all I've got left!"

Cade stopped and looked at him.

"You could lose more."

Lane took the hint and collapsed back into the sand.

Not long after, he got a job selling cars.

SIXTEEN

Nation . . . Nation . . . You know I'm no fan of [MAKES AIR-QUOTES] "President" Samuel Curtis. And now we have even more proof of his unfitness to take the office that he was never actually elected to in the first place. Curtis is spending millions of your hard-earned tax dollars on a roadtrip in what appears to be the bastard offspring of Darth Vader's helmet and the bus from the 1994 Damn Yankees 12-city reunion tour. "Ooooh, look at me, I'm the president, I'm so special, I have to ride in a big armor-plated bus instead of wandering from city to city on foot." Frankly, this is outrageous. I mean, look at this list of things we're paying for on the Magic Curtis Carpet Ride: Secret Service agents; bottled water; air-conditioning; even a traveling physician and a supply of the president's own blood. As Future President-for-Life and Man's Man Skip Seabrook pointed out, Curtis can't even go among the people without a bulletproof vest. What a little girl! Listen, Mr. Curtis, if you can't dig a bullet from your flesh with a sharpened stone like Davy Crockett or John Wayne, then you have no place in the White House. That's why we have moonshine and leather belts to bite on, sir.

—*The Colbert Report,* Wednesday, October 10, 2012

October 12, 2012, Curtis Campaign Headquarters, Chicago, Illinois

Zach breathed it in: the smoke-and-Pine-Sol odor of hotel carpeting; the new-car scent clinging from airport shuttles and rentals; the slight chemical aroma of the wash-and-wear, wrinkle-free shirts pulled straight from the plastic that morning; the barely contained stink of gas pains from fast food and stress and too little sleep; mouthwash fighting with halitosis, deodorant against flop sweat.

The smell of the campaign.

He didn't regret his work with Cade—well, not much, anyway—but as vital as it was, it would never sing to him the way this did. Being this close again brought it all back.

Politics. The highest and lowest form of human expression. God, he didn't even realize how much he'd missed it.

He walked into the Curtis campaign headquarters in Chicago. It made sense to be here, given Curtis's roots in Illinois, but it was also the closest major city to the launch pad for Curtis's Heart of America tour. (Zach had not been consulted about the name. He thought it sounded like a country music song.)

The room was filled with the low buzz of gently trilling phones, tapping keyboards and the occasional outburst of disbelief:

"You're kidding me! He was wearing what? A Klan robe? How is that historical reenactment?"

"No, no, no. Please don't tell me he— He did. He forwarded the pictures to everyone on his campaign's e-mail list. Oh, that's it. He's toast."

"Sir, for the last time, I don't know anything about any conspiracy or lizard-men or the CIA. Don't call here again."

Curtis was not coming here. He was flying direct to Malmen, Illinois, for the kickoff rally.

But first they had to get the buses there. And the press.

Zach found Butler and his agents in the fenced-off parking lot behind the building. Ordinarily a pay lot, the space had been rented out by the Secret Service as a staging area. The chain-link fence had been erected overnight and topped with razor wire. Massive, portable floodlights sat on their wheels to illuminate every square inch of concrete. At the center of the lot, lined up side by side, were the three Greyhound-size luxury campaign buses. One for the president and select staff, one for support staff and one for the media.

The president's limo—affectionately known as The Beast—was being airlifted to Malmen. It would follow the buses in case the president needed it. Bulletproof, bombproof and able to run even if its tires were shot out from under it, The Beast was much more secure than any of the buses. The Secret Service had only insisted it come along on the trip. Butler wanted a place he could stash the president in case everything went pear-shaped on them.

Zach saw the detail leader and waved. Butler nodded back. He was checking the buses again with Latham and Dunn. No one had been near them except the Secret Service, but Butler wasn't taking any chances. They were using mirrors to sweep for bombs and testing the cargo areas for gunpowder residue.

Zach's job, by way of contrast, was simple. He just had to get some luggage on board.

Lanning appeared from the rear door of the building. Despite the no smoking signs everywhere, he was puffing away on his unfiltered Camel. Half of it was ash with a single deep breath. The president was chewing nicotine gum like Hubba Bubba to keep his promise to the First Lady and his kids that he'd quit, but there was no way Lanning was going to abstain. He was an unrepentant four-pack-a-day man. Zach had not seen anyone smoke like Lanning who wasn't already being treated for emphysema.

Lanning was just finishing a conversation on his cell phone. "You know what? Fuck the liberals. No, seriously, fuck them. They don't like it, they can go back to tiptoeing over the homeless on their way to get a fair-trade foam latte in a recycled cup at Starbucks. What are they going to do, vote for Seabrook?" He ended the call and exhaled a huge, toxic cloud of smoke. Then he saw Zach.

"Christ almighty, Barrows," he said. "Did you bring a surfboard?"

He pointed to Zach's luggage: a seven-foot-long, sleek fiberglass trunk. It had wheels at one end so Zach could drag it along easier.

Butler and Latham walked over and hoisted the trunk away from Zach and loaded it into the cargo bay of the president's bus.

"Sorry, Dan," Zach said. "The contents are classified."

"My three ex-wives together didn't pack that much crap

on a trip." Lanning lit another cig off the one in his mouth. Zach honestly didn't know how the man's lungs were anything but tumor at this point.

"You going to be okay with Lanford?" Lanning asked.

"What do you mean?"

"You know what I mean, Zach. If you run into your old man?"

Zach stiffened a little despite himself. "It will be fine."

"Good. So are you busy consulting, or you got time to do some real work?"

"What do you need?"

"It's time to throw a cheeseburger to the crocodiles."

"Oh," Zach said. "The press."

THE PRESS. Zach felt an instinctive and not-quite-irrational loathing for all of them. It was like seeing a weird colony organism out of some bad made-for-Syfy TV movie: a hundred yammering, hungry, belching, shouting, chattering heads on one fleshy body, all demanding food, oxygen and attention, with sharp teeth and strong jaws to devour anything stupid or slow enough to fall in the middle of them.

As James Carville once said, if you don't give the beast a cheeseburger, it's going to start munching on your leg. Sometimes, this seemed almost literal to Zach. He'd never had anyone scream at him like a journalist who missed his or her complimentary packed lunch.

But even if they swallowed what you fed them, you could not trust them. Journalists were loyal only to themselves and, by extension, their stories. Reporters were excellent at weaseling their way onto your blind side, and using that proximity to find stuff you never thought anyone would notice. You were stuck in the tunnel vision of the campaign, while they knew how to craft the narrative so it told a completely different story to outsiders.

So if a story was really big, then all the warm and happy secret handshakes didn't mean dick anymore. You could give a reporter a seat at the candidate's Thanksgiving dinner, and the next day they would still run a story that linked the campaign to a child molester if it meant readers or ratings. It went from "Zach, my main man" to "Mr. Barrows" in under sixty seconds, with stiff-necked outrage where it was all smiles and jokes a day before. There was nothing like a good, dirty scandal to remind them all that they weren't on the same side. And the media were always looking for a scandal.

They filed onto the bus, the difference between the print crowd and the TV people like Morlocks and Eloi. Lanning greeted them all with the same good-natured cynicism. Every news outlet had sent its top talent, best known by their nicknames: the Mustache of Understanding; the Mean Girl; Blonde Ambition; the Silver Fox; America's Sweetheart. They took their seats and studiously ignored one another.

Then Lanning grimaced like he had heartburn. "Oh Christ. That's all we need."

Heading down the aisle was a grown-up cheerleader—perky and taut and bouncy from head to toe—except for the look on her face. She showed her teeth and narrowed her eyes in something that was less a smile and more a joyous kind of hostility. Zach couldn't get the idea of a teddy bear with fangs out of his mind.

"Who is she?" Zach asked.

Lanning barked his short, harsh version of laughter. "You're kidding. That's Megan Roark."

Zach did a double take. He'd been on the cutting edge when he was still in politics. Now he needed flash cards to identify the players. "*That's* her?"

"Lois Lane with thirty-two double-D's, a million and a half daily pageviews and zero soul. That's her."

Lanning shut up then, because Roark had walked right up to them both.

"Daniel," she said. "I'm sure you didn't expect to see me here, after all the roadblocks your little elves put in the way of my press credentials."

A lot of political hacks would have danced away from the accusation. Lanning beamed with pride. "The problem, Megan, my dear, is that we usually only give access to journalists."

"More people watch my show—"

"YouTube channel," Lanning said.

"—*my show* than those limp dicks you've got here from CNN. Internet? Wave of the future? Maybe you've heard of it."

"Yeah, and a million people watch online porn, too," Lanning said, deliberately looking down at Roark's low-cut blouse.

"What a good feminist sentiment. Sure explains those sexual-harassment complaints from your staff."

Lanning scowled and pushed Zach in front of her. "Have you met Zach Barrows?"

She ran her eyes up and down Zach, taking in everything, and then dismissed him utterly, all in the space of a second. "Barrows? You were dumped by Curtis two years ago. They must be desperate if they're going back to the junior varsity."

Zach blinked. "I'm just happy to be on the team," he said.

"I'll bet. Wasn't Starbucks hiring?"

"They're still looking over my résumé." He crossed his fingers in front of her.

She frowned. "Cute. Real cute. Too bad you're working for the Devil." She turned back to Lanning. "Your boy is going down. You can't stop the truth."

She turned and bounced back down the aisle. Lanning and Zach both watched her go.

Lanning recovered while Zach was still staring. "Easy there, kid."

"You couldn't keep her off the bus?"

Lanning sighed. "More traffic than the *New York Times.* If we kept her off, she'd make it into a story. Pretty soon the rest of these jackals would take up her cause, because it's easier than doing their goddamn jobs, and then we'd have to explain why we were censoring the press."

Zach looked at Roark again, laughing and flipping her hair at something Brian Williams said to her. Lanning smacked Zach on the shoulder, not gently, and leaned close.

"You know reporters are the enemy, but in the end, we're all in on the same joke, right? Not her. She's a crusader. She'll do anything to take us down," he warned. "So don't you dare sleep with her."

Zach was offended. "Goes without saying."

"It would," Lanning said, "with anyone else but you."

SEVENTEEN

Friday, October 12, 2012
All Times ET
10:00 AM
The President meets with Secretary of State Rusk
Oval Office
Closed Press
10:35 AM
The President departs the South Lawn en route Joint Base Andrews
South Lawn
Open Press
Gather Time 10:15 AM—North Doors of the Palm Room
10:50 AM
The President departs Joint Base Andrews en route Illinois
Travel Pool Coverage
12:55 PM
The President arrives Illinois
Local Event Time: 11:55 AM CDT
Quad City International Airport
Open Press
1:45 PM
The President departs on Campaign Bus Tour
Local Event Time: 12:45 PM CDT
3:00 PM
The President arrives Malmen, Illinois
Meeting with Malmen Chamber of Commerce

Local Event Time: 2:00 PM CDT
Malmen Downtown Business Association
Open Press

Vice President's Office, White House, Washington, D.C.

It was sort of funny when he thought about it. Vice President Lester Wyman only felt welcome in the White House when the president wasn't home.

He had an office in the West Wing. But it was signaled in all sorts of subtle ways that Wyman shouldn't spend much time there. For instance, the staff stopped emptying his wastebaskets for a whole week once. People glared at him as he walked through the halls. Aides stopped using his title. Little things like that.

So Wyman spent most of his time in the Executive Office Building, where VPs traditionally waited for the funerals of foreign dignitaries.

The president arranged his schedule so they'd never have to speak. Everything was communicated through intermediaries these days. Wyman heard FDR did the same thing to Truman.

But it wasn't supposed to be like this between him and Curtis. They'd come into office as a team. He'd been the political knife-fighter, while Curtis got to be the inspirational figure.

Wyman supposed he had to take some of the blame for

the rift between them. After all, he did—technically—betray Curtis and very nearly got them both killed. Curtis had never been able to prove it. But he suspected.

Wyman didn't feel that guilty about it. In fact, he mainly felt bad that it hadn't worked out properly.

Wyman, when he looked at himself unemotionally, knew he was not a very good man. He accepted it. He assumed it was genetics or destiny or whatever people thought decided the course of their lives these days. So be it. No one had ever embraced him immediately—not even, he thought with surprisingly little bitterness, his parents. He never doubted they loved him; they bought him every toy, indulged his whims, lavished him with affection. They simply never seemed to like him very much. And in the cold moments, when he was brutally honest, he couldn't blame them. They seemed to know the same thing the kids at school did from the very first day he was plopped down in kindergarten. Perhaps he was too watchful. Perhaps he was too honest in putting his own needs first, as most normal kids do. But whatever it was, a hollowness grew in the place where other people might have had the warmth of easy affection and regard from others.

However, he was smart—smart enough to know that he could fake being nice long enough to get what he wanted.

It made things easier for him. He never worried about losing friends, because he believed he'd never really had any. He was capable of breathtaking selfishness without guilt. And he discovered that ambition warmed him even more than love. Maybe that's why he set his sights on politics at such an early age.

By high school, he was a winner by any definition. Student body president. Prom king. Perfect GPA. He was accepted at Yale and tapped for its most elite secret society. He turned it down to join another fraternity, almost as prestigious, where it would be easier to rise to the top.

After college and law school, with the same unsentimental clarity, he immediately married and knocked up his girlfriend. Without student deferments, he needed a reason to stay out of Vietnam. He entered the protest movement as well, mainly because it was a quick way to advance in the Democratic Party without working his way through the ranks of the old guard. He was elected to statewide office, then the House, then the Senate.

And that's where he stalled. It chafed him. It seemed that he could get pretty far without charm or charisma, but not all the way to the top. He sat on the panels of the Sunday talk shows, he tried to become a national figure with his speeches and carefully selected bursts of moral outrage. But he never quite found the magic vehicle that would carry him in front of the cheering crowds. His one attempt at running for president himself was stillborn in the primaries with a dead-last finish in New Hampshire.

That's when he met Samuel Curtis. He was selected to be the freshman senator's mentor. Curtis was handsome, smart and magnetic. People wanted to be around him. They liked him, while they merely tolerated Wyman. Even Wyman had to admit he liked Curtis.

It made it easier to bear as the younger senator bypassed him effortlessly in his first term. Or, at least, it made it easier to choke down the resentment in public.

More important, Wyman knew that Curtis was going to be the star he'd never be himself. He stifled any anger and stayed close, becoming Curtis's trusted hatchet man: the guy who would do the awful things so Curtis could remain beloved.

When he was chosen by his Senate protégé to be the second man on the ticket, he'd accepted with a shit-eating grin. He knew the VP spot with Curtis was a surer way to the presidency than trying to crawl into the Oval Office on his own. His previous attempts at presidential campaigns had proved that.

Then something interesting happened. A group he'd heard rumors about during his time on the Senate Intelligence Committee reached out to him. A man in glasses met with him privately and hinted he could be president in much less time than eight years.

Wyman had never thought of himself as a particularly bad person. But he knew what that meant and he shook the man's hand anyway.

Of course, nothing had worked the way it was supposed to. He'd fed the Company classified info about the president's security and schedule. He told them all about Cade and the treasure trove of occult objects under the Smithsonian. He gave them everything short of a key to the front door of the White House.

And yet Curtis had survived the attempt on his life—an attempt that would have killed Wyman as well. The Company began telling him what to do, like he was their servant. Even worse, the president seemed to suspect something and Wyman's exile into political limbo began.

Wyman knew Curtis wouldn't dump him at the convention, but it was a surprisingly close call. In the end, it was decided by the party bigwigs that changing out VPs would be seen as a sign of indecision and weakness by the pundits.

So Wyman was put on the campaign trail. He was never in a position to do any damage with his big mouth. He either spoke to the rabidly loyal base in secure blue states or endured hostile protesters in the flaming red districts where they didn't have a chance anyway.

He still made the rounds on the Sunday talk shows, but there was no question he was out of the loop. For a politician like Wyman, this was living death.

More than that, it worried him. He didn't know why, but the Company had stopped using that secure phone in his desk drawer. They never asked for favors anymore. They never gave orders. They simply didn't contact him anymore.

Until today.

The secret phone rang. It wasn't good news.

He tried to make a joke of it. "You must have been going through a tunnel," he said. "I couldn't have heard that right."

The voice on the other end—the man in glasses, sometimes called Proctor—didn't sound amused. But he repeated himself anyway. "Consider yourself free. We don't need you anymore."

"But I don't understand. I'm right in position. I can—"

"We don't like your chances in November," Proctor said. "We've crunched some numbers, looked at some entrails and rolled some bones. We don't think you're going to win."

That chilled Wyman. It was one thing to hear a TV airhead blather on about poll numbers. The Company had much more accurate ways of divining the future. The talk about entrails and bones wasn't any kind of metaphor.

"We might surprise you," Wyman said. "Our internal tracking shows some gains."

"It's wrong. You should consider renewing your law license. You won't hear from us again."

"Wait." Wyman hated the pleading in his voice. "After all I've done for you, that's it? You're cutting me loose?"

"You've had more than enough chances, Lester. You were given every opportunity to close the deal. You failed. But you're walking away. Count your blessings. You get to keep that shriveled little thing you call a soul."

"I refuse to accept this. I will be president. You'll see. And then you're going to have to beg me for favors."

A laugh. The kind you hear at a cocktail party when a drunk coworker says something stupid. "Okay, Les. Whatever you say. You take care."

The phone went dead. Wyman stabbed at the buttons, but it was nothing more than a hunk of plastic now.

He'd been utterly abandoned. Even as a traitor, no one wanted him. He had nothing left to bargain with.

Wyman sat for a long time in his office, watching the sun go down over the Potomac. He ignored the calls that came from his scheduler and his assistants. Let them wait at the damned fund-raiser.

He was alone with nothing left to lose. Good. He'd been relying too much on other people. Ask anyone: Les Wyman was at his best with his back against the wall. He would do it himself. He would be president.

He just had to figure out how to make it happen.

EIGHTEEN

BULLETS, NOT BALLOTS

"THE TREE OF LIBERTY MUST BE WATERED WITH BLOOD OF TYRANTS"

9/11 WAS AN INSIDE JOB

WE CAME UNARMED (THIS TIME)

SAVE THE PLANET: KILL A REPUBLICAN

GET THE BLOODSUCKER OUT OF THE WHITE HOUSE

SEABROOK = HITLER

CURTIS = HITLER

IT'S 1939 GERMANY ALL OVER AGAIN

WHERE'S LEE HARVEY OSWALD WHEN YOU NEED HIM?

—Signs carried by protesters at 2012 campaign rallies

October 12, 2012, Malmen, Illinois

Zach and Candace sat with Lanning in the back of the president's bus. They were on their way to meet with the Malmen Chamber of Commerce. The Chamber was going to give President Curtis ideas for boosting small businesses in America.

At that moment, Curtis was on the other side of the door, giving an exclusive interview to a couple of reporters from the *New York Times.*

Lanning had the window open to vent his cigarette smoke. He looked out as the bus crawled along the town's main drag. Empty storefronts. Midwestern imitations of L.A. gang tags spray-painted on street signs. Garbage overflowing from corner trash cans. Broken bus benches.

Lanning smiled, the smoke flowing out over his teeth. "Christ. Look at this town. The leading industries are meth labs and yard sales, and these geniuses want to lecture the president on how to jump-start the economy."

"Jesus, Lanning, someone could hear you," Candace said.

Lanning snorted. "The press? You think they don't know this already? Another free tip from your uncle Dan, sweetie: hypocrisy is the secret ingredient that keeps American politics healthy and strong. We all agree to the basic story line: 'America is a good and great nation founded on the strength of its people. Democracy is all about the common sense of the common man.' But you ask any one of those jackals out there what they really think, they'll tell you the same thing: most Americans can barely figure out how to program their universal remotes, and we would be in dire fucking straits indeed if we had to rely on them to steer the ship of government."

Lanning pointed out the window with his cig.

"Take any one of these dipshits in their easy-fit pants and triple-XL T-shirts. Ask them what we should do about the Middle East, or health care, or abortion, and they've got all the answers. Half of the voters can't find Iraq on a map, but they know just what to do about the War on Terror. Sixty percent of them are on some kind of government handout, but they can't stand freeloaders. And ninety percent of them don't know what the Fed does, but they're ready to abolish it. Meanwhile, they're bouncing paychecks to firefighters and teachers and their kids are all watching double-anal penetration on the Internet. I've got an idea: let's see if they can build something other than a shopping mall for a change. I would dearly love to see a single one of these bastions of homegrown wisdom show us all how it's done. Manufacture something again. Invent something. Create a few jobs that don't require a fucking name tag. Hell, I'd be impressed if just one of these crusaders refused to cash their Social Security check. They pull that off, then they can give us their deep thoughts on how to save America. Until then: fuck them."

Candace frowned deeply and checked again to make sure the door to the rest of the bus was closed. "Awesome. That will look great on Drudge: 'Curtis campaign says "Fuck the Heartland."'"

Zach could see this getting ugly. He tried to defuse it. "I know you've got to blow off steam, Dan, but Candace is right. We don't want anyone to overhear and spice up a slow news cycle."

For a moment, Lanning looked like he was gathering his breath for a tirade that could crack drywall. Then he chuckled.

"Look at the two of you kids, all grown up. You think you can run this damn ship by yourselves? Just remember, I was there when you were caught in the Lincoln Bedroom. So don't lecture me about discretion, all right?"

He tossed his smoke out the window and pushed past them. Zach and Candace stood there, a bit sheepish.

Lanning turned back. "Oh Christ, don't look like that. You'd think I just killed your puppy. Come on. I'll buy you some ice cream."

7:14 P.M., OCTOBER 12, 2012, MALMEN UNIFIED HIGH SCHOOL

Everyone was strung tight. It wasn't just the usual energy of the campaign. That would have been enough. A presidential campaign was like doing shots of pure adrenaline every morning at breakfast.

But on top of that, there was the fear.

Zach saw it in the tightness of the agents' moves, heard it in the clipped tones of their speech. They were all wondering the same thing: when is the Boogeyman going to show?

Butler stood behind the curtain of the stage that sat at the front of the high school gym. The president was waiting in The Beast outside. He would be hustled in through a portable tunnel stretched from the door of the limo to the door of the gym; no sniper would be able to get a bead on him even if they managed to find a high point that hadn't already been secured by the Secret Service.

Butler's attention was on the array of screens in front of him. Earlier that day, the agents had put wireless cameras in a dozen locations through the gym and the school. He kept an eye on both the locals and his own people, watching for the slightest aberration, for anything that might present a threat.

The guest speakers warmed up the crowd. Loud cheers erupted every time the president's name was mentioned. Some idiot had handed out noisemaking sticks, which didn't help calm anyone's nerves.

Then the sun dropped below the horizon. Zach didn't see it. He didn't have to. Cade appeared backstage like clockwork.

He stood there for a moment. Cade didn't require Butler's orders. His job was simple. Wait for the Boogeyman. Try to kill him if he shows up.

But they nodded at each other anyway.

"Good hunting," Butler said.

Cade's mouth twitched. "You too."

He walked out into the gym and into the crowd.

CADE THANKED GOD every day for soap.

When he'd been turned, people didn't bathe. Their sweat built up over days, even weeks, working into the crevices of unwashed clothes and skin. The gases in their stomachs, the oils on their skin and in their hair, it all formed a cloud that saturated the air around every person, each one reeking of different flavors.

To Cade, it was like the aroma of a steak on the grill. Everywhere he went, he had to restrain himself. His mouth constantly filled with saliva as the bloodlust hit him with each person he met. He focused on the pain of the cross at his throat, thinking of it like a vise that would cut off his thirst.

As the years went on, however, Americans began to bathe every week, then every day. They invented fantastic chemicals to erase any hint of odor. Cade could still sniff out a person under the sterile wrapping of clean clothes and air-conditioning, but it was light beer compared to twenty-year-old Scotch. Sometimes, he even missed the old days when he could at least smell the food if not taste it.

A pack of humans in close quarters, however, erased a century of progress. Air-conditioning was impossible or useless in the great convention halls and auditoriums on the campaign trail. The adrenaline flowing in the crowd's veins overpowered all their colognes and antiperspirants. After a few hours, a campaign event began to smell like an all-you-can-eat-buffet to Cade.

It made his job even more difficult.

He walked through the crowd and scanned for any

likely candidates for his quarry. But he couldn't escape the feeling that he was wasting his time.

The Boogeyman liked to catch its prey off guard and isolated. It would never be spotted under these bright lights, battered by the thumping music coming from the speakers in every corner.

The Boogeyman preferred to work in darkness and silence.

For that matter, so did Cade.

So why was he here?

He could not escape the feeling he was being played. That they all were.

THE BOOGEYMAN stood in the crowd, waiting. He had the advantage. He knew what Cade looked like. But with all these people, he couldn't see a blessed thing.

Time to see just how prepared Cade was.

Time to make his move.

CADE SCANNED FOR THE PEOPLE who stood apart, who seemed alone even in this great wadding of exuberant flesh.

His eyes locked on a little man in a heavy green camouflage jacket. He was near the back of the auditorium, pushing his way slowly and unsurely toward the stage. The crowd was packed in, standing shoulder to shoulder, wall to wall. He wasn't making much progress. But he was determined. And he kept one hand clutched in his pocket.

There was no way Butler's people were sloppy enough to let this walking checklist of warning signs through. How did he get inside?

Then Cade saw. Someone had unlocked the emergency exit at the side of the gym and was opening it to let more supporters in. For whatever reason, the alarm was not working.

It was one of those random little gaps. One of the ways in which events just seemed to break in favor of an assassin.

Cade began moving through the crowd toward the little man.

"GOT MOVEMENT," Butler said, watching the screens. "Cade's going after someone."

Zach looked over his shoulder.

"What the hell . . . ?" Butler muttered. "South entry, what's going on over there? Why is that door open?"

The radio buzzed to life. "Fire codes. We should hear the alarm if anyone opens it."

"You should? Well, maybe we've all gone deaf, because some stoner kid is opening and closing the goddamned thing. Get over there!"

Butler switched channels. "Cade," he said. "Cade! Where are you going? Who is that?"

No response.

"What the hell?" Butler said.

"Yeah, he does that," Zach said. "Don't take it personally."

"Come on," Butler shouted to Zach and the others

nearby. "Keep the president in the car. Prepare to get him out of here if I give the word. The rest of you, with me."

Zach ran after them as they went out the backstage door.

THE LITTLE MAN saw Cade and began hurrying in the opposite direction. He was closer to the door. As the teenager opened it again, he squirted out before another group of supporters could get in.

Cade was caught in the crush of bodies. He began making eye contact with people. All but the most fervent supporters, the ones blissed out on the excitement and spirit, shrank away from Cade. He reached the door in no time after that.

It opened. Latham and Thomason were on the other side.

"Where—" Thomason said.

"Move," Cade snarled.

The little man was running to a beat-up car in the distance.

Cade slipped between the two agents and was after him in a second.

He caught him easily and yanked him back by the collar of his green jacket.

The little man yelped. He closed his eyes and screamed, *"Sic Semper Tyrannis!"* and pulled his hand out of his pocket.

There was the gun.

Cade covered the man's fingers with his own, almost

like holding hands, preventing him from pulling the trigger or pulling away.

He looked deep into the face of the little man, nearly touching him nose to nose.

"Not you," he said.

Behind him, Butler and the others arrived in a clatter of hard shoes and heavy breathing.

Cade tossed the man over his shoulder as if discarding trash.

The little man tumbled through the air. The shock was evident on the faces of Butler and the other agents.

He hit the surface of the parking lot hard. Butler and the other agents scrambled to cover him. Butler was shouting, "GUN GUN GUN" over and over. Just as the would-be assassin wobbled to his feet, he was taken down in a pile of suits and uniforms.

Within a few seconds, Butler was up from the scrum, his clothes and hair askew. Four men had the would-be shooter down and were cuffing his hands behind his back. Butler held the man's pistol in one hand.

"What the fuck, Cade?" he shouted.

Cade only seemed to notice the commotion when his name was mentioned. He looked back at Butler, face completely uninterested.

Butler was furious. He stomped into Cade's personal space, still shouting. "You just drop an armed man into the middle of my agents? What the fuck was that?"

Cade looked at Butler, blinked slowly, then looked at the gunman being dragged away by the other agents.

The silence dragged out for a moment. Butler seemed

to realize who and what he was shouting at. He still looked pissed, but he stepped back from Cade.

"He's of no interest to me," Cade said.

"Well, that's fucking great," Butler said. "You ever stop to think about disarming him before you let him go?"

"It seemed within your capabilities," Cade said. "He's only human."

Cade walked away.

Butler puffed up his chest to shout something else but thought better of it. Instead, he wheeled on Zach.

"What the hell is with him?"

Zach shrugged. "You get used to it."

"Really?"

"No," Zach admitted.

THE BOOGEYMAN HAD watched the whole thing. He'd seen the little man with the green jacket lingering around the entry to the gym. He knew the twitchy little bastard would never get within a thousand yards of the president. Probably never work up the courage to use that cheap .22 pistol in his hand.

So the Boogeyman had given him a little push. It was easy. He talked a little bit with him about the "goddamned federal government," got him worked up, and then found the hole in security right when he needed it. He'd always been lucky like that.

He'd pushed the man through the door and followed, then allowed the crowd to pull them apart.

Now he knew. Cade was staying close to the president.

Even with his obscene luck, he was not going to be able to breach that final wall of security. Not as long as Cade was around.

He had to admit, everything was working out just as Holt had predicted.

NINETEEN

No one need think that the world can be ruled without blood. The civil sword shall and must be red and bloody.

—Martin Luther

OCTOBER 12, 2012, SEABROOK CAMPAIGN EVENT,
PITTSBURGH GRAND HILTON,
PITTSBURGH, PENNSYLVANIA

Seabrook kept smiling as he backed into the private room of his suite. He'd learned from experience never to let anyone see his irritation until he was on the other side of the door.

Once the lock clicked, his face fell into a dark scowl. He could still hear the local party hack's braying laughter [illegible]bove the gobbling noises of the fund-raiser in the adjoin[illegible]g room.

Judas Priest, what a jerk, he thought. Seabrook couldn't [illegible]ear, even in the privacy of his own head, without his [illegible]ther's sad look of disappointment flashing before his [illegible] But guys like that made it tough to keep his temper. [illegible] long since learned to put up with such people. They [illegible] good money for his time ($5,000 minimum donation to attend, drinks included). But what kind of ignorant turd still tells jokes like that in public? *The hardest part is changing the diaper*? Jerk.

The media liked to portray him as a stuffed shirt, a robo-candidate with no real emotions of his own. Just another thing they got wrong. He had to keep his temper in check, especially at times like these. He knew that there were knuckle-draggers and mouth-breathers in the extreme wing of his party. He didn't like them. But if they wanted to vote for him because of whatever image they'd already created in their bent little minds, then he wasn't going to say or do anything to dissuade them. He was too close to the prize this time and every vote counted. Besides, it wasn't like Curtis was doing anything to discourage the far-left whack jobs on his own team, like the Occupy Wall Street people. And that crowd was *really* dangerous.

Seabrook took off his jacket and began unbuttoning his shirt. He wanted to get out of the bulletproof vest before rejoining the party. The Secret Service insisted he wear it for the speeches, but he figured he was safe enough in a room full of vetted and screened contributors. It wouldn't look right for him to be wrapped in body armor while he was hammering Curtis for being afraid of his own constituents.

To tell the truth, he was uncomfortable with the entire line of attack. The vest was a reminder of the reality they both faced: they were targets for anyone with a grudge or a wish for sudden fame.

Seabrook had his own troubles with the hair-trigger rage of the voters. He'd been as careful as a bomb-squad technician during the primaries and he was still attacked every day by the Tea Party, the patriots, or whatever else they called themselves.

The same inarticulate rage that battered Curtis found a target in Seabrook, too. The rank and file of his own party distrusted him. A former Wall Street investment banker himself, Seabrook was too perfect, too polished, too rich. They doubted his commitment and zeal. He wouldn't romise to shut down the federal government or return he country to the gold standard. His primary opponents eefully threw red meat to the crowds because they knew ey'd never win a general election. Seabrook, on the other nd, had a chance. So he spent every day on a tightrope sperately trying to find a balance between the extreme nge and the swing voters in November.

As a result, he'd had to fight for every vote in the naries—donations dried up after a disastrous third-place sh in New Hampshire, a state he was expected to win in alk—and he spent a considerable amount of his perl fortune just to stay in the race. His closest rival pped out, thankfully—she was still making appearances, she'd more or less thrown her support behind rook. The campaigning was really just to provide more ge for her reality-TV show, *The Candidate.* She'd told nedia, with a straight face, that she could do more with that than she could in Washington. And the candidates fell away, just as he knew they would.

er the convention, his advisers flipped the script and the same attacks on Curtis that Seabrook had suf- They said the president was out of touch, an elite, to talk to the real Americans out there in the heartland (and Seabrook's campaign deliberately left it vague as to how they defined "real Americans"). They mocked the tailored suits, the Ivy League education, the bombproof limo, even the "extravagance" of Air Force One. ("When was the last time *you* flew first class? President Curtis does it every day—and you foot the bill.")

It made him uncomfortable. It was undeniably tawdry. But he hadn't said no to any of it. Because the polls said it worked, especially in Ohio, which was going to be crucial in the final electoral count. So he let his campaign keep hammering away at it.

But he wondered how he would feel if something did happen to Curtis—if the responsibility would nag at him, or if the media would blame him.

He shook off the thought. The campaign had its own momentum now. He felt more like he was being dragged along than steering it.

Seabrook was undoing the Velcro straps on the vest when a man cleared his throat.

He spun around, heart suddenly racing.

The mild-looking man sat quietly in one of the hotel chairs, blending in with the decor like another shade of beige. He wore old-fashioned wire-rimmed glasses.

"What the Sam Hill are you doing in here?" Seabrook demanded. He almost reached for the panic button the Service had given him, but it was still in his jacket, which he'd tossed on the bed. And anyway, this guy didn't look like he could threaten anyone.

"My apologies, Governor," the man in glasses said. "I thought your staff would have told you I was here."

"Obviously not. Who are you?"

The man gave him a bland smile. "My name is Proctor. We met at the briefing last week."

Seabrook blinked, suddenly off balance. He couldn't quite remember this guy, but he remembered the briefing. As a courtesy, the CIA and other intelligence agencies gave classified updates to the opposition candidate, supposedly so that if he did win, he'd be up to speed on vital matters of national security. Seabrook suspected it was just an ego-stroking game of charades.

"That doesn't explain why you're here," Seabrook snapped. "Unless we're at war with someone you forgot to mention, this could have waited." He didn't like being surprised. And he especially didn't like the way the little man had watched him undress.

Proctor frowned. "I'm very sorry to have upset you, sir," he said. "To be perfectly honest, I'm not exactly here on official business."

Now, this just stank of wrong. Seabrook was ready to throw the pencil-neck out of the room himself when Proctor said, "What would you do to win this campaign?"

"Excuse me?"

"You heard me, sir," Proctor said, a hint of steel in his voice now. "What are you prepared to do to win?"

Seabrook shook his head. "I'm not sure what you mean by the question."

Proctor smiled. Seabrook thought there was a hint of mockery behind his lenses now. "There's no need for that kind of politician's answer. I assure you, there are no bugs in this room. I'm not recording this conversation. This might be the one time in the next eight years you can speak freely. If you accept what I'm offering, I can almost guarantee you victory in November."

"'Almost'?" Seabrook repeated. "You talk about me being a politician. That's a fairly big weasel-word."

The man with the glasses nodded, acknowledging the point. "It's a big country. We can't push every lever everywhere. Besides, we've tried it in other places often enough to know that stuffing ballot boxes never works. It's stupid and crude. Even with the new machines, people remember how they voted. What I *can* give you is advice and information. I could give you the inner workings that you're not privy to—and never will be, unless you win. Believe me, you'd find a way to use them. Some of these disclosures would sink Curtis. Of course, the choice would be entirely up to you."

For a moment, Seabrook was tempted. Like any decent politician, he'd studied Reagan's 1980 campaign. The hostage crisis and the debates were what sealed it for him. And there were persistent rumors that the CIA helped Reagan into office by tampering with both. Until this moment, Seabrook would have called those rumors the typical whining of the losing side.

Now he wasn't so sure.

"What would you want in return?"

"That's something we'd have to discuss after your inauguration. All I can tell you: it will be well within your powers, it will not threaten you or your family's safety, and it's completely nonnegotiable."

"How do you know I'd keep my end of the bargain?"

Proctor smiled again. This time there was no mistaking the mockery in it. "Because everyone always has."

Seabrook had made many compromises to get where he was; he didn't lie to himself about that. He smiled and choked back his indignation and disgust at certain people. He turned a blind eye to things that went against his personal morals.

But he knew this was different. This wasn't a compromise. This was a buyout offer. And he had a nagging feeling all sales were final.

"Get out," he said.

The man in the glasses shrugged and stood up. Seabrook stepped back to give him a wide berth as he walked to the door, as if watching a poisonous snake make its way across the floor.

TWENTY

HE'S NOT CHICKEN—HE'S A DUCK! QUIT DUCKING THE DEBATE, CURTIS!

—Sign carried by Seabrook campaign worker criticizing President Curtis for refusing to debate

EMBASSY SUITES HOTEL, MALMEN, ILLINOIS

Megan Roark was stuck.

In her hotel room she finished uploading her last bulletin of the day to her website, The Roark Report: CURTIS CAMPAIGN CATCHES GUNMAN—A FALSE FLAG OPERATION? (Copyright, Breaking News, Must Credit.) The Net was an even more demanding beast than the cable news cycle. Every minute of every hour, there was someone awake in the world looking for a new story, a new hit of information and outrage. According to the software that monitored her site, some members of her audience hit refresh on their browsers every minute just to make sure they hadn't missed anything she might have added in the last fifty-nine seconds or so.

Over a million people daily came to Megan's site, read her quickly typed blog posts and watched her videos. They came for her vicious attacks on the Curtis administration.

They came for her blunt-instrument sarcasm and humor. They came for scandal that the MSM—mainstream media—wouldn't touch. And, she admitted freely, they came to look at her perfect rack and cute-as-a-goddamned-button smile.

At least when she was on cable, she had staff and producers to shoulder some of the load. Back then, she was one of a dozen forgettable blond anchors better known for their looks than their journalistic creds. Megan had carved a small niche as the one who was really snide in interviews with anyone perceived to be on the side of President Curtis. She was moved up to a spot during the morning news block on a trial basis.

But Megan lost her spot due to an unfortunate on-air freak-out after the terrorist attack on the White House. She'd been awake for twenty-four hours covering the story and had spent her off-air time gobbling Adderall to stay awake and reading Internet message boards that tracked the inconsistencies in the official timeline of events. Megan still wasn't quite sure what had happened. She had only intended to bring up a few of these discrepancies while interviewing a White House spokesman in the aftermath. The next thing she knew, she was screaming at him, accusing him of orchestrating a cover-up. "The facts don't add up!" she screamed into the camera. "You keep changing your story!"

She was yanked off the air and suspended. While she wallowed in misery in her apartment, waiting for the official word that she'd been fired, she spent even more time on the Net. And she found that a YouTube video of her tirade had become one of the most popular videos on the Web. Sure, some people just laughed ("LOL! Bitch be crazee! OMG!"), but others—many others—called her a hero. "she has the GUTS to aks the real ?s noone else will" was a typical comment.

Megan looked at the counter on the video and saw that more than two million people had watched it. That was about twice the number of viewers she normally pulled on cable. Within an hour, she set up her own website and began recording herself through her laptop's built-in camera. The network shitcanned her as soon as her first home video hit the Net. They figured she was doomed to become another frayed thread on the lunatic fringe.

That was two years ago. Now she had a professional studio in one corner of her new $1.5 million condo and an advertising deal with a major media buyer. The lunatic fringe, as it turned out, was a very profitable place to be in America these days. But it was still only her doing it all: researching, reporting, writing and shooting and editing. And sometimes the content got a little thin.

The campaign trail was unbelievably boring to both her and her fans. She'd been reduced, in the last week or so, to rehashing some old conspiracy theories: Bin Laden had actually been dead for years and his corpse was kept on ice until the president's poll numbers needed a boost; a hospital ship that sank in the Gulf of Aden last year was actually sunk by a U.S. Navy submarine; and her old standby about the suicide bombing run at the White House being an inside job.

None of it was dragging eyeballs to the site the way she'd like. She hadn't seen a drop in overall unique users, but growth was no longer ramping up like before. She wondered if she should start showing even more cleavage.

But first, she checked her crank file.

She had a dedicated mail account that accepted public messages. She only opened it on a spare laptop that had no other purpose. It received thousands of e-mails. Maybe 50 percent were spam: get-rich-quick schemes, offers of Viagra and penis enhancement (she thought her balls were big enough, thank you very much), viruses, and porn, porn, porn, porn. Then there were offers of marriage from prisoners and would-be stalkers. Those went right into the trash. There were poorly spelled manifestos from true believers who wanted her to expose the alien tunnels under the Southwest, and a few obscene messages from unhinged liberal types.

Tonight, however, at the top of her in-box, she found something different. Sent from a random overseas server, it contained one massive attachment and a simple message:

The president doesn't want you to know about this.

If it was a virus, it was the most ingenious one she'd seen yet. There was no way for her to resist that.

She clicked on the attachment and it began unpacking itself onto her computer.

It was huge. Reams of documents, plus video and photos. She recognized the first file almost immediately from her days as a cop reporter.

It was an autopsy report. Intrigued, she kept reading before shuddering at the description of the horrific wounds inflicted on the victim. Then she moved on quickly to the police report.

She checked her newsfeeds and archives just to be certain, but she was right. No one had covered this. No one had even mentioned it.

Someone had carved up a campaign worker for Curtis like a pig in a slaughterhouse. And while he was banging a local volunteer.

Then someone had tried to cover it all up.

Megan's face split into a shit-eating grin. She did a little spin in her chair and squealed with delight.

She had her next big story. And it went all the way to the White House.

TWENTY-ONE

The question before us is: if these incidents are mere border skirmishes in this conflict, what would a full-scale invasion from the Other Side look like? For an answer, we should look back to the medieval period (5th century CE to 15th century CE), more commonly known as the Dark Ages. In that time, it was quite common for people to see demons, monsters, fairies, and the effects of black magic on a daily basis. It would be no real surprise for a 13th-century miller to see the Devil on the road in broad daylight. The supernatural was considered as normal as the weather, if less predictable.

Modern historians tend to discount these eyewitness accounts as fantasy, hyperbole, or simply the misunderstanding of a more primitive time. But this is a facile and simplistic explanation. One of the great mistakes of historical investigation is to assume people of earlier times are stupider than people in modern times. In fact, people in the medieval period, while largely illiterate, were no less intelligent than people today. The lack of formal education systems does not mean people in the past were any more likely to be prone to fantasy or delusion; if anything, they would be more likely to trust the evidence of their own eyes. And in the darkest parts of the Dark Ages, they would be much more aware of their surroundings, since fatal threats were far more commonplace.

We have to consider the possibility if thousands of eyewitness accounts of supernatural beings exist from the

Dark Ages, it's because thousands of people were actually seeing these things. The sheer number of sightings, the existence of the old European "witch-cults," the records of mass killings by unknown creatures—all of these point to a climate where the Other Side crossed into our world with impunity. The populace was consistently in terror from the things that walked in the dark, and had to take precautions every day to avoid them. Indeed, such a state of constant fear is less a hallmark of an invasion, and more like what is observed during an occupation by a hostile force.

—Dr. J.R. Berger, emeritus professor of history, "Them: An Examination of Human/Non-Human Contact Throughout Recorded History and Its Implications" (Specially Commissioned Report/Classified ABOVE TOP SECRET)

4:23 A.M., October 11, 2012, Presidential Campaign Bus, Outside Lanford, Illinois

The president was doing an admirable job of controlling his temper. But there was no mistaking the volcanic anger under the surface. He was pissed.

"How did this get out?" he demanded.

He pointed to the flat-panel computer on his desk, the screen turned outward to face his staff.

CURTIS CAMPAIGN WORKER KILLED DURING SEX ROMP WITH VOLUNTEER

Is there a "Campaign Carver" at work on the trail?

THE REPORT HAD gone up at 3 A.M. on *The Roark Report.* She'd run it without waiting for confirmation or a response from the campaign, of course. But the police records and autopsy photos were enough. She had the whole sordid story of Kirkman and Ohio in excruciating detail.

The other media outlets were only asking tentative questions so far. They didn't want to get their hands dirty on such a sleazy story if it turned out to be a complete hoax. So far, the campaign had been able to stall them with the tried-and-true "We won't even dignify that with a reply." But it wasn't going to work for long. Pretty soon the Mansfield Police Department would have to issue a statement. And so would the campaign.

Lanning finally answered the president's question. "We don't know. But it's out now. So we have to deal with it."

"That's not a very good answer, Dan," Curtis said.

"That's all I've got."

Curtis clenched his jaw, then nodded. "Fine. Dan, I want you to prepare an official statement. We are allowing local law-enforcement to deal with what appears to be a completely local matter. The victims have our prayers and support. Off the record, you tell people what Ms. Roark is calling a cover-up has simply been discretion. We haven't wanted to turn this into a sideshow by getting involved. The Secret Service offered its help but was refused. Also, I seem to recall the woman was married. See if you can float the idea of a jealous husband."

Lanning scratched out a few notes on a piece of paper

and got up. "Got it. I'll have a draft out with the morning schedule."

"No," the president said. "You'll have it out in ten minutes. I want people to have our response before they even wake up."

Lanning hesitated. He noticed that Zach and the others were not being dismissed.

"Did you need anything else, Dan?" Curtis asked.

"No, sir," he said.

"Right now, there's a security issue I want to discuss," Curtis said.

Lanning looked at the president, the disbelief clear on his face. "Right," he said. He took a few steps toward the door before turning back to Curtis.

"I know you're keeping something from me, Sam," Lanning said. "It's fine. I'm used to that. But I'll be fucked if I can figure out what it is. Anyway. I guess I just want credit for going quietly out the door."

The president smiled at him. "I know how hard that must be for you, Dan."

Lanning left. Curtis turned back to the rest of them.

"What now?" he asked.

"We haven't found him," Butler said.

"I could guess that much," Curtis replied. "What I want to know is how many more funerals I have to attend before you do."

"It has changed its pattern," Cade said.

As always, everyone stopped to listen when he spoke.

"It has never behaved like this before. It's never been this mobile. It's never gone this far afield from one hunting ground. And it's never been able to contain itself this long between kills. I should have been able to find and kill it already."

"You're not filling me with a great deal of confidence, Cade," the president said.

"My apologies, sir," Cade said. "I have no good answers for you."

Curtis blew out a sigh of frustration. "Then I guess I just keep taking it."

Zach had a question, however. "You're going to warn the local campaign offices, right?"

The president didn't reply. The silence lasted a few seconds too long for Zach's comfort.

"I mean, you don't have to tell them the Boogeyman is after them. Obviously. But you could tell them there have been death threats. . . . You don't have to be specific. They could still be more careful that way."

The president shook his head. "We can't take the chance of this getting out to the public."

Zach felt a small bloom of anger open in his chest.

"You're not going to tell them anything?"

"No," Curtis said. "We cannot allow this knowledge to spread. And I know Cade agrees with me."

Cade gave a curt nod. "Hunting the Boogeyman has never been easy. The more people involved, the more bodies. It's that simple."

Zach tried not to be pissed at Cade; he wasn't human, after all. He didn't have the same emotional range as a human as a consequence of the change into a vampire. Whatever had designed the operating specs for bloodsuckers seemed to know that it would be a serious impediment if vampires had feelings for their prey, so Cade's empathy was at best stunted, at worst nonexistent. All he cared about was catching and killing his prey.

But the president was more concerned about what a leak might do to his poll numbers. It would confirm everything Roark had said in the story. It would throw gasoline on the fire.

This was why, in some ways, Cade got along better with the president than with Zach. Zach was the closest thing Cade had to a friend or colleague, but on a fundamental level, Cade understood this president and the ones before him. It wasn't fear that united them. Cade was not afraid of anything, as far as Zach knew.

Cade, just like the president, hated to lose. On this, he and Curtis were instinctively in agreement: they'd both do whatever it took to make sure they won.

"There's another alternative," Candace said.

The president, then everyone else, turned to look at her.

"Disclosure," she said. "We go public. We tell everyone."

The room was silent. She had a look on her face. Zach recognized it from her appearances on the talk shows: a slight smirk with a practiced calm. She believed she had just jumped outside the box.

"I mean, we tell people what we're really up against," she said, as if nobody understood what she meant. "We give people the information they need about the Other Side. At the very least, we'll give them a fighting chance. And you"—she pointed to her father—"go down in history as the guy who led us in the ultimate battle between

Good and Evil. You tell me that wouldn't get you re-elected."

Zach searched for the right words. "It's not that simple," he said.

"Oh, bullshit," she shot back. "Who are we protecting? Sure, it will be hard to believe at first, but people will have to accept the evidence. Hell, we can bring out Cade if it comes to that. If this really is a war, shouldn't the people know about it?"

She wasn't done, but Zach started talking over her. And then Cade spoke, silencing both of them.

"No." One word, dropped like a stone.

Candace recovered fast. "Why not?" she shot back.

Cade looked at her for a long moment. She squirmed a bit. Cade seemed to be determining if the question was serious.

"It would break you."

She blinked. "Excuse me?"

"The Other Side feeds on your fear," Cade said. "It grows stronger as each one of you succumbs to superstition and despair. This is a war where territory is measured in minds and souls. You admit the truth, and you open a floodgate of pure horror. You've had this explained to you before, Ms. Curtis."

"But we could still—"

"I wasn't finished," Cade said. "Even if that were not true, you cannot face what I represent. You would not survive in a world that admitted things like me exist."

Candace frowned. "You're pretty scary, Cade, but I seem to be doing okay so far."

"No," Cade said. "You're not. I'm on your side. I'm leashed. And you're still terrified of me. You literally cannot imagine living in a world where the things like me—the ones that do not have to obey and protect you—are part of your everyday life. You try, in your movies and your stories. You rehearse the Apocalypse over and over. And all of those efforts are too small. Too human to grasp what any of it would mean. Those stories still have heroes and hope. You cannot fathom what it would do to you, to actually live in that world. Could you kill your six-year-old child when she woke with blood on her lips? What would you do when you found the place in the cellar where your husband stored human flesh? Could you do what it takes?"

The room was quiet again.

"You couldn't," Cade said. "Because if you did, you would no longer be human. You'd be amputating your souls, one cut at a time, every day. You might continue to function—but only as monsters. You cannot live in that world. That's why you have me."

Cade looked at Candace, who had gone quite pale, waiting for a response. She didn't open her mouth.

"It would break you," Cade said again, and left the room.

"I guess that answers that," President Curtis said. He stood and went into the bedroom in the back of the bus. He paused only to place a hand on his daughter's shoulder and give it a squeeze. She didn't respond.

Butler followed the president. Candace and Zach were the only two left.

Neither of them spoke for a while.

"To be fair," Zach finally said, "you *did* ask."

CANDACE WALKED OUT OF THE bus and through the hotel parking lot quickly. Zach followed, calling after her. She ignored him.

Candace went through the lobby doors. Zach followed. The Secret Service dogged their steps a few feet behind. Zach caught up to her just past the bar.

"Candace," he said, grabbing her arm. "Come on. Talk to me."

She spun around quickly, looking like she wanted to slap him. Her hand came up, but all she did was point a warning finger at Zach. "Don't touch me," she said sharply. "I mean it."

A few of the late-night stragglers were still around, finishing their drinks and looking for any excuse to avoid returning to their empty rooms. A cop stood in the lobby and looked concerned as Candace passed. A drunken businessman. An airline pilot. Their shadow from the Seabrook campaign. They all gawked.

Candace noticed, and stormed back out the lobby doors, into the parking lot again.

Zach turned to the agents. "Guys. Please. Give us a minute."

The agents, Fisk and Dunn, looked at each other. Dunn nodded at Zach. "Get her back inside fast," she said.

Zach went through the doors.

Candace stood in the cold, staring at nothing, hugging herself.

"I want you to know I don't appreciate your lack of support," she said without turning to him.

"You were wrong. Deal with it."

"You really believe this should be swept under the rug?"

"And stomped flat."

She turned away. "I have more faith in people than that."

"Oh, bullshit," Zach said, more tired than angry. "It's not about faith in America. It's about what's out there. I've seen it. You haven't."

Candace opened her mouth to argue, but Zach cut her off.

"No. You've seen the warm-up act. You haven't even been close to the headliners. None of it belongs in this world. And just looking at it makes it stronger—gives it a little more space that it shouldn't have. This isn't about your feelings. I agreed with Cade because he was right. This isn't about scoring points in a debate. This is beyond human. Nobody should have to live in the same world as this shit. If I didn't have to know about it, I'd gladly go back to blissful ignorance. But I do. So I take the responsibility until we beat it back to the Other Side. That's our job. You need to get on board with that now or go home."

Candace looked at him for a long moment, then stared back out into the night.

"You've changed," she said.

Zach shrugged. "Beats the alternative."

"Which is?"

"Dying."

She thought about that for a moment.

"Secrets," she said. "Since I was five years old, my life has been nothing but secrets. Things Daddy wouldn't talk about. Things we were never supposed to say when there were other people around. Smiling for the cameras. Every year, every election, more things we had to keep secret. I just get so sick of it sometimes."

Zach touched her arm so she could see he was smiling at her. "Join the club," he said.

"You know, I had a crush on you when we were kids," she said.

Zach blinked. Christ. Her father could take lessons from her in keeping someone off balance. But he remembered Candace as an eleven-year-old girl during Curtis's first run for Senate. Zach was still in high school and the closest person to her age on the campaign. He spent a lot of time getting her sodas, helping her with her homework and keeping her occupied while her father and mother began their path toward the White House.

"No. I didn't know that."

"Yeah. Imagine how disappointed I was when you grew up to be such a dick."

Zach laughed.

"I'm serious. You finally worked up the balls to take me into the Lincoln Bedroom and then you vanished. Why didn't you ever try to see me again?"

"Really? You want to have the 'Why didn't you ever call me?' conversation now?"

"You have something better to do?"

He exhaled, sending a billowing cloud of vapor into the cold air. "Let's put aside the fact that your father had the

Secret Service escort me out of the White House and I thought I was going to be shot and dumped in the Potomac. You immediately took off for California. A week later, I'm watching you make out with some D-list celeb on TMZ."

"I wouldn't call Topher D-list."

"Whatever. You didn't seem to miss me."

She looked directly into his eyes. "I missed you."

That threw Zach again. "Well. A week later I was working with Cade. It didn't seem like a good idea to pull you into my life. Especially after what happened at the White House."

"Maybe you should leave that decision up to me. After all, I'm here now."

"Yeah. You are."

The silence stretched between them. Neither one looked away.

Zach leaned in to kiss her, but hesitated. "Are you trying to make a point about going public again? Trusting people to know what they want?"

She laughed. "You can shut up now."

She grabbed him by the back of the neck and pulled his mouth to hers. Her skin was cold at first but was warm by the time they broke away.

She took his hand and they walked back into the hotel together.

ZACH MADE SURE THE DOOR was locked behind them this time.

He turned around and saw Candace taking down her underwear while pulling down her skirt. His mouth might have dropped open, because she laughed when she saw the look on his face.

"What?" she asked, still smirking. "Not romantic enough for you? Did you want to talk about our feelings some more first?" She reached behind her back and popped the clasp on her bra.

Zach felt the blood rush away from his face and into other parts. "No," he said, unbuttoning his own shirt. "This is good."

"Glad to hear it. If you'd decided to get sensitive on me now, I'd probably have to kick your ass right out of here."

Zach looked up from removing his pants—there was no way on earth to do this with dignity, he thought—and caught his breath.

"See anything you like?" she asked. Candace stood naked except for her heels and hose, her eyebrow cocked at the same angle as her hip, completely at ease. Her skin was flawless. Every inch.

She looked down at him. "Now, that's the response I was looking for."

Zach stepped toward her. She kissed him hard and quick, then pushed him to his knees. His head was level with the cleft of her thighs. He looked up into her eyes. Her smile was a little feral now.

"Come on, Barrows," she said. "What are you waiting for? A dinner invitation?"

He couldn't keep from laughing. "Jesus, Candace."

"Don't," she said. "I mean it. Don't get all wishy-washy

PROMENADE
3555 LAS VEGAS BLVD.
LAS VEGAS, NV (702)735-3551

3101731 BETELEHEM

CHK 4450
DEC02'12 5:58PM

4000J2641810
**T BOOKS/MAGAZI 9.99

MERCHANDISE 9.99
TAX 0.81
TOTAL PAID 10.80
CASH * 11.00
CHANGE DUE 0.20
3101731 Closed DEC02 05:58PM

ROOM#: ____________

NAME ____________

SIGNATURE ____________

THANK YOU FOR SHOPPING @
FLAMINGO LAS VEGAS
VISIT US AT: WWW.HARRAHS.COM
EXCHANGES ONLY ON OUTLET REGARDS
RECEIPT PROVIDED FOR RETURNS

and lovey-dovey on me right now. With everything we've seen lately, I don't want to have to worry about your feelings or think about monsters or what's waiting out there in the world. Not right now. I just want to come and sleep."

"That's all?" Zach said.

"That's all," she said, hooking one leg over his shoulder, pulling him in tighter and putting her weight on him at the same time.

"I can do that," he said, his lips brushing hers now. She shuddered and growled a little in her throat.

"So get to it," she ordered.

Zach did as he was told.

THE BOOGEYMAN COULD SMELL the anticipation on them both. It had been so long for Barrows it was practically coming out his pores. And the woman, Curtis's daughter, she was practically in heat. It filled him with an elemental level of disgust.

But he'd stuff it down for now. He knew he could easily make it up to their rooms and catch them in the act. What would that do to Cade, to have his pet human sliced like a Christmas ham? It was so tempting.

But no. He'd agreed to Holt's plan. This time he would be more than a creature of instinct. This time he would wait.

After all, when everything was finished, he'd have all the time in the world.

TWENTY-TWO

NATIONWIDE POLLING NUMBERS, W/E OCT. 12, 2012

CURTIS—44

SEABROOK—46

UNDECIDED—6

(Margin of error +/-5 percent. Totals may not equal 100 percent due to margin of error. Based on poll of 1,576 likely voters who expressed a preference between the two major parties.)

October 12, 2012, Lanford, Illinois

Lanford, the town where Zach grew up, had undergone something of a rebirth. Solidly lower-middle-class all through Zach's childhood and adolescence, it was now a community for those looking for a yard and a four-bedroom house within driving distance of Chicago. The new arrivals had brought money with them. They had turned downtown's pawnshops into coffeehouses, built a new mall with an Apple store, turned the grimy diners into coffeehouses, replaced the U-Sav with a Whole Foods and the cheap watering holes with brewpubs, and turned the convenience stores into coffeehouses.

Really, there were a lot of damn coffeehouses.

Zach was somehow insulted. He'd grown used to being slightly ashamed of his hometown. Now it looked practically respectable. He was surprised to find the Civic Center had been completely refurbished. The leaking old mausoleum where he'd graduated from high school had been renovated, dragging it, if not all the way into the twenty-first century, at least into the late 1980s.

It was while he was watching Butler and others do their security checks for the campaign rally—in daylight, so Cade was confined to his box in the cargo section of the bus—that he heard the familiar voice call his name.

Despite his reflexive self-confidence—some would call it arrogance—Zach didn't really understand just how good he was at finding information. Every time someone else threw up their hands in frustration and pushed back from the keyboard and computer screen, Zach simply assumed they didn't know where to look. He was right, but he had an innate grasp of the right places to dig for skeletons. It was a great gift when he was still in politics; he could find the buried DUI record of a born-again moral crusader or the hidden bankruptcy of a fiscal conservative with just a few minutes and a wireless connection.

Zach never put it into words, but he saw people's inner fears underneath all the shiny armor piled on top to hide them. He understood hidden shame. This gave him an almost intuitive ability to break open secrets.

If he'd ever stopped to think of it, he would have realized that his own hidden shame would have to come out. It was just the way it worked. Nothing stays buried forever, no matter how hard you try.

But somehow, it still surprised Zach when his own worst secret stood in front of him, grinning that idiot grin, smelling of Marlboros, Old Spice, and his usual lunch of Coors Light and stale bar popcorn.

He was still handsome. Maybe not movie-star good-looking anymore, but definitely aging-TV-star level. In fact, one of the young women who volunteered in the local office followed him with a proprietary eye. He winked at her before offering Zach his hand.

"Hello, Zach," the man said. "Been a while."

Zach shook it. He didn't know what else to do.

"Yeah," Zach said, his throat suddenly dry. "Been a while, Dad."

In recovery and therapy programs, they call it "inappropriate loyalty." It's the tendency shown by many children of narcissistic alcoholics to stick with people long after it becomes destructive. The thinking being that because they were let down and abandoned so many times in their childhood, the grown-up kids decide it's the highest virtue to remain steadfast to someone no matter how much shit piles up.

That was probably why he agreed to Frank's request to have a beer.

"Beer is all right," Frank insisted. "It's the hard stuff that gets me into trouble."

Zach was pretty sure there were any number of things that got his father into trouble. But he let it slide.

After all, they were working on the same campaign together.

Frank had, after years of political exile, been chosen as the guy by the Lanford Democratic Party to reach out to the Tea Party and other disaffected voters. That seemed fitting to Zach. If there was anyone who could tap into a reservoir of resentment, it was his dad.

If pressed, Zach would admit that there must have been good times when they were a family. He just couldn't name any off the top of his head.

Zach's father had served as a city councilman, a state representative, and a county commissioner despite a complete lack of accomplishments in any of those offices. But he looked right and sounded right. He inspired trust. He radiated such confidence that even people who were spitting mad when they confronted him would stop and listen. A few minutes later, they were nodding in agreement. Only when he was gone would they realize everything he'd said was complete bullshit.

Frank had the gifts to go far in politics. His lack of interest in actual policies or issues wouldn't have been a problem. Even his fondness for young women and aged Scotch could have been managed. But Zach, who developed his own political instincts very early, knew that Frank's biggest problem was his ego. Frank Barrows could never admit he was not the biggest man in the room, even when he knew he wasn't. This got him into trouble, especially when combined with his other bad habits.

Zach remembered the first DUI that went public. He'd been in junior high. The cop might have let City Councilman Barrows off with a warning, Zach knew. He'd seen his father talk his way out of other scrapes with the law while sloshed, starting at the very young age of six when Frank picked him up from school while half in the bag and then dented the fender of the principal's car in the parking lot. (Zach sometimes looked at all the safety gear parents used now and wondered how he made it through his childhood alive.)

But Frank had threatened the cop. And so all the sordid details came out. The "exotic dancer in the passenger seat of the councilman's family sedan," as the local paper put it. The mug shot showing Frank's idiotic, bleary grin. The inevitable quote from the police report: "Don't you know who I am?"

That was the first DUI, but the last straw for Zach's mom. She'd put up with other girlfriends, unpaid bills and drunken fights. But when her humiliation went public, she kicked Frank out. He still managed to win reelection—he blamed a vindictive police chief angry over cuts to the city budget—but that was the start of the downward slide. City councilman was only a part-time job, and Frank's drinking began to take up all his remaining attention. Zach's mom had to go to court to get the child support she was owed, and this showed up in the press as well. Eventually, the local party hacks convinced Frank it was time to retire and a new candidate ran on the ticket in his place. Then he changed his mind and ran as an independent and was crushed in the general election despite his years of service.

Frank survived on small-time patronage jobs and miscellaneous city contracts from old friends who took pity on him. But he was still owed favors, and he called them in when Zach was arrested for grand theft auto in high school, and again when Zach needed an introduction to then-Senator Samuel Curtis.

Zach cut the old man off when he failed to show up, even once, at his mother's deathbed in the hospital. Not that she would have wanted to see him, or would have been able to respond after she slipped into the coma. But still. Zach felt his father owed her at least an attempt at an apology.

They'd spoken only once since Zach left for D.C., not long before Zach began working with Cade.

The phone had rung at 3 A.M., and Zach had answered it before checking the caller ID. Rookie mistake. Frank had been drunk-dialing him since Zach went to college, and the conversations never ended well.

This one started well enough. Frank went on and on about how proud he was of Zach. Then Frank got to the point.

"Makes me proud, son. It really does. Who'd have thought you would have come back from being a car thief?"

Zach knew both politics and his father too well to believe that was just a random comment.

"What do you want, Frank?"

"Hey. You watch your tone. You owe your career to me, Mr. Big Shot White House. I helped you out when you needed it. Now all I'm saying is, maybe you could help me out."

"Or else what?"

"You think I'd threaten you?"

"I want to hear you say it out loud. I want to hear my father say it out loud."

Frank's face darkened. "Ah, this is just like that crap you spouted after you went to that goddamned therapist. And who paid for that?"

"Mom did. What happens if I don't help you out, Frank?"

"Well, I hate to say this, but there have been a few calls. Reporters. Some of them say they'll pay big money for any dirt on Curtis."

"You don't have any dirt on the president."

"I know one of his staffers is hiding a criminal conviction."

And there it was. In the end, there was nothing Frank would not use as a bargaining chip. Zach was not disappointed. He was not even surprised. All he felt was the grim and useless pleasure a person gets when he gets to say, I told you so. All he got out of this was the proof that his worst expectations were, once again, dead right.

By the end of the haggling, it wasn't much. Zach was able to cover the amount with what he had in his checking account. They could call it a loan, a gift, a long-overdue Father's Day present. Whatever.

It was a small price to pay for the solid proof that his father was exactly the person Zach always suspected him to be.

Since then, there had been other calls—Zach let them all go to voice mail. Zach had grown practiced at turning enemies into allies, or at least defusing their anger. Drop him into a congressional hearing or a fund-raiser and he'd be able to work the room as if he'd known everyone in it for years. But he never knew how to handle his father.

ZACH WAS ODDLY comforted by the fact that the bar Frank had made his second home hadn't been transformed like the rest of Lanford. It was still a dive: same cracked leather banquettes; same pool table with a phone book under one leg; probably even the same phone book, Zach was willing to bet. The bartender brought them ice-cold Pabst from the tap and Zach paid with a five and got change.

Frank smiled at his son as if five years hadn't passed without them speaking face-to-face. Frank's smile had, in fact, kept many people from punching him over the years. Zach had to admit, his dad looked a decade younger than the last time he'd seen him. Maybe all he needed was a little time in the limelight again.

"So," Frank said after draining half his glass in a single gulp, "you getting any?"

Zach had a brief, painful vision of Bell, smiling, naked and sweating, straddling his hips, leaning back and displaying her entire body for him.

"I was seeing someone for a little while. It didn't work out," he said.

"What happened?"

"Career stuff. She and I . . . we were on different sides of the issues."

"At least it was a she. God, for the longest time I worried you were queer."

"That term isn't an insult anymore, Frank. The queers took it. But you could probably still be offensive if you went with 'faggot.'"

Frank's grin went a little stiff. "Ease up, kiddo. No need to get all politically correct on me. I just wanted to know if I'm ever going to see a grandchild."

Zach stifled a laugh. It wasn't just his lack of a social life (He could barely imagine what a date would even be like anymore: "So what do you do?" "Oh, I work with a vampire who protects us from ungodly things that want to feed on our souls. You say you're in marketing?") or the thought of Frank playing grandpa. It was trying to justify bringing a child into the world now that he knew there really were monsters lurking under the bed.

All he said was, "Maybe someday."

"Well, you better get on it."

"Work's keeping me busy. I'm not really seeing anyone right now."

"That's not what I hear," Frank said.

"Really? What do you hear?"

"You've been fucking the big man's daughter."

Zach hesitated a beat too long. "Who told you that?"

Frank laughed, filling the bar with the sound of real delight. "So it's true. You never could lie to me, kid."

He signaled for another round. Zach waited while the bartender delivered two fresh glasses and then left.

Frank raised his drink in a toast. "Well. Congratulations. She's some kind of piece."

"Hey. I don't appreciate that."

"Come on, just a couple details. I bet she's taught you some things already. She's been around. All those Hollywood guys."

Zach slammed down his glass. "Frank, are you trying to find out if I'll kick your ass? Because you're not going to like the answer."

Frank put his hands up in a gesture of surrender. "Sorry. Sorry, son. I just—well, we never did this when you were running around in high school. Guy talk. I thought maybe, I don't know, you missed out on it. Because I wasn't around."

He really sounded contrite. Between Frank's improvement and the second beer, Zach almost felt bad for a moment. It seemed like his father, in his own fucked-up way, was actually trying to bridge the gap between them.

Zach sighed. "It's not like that between me and Candace, Dad. I'm not in this with her for the entertainment value."

Then, of course, Frank hit him with the sucker punch.

"So you are doing her," he said. "Good to know."

Zach immediately realized he'd made an enormous mistake. "Frank. You can't tell anyone this."

"Why not? Hell, if I were you, I'd put it on fucking billboards. You got any pictures? I know some people who'd pay big for them."

Zach ground his teeth. He was an idiot. Like his father was going to change now?

"She doesn't need the political sideshow. Neither does the president. Aren't we supposed to be on the same side?"

"There's only one side, Zach: your own. You've been in politics this long and you still haven't learned that?"

Zach sighed again. "What do you want, Frank?"

"I'm not getting any younger, son. I'm tired of bouncing from one thing to the next. I could use a nice, protected, civil service job. Something with a good pension. Six figures. I know you can tell the president to make it happen. Hell, you're practically family now."

Zach stood. Goddamned moron, he told himself. How did he not see this coming? For a moment, he considered just stuffing Frank into an administration position somewhere until he died. It wouldn't be that hard. Zach had done much more difficult things with a single phone call.

But no. Not this time. He was really finished this time. He was done looking for his father in this man. He didn't want to waste another second on him.

"You know what? Tell whoever you want," Zach said. He threw a twenty on the bar. "Drink up. It's on me."

"Come on. Zach. Zach," Frank called after him as he stalked away. "It's the least you can do for your father."

That nearly sent Zach right at Frank. But he restrained himself. "No. The least I can do is nothing. But if you don't stay the hell away from me, I'm going to tear your fucking arm off and beat you to death with it."

The bartender and the few other drunks all stared at him. Zach realized he was shouting. He stormed out of the gloom and into the daylight. He began walking blindly the streets of the town where he grew up, on autopilot, following the sidewalks by memory.

But that was okay. Nothing here ever really changed.

CADE FOUND FRANK BARROWS at the same bar where his son had left him. He'd either been celebrating or drowning his sorrows ever since.

Barrows was alone aside from the bartender. Cade showed the Secret Service credentials he'd been given by Butler. "I'd like to talk to Mr. Barrows in private for a moment."

The bartender took a pack of Marlboros from behind the register and walked outside. Barrows straightened up at his bar stool as much as he was able and turned both bleary eyes on Cade.

"This ought to be good," he said. "My little shit of a son call you in? Afraid to stand up to his daddy? I should have whipped his ass more when he was a kid."

"Your son didn't ask me to come here, Mr. Barrows," Cade said.

"Well. Sit down. Have a drink. Call me Frank."

"No," Cade said. "I'm here to deliver a message."

"Well, let's hear it."

Cade took a step closer. "You're going to keep silent about anything your son told you. And you will never contact him for any reason. Ever again."

Barrows looked uneasy. The effect of Cade's presence was making its way through his protective shell of booze. But rather than back down, he decided to try for intimidation.

"So you here to put the fear of God into me?"

"I'd appreciate it if you did not take the name of the Lord in vain," Cade said.

"Oh Lord. You're one of those Bible-thumpers? Well, Jesus H. Motherfucking Christ on a Popsicle stick. Please forgive my goddamned manners."

He grinned. Cade said nothing. The grin faded. Barrows reached behind the bar and picked up a bottle. Absolut. He poured more vodka into his glass and slurped it down quickly.

"Fine. Let's get this over with," Barrows said. "You're here to tell me to back off. To keep quiet about my son and the prez's slutty daughter. Mission accomplished. You can go. But I find it hard to believe you're stupid enough to think that you can scare me into shutting up."

"Why?" Cade was genuinely curious as to how this man's mind worked.

"Because you just made it worse!" He laughed loudly. "You telling me to keep my mouth shut just makes the story better! Now I can say the Secret Service threatened me. This just went from the front of the *National Enquirer* to the *Washington Post.* Tell my son to forget the job. I'll wait for the book deal instead. I should thank you. You just made me famous."

"I don't think so," Cade said.

"Yeah?" Barrows laughed again, but not quite so loudly this time. "What makes you think that every newspaper and network in the country won't beg me for an interview once they hear about this?"

Cade took a final step closer. He was face-to-face with Zach's father now.

"Because they would never believe you," he said.

He bared his fangs.

The shock hit Barrows like a two-by-four to the face. He stumbled off the bar stool and staggered backward.

"Don't try my patience, Mr. Barrows. Zach is under my protection. And his sentimental attachment to you means less than nothing to me. Do you understand?"

Frank Barrows didn't say anything. He shook violently and opened his mouth without speaking. Then his eyes rolled up into his head and he fainted.

Cade looked at the man on the floor. His almost-smile flickered on his lips. "I'll take that as a yes."

TWENTY-THREE

Hitchhiker drinks:
"I call again on the dark
hidden gods of the blood"

—Why do you call us?
You know our price. It
never changes. Death of
you will give you life
& free you from a vile
fate. But it is getting late.

—Jim Morrison, "Lamerica"

October 13, 2012, Fort Madison, Illinois

Stacy felt the gloom of the strip club wrap around her like a familiar blanket. It was always the same: the AC cranked high, the fog machines cranking, the too-clean antiseptic stink of the sanitizer the dancers used on the poles, the flat wall of bass notes from the speakers. It could have been the club she'd worked the night before, picked up and moved almost three hundred miles west.

Stacy and her friend and fellow dancer Annie (stage name: Cristal) had both quit school after getting their high school diplomas, but they knew economics better than most college students. Raising a kid on your own tends to teach the subject hard and fast. They both lived in the same crappy apartment complex and became friends around the laundry room and what was left of the lawn by the parking lot. They watched each other's kids, commiserated about deadbeat ex-boyfriends and realized, at about the same time, that they were always going to be in debt or on food stamps working minimum-wage jobs while paying for day care. There was no shortage of guys who wanted to be the next deadbeat ex-boyfriend, at least for a night, so Stacy and Annie knew they were still hot enough—for Peoria anyway. They bought some cheap lingerie, hired a reliable babysitter, and began earning three to five hundred at night dancing in platform heels while their kids slept.

The problem was, there were a lot of other women who got the same idea when the economy went straight into the crapper. She and Annie watched as their number of shifts dropped to one or two a week.

But Stacy did a little Internet research and a little math. She counted up all the clubs in a 500-mile radius and figured that as long as gas stayed under five bucks a gallon, she and Annie could find a place to work every night.

True, it often meant a 600-mile round-trip before dawn, but that was easily solved by a little crystal meth.

The strip clubs out on the fringes were happy to see them. Smaller towns had a problem that the bigger cities didn't: everyone knew everyone else. No matter how bad the economy got, there were always more men who'd pay to see naked women than local women willing to be seen naked. Stacy and Annie didn't have to worry about running into the Sunday school teacher while in line at the supermarket after giving him a three-for-two lap dance in the Champagne Room.

In economic terms, they'd found a niche market. The local strippers didn't even mind too much, because they took the shifts nobody else wanted, like Tuesday nights.

Of course, this meant they had to work harder to get dollars out of the cheaper customers, but they were motivated and they were pretty good at their jobs. Plus, hot enough for Peoria was usually way hotter than guys got to see in Fort Madison or Waterloo.

Stacy waved to the DJ in the booth and pointed at the women's room door, signaling she was off the floor for a few minutes. He barely nodded back. The club was slow, even for a weeknight. Annie had struck pay dirt, however—an old guy who appeared ready to spend his entire Social Security check in pursuit of a heart attack while underneath her.

There were no lockers inside the restroom. There wasn't even a door on the stall. This was just a place for the girls to change from their real clothes to their stripper-wear. Management had thoughtfully provided hooks on the wall for their bags, but Stacy carried everything valuable in her tiny stripper-purse. She'd been ripped off once before, and that was once too often.

She opened the little bag and found an even tinier envelope. She dumped a little of the crystal powder onto her hand and snorted it. Just a little bump. Annie worried she was doing too much, but she didn't have much room to preach. They both needed something extra to get through the week.

Just twelve more years of this, Stacy thought, and then Evan's college will be paid for. It almost made her laugh. There was no way she'd be able to make decent money at this even five years from now. She was saving some, but not enough. She knew she'd have to find a real solution soon. But it was too much work just staying awake these days.

Then the electricity shot from behind her nose to the front of her brain and pushed out all the weariness and fear. She walked back into the club like she owned it.

A new guy had come in. He was wearing a suit. The fat girl on the stage tried to get his attention, grabbing at her crotch, but Stacy locked onto him before he even ordered a beer.

A suit was always a good sign. Suit usually meant money. Suit also usually meant out-of-town, which meant lonely and horny and often willing to do something stupid.

She sat down and kissed him on the cheek. "I'm Amber," she told him. "What took you so long?" It was her best line, and he was charmed immediately. Up close, he was younger than he appeared at first. He had doughy lumps under his dress shirt and dark rings under his eyes.

She learned why right away. His name was Lawrence—not Larry, never Larry—and he was eager to talk. He was in politics, racking up frequent-flyer miles and hotel and rental-car points across the country. He was spending a lot of time over the border in Iowa now because of the election. He really believed the president had a chance to take the state this time—he could see it in people's faces, he really could. He'd just come from arranging a big campaign event. He couldn't go into detail, he said, but he'd talked to the Secret Service, and he knew this was going to be huge for the president, just huge.

Stacy couldn't care less—she didn't follow the news, didn't vote—but she felt the buzz coming off him. He felt important, needed, *alive.* Maybe it was the drug, but she felt some of his energy too. He was pumped up and ready to celebrate. And he was harmless. She could feel it. So she decided to cut to the chase.

"Lawrence," she said. "Why are you here?"

"Well," he said. "That's obvious, right?"

She leaned in. "Say it. I want to hear."

His voice shook a little. "I wanted to see [illegible]."

"Just to see?" Her voice was mocking now. She lazily traced the outline of her nipple through the black, deep-cut camisole she wore. "You sure that's all?"

"I, uh, I thought that was all I could get."

Her hand slid down the curve of her own body, across her bare thigh and up his leg. Her thumb barely brushed his erection, straining at the seams of his pants. Still, he shuddered like he'd been Tased.

"But that's not all you want," she said, drawing her hand back.

He nodded.

He was hers now. It was too easy. "Tell you what," she said. "It's about time for my smoke break. You have a car?"

He nodded even harder. "Out back."

"Well," she said, standing up. "Maybe I'll see you out there."

Stacy went to the bathroom again, got her coat and waved her pack of cigs at the DJ, who again barely acknowledged her.

Lawrence Edwin, advance campaign coordinator for Americans United to Re-Elect President Samuel Curtis 2012, could barely wait two minutes before too-casually going out the door after her.

Lawrence made a show of checking his pockets and picking up his jacket before he left. Only one person cared enough to watch his act.

The Boogeyman heard everything. His hearing was so acute now, he could pick up the click and slurp as a stripper chewed gum on the stage. He could hear the fiber of the cheap industrial carpeting being crushed under the waitress's heel as she went out of her way to avoid him, sitting in the corner. He could hear the beating of Lawrence Edwin's heart as the blood rushed away from his brain.

He waited three minutes before he got up and followed them to the parking lot.

ZACH COULDN'T IMAGINE a parking lot of a strip club that didn't look like a crime scene. This one just happened to have two dead bodies in it.

They were hacked up in the backseat of a rental car. Despite the chunks taken out of their bodies, it was left very clear what they were doing before the blade had come down on them: her head rested in his lap, separated from the rest of her body.

The local police had called the state troopers, who'd found Edwin's wallet and business cards and called the Secret Service. Cade and Zach had backtracked along the highway to take a look for themselves.

"Is it him?" Zach asked.

"It. Not him."

"Right. Well?"

Cade nodded. "This isn't right," he said.

"Preaching to the choir, Cade."

"No. It shouldn't be doing this. It's never traveled this far before. It usually stays in one area. Usually limits itself to one hunting ground at a time. This is different."

Zach wasn't quite sure what Cade meant. "Things change, I guess."

"No," he said again. "Not things like it."

"You've changed," Zach pointed out. "You adapt. You improvise."

"Because it's in my nature to do so. It's not in the Boogeyman's."

"Apparently it is now. Oh, just so I know, does it have to attack someone having sex? Is that a rule I missed?"

"Griff had a theory about that," Cade said. "He believed it hated sex because it hates life. Sex is the ultimate expression of life; it's what your species is designed for, and it's what most of your lives revolve around."

"You're one to talk. I've heard the echoes when Tania comes to visit you."

Cade didn't reply. Zach knew this was a touchy subject.

Tania had not responded to any of the messages Zach had left on the encrypted phone he'd given her in the past couple of months. For all he knew, it was in a landfill somewhere. Cade, when asked, would only grunt that he was not her keeper. Zach assumed from the surliness that Cade wasn't getting any.

This was troubling, because Zach felt a lot better when he knew where something as dangerous as Tania was. He hated the idea of her springing out at them from the dark if she finally decided to turn on them.

Whatever, Zach decided. They'd leap off that bridge when they got to it. There were more pressing matters right now.

A car pulled into the lot. Before the local police could intercept the driver, she hopped from the front seat and began taking pictures with her phone.

Megan Roark.

"Son of a bitch," Zach said. "That's all we need."

He ducked under the crime-scene tape with Cade as she came running after him.

"What are you doing here, Mr. Barrows? Is it true that another campaign staffer has been killed?"

She must have been recording. It was the only time she'd call him "Mr. Barrows" and not "Junior" or "Sparky."

Cade kept his back to her.

"All right, ma'am, you're going to have to step back," a policeman said to Roark.

"Don't you touch me, don't you touch me!"

"I'm not touching you." The cop sounded almost hurt.

"You can't cover up the truth, Mr. Barrows!"

Then Roark pressed a button on her phone and put it back in her bag. She stopped pushing against the cop and became almost calm.

"Okay, I've got enough of that, I think. You got anything to tell me, Sparky?"

"Nothing you'd want to print," Zach said. "You're freaking insane, you know that?"

She gave him a radiant smile. "Got to get those page-views up. You want to tell me why one of your people was getting a hummer from a lap dancer in this shithole when he was killed?"

"No comment."

The cop had had enough. "Ma'am, you're going to have to leave this area now."

"I'm not old enough to be called 'ma'am,'" Roark said.

He popped the button on his handcuff case.

"I'm going, I'm going," she said. "I've got what I came for. See you back at the hotel, Junior."

Zach watched her get back into her car and drive away. "I wonder who's leaking to her."

"It doesn't matter," Cade said.

"It doesn't?"

"We stop the Boogeyman. No more story. Cure the disease, Zach. Not the symptom."

Cade turned away and headed back for their own car.

Zach looked over at the body bags now being hoisted into an ambulance.

Yeah, he thought. And what if we can't do either?

TWENTY-FOUR

Welcome to *The Daily Show*, my name is Jon Stewart, got a tremendous show for you tonight. Apparently I am going to eat a tub of rice pudding bigger than my torso. [LAUGHTER] No, seriously, we're going to have Denis Leary on later and he'll ramble on about his cooking show on the Food Network. [LAUGHTER] But first, let's look at the presidential race in our award-adjacent coverage, Indecision 2012. It's getting rough out there on the campaign trail. What's that, you say? Because of the hard-hitting questions about our plummeting economy, overseas wars and massive federal debt? No! Because working for the Curtis Campaign has turned into a really horrific good-news, bad-news joke. The good news is, you will get laid. The bad news is, someone will probably kill you. [LAUGHTER] Now I know there are those in the audience who will say, 'Jon, I likes them odds . . .'

—*The Daily Show with Jon Stewart*, Monday, October 15, 2012

October 15, 2012, Lafayette, Illinois

Crystal Waddell was working late in the campaign office again when Dustin came to her desk. He looked determined. The beautiful, blond lummox of an intern had made excuses to stay late at the campaign office with her all week. Every night, she would let him walk her to her car. He was worried about her after the recent killings. She told him she didn't have any plans to get caught in the parking lot of a strip club, and he blushed. Such a gentleman. His mother trained him well. And every night, he would look at her wedding ring when he was about to lean in for the kiss before his nerve failed him. She thought it was sweet. Annoying, but sweet.

Tonight was different. They were alone in the office, about to turn out the lights and lock up. Only this time, he approached her at her desk. She could see it in the way he moved—almost marching up to her, dead set on making it happen this time, right here, right now. Crystal was torn.

She never, *never* did anything at the office. Campaigns were gossipy enough. She preferred cheap motel rooms where her rental car was one of a dozen others in the lot.

The fact was, Crystal had decided she was going to sleep with Dustin the moment she saw him. He was going to be her plaything and reward, her tension-breaker from the stress of the campaign. She'd come to look at the boys like Dustin as an expected—and well-deserved—perk of her job. Crystal was a brilliant campaign fund-raiser. She could pump dollars out of donors long considered dry wells. More than that, she was expert at the minutiae of campaign finance laws, and her disclosure forms were works of art. She knew exactly when to file and exactly how much info to give. She knew exactly where the line of legality was and how far over it she could go when juggling checks from other candidates, PACs and independent pressure groups. Crystal held and dumped money in a half-dozen accounts and could always be relied on to find cash for a last-minute TV buy if necessary. It was exhilarating and enervating work. She was required to be dazzling for at least eighteen hours a day. So she had no guilt about a little illicit sex if that's what it took to recharge her batteries.

It wasn't that she didn't love her husband and her wee darling son at home. She'd been genuinely grateful to leave the campaign trail when she got married at twenty-eight. Before that, she'd lived on Diet Coke and ephedrine tablets, flying from one state to the next, raising money for the National Committee and a string of candidates, stopping at her apartment in D.C. only long enough to get her suits dry-cleaned. It had been that way since she graduated from college and sprang into her first job as an assistant to a congressman. She'd been amazed at how much time was spent begging for cash and found she had a gift for opening wallets and checkbooks. So she made that into her career.

But she'd looked around at the people in her profession—the other fund-raisers, direct-mailers and year-round campaigners—and been discouraged. By the time they hit forty, they were burned down to wire-frame versions of their previous selves. Only their charm kept people from noticing how much they'd devolved.

When her boyfriend, a handsome policy analyst from a good WASP family, finally proposed, she'd said yes. She got pregnant almost immediately. For a couple years, it was domestic bliss.

Then one day, Crystal got a call from an old colleague who was raising money for then-Senator Curtis. She was going to turn him down when it hit her like a bolt from above: she was bored out of her skull. Her darling boy was in preschool. Her hubby spent all day at his think tank and most nights buried under reports and books. She wanted back in the game.

Once on the trail again, she discovered something else. Crystal was, for the first time in her life, insanely horny. She'd never thought of herself as someone who needed a lot of sex. It just wasn't that big a deal to her. One of the reasons she'd married her dull but reliable hubby was that he wasn't exactly an animal in the sack, either. Most nights, they were both more content to get an extra hour of sleep.

But whether it was passing thirty or just being out of the house again, she found herself constantly, ravenously and indiscriminately aroused. She'd watch gym-toned men walk in airports on business trips and feel almost like pouncing on them like a lioness would a gazelle, tearing open their suits to see what was inside. She did her best to resist temptation, becoming a compulsive masturbator after a lifelong hands-off policy toward her own body. She'd go into the tiny, cramped airplane restrooms and jill herself off repeatedly in a single flight, then spend all night watching hotel-room porn. She even bought a vibrator on one of her trips and had it out of the packaging before she started the engine of her car.

But Crystal was basically a practical woman, and she found doing anything halfway ridiculous and frustrating. She saw no reason to deny herself what she wanted. After all, she still ate ice cream straight out of the container. She just worked it off at the gym.

So, four or five days in a row, she was the perfect wife

and mom. Then, four or five days away from home, she would get what she needed.

Crystal could have had any number of affairs with any number of donors or other political operatives; the host of one of the talk shows passed her his hotel key card when they met at an event. But she had standards. She didn't want a doughy guy who'd spurt himself dry in fifteen minutes and then talk politics for the rest of the night. She didn't want an affair. She wanted to fuck.

Luckily for her, politics tends to draw young, idealistic people who confuse their political passions with their raging hormones all the time.

Crystal knew that some of the boys she took to bed were only there for what they thought she could do for their careers. She'd overheard others talk about her as a "MILF," which didn't hurt her feelings, or a "cougar," which did. She knew that at thirty-six she represented age and experience to horny college students barely out of their teens.

But she didn't really care as long as they could perform. And thank God, most of them could. Over and over and over again.

Dustin was really too sweet for her. And moreover, it was possible he'd get dangerously attached. She'd been working the Midwest and spending more and more time away from home. Curtis was going to need every dollar he could get to pull out a win in November, especially with those killings. So Crystal was consulting with a half-dozen different state offices, spending a week or two at each one in rotation, helping them massage their finances.

She hadn't been home for almost a full month. Worse, she hadn't ridden some young guy like a pony in almost twice that long. She was due to return to Washington, D.C., the next day. If she was going to take Dustin, it had to be tonight.

He gave her a look that loosened her bra straps and she made her decision. Even though they were in the office, she jammed her tongue in his mouth. Just so he wouldn't get the wrong idea.

"Oh wow" was all he said when she let him up for air.

Crystal maneuvered him around so that his back was to the desk. Dustin lost all his timidity. He grabbed her, pawing at the buttons on her blouse like a poorly trained circus bear. She let him try for a while, then pushed him back hard. His thighs hit the desktop and he had to fall on his back onto her carefully arranged papers.

"Oh man, oh wow," he said again as she slowly unbuttoned her blouse, then stripped off her skirt. He fumbled with his own khakis, his cock bobbing up and down like it was spring-loaded.

She smiled. This was the kind of enthusiasm she was looking for.

Crystal swung a leg over his hips and guided him in. It felt perfect. Exactly what she needed. She tried to start slowly, because she knew kids his age had a hard time containing themselves. But she knew he'd rise for her again. And again and again and again.

Crystal didn't hear the door at the back of the campaign offices open. Dustin probably didn't hear anything, either: his voice was a constant stream of "Oh God, oh man." Her eyes were closed while she worked herself back and forth on him, so she didn't see the figure that crept up behind them, or the blade he carried.

It might have been almost merciful if he had brought the blade down at that moment.

But he wanted them to see it coming.

Crystal felt a tap on her shoulder and nearly fell off Dustin. He was too close to coming, couldn't stop pumping even if he'd wanted to. Entangled and struggling, she tried to pull on her top. She was trying to figure out how to deal with this, whether or not to shriek in outrage or laugh it off with embarrassment. Then she saw him.

A man stood there with something like a machete but with a curved blade, held high and ready to strike. His entire head was covered with a rubber mask. It was a dirty-yellow latex version of a smiley face, some kind of bargain-bin Halloween remainder item, stuck on the man's neck like the top of an obscene, fleshy lollipop.

She saw him lift the blade and her breath was vacuumed from her lungs. She couldn't scream.

Crystal heard Dustin, who had finally opened his eyes, say, "What?"

She had a second to think about what this would do to her husband. Then there was blinding pain and that was all she could think about. It lasted much longer than she thought possible before everything went utterly, finally black.

TWENTY-FIVE

Reporting from Lafayette, Illinois—

The Campaign Carver has done it again.

Almost as soon as President Curtis's million-dollar campaign buses left this tiny town where he gave his usual promises about jobs and a better tomorrow, the bodies of two innocent victims were found.

They will never see a better tomorrow, thanks to the mysterious serial killer who just so happens to follow the President of the United States like the discarded confetti and signs from one of his rallies.

Crystal Waddell, 36, and Dustin Nichols, 22, were discovered by a campaign staffer upon opening the Curtis for President offices in the morning.

She called police, who found most of their bodies in various places around the room. According to one police source, "it looked like a goddamned slaughterhouse."

Waddell was a regional committeewoman for the Curtis re-election effort. Nichols was a volunteer taking a semester off from his senior year in college to follow the campaign.

Waddell's husband, Stephen Waddell, had no comment on why his wife would have been found naked with the much younger man.

The Curtis campaign has refused to answer any questions from THE ROARK REPORT, but when questioned by other media, spokesmen have said that the rapidly increasing body count following the president is nothing more than "coincidence."

Coincidence? Six bodies in three months is a coincidence?

How many more people have to die before the lamestream media will stop buying the spin from Curtis's hired mouthpieces and start asking the tough questions? Maybe they're afraid of losing their place on the White House Christmas Card list, but THE ROARK REPORT is willing to be a little impolite if it means stopping a serial killer.

—Megan Roark, The Roark Report, October 17, 2012

9:23 P.M., OCTOBER 17, 2012, PRESIDENT'S SUITE, HOTEL PÈRE MARQUETTE, PEORIA, ILLINOIS

"We're getting killed," Lanning said. "No pun intended."

No one laughed. Butler, Cade, Zach and Candace sat with the president in the conference room attached to his suite in the hotel, listening to Lanning tally up the political damage.

The murders were the lead item on every network newscast. CNN was doing round-the-clock coverage. Fox had created its own graphic: a ballot marked with a check written in blood. The Net already showed what tomorrow's headlines were going to be: MURDER ON THE

CAMPAIGN TRAIL: DOES A KILLER STALK THE PRESIDENT? Even NPR went with the blood and guts. "*Et tu*, Robert Siegel?" was Lanning's reaction.

The media had burrowed into the story like a tapeworm. And in a way, Zach could not blame them.

The "Campaign Carver" angle was too good for them to pass up. It guaranteed them headlines and lead position in the broadcast or at the top of the hour. Careers could be made from something like this. And it slid so neatly into the narrative they'd already created, the one-term wonder. What better symbol of Curtis's impotence than the fact that someone was killing his staff? How could he keep the country safe when he couldn't even keep his own people alive?

Even Zach had to admit—it was a hell of a story.

And in all honesty, print reporters did not have the time to go out and find a new narrative; they were pressed to write a story a day, plus blog updates plus graphics plus a Sunday piece plus whatever else it took to convince the bosses that they were worth the added expense on the bottom line. The TV people had it just as bad, if not worse. Five or six updates a day, trying to milk news out of the same canned speeches, the same generic crowd scenes, knowing that they were only there to catch the candidate saying something unforgivably stupid or if someone took a shot at him.

They were all bored out of their skulls, wired from too little sleep, constantly uncomfortable and in direct competition with a bunch of other people who were crammed in the same buses and planes and hotel rooms. No wonder they were psychotic. Fortunately, they were easily distracted.

Throw something shiny and easy to get in front of them, and they were off like hyperactive puppies.

The trick would be to find something even better for them. At least until Cade could stop the killings.

"Have we got any reliable numbers yet?" the president asked.

"Still crunching the latest phone poll. Very preliminary numbers. We should have something more solid by morning."

"What's the damage?"

"As I said, it's very preliminary—"

"Dan. Come on."

"You're down seven already."

Seven points in less than a week.

Curtis actually smiled. He turned to Candace. "Is my nose bleeding?"

She looked puzzled. "No."

"Thought it might be, considering the shot I just took."

There was a little laughter at that.

"You're taking this pretty well." Lanning looked suspicious.

"No, I don't think so," the president said. "I think I'm taking it the only way I can. I cannot be responsible for the acts of a psychotic. If that's what controls the outcome of this election, then so be it. All I can do is my job. And that's all I can ask of any of you. I apologize for my earlier displays of temper. That was inappropriate. By now I should know that evil does exist in this world. We do our jobs. We go forward. There are some things more important than winning elections."

The president stood.

"I'm going to see my wife."

On his way out, he gave Candace a kiss on her head.

There was silence in the room after he left.

Lanning spoke first. "Anyone here want to see that guy lose in November?"

Silence.

"Then it's time we got to work, kiddies. Zach, you and Candace will go out to the press bus. They're tired and pissed off. I don't care if you both have to blow them all in their seats, but you work the refs. All night if you have to."

Candace and Zach got up to leave the room.

Cade followed them.

In the hallway, Zach said, "Shouldn't you be with the president?"

"He's surrounded by the Secret Service."

"Yeah, but still—"

Cade allowed a small scowl to cross his face. "I need to get back out there. If I can find it, I can stop this."

Zach turned and blocked Cade's path.

"I think you should stay here, Cade. You haven't found him so far. And for all you know, that's exactly what he—sorry, it—wants: to get you away. To distract you. Maybe you shouldn't take the bait."

Cade turned dead eyes onto Zach. "Are you giving me a direct order?"

"Yeah. I guess I am."

"So you're the strategist now?"

"Well, maybe it's time for a new plan. The old one isn't working."

"Thank you for that," Cade said. He turned away quickly, coat snapping in the air with the sudden movement.

Zach had honestly never seen him so out of sorts, so easily irritated.

"Hey," he said. "I'm only trying to help."

Cade turned back. His mouth was clamped shut. Zach realized Cade was trying to keep his fangs from popping out of his gums.

"You want to help?" he hissed. "Explain to me why it's changing a century's worth of habits. Explain to me why it's nibbling at the periphery instead of launching itself at its target. Better yet, tell me where I can find it. Tell me where it lives, so I can kill it."

Cade's fangs jutted forth, right there in the hallway of the hotel.

"You want to help?" Cade repeated. "Give me something I can *bite*."

Zach stepped back. Candace simply looked scared.

Cade saw their faces. He took a moment and visibly brought himself under control again.

"Cade," Zach said. "You'll find him. You'll stop him. I know you will."

"It," Cade said. But he seemed to relax somewhat. "You're right. Thank you."

Candace and Zach turned again to go out to the press bus. Cade began to follow.

"The president is the other way," Zach said.

"I thought I would walk you out. I can't have anything happen to my strategist now, can I?"

Zach smiled at that, even though Cade remained stone-faced.

"Pretty sure we're going to be safe with the press, Cade. They only assassinate character."

Cade got the hint and walked away.

Zach never ceased to be surprised by Cade. Sometimes he could be almost human.

Megan Roark would never admit it, but she loved meeting with her source inside the Curtis campaign. He was actually very good in bed. She let him believe it was a chore.

She didn't wonder why he was here with her. Betrayal, jealousy, revenge, yadda yadda yadda, all that psychological stuff? So much bullshit. One look at herself in the mirror naked was all the answer Megan really needed to that question.

But lying sideways on the bed, one leg thrown over him, both of them sweating and spent, she felt pretty great.

Every news outlet in the world was following her lead. Everyone who'd ever looked down their nose at her after she left the lamestream media now wanted an interview, a tip or a link back to their own struggling and pathetic sites.

A decent orgasm was just the cherry on top.

Besides, even the pillow talk was fun.

"All right. Pay up," she said.

"What more do you want? Doesn't the story of the year get me at least a little credit?"

"Coal into a furnace. You know that. I want to know who's doing this."

He frowned. "You and me both."

"Still no leads?"

"Nothing."

"I suppose that's enough for a follow-up. But it's not much of one." Megan stretched, rolled over and saw the hotel's clock radio. "Shoot. I've got to get back."

She bounced out of bed. His eyes followed every move hungrily as she collected her clothes from the various places they'd been thrown across the room.

She smiled at him. "Nope. No time for another round. Plus, you still haven't given me anything really good."

"Open my bag," he said.

She slid into her thong before crossing to his laptop bag on the desk. Unzipping it, she found a file.

"Everything I could get on Zach Barrows. As you requested."

"Oooh," she squealed. "Interesting."

"You're not stalking him, are you?"

"I find it awfully convenient that he's rejoined the campaign just as the killings have started."

His laughter turned into a hacking cough. She really wished he'd quit smoking. The old joke about licking an ashtray was, unfortunately, true in this case.

"Barrows? You think Barrows is the killer? Come on. He couldn't give anyone a paper cut."

"How would you know? You haven't seen him since he was fired. And you were the one who told me he'd been bouncing around all these places where people turned up dead. And on top of that, you just happened to have all this information gathered and ready for me."

"I got curious," he admitted. "I don't know why the kid is inside Curtis's inner circle again. Frankly, he shouldn't be there."

"Right. Your motivations are pure. I get it."

"Hey, I'd be happy to see the kid go back to obscurity again. I've got enough competition. You should head back to Lanford, actually. His old man lives there. He's probably got lots of dirt on the little snot."

Megan's eyebrows shot up. Still half-dressed, she found her phone. Thumbs flying, she made a note on the device.

"Thanks for the tip. Tips. Gotta run."

"Megan. You know there's no evidence that actually links the killer to the campaign," he said.

Roark buttoned her blouse and tucked it into her pants. She wondered why he said stuff like that. He also swore up and down that he hadn't sent her the initial e-mail about the killings with the police reports. Just making the best of a bad situation, he insisted, and getting a little nookie out of it. At times, it made her wonder if he was just playing her.

But no, that would be absurd.

"You know that, right?" he repeated.

Roark checked her makeup at the mirror. "So?"

He laughed. "Wow. You really are a horrible person."

She smiled at him from the door and blew him a kiss. "You're the one who's fucking me."

"You've got a point," Lanning said.

TWENTY-SIX

Music World is built on the site of an old slaughterhouse (complete with a well underneath the building that received the drained blood of the slaughtered animals) dating back to the nineteenth century, and indeed, it was a site for satanic activity and a cult murder in 1896 when the headless body of five-month-pregnant Pearl Bryan was found. Two men—Alonzo Walling and Scott Jackson—were arrested for murder after confessing to the crime. Self-proclaimed devil worshippers and occultists. They refused to tell investigating authorities the location of Pearl Bryan's missing head, saying it would bring the wrath of Satan upon them. They feared Satan more than death, because they were offered life in prison instead of execution if they gave up the head. . . . If . . . some sites in America are sacred, then perhaps Music World is evidence that others may be just the opposite: unholy and profane.

—Peter Levenda, *Sinister Forces*

October 17, 2012, Lanford, Illinois

Frank Barrows had spent the last week working his way to the bottom of the vodka section in the liquor store.

He always started near the top when on a real bender. It was important to prep the system with some high-quality stuff, preferably taken as close to freezing as possible and served straight up. So he began with Absolut on day one. On the second and third days, it didn't matter as much. Everything was going numb, including his taste buds. He moved down a shelf or two. By Friday, he was drinking the generic stuff in the big bottles marked VODKA stored on the floor.

He'd tried to explain this method to his son once back in high school. Getting drunk—properly drunk, the kind of drunk that blunts the world's thorns while brightening the roses—took planning and effort. Like anything else in life, it required practice to get it right.

But did Zach appreciate this? Of course not. He'd just looked at his father with that snide, know-it-all expression on his face and gone back to his debate briefs or his term paper or whatever he was doing then.

Franklin Pierce Barrows had tried to help his son out. He really had. He remembered the thrill he felt, looking at the kid through the fish-tank glass where they kept the newborns at the hospital. A boy. His own boy: Zachary Taylor Barrows, continuing the tradition of naming the men in the family after presidents. He swore right there he would teach the kid everything he knew. Take him to football games. Play catch. He'd be the first dad there to cheer when his son won a race or a wrestling match or whatever sport he chose.

But it didn't turn out that way. Even as a toddler, Zach looked at balls with the hardened suspicion of an ex-con facing a traffic stop. He was happier reading than watching football. And he was smart. Christ, he was way too smart.

Zach began correcting his father on grammar when he was still in grade school. Frank knew it wasn't intentional, but he couldn't help feeling like the little shit was making fun of him even then. Like, "I'm a kid and I know this. How are you the grown-up here?"

He could tell the boy had the important stuff down cold. Frank reluctantly concluded that his son would not need his help with homework or school or pretty much anything that would matter in the long run. This made leaving Zach and his mother a little easier, actually. He suspected he wasn't necessary in their lives anyway. And the ease with which they both went on living after he was ejected from the family unit only proved it.

But he could also tell there was an element of social awkwardness to Zach. Frank could help with that if nothing else. He might not have been the role model he wanted to be, but making people like him was always easy.

Except, as it turned out, with his son. He tried to teach his son what it was like to be popular. You'd think that would come in handy for a kid who said he wanted to go into politics. But no. Every overture was greeted like it was some kind of insult. Zach only got more clenched and snotty with every bit of advice. Frank eventually gave up. Let the kid do it himself, then, he was so damn smart. Probably didn't get laid until he was twenty-one, but that's the way he wanted it.

Frank sighed and looked around his town house. He knew there was a reason for this drunk. He'd buried it carefully under the layers of alcohol. Something that happened in the bar. Frank shuddered involuntarily. He had been humiliated and he knew there was nothing he could do about it.

He didn't want to bring that back. He'd blotted out a lot of crappy things in his life. This was just one more of them.

As if in response, Frank felt the familiar tidal pull from the region of his groin. Women and whiskey. His two great weaknesses. He was a little proud of his physical endurance. Despite the years of abuse he'd forced on his liver and his dick, neither had failed him yet. Science would probably want to study his corpse to figure out how a man pushing sixty could down a quart of booze and still get it up.

It had been a while since he'd been this drunk, though. He hadn't been lying to Zach. He really had started to pull himself together. The job with the campaign had given him a steady paycheck and a little self-respect. People listened to him again. He'd even managed to draw attention from the young campaign volunteers. One of them, younger than Zach, came over to his place two or three nights a week.

Her name was Juliette, and they both knew he was not the kind of guy she really needed. He was not surprised when she went through the inevitable rundown of her family history: divorce, bad stepdads, wicked stepmothers, emotional abandonment, escape to college and grown-up issues like politics.

It occurred to him that because the men of his age had been such shitty fathers, they'd created a whole generation of young women looking for a male figure to give them the security and love they never got at home. And since these young women would often become the mistresses or second wives of married men, they were helping to perpetuate the cycle of broken families and absent dads. In twenty more years, those daughters would go out and do the same thing. He felt like writing this down for his son so he would remember to be grateful when he started screwing his own damaged twenty-two-year-olds with perfect tits.

Despite knowing this, Frank was a little stunned at how readily Juliette had started sucking him off in the car on their way home from a late night at the bar. The girls he'd grown up with required weeks of effort before they would so much as remove their bras. Juliette took his cock in her mouth the same way someone else might shake hands. She'd tried to explain it to him once in bed. How oral sex was no big deal. How kids started doing it in junior high now. It made him feel old, and that was not the right time or place for it. So he'd flipped her on her stomach and slid deep into her.

Just remembering it was getting Frank hard. He picked up the phone and dialed.

Juliette answered after three or four rings. She sounded confused. When he looked at the clock, he realized why. It was close to 2 A.M. He wondered what had happened to the rest of the night.

"Frank?" she said, voice foggy with sleep. She shared an apartment with several other young campaign workers. (In his shower, alone, Frank had imagined orgies, flexible young bodies testing new positions and partners in the small hours after long days of envelope stuffing and door knocking.)

"Sorry," he said. "I didn't mean to wake you." Lying.

"What's going on?"

"I just wanted to hear your voice."

She giggled. God, she was young. She still giggled. "Was that all you wanted?"

He could hear the smile in her voice. "Well . . ."

"I'll be right over," she said, and hung up.

Thank Christ for girls with daddy issues, Frank thought.

She arrived twenty minutes later, still wiping the sleep from her eyes, and planted a warm kiss on his mouth. She looked around the town house. Her eyes opened a little wider.

"Frank. What's going on?"

He looked at the bottles on the kitchen counter. He really was out of practice. He would have hidden them in the past. "Bad week," he said.

To his surprise, he found himself telling her about Zach. Not about the reasons for their fight. And certainly not about the weird Secret Service agent, no, thank you, let's not go there again. She listened. She held his hand.

"You're a good dad," she said. "I wish mine would make that kind of effort."

That was almost too much for even Frank to take. Before her words could start him thinking about his long, failed history of fatherhood, he began stroking her back.

She giggled again. He put aside his annoyance at that,

because she also stood up and pulled her sweatshirt over her head.

She was a little chunkier than he liked his women. Even now, he took pride in the tightness of his abdomen and his muscle tone; he'd never been a fleshy drunk. But she was also twenty-two years old, and that made up for a lot. Her breasts were still high and full and perfect, untouched by gravity or children or age.

And she could suck the chrome right off a fender.

Then he got a weird sensation. He looked at the town house window. His reflection looked back. But it was in the wrong position. Its eyes were not level with his eyes. It moved closer to the glass, and that's when he realized it *was not his reflection at all*—

The window shattered and a heavy man wearing a bizarre latex mask shaped like a smiley face leaped inside. Frank and Juliette both screamed. Somewhere in the back of his head, Frank knew this would not help, because his neighbors in the condo association studiously avoided one another. He'd had some real screamers up here before, louder than this, and no one ever said a word.

While this ran through his mind, he and Juliette fell to the floor, bleeding from a dozen small cuts from the shards of glass. The smiley-faced man stood above them on the bed.

Frank tried to protect Juliette. He pushed her toward the door and lunged for his nightstand. Inside was his gun. It wasn't much, just a .38 snub-nosed Bulldog that he hadn't even test-fired in years. He honestly thought he'd end up putting the barrel in his mouth one day, but now he knew he had to use it or die.

As he reached out toward the handle of the drawer, metal sang through the air.

He looked at the result for a moment, unable to comprehend. He was still reaching for the drawer, but there was nothing he could use to grab it. His hand was gone, along with most of his arm: severed neatly above the elbow.

The blood pumped out and the pain started. It seemed to take forever. He supposed he must be going into shock.

Frank looked up. He saw the smiling mask right above him.

The Boogeyman raised the curved blade. Frank could hear the laughter from under the mask. It sounded like a garbage disposal chewing on a tin can.

He turned and was surprised to see Juliette was still there, still crawling in an effort to get out of the bedroom. He thought he could buy her life at the cost of his own.

But he'd failed. He couldn't stop the killer. Frank couldn't even slow him down.

Frank Barrows had made the mistake many times in his life of preferring to believe in his version of events despite all evidence to the contrary. He'd always thought there would be more time. He thought there was always another job, another day, another chance to get it right. He believed, against all evidence, that someday, when he was finished fooling around, his now-dead wife would take him back and his son would embrace him as the father he should have been and always meant to be.

This was no exception. Despite what Cade had shown

him, he refused to accept the idea that anything like that could be real. The world could not include things like Cade. They were horror stories and fairy tales. They couldn't be real.

He was wrong. The world did include things like this. They were real. And they could hurt him.

It was not the first time he'd been wrong. It was, however, the last.

TWENTY-SEVEN

CURTIS CAMPAIGN PRESS BRIEFING, OCTOBER 18, 2012

JEFF CALLEY, CAMPAIGN SPOKESMAN: There's the weekend schedule. We have time for a few questions before we go.

Q: So when does the president plan to speak about the murders of his campaign staffers?

A: The president believes in allowing local law enforcement to do its job without interference from the White House. He has, of course, already extended his condolences to the families of the victims. But he has faith in the men and women of the local police and sheriff's departments to deal with these matters.

Q: So you're saying he plans to ignore them completely?

A: Hi, Megan. Nice to see you here. No, that's not correct. He's busy doing the job the voters elected him to do, and he's going to let the police do theirs.

Q: Oh come on. It's obvious they're all connected to one another. The method, the similar nature of each killing—

A: At this point, it would be irresponsible to speculate on what connection, if any, there is between these horrible, heinous crimes. And I certainly wouldn't want to increase the pain of the victims' families by throwing out wild theories. That said, you're talking about incidents that happened in different states, weeks and months apart, to very different people. I don't see how you can jump to any conclusions from that.

Q: Has the FBI been called to assist?

A: I have no idea. You'd have to ask them.

Q: Why is the president ignoring clear evidence of a serial killer stalking his campaign?

A. As I said before, there's no evidence of that. It sounds like a great movie, though. Can't wait to see it. [LAUGHTER] And I think we've given you enough time, Megan. Let's move on to someone else.

Q: Does this violence mean that the president can't even manage to protect his own people from criminals?

A: Ah, come on, that's just sleazy, even for your paper. [LAUGHTER] Look. Violent crime is a terrible, tragic fact of life. But I'd like to remind you all that the national crime rate, and this is for all crimes, including homicides, has in fact declined four years in a row under President Curtis—

Q: Hey, Jeff, you double-locking your door at night? Worried at all about your own personal safety?

A: I think the most dangerous part of my day is right here. [LAUGHTER]

Zach woke with a start on the press bus.

He checked his watch and realized it was 5:45 A.M. He had fallen asleep only an hour or two before. But nothing quite made sense as he blinked away the sleep. He looked up and saw President Curtis. Only, the reporters weren't mobbing him or throwing out questions. Instead, they gave him a wide space. Some even looked embarrassed.

"Zach," the president said, face somber, "would you come with me, please? I'd like to talk to you alone."

It reminded Zach so much of being called to the principal's office he almost laughed. But he realized what it must be about: someone had spilled the news about him and Candace. God. He'd be lucky if Curtis didn't order Cade to kill him.

Only, Candace was standing at the front of the bus, waiting. She didn't look flustered or humiliated. She only looked at him with deep concern.

And if the news had broken, then the president would be nowhere near the press. They would have broken into their regular programming, done special graphics and assembled expert panels on what it all meant that a minor-league staffer was banging the president's daughter. Setting foot on the press bus would have been like wearing a gravy suit in front of a pack of starving poodles.

Zach followed the president off the bus. Candace came with them.

They stepped around to the side of the highway, Secret Service watching everything carefully in the predawn gloom. The buses sat chugging exhaust. There was nothing but empty fields in every direction.

And the president told him what had happened.

Zach thought idly that he wished all of the bad news in his life had been delivered by Samuel Curtis. He was direct without sacrificing compassion or kindness. He gave an impression of strength even in grief. His hand on Zach's shoulder was steady and warm.

Then the actual meaning of the president's words finally penetrated the thick haze clouding Zach's brain.

Candace was there to hold him before he fell.

THE FUNERAL WAS SMALL and sparsely attended. There was no casket. Frank Barrows's body was still in a coroner's locker. Not that there was any question about cause of death, but bureaucracy moved slowly, and Zach had wanted to be done with this ceremony as quickly as possible.

The wake, at the same bar where he and his father had fought for the last time, was much more crowded. After the sun set, it seemed, Frank's friends came out and took advantage of his son's open tab for drinks.

Zach got very drunk. He would play the part of his father's son for one night at least. The press, thankfully, stayed away. Frank's murder was enough of a story on its own. Out of some kind of professional courtesy, they didn't feel the need to add Zach's name to it. Zach was grateful for all the favors he'd never cashed with the media during his time back in the real world.

Everyone had a story, it seemed. They genuinely seemed to love and miss him. The owner of the bar kept the doors open well past closing. He talked about retiring Frank's regular stool. The others remembered his time on the city council; his ability to charm the pants off almost any woman; his inability to keep himself out of trouble. The women he'd bedded said they felt he truly cared about them. And that he was great in the sack. Everyone laughed. Everyone had a great, funny memory of Frank.

Everyone but Zach.

Try as he might, he couldn't think of a single good time with his dad.

Someone finally shouted for him to make a speech. Zach panicked for a moment. Then, like magic, in the time it took him to take another drink of vodka—the top-shelf stuff, served close to freezing—the memory came to him.

"It was my first debate tournament in high school," Zach said. "Yeah, I was that much of a geek. I was over at my dad's that weekend. I was standing there in my jeans and shirt, and he said, 'You're not going like that.' We went to a tailor downtown—the guy opened early, just for Frank—and he suited me up. So I was there in this custom-tailored suit and I realized I didn't know how to tie a tie. Frank knotted one up for me. He tried to show me, but I was too nervous, I guess. I couldn't get it right. So he bought five more and knotted them all as well. He said if I never learned, no matter what, he would tie them for me. I'd just have to mail them to him after I moved away, and he'd mail them back, all tied up."

There was silence.

Then someone yelled, "To Frank!" and there was a drunken roar and the sound of broken glass.

Zach saw Cade then, standing at the door.

He pushed through the crowd and made his way outside.

Cade was waiting there. Zach knew it must have been

freezing out, but he didn't feel it. His mind only registered the vapor forming in front of his mouth as he breathed. There was no cloud of vapor over Cade's head.

"I'm sorry for your loss," Cade said.

"Right," Zach said. "You didn't have anything to do with this, did you?"

Cade looked disappointed. It must have been crushing for Zach to see it that plainly on his face.

"I will pretend you didn't ask me that," he said.

"Yeah. Should have known better. After all, nobody tried to drink their blood."

Cade said nothing.

"Hey, help me out with something, Cade. If you were to drink Frank's blood, would you get drunk? I mean, the guy always had a load on. Does it work like that for you?"

"Why are you doing this?" Cade asked.

"Don't pretend your feelings are hurt," Zach said. "We both know that's not possible."

"You're right," Cade said.

"Why are you even here?" Zach said, suddenly, incredibly, volcanically angry. At Cade. At the whole insane nightmare his life had become over the past three years. "What the hell do you want?"

"Only to tell you that I will kill it. I thought you would find some comfort in that."

For a moment, Zach was so angry he wished he had a stake he could ram through Cade's chest, to watch him choke and die on his own black blood . . . and then the anger vanished, like the air from a popped balloon.

"At this point, I'll take what I can get," he said.

Cade gave him the nanosecond smile. "Who's got your back, homeslice?"

Zach coughed out a laugh. He staggered toward the door.

When he looked back, Cade was gone.

CANDACE CAME AND COLLECTED HIM. He didn't know when.

He was facedown at a table. He opened his eyes and managed to focus on her face before the room spun away from him again.

"You here for the pity lay?" he said.

He could just make out a sardonic grin on her face. "Would you turn it down?"

"I seem to be saying this a lot, but I'll take what I can get."

She helped him up and poured him into a car. In the morning, he found himself in the bed in the back of the staff's campaign bus, far away from Lanford.

He showered in the closet-sized stall of the bus. He found his suit, dry-cleaned and crisp, under a plastic wrapper and hanging from the door. He took a wash-and-wear shirt out of a box. He drank many, many cups of coffee.

Then he went through the door into the main cabin of the bus and went back to work.

TWENTY-EIGHT

FADE IN: A montage of video clips of Governor Skip Seabrook: talking at Town Hall meetings; shaking hands with passersby on a sidewalk on a sunny day; listening intently as an elderly man in a military uniform talks to him.

VOICE-OVER: You know, it seems like there are a lot of people who want to tear this country down. There are a lot of people who will say we should worry about what's coming. That we can't trust anyone. Maybe I'm old-fashioned, but I think the real strength of our nation is in its people. I am not afraid of America. I am willing to tell the public what I believe, face-to-face. I believe in democracy. I believe in giving the voters a chance to be heard. And I believe our greatest days are yet to come.

[Montage fades into SEABROOK 2012 title card.]

VOICE-OVER: My name is Skip Seabrook. And I'm running for president.

CAPTION: PAID FOR BY THE SEABROOK FOR AMERICA CAMPAIGN

VOICE-OVER: I'm Skip Seabrook, and I approve this message.

—Seabrook campaign ad

The morning press briefing started out normally. Lanning was feeding the maggot farm today, so it promised to be a little more entertaining than usual. Zach hoped it would distract him from his hangover. He felt like someone had dumped toxic waste into his skull.

"Hey, Lanning! Any comment on Seabrook's latest campaign ad?"

"The one where he says he's not afraid of America? He might reconsider if he took a walk on Chicago's South Side at night."

Laughter.

A hard-eyed little man shouted, "What about the latest job numbers? When do we see someone actually get hired as a result of all this spending?"

"Well, I'm working again," Lanning said. "But no, this is a serious issue, and the president—"

Then there was a slight commotion as Megan Roark shoved her way to the front of the pack. The other members of the media gaggle looked mildly annoyed, but they'd learned to expect a little crazy behavior from Megan.

Nobody was expecting what came next, however.

"I have a question," she said. Her voice was trembling. But she didn't look afraid. If Zach had to name what he saw on her face, he'd have to say it was elation.

He got a sinking feeling. This wasn't going to be good.

"I've been doing a little research," she began. "I've found proof that over the past three years, there has been a White House employee connected to a dozen different killings that have resulted in at least nineteen people dead."

Zach could practically see the ears of the other reporters pricking up. Megan was obnoxious, but she delivered the red meat. They were willing to listen.

"I have photos of this employee placing him conclusively at the scene of murders in Los Angeles, Mexico, Virginia, Iowa—"

Oh shit, Zach thought. That was a highlight reel of Cade's itinerary over the past few years. Roark might have stumbled onto the biggest secret in White House history.

He shot a glance at Lanning up at the podium. Lanning didn't have to feign his expression of boredom and bafflement. He didn't know what she might have blundered into. Zach tried to think of a way to shut this down.

But Roark was really in a groove now. "—And there are even reports of this staffer being on-site during the attack on the White House. I have reason to believe that the White House is shielding this man from inquiries and criminal prosecution related to these killings. And I believe this man is also involved in the deaths that have been following the president on the campaign trail. He has been at every location. He has worked with local police to cover up details. And he was seen arguing with the most recent victim on the day of the killing."

Oh boy. This was bad. He should have ordered Cade to stay away from his father. This was a textbook example of unintended consequences. Roark could make a pretty strong case against Cade just from the circumstances. She didn't even have to know his name. But wherever he was, there were plenty of bodies.

Lanning shook his head. "I believe you said you had a question, Megan?"

The other members of the press weren't impatient, though. They were intrigued. They wanted to hear the rest.

Roark smiled, vicious and triumphant. She turned and pointed right at Zach. "What I want to know is, where was Zachary Barrows on the night his father was murdered?"

Wait—what?

Zach, standing to one side of the stage, looked so pole-axed that most of the press burst out laughing.

They didn't stop. The smile began to ebb from Roark's face as she realized: they were laughing at her.

"This isn't a joke," she said, suddenly nowhere near as sure of herself. "I have photos, dates, times—" She waved a sheaf of papers at the people closest to her.

Lanning, leaning down over his podium, wasn't laughing. His look was one of barely contained rage.

"Ms. Roark," he said quietly. The chatter of the press died down. They leaned in to hear. "You've suggested that a campaign consultant—who has not been employed by the White House in three years, I might add—has a record as a serial killer that would rival Ted Bundy's. You've suggested he's had the assistance of the office of the President of the United States in these crimes, which only you, out of all your slow, benighted colleagues, have been able to uncover. And now you've accused him of killing his own father. So I thought you might, if you'd be so kind, allow me to answer your deeply insulting and slanderous question."

Roark just blinked. Everything had flipped on her, but she still didn't know why. Zach knew it was small of him, but he really enjoyed the look of utter confusion and fear on her face. She wasn't that wrong, if you looked at it through her distorted lens. She'd missed only one detail.

"Zach Barrows was on the press bus all night, answering questions after the rally and then riding with the other members of the media to the next campaign stop," Lanning said.

One really important detail, as it turned out.

Just like that, Megan Roark was finished. The other reporters moved back from her. She couldn't have been more alone if she was on an ice floe cast off into an arctic sea.

She opened her mouth to speak. Lanning cut her off.

"You were out gathering this evidence, I assume. Too bad you didn't ride the bus that night. Why, you might have caught him in the act."

His tone was withering. Zach didn't say anything. He didn't have to. Many of the members of the press knew him from the old days. They would have found it inconceivable that Zach could throw a punch, let alone carve up his own dad. Even if Zach hadn't been doing background briefings all night with the media, they probably wouldn't have believed Roark. It was very hard to get a reporter to admit his first impression might not be accurate. The media had a lot invested in their ability to make snap judgments. Zach was a soft, political flack. That's all they saw when they looked at him.

Roark didn't help her case just then. She began shrieking like a banshee: "Oh no. I know what I've found. You can't explain all this away. I have proof! I have—"

"Sorry, sweetheart," Lanning said. "You've gone too far this time." He nodded. Two large, black-suited men from the Secret Service slid through the crowd as if greased. They gently but firmly lifted Megan Roark off her feet and escorted her away. She didn't stop screaming. "You can't silence the truth! You can't silence the truth! You assholes, let me go—"

The hole where she'd been was neatly filled by the other members of the media. They looked expectantly at Lanning.

"Any other questions?" he asked.

That got the laugh he wanted, a release of nervous tension, and it was as if Roark had never been there. If anyone saw the relief on Zach's face, they probably assumed it was because he'd just barely escaped an encounter with a crazy woman and national disgrace.

That was fine by Zach. What the press didn't know wouldn't hurt them.

TWENTY-NINE

A month after his transfer to [the Federal Reformatory at] Chillicothe [Ohio], Manson suddenly became a model inmate . . . It is a mystery. What happened to Manson in Chillicothe, that he suddenly became studious (he was still illiterate when he was transferred there), learned to read and write and do simple arithmetic, mellowed out and became a star "prisoner"? . . . Manson became a different person and maintained that identity for over a year and a half, until his release. That degree of conscious control—especially in a disturbed, uneducated, illiterate, violent, sodomitic bastard child of an unmarried, alcoholic mother—is suspicious, if not alarming . . . Chillicothe is, of course, the center of the American Mound culture . . . the remains of our Old Ones, the original people, the deep ancestors of our forgotten history, the history before Columbus that is never taught in the schools because we don't know it ourselves . . .

—Peter Levenda, *Sinister Forces*

MIDNIGHT, OCTOBER 22, 2012, CHILLICOTHE, OHIO

After Megan Roark's spectacular public meltdown, the campaign seemed to gain a little breathing room. The press was not eager to roll around in the same muck as she did. And no one on Curtis's staff had died in several days.

The Boogeyman watched the buses leave the rally outside Chillicothe, Ohio. He turned on his cell phone and dialed the only number it contained.

Holt answered on the first ring.

"Now?" he asked.

"Now," she said.

He hung up. It was about time. The relief he felt was as close as the entity would ever get to sex.

He went to find a car.

ZACH FELT ALMOST NORMAL AGAIN. They'd had a good couple of days. No more deaths. The press had backed off. The rally in Chillicothe had been full of warm and responsive supporters. They got great footage of small-town America cheering for Curtis to use in the next round of campaign ads.

He supposed he was still numb about Frank's death. He never really believed he'd outlive his father. The man seemed impervious to everything but nuclear radiation. But he was handling it. He supposed it helped that he and Candace, throwing caution to the wind, spent every minute they could in bed together. He knew it was tempting fate and the Boogeyman, but he wasn't about to stop.

Cade had withdrawn to the fringes of the campaign. They hadn't spoken much, although Zach suspected Cade guarded him and Candace when they went back to her hotel rooms at night, which was somehow creepy and reassuring at the same time. Zach went about his fake job on the campaign as if it was his real job. It felt surprisingly good.

He heard a grunt of surprise from the driver right before the bus seemed to crank on its own axis. He was flung into the air and then the floor came up and met him again. He blinked and saw a discarded candy wrapper under one of the seats. It was over that fast.

He got to his feet. He didn't feel anything broken. The inside of the bus looked like a landslide made of paper and coffee cups. Laptops were tossed like glowing dice. Zach found Candace and helped her up. The bus was off kilter, the floor at an angle. She didn't seem hurt. Her eyes focused on him.

"You all right?"

"Yeah. Think so. What happened?"

"Stay put. I'll be back."

Zach hopped up and walked over the mess, using the seat backs as stepping-stones. He ignored the calls from the other campaign staffers. Nobody looked seriously hurt. He got to the driver. There was blood down the man's shirt. He sat in front of a deflated air bag, yellow powder over his hands and arms.

"Da'd t'ing broke by node," he told Zach, holding his face.

"Anything else? You feel any other pain?"

The driver shook his head.

"What happened?"

The driver gestured with his elbow toward the windshield. The bus was sideways, its front half in a ditch alongside the road. Only the rear end of the car that had hit them was visible—the rest appeared to be under the bus's front grille, which poured out steam from its shattered radiator. The driver had managed to turn, but the car still hit hard.

"He swer'bed right into be," the driver said, still blocking the nosebleed.

Zach realized what was missing.

No one's phone was ringing. After something like this, every ringtone in the bus should be blaring with calls from the other vehicles in the convoy.

Instead, there was just the hiss of the radiator and the wind yowling like a cat caught out in the rain.

Zach checked his own phone—another piece of spy tech, linked to secret satellites and black ops networks hidden across the nation. Ordinarily, it could place calls from the inside of a coffin six feet under.

No signal.

He suddenly felt like he had ice cubes in his guts. He hit the lever to open the door.

"Zach, wait." He looked back and saw Candace struggling to climb the seats after him. Her skirt was making things difficult.

"I'll be right back," he said. He went out into the cold. The driver closed the door behind him without being told.

ZACH LOOKED BACK at the other cars. The road was hopelessly jammed. The other vehicles in the motorcade had only managed to avoid a massive pileup by swerving wildly. Now they were all spun around at odd angles, parked like they'd been left by drunks at a Fourth of July picnic. Exhaust vapor rolled over the ground, forming a thick gray fog. In the glare of the headlights, Zach could see tiny single flakes of snow, whipped around by the sharp winds.

Then Cade was standing beside him. Zach jumped, then cursed. He was going to have a heart attack by the time he was forty, he just knew it.

"Get back," Cade told him.

Zach saw Butler running through the dark, gun out, his silhouette briefly appearing through the headlights.

Cade moved past Zach like silk, around to the front of the bus.

Butler didn't stop to talk. He ran after Cade.

Zach came around the side of the bus a step behind. They both found Cade standing alone, staring at the wrecked car. The smaller car, a Honda, had been jammed under the fender and above the bus's axle by the crash. They were stuck together like puzzle pieces forced to fit in the wrong slots.

The driver was halfway out the shattered windshield, far beyond caring about the wiper blade that kept swiping up and into his face. His neck was twisted so that his chin touched the back of his own shoulder. His eyes stared blankly at the sky, mouth open.

The engine of the Honda was still racing, as if the car itself was trying to keep moving through the bus.

"Must have been drunk," Butler said.

"He was dead," Cade said.

Butler stepped back. "What?"

"Almost no blood," Cade said.

He was right. Trust a vampire when it comes to that, Zach thought. Despite all the tears and cuts in the driver's flesh, there was barely any bleeding.

"His neck was broken before he was put behind the wheel," Cade said.

Butler leaned in the open driver's door and swept it with his Maglite. "Cinder block on the gas pedal," he told them.

Zach finally noticed the bumper sticker. Cade kept staring at it. It was in the rear window of the Honda. The lights from the bus lit it up.

It was a simple message: HAVE A NICE DAY. Punctuated by a smiley face.

"It's him," Cade said.

Something under the hood began to shriek, blotting out all other sounds. A metallic clank cut it off at the top of its scream. The Honda bucked and shuddered, and the wiper finally stopped its arc into the corpse.

Silence.

Then Butler swore. He pressed a finger to his earpiece, then pulled it out and put it back again.

"Coms are down," he said.

"Of course they are," Cade said.

Zach checked his phone again. "No signal."

The lead bus's door opened again and Candace got out. She hugged herself against the cold.

"What's going on?" she asked.

"Get back in the bus." The three men said it almost simultaneously.

She ignored them and walked closer.

"Agent Butler—" Cade began.

Butler turned to Candace. "Ms. Curtis. Please. We've got a situation."

"And I want to know what it is," she snapped back. "I'm not the damsel in distress, guys. My father is."

"We don't have time for this," Cade barked. They all looked at him. His tone meant the screwing-around portion of the evening was over. "Butler. Get the president into the limo. Lock the doors. Do not open them for anyone but me. Have the other agents set up a perimeter. Guns out. Shoot anything that approaches. Anything at all."

Candace tried to object. "Wait—"

But Butler wasn't about to argue. He simply ran back toward the motorcade.

"What are you going to do?" Candace asked.

This time Cade deigned to answer. "I'm going to find him and stop him."

"What about the press?" Zach asked.

Cade nodded. "Good point. You and Ms. Curtis go to the press bus. Tell them we are waiting for assistance. Hand out drinks."

"I'm not a damned waitress," Candace protested again.

Cade looked directly at her. She shut up. "Make sure you use the drinks from the blue cooler. Only the blue cooler. *Do not* drink anything yourself."

Zach and Candace exchanged glances. "Are you telling me we're going to drug the press corps?" Zach asked.

"It's hardly the first time."

"Is that a good idea?" Candace asked. "I mean, if the Boogeyman gets past you. What then?"

"At least they'll die in their sleep," Cade said.

Then he was gone.

THE MEDIA WERE GETTING RESTLESS. They quickly discovered nobody had any coverage out here. None of them had very long attention spans to start, and the thought of being stuck in the middle of Ohio in a snowstorm without wireless access didn't help.

One of the reporters looked out the window. He saw one of the Secret Service agents pass by. He did a double take. The agent was definitely carrying her weapon in one hand and a flashlight in the other.

"Hey," he called to the others. "Hey. The Secret Service is out there. I think they've got their guns out."

There was a general groan of disbelief. "Oh, shut the fuck up, Taibbi," one of the anchorbabes said. "Nobody wants to hear your conspiracy theories."

The reporter started to protest, but then Candace Curtis showed up with free drinks as an apology for the delay. The lead bus had been hit by a drunk driver. Nobody was injured. Everything would be cleared up as soon as the tow trucks arrived.

The members of the media accepted this and settled into their seats to wait. The one reporter who'd noticed the gun kept looking out the window, trying to find anything new as the glass fogged over.

A few minutes later, Candace Curtis and another couple of attractive young campaign staffers showed up in the aisle of the bus, wheeling a big cooler of drinks behind them.

"On the house, everyone," Candace said. "Just our way of saying sorry for the delay."

"You gals should work for the airlines," the reporter from Fox barked. "You're a lot better-looking than most stewardesses."

Candace laughed and gave him a mock slap on the shoulder. Pretty soon every reporter on the bus had a drink in hand. Even the guy looking for the gun took a Heineken. What the hell, he figured. It wasn't like they were going anywhere.

CADE FOUND HIM IN MINUTES. It wasn't hard. He wasn't hiding.

The Boogeyman was out in the fields on the side of the highway, walking across the frozen ground as if simply out for a stroll. He wore civilian clothes and a yellow latex mask.

They faced each other like gunslingers, a dozen feet or so separating them, their hands loosely at their sides.

Cade felt his fangs emerge and his lips peel back in imitation of a smile.

It's about time, he thought.

MEGAN ROARK WAS happier this way. She really was.

Sure, she'd been forced to follow along behind the buses since Lanning had banned her from the campaign press. Fucker. She was almost certain he'd set her up deliberately. But it didn't mean that she was wrong. There was something very weird about Zach Barrows, and she was sure it tied in to the Campaign Carver. She was going to prove it.

If that meant dogging after the campaign in her own rental car, so be it. Maybe the Secret Service wouldn't let her into the private events, but they couldn't keep her out of the public spaces. She would find the connection between Barrows and the killer. No matter what.

And she preferred to drive herself anyway.

Roark suddenly slammed on her brakes and skidded to a halt on the shoulder, tires spitting up gravel.

The bus caravan had come to a dead stop in the middle of the road and the Secret Service had set up barricades and road flares.

For a second, Roark just sucked in deep breaths. She tried not to see herself mangled in the wreckage of her rental Hyundai.

She rolled down her window as an agent jogged to her car.

"What the hell?" she screamed as the wind blew snow and road grit into her eyes.

"Mechanical trouble, ma'am," the agent said. "You're going to have to stay in your car or turn back around."

This was the last fucking straw, Megan thought. She flipped out her press ID—the one she'd made herself, with the logo of her Internet channel laser-printed in full color.

"Do you know who I am?"

The agent looked at her badge, then back at her. "Yes," he said. "You're not going any further. It's for your own safety."

Roark had heard that line before. It screamed "cover-up" to her.

"What are you going to do if I try to get past? Shoot me?"

Then she looked down and realized the agent already had his service weapon out of its holster.

"I'd rather not," he said. He turned and started walking away.

He was serious. Her hands still shook from the near-accident, and now another wave of fear and nausea washed over her. In all her time revealing the truth—in dealing with the shadowy machinations of the Curtis administration, which she knew was trying to destroy the nation she loved—this was the first time she'd ever felt the presence of real danger. They had actually *threatened* her. She must be closer than she even dreamed.

At that moment, her car sputtered and died.

Roark looked at the barricades. The buses were farther down the road. She couldn't see anything. But with the flares, the agents and their guns, it all reminded her of scenes she knew from TV.

Crime scenes.

The Campaign Carver. It had to be. They were trying to hide it. My God, wait until her followers heard about this.

Before she knew it, she'd popped the door of the car

and was following the agent, recording everything with the video function on her phone.

"Hey! HEY! I don't know what kind of shit you're trying to pull, but you can tell Curtis for me that he's not going to get away with this! The truth will come out!"

He turned back to her. The wind whipped his tie up over his shoulder. It was too dark for him to wear his standard-issue sunglasses. His eyes seemed very, very tired.

"Look," he said. "If you can get out of here, do it. Believe me. I would if I could."

The other agent at the barricades yelled something at him, and he jogged away, leaving her there.

Roark stood there in the biting cold. The agents had their backs to her. She knew this was her only chance to get proof. She had to act fast, before they got the cover-up in place.

She walked back to her car and opened the door. The agent with the tired eyes looked over his shoulder at her. She waved. He turned away.

She slammed her door hard and immediately ducked down by the side of the car. She hoped that would be enough to convince him she'd chosen to sit quietly and wait. As quickly as she could, she slid down the side of the embankment beside the highway.

As soon as she was at the bottom, she was swallowed by the dark. She didn't think the Secret Service would spot her. She could barely see her own hands.

The cold began to bite its way through her clothes. She wished she'd grabbed her coat before coming up with this plan. But it was too late now.

She moved carefully over the rough, frozen ground. She

had her phone in one hand, ready to take pics before Curtis's goons could hide the bodies. She was going to blow this story wide open.

THEY PAUSED, watching each other. Cade could hear the heavy breathing behind the smiley-face mask.

The Boogeyman's weight shifted back to its right.

Cade took a step in that direction.

It shifted its left foot a fraction of an inch.

Cade pivoted slightly in response.

They knew each other. Each knew the other had the raw power to hurt him badly. They knew the first steps in any of their dances were crucial.

Cade began to feel something was wrong with this. He had always been a little stronger and a few seconds faster. But if anything, he was at a disadvantage here. Since Cade had not encountered the Boogeyman in this incarnation, he didn't know exactly how strong it was or how it would react.

On the other hand, Cade had won every previous matchup. That had to factor into its considerations as well.

As if it could sense what he was thinking, the Boogeyman stopped circling and put its hands up.

It couldn't possibly be surrendering, could it?

Cade remained where he was, watching carefully.

But the Boogeyman still didn't move.

Now Cade's instincts were fairly screaming at him.

The Boogeyman dropped his hands. Cade heard muffled laughter under the mask.

It wasn't a surrender. It was a signal.

By the time Cade heard the shot, it was already too late.

CADE REALIZED HE'D MADE a mistake as he stepped out of the way of the sniper's bullet, fired from nearly a thousand yards. At that distance, anything less than a .50-caliber cartridge was not a threat to him, and anyway, he could simply move before the bullet hit him.

That was what they were counting on.

The fibers of Cade's skin, when he was fully fed, swelled with blood and interlocked to form a kind of weave as tough as Kevlar. These unnaturally dense layers could stop a bullet with little more than a bruise. But even Kevlar has its weaknesses. An ice pick can pop through a Kevlar vest by focusing all its energy on one tiny spot, robbing the netting of its ability to spread and deflect the impact. So can knives, arrows, crossbow bolts and very sharp wooden stakes.

The Boogeyman used something like an ice pick. He took full advantage of the distraction of the sniper's shot, moving with inhuman speed and strength to slam a narrow steel rod through Cade's skin, his ribs, and his lung. Only a last-second twitch kept him from piercing Cade's heart.

Cade backhanded him away and plucked the weapon out of his body. It was not an ice pick. If Cade had to describe it, he'd have to call it a combat syringe: a specially designed chemical delivery system with a reservoir in the handle behind a hollow, surgically sharp needle.

And then Cade started dying.

At first, he couldn't understand. Poison meant nothing to him. His hyperactive immune system had dismissed Ebola variants like a slight cold.

Then he realized: the Boogeyman hadn't injected him with poison. He'd been hit with something that was already in his blood.

In humans, blood clotting is activated when damage to the tissues prompts the release of proteins that cause the platelets to stick to one another and to the damaged area. One of these proteins is fibrin, which essentially turns blood from a liquid into a solid, causing a scab or clot to form.

Cade's blood-clotting response was inhumanly fast and effective. The proteins in his blood that activated fibrin were already hypersensitive. A vampire, after all, doesn't want to lose so much as a drop.

The Boogeyman had flooded his system with the activating proteins for fibrin, sending his clotting factors into overdrive. It spread throughout every vein and artery like a chemical drought. His blood thickened to cake batter, then wet cement, then sand. He was being petrified from the inside out.

His heart stuttered, desperately trying to churn sludge. A series of strokes popped like bubble wrap in his brain, blacking out details as his body seized underneath him. He bit through his lips, spilled rust instead of blood. The world flickered in and out as he thrashed on the ground, learning an entirely new vocabulary of pain.

Cade's head flopped to the left. He caught a glimpse of the Boogeyman, strolling as if he didn't have a care in the world, moving toward the bright lights of the buses trapped on the road.

FROM THE SMALL RISE BEHIND the farmhouse where they'd camped, Helen watched Cade through her night-vision optics. He was still squirming in pain as she took off the lenses. Reyes was fumbling on the ground, trying to get the sniper rifle into his gear bag, his fingers clumsy with fear.

"No rush," she told him. "He's not going anywhere."

Reyes muttered something in Spanish without looking at her. She put the optics back up to her eyes. The Boogeyman moved toward the buses. Part of the deal. He wanted to kill the president. Helen had tried to argue, but it was worse than the time she tried to talk to Cade. Cade at least responded with anger or contempt. The Boogeyman simply sat like a tree stump until she agreed.

It wasn't that Helen gave a damn about the president. She even held a slight hope that Barrows would get in the Boogeyman's way before Curtis was killed. But this was all a distraction from her main goal, now that Cade had been dealt with. She wanted to begin using her new ally against the Shadow Company as soon as possible.

Still, she respected his need to finish what he started. It showed a certain bloody-minded stubbornness, an inability to let go of a grudge. It was a quality she could use if they were going to work together in the future.

Reyes was packed and ready. "We going over there?" he asked, shrugging toward the place where Cade had fallen.

He looked into the darkness. Helen turned and followed his gaze. Cade was barely visible, but they could see him, crawling slowly toward the highway.

She checked him through the night-vision again. He'd made the edge of a stand of trees just below the highway. He kept trying to rise. Kept falling.

She lowered the goggles again. "Either he dies now or the sun will get him," she told Reyes. "Come on. I'm freezing."

She walked across the field toward their car, dragging her dead left foot along with her. Reyes followed.

Inside the car, Reyes hesitated. He made a noise in the back of his throat.

"What?"

"Maybe we should go look at him. To be sure."

Helen smirked with one side of her face. "What are you going to do?" she asked. "Check his pulse?"

Reyes didn't say anything. He stared at the trees, even though Cade's shadow was no longer visible.

Helen sighed heavily and checked her watch. Reyes put the car into gear. They drove away.

CODY FELLOWS WALKED along the old ruts in the field. Frost and dead weeds crunched under his feet, and the furrows were frozen as solid as concrete. It had been years since anyone plowed this land, even longer since anyone had grown crops here. Like most of the farms around town, this one had been foreclosed or abandoned.

Cody watched his steps carefully in the dark, the toes of

his sneakers dancing in and out of the small circle of light from his Special Forces flashlight ($7.99 at the local Gas N' Go, free with a five-finger discount). If he twisted his ankle in a rut, no one would come looking, maybe not for days. His mom and Carl did not want him in the trailer when they were cooking. Said it wasn't good for him to breathe in the fumes. Mom's final, eroded effort to be a parent. Cody didn't need the warning; he saw the results: his mom's face looked like a skull eating its way out of her skin, chewing relentlessly at her chapped and bleeding lips. But if Cody were ever to say that, his mom would smack him, then cry, then complain again about Cody's dad, and where the hell was she supposed to get any money from anyway. Then she'd start using the stuff again.

Cody spent a lot of time in the fields. He was eleven years old.

He suspected he'd start using meth, too—maybe not anytime soon, but before too long. His school attendance had dropped down to seldom at best, and he was smart enough to recognize that his options had narrowed to the same tunnel his mother had crawled inside. Some of the girls in his class were already hooking up with guys from high school, the ones who had cars and clothes they bought with what they made from dealing or delivering. Cody was small for his age, so he'd managed to avoid any offers to make extra cash. But he knew it was coming. Sooner or later, someone was going to put him to work or offer him the drug. And Cody knew that if the offer came in the right way, couched in friendship or as a demand from his mom, he would say yes and his life would pretty much be over.

It occurred to him that maybe what he was looking for, out on these late-night walks, was his own death. People succumbed to hypothermia every winter. He'd heard it was like falling asleep.

There were worse ways to go. Home-brew meth operations were not exactly designed for safety. Mom's previous boyfriend, Jerry, had blown a hole in their old house and run outside, his skin on fire. Cody had been over at a friend's, but he'd run home when he heard the explosion. By then, Jerry was dancing on the remains of the front lawn, firemen and police looking at one another, unsure of what to do. Everyone knew you couldn't pour water on a chemical fire. Jerry tried to hold on to his skin as it melted off his body, falling in great sizzling drops like grease on a skillet.

Someone turned Cody away before he saw how it ended. He didn't miss Jerry—he was the guy who first introduced his mom to meth—but he still couldn't hear bacon fry without starting to shake.

His flashlight caught a burst of color on the gray dirt.

Red. Blood.

It didn't look fresh—it seemed to be turning the color of a scab—but he cast his flashlight around to see where it came from.

The blood traced a path in a long line from out of the field back toward the highway.

Unsure of exactly why he did it, Cody began to follow.

He went toward the road, although he supposed the trail could just as easily have been made by someone going the other way. If it was a wounded animal, he thought maybe he could nurse it back to health. Maybe it was a dog. He'd always wanted a dog. He had vague, warm memories of his father's hunting dogs in the time his folks were still together.

He allowed himself to imagine it. The dog—it would be a male—would be nervous and snappish at first. That's how these things went. But he'd let it sniff his hand and it would see that he meant no harm. Then he'd tear a piece off his T-shirt to wrap like a bandage around its wound, which was going to be on his front leg, he decided. He would bring it to the trailer and give it a blanket and let it sleep in a crate out back and smuggle some food from inside. Probably beef jerky, that's all Mom and Carl seemed to eat when they were tweaking, anyway—

He heard a growl and stopped short. He was almost at the grove of small cottonwoods that grew like weeds in the gully by the highway. Inside the stand of trees, he could see a dark, hunched shape.

It was a *very* big dog.

But he was determined. He put his hand out, palm down, for the dog to sniff.

"It's all right," Cody said, his breath steaming in the air. "I won't hurt you. Here, boy. I'm here to help."

The hunched shape moved, lurching toward him with a sudden and awful speed.

Cody only caught a glimpse before he dropped his flashlight.

He saw teeth. Fangs.

But it wasn't a dog.

CADE WAS HALF MAD with thirst and pain now. His heart and veins were clotted nearly shut. Blackness danced around the edges of his vision. His thoughts came in clusters while his body moved on instinct.

The vampire side of him was forced to the surface—there was very little of him human enough to disguise it now. He could feel the sludge inside him, curling and shrinking him like a spider caught in a candle's flame. In another few minutes, he knew his muscles would crack as his veins and capillaries contracted and then sealed. His bones would split under the pressure. Whatever was left would be a dried-out husk until the sun rose to finish him.

But even through the pain, Cade felt the oath tugging at him.

The president is in danger. The president will die. You must protect the president.

He struggled to his feet. Fell again. Impossible. They had killed him. He had failed. The one coherent thought that came to him: he needed fresh blood. But Zach, and the containers he kept, were back on the bus, and Cade could not move any closer.

And then he'd heard the boy.

Something inside him recoiled, even as he stopped moving, stopped doing anything that might spook the prey. His fangs emerged. He could smell him now. Small, but filled with enough to save him. Enough to heal him so he could fulfill his duty.

Now he began to fight himself. His oath, which had given certainty and strength in the past, was now working against him. He had the excuse he'd always wanted. He could drink. He could feed. And he had to do it. He had to, or the president would die.

A dim thought. A memory. Cade had once promised himself, never again.

He should warn the boy. Tell him to get away. He couldn't hold out against this kind of hunger. Just one word. Tell him to run. That's all it would take.

But he stayed silent. Inside his head, the argument raged.

You have to live, the vampire and the oath both told him. *You have to carry out your duty*

He's just a child.

And what is one small life against all the lives you have saved? Blood is always spilled to protect the nation.

No. I won't. I can't.

The boy stepped closer. Cade realized he was already losing. Every step the boy took, every inch he moved nearer, the decision was being made. If he was close enough, the bloodlust would overpower Cade. He would devour him.

What are you protecting? Your vanity? You are a monster. You think anything will change that? You have to give up the pretense now. You are a monster. And a monster is what is needed.

I can't. Not like this.

It is a necessary sacrifice.

The boy was only a few feet away now. All the blood he

needed. He heard a small voice. "It's all right. I won't hurt you. Here, boy. I'm here to help."

You must.

I can't, Cade thought. But he knew that was a lie.

THE BOY SCREAMED as Cade knocked him to the ground. Part of Cade wanted to laugh. There was something thrilling about the terror, the sheer helplessness. He stared right at the boy's face, and his scream died. He was frightened beyond any sound now. The boy couldn't even move except to tremble in his grip. He wet himself. Cade could smell it. Tears rolled down his cheeks. Cade could almost taste their salt.

The boy wasn't dead yet, however. He thrashed and punched. His fingers clawed at Cade's throat. Cade's absurd clip-on tie popped off. Cade almost smiled. Butler was right about one thing, at least.

He slapped away the boy's hands, opened his mouth and leaned over the boy's throat, the sound of his pulse like a roaring ocean in Cade's ears—

Cade felt a mild sting against his chin.

He tried to shake it off. It stung him again.

He knew he should feed. But the irritation wouldn't go away.

He reared back, clawed at the tiny thing under his neck. His hand burned as he yanked it from his skin. It glinted slightly, a reflection from the boy's dropped flashlight.

It was his cross. When the boy tore off his tie, he'd opened Cade's collar. And the cross had come loose again.

Cade looked at the boy. He sat only a foot away, eyes wide, still frozen with fear. Cade could recapture him without any effort at all.

And he knew he'd do it if he waited another second.

A single word escaped his throat before he could think of anything else. It sounded like a stone dredged from under miles of earth and gravel.

"Run," he screamed.

The boy broke from his stupor. He scrambled with his hands and feet like a sprinter on the blocks. A dozen feet away within seconds. Still too close.

Get up. Get him.

Cade forced himself to watch until the boy was well out of range.

He fell back, curling in on himself like a pill bug. The oath tried to prod him up. The vampire in him howled with rage and need and fear.

He'd failed utterly. He would die. The president would die.

His last act was that of a traitor.

The pain of the oath washed over him, the seizures blotting out everything else.

Except the cross. He felt it burning in his hand, a tiny star in an endless black night of pain.

ROARK KEPT TRIPPING as she tried to run, certain she heard someone scream in this direction. She didn't for a second consider calling 911. That was the quickest way to blow a scoop, and she'd never want to alert the rest of the jackals to her story. They had laughed at her, shunned her and mocked her. She was looking forward to all of them having to beg for scraps after she broke this open.

She slipped and fell flat on her ass. She let out a loud curse, then clapped a hand over her mouth. She waited for a few precious seconds, expecting the Secret Service to pounce on her at any moment and drag her away.

In Roark's mind, there was an infinite number of enemies lined up against her. She knew the president was covering for a murderer. She knew her competition would undercut her at every turn.

But for all that, she still had faith that the world would have to pay attention when presented with irrefutable proof. Maybe it had ignored all the proof she'd already presented—the truth behind JFK, the New World Order, the Bilderbergs, 9/11—but this was going to be different. This was actual blood and guts. People paid attention to murder even if they didn't care about politics. For the President of the United States to cover for a killer would be the domino that toppled everything else. And she would be the messenger.

She composed her Pulitzer acceptance speech twice in her head before she felt safe to stand up again. The lights of the buses were far away. No one had heard her. The wind grabbed any sound out here and smothered it.

She smiled. She was still safe.

Roark turned. She heard thrashing in the stand of trees that grew in the ditch, just a few yards away. They were close and thick enough to obscure whatever was moving. But something shook them hard enough to knock the last dead leaves off their branches.

He got another one, she thought. A new victim. She kicked herself for leaving her camera in the trunk, but hey, that's why God invented cell phones. She held it in front of her like a shield.

She stood at the edge of the trees. The branches were shaking wildly now. Sounds more animal than human were clear to her now. God, whoever it was, they were really going nuts. Bad news for whoever was unlucky enough to get caught by the Presidential Assassin. She decided that's what she'd rename the Campaign Carver. Just so no one would be confused. She steeled herself for the blood and guts. But they wouldn't die in vain. They were going to provide the proof Megan needed.

Her plan was simple. Get in, take the pics, get away. No problem. Piece of cake.

She took a deep breath and plunged into the dark.

She saw the killer lit up like a strobe by her cell's tiny flash. Horrible red eyes glared at her. A scarecrow wearing the suit and earpiece of a Secret Service agent, splashed with blood and gore.

She couldn't stop herself from shrieking the most orgasmic phrase of any conspiracy theorist: *"I knew it!"*

She meant to turn and run like hell. Instead, she hesitated, only for a second, because something was missing. There was no body. Nobody else there. Where was the victim? How could she catch a murderer without a victim?

That was the last thing she thought before Cade ripped out her throat.

THE WRITERS WHO DESCRIBED a vampire's bite as two neat puncture wounds in the neck were either being polite or had never really looked at their own teeth. A vampire, when he bites, hyperextends his canines, the third tooth on each side from the center. They are necessary for any carnivore, designed by evolution for the express purpose of rending flesh. Canines are used for only one thing, even by humans. Canines tear.

Megan Roark's head was attached to her body only by her broken neck and some gristle. Snow fell and melted on her still-open eyes.

There was blood on her blouse, on her chin.

Cade restrained himself from lapping it up. His body was working again. And so was his mind.

He'd been moments—perhaps seconds—from true death when the annoying flash of the camera had fired in his eyes. His body rose by instinct. It wanted blood. And there was a whole bag of it, standing and waiting for him.

Easy prey.

The cross had fallen out of his hand. But even if he'd been holding it, Cade doubted he would have stopped. The vampire in him was not about to die. It would not surrender another easy meal.

The vampire. As if it was something separate. Even as he thought it through, Cade knew he was lying to himself.

His body was capable of amazing things, running on instinct buried in a place deeper than he could name, but it was still him. He had been there—small and fragmented, delirious with pain, but he had been a part of it.

Instead, he guzzled her down. Human blood poured into him. What he was built to consume. It sang in his veins as it remade him, stronger than ever. The brown rust clogging his cells turned fresh and red, a river quenching the drought. His bones and tissues knit their millions of tiny fractures. His skin tightened and stacked into layers of armor plate. His muscles hardened like steel cords. Neurons regenerated and multiplied, filling the dark gaps blown in his brain, and the world danced before his eyes in Technicolor again despite the moonless sky.

It was all he could do not to leap up and laugh with joy.

Instead, he fell to his knees. His hand scrabbled through the dead leaves for his cross. A question echoed across the years to him: "This thirst . . . is it stronger than your faith?"

He felt the sting of the cross in his palm, but it was nothing compared to the power and the glory thrumming in his heart. He knew the answer. Knew no matter how long he lived, he would never reclaim anything but a pathetic mockery of humanity.

Over a century of clinging to his promise never to feed again on a human. Gone in an instant.

He was a monster, playing at being a man. But his body would not let him lie to himself. He felt better than he had in decades.

He felt whole.

Then, above it all, he heard the oath pushing him again:

"By this blood, you are bound to the President of the United States; and the orders of the officers appointed by him; to support and defend the nation . . ."

He didn't have time for the luxury of guilt. Cade leaped to his feet and aimed himself like a bullet for the buses. Right now, he had a job to do.

He hesitated only long enough to scoop up Roark's phone from beside her corpse as he left. Cade knew he was a monster, but that didn't mean he had to be stupid as well.

AGENT CAM BUTLER, like every other member of the Secret Service, knew his professional code of ethics. He was prohibited from a number of activities that would have been perfectly normal if he'd worked in an office. For instance, he couldn't wear a T-shirt with a political slogan on it, even while off duty. He couldn't have a Facebook page or Twitter account (someone might track his movements). He could not have a beer while on protective detail, even if he was not on duty (the agency was very sensitive about that since JFK).

And, of course, he was definitely not supposed to be having an affair with a fellow agent. Particularly one who was under his direct supervision.

Not only was it against the rules, it was really, really stupid, he reminded himself.

Butler's job, he knew, was to protect the president. If he was more worried about one of his agents, then he wasn't doing his job.

And yet, Butler found himself taking a quick detour on his way to The Beast to check on Alison.

He didn't know he'd been clenching his fists until he saw her and something in him relaxed. "Agent Dunn," he said.

She turned. She was on the perimeter with Gary Fisk. Fisk was an incredible shot. He could snap off a bullet one-handed and still hit the 10-ring from a hundred yards. It made Butler feel better about having Alison on the outer limits of the caravan. Yes, he knew that was sexist and insulting. He didn't have to tell her that's why they were paired so often on the schedules.

"Chief," she said. Fisk nodded and turned back to face the dark. In addition to being a good shot, he was smart enough to know they'd want a little privacy. It was impossible to keep secrets in the Secret Service, especially when on protective detail. They were simply stuck together too much, spending far too much time on the road, in the same hotel rooms, awake for days at a time.

That's probably why he was with Alison. Or, more accurately, why Alison was with him. She was a knockout, twelve years younger than he was, and funny as well as smart. She could drink beer and dissect the action in a Redskins game better than he could. If she'd been on the market in any kind of a normal way, rather than trapped on the road for months with him, he doubted she would have chosen her slightly over-the-hill supervisor.

He'd said as much to her once, and she'd hit him in the gut. "Dummy," she told him. "You think I'm settling? You think there was no one else on the detail I could have gotten? It's damn lucky you're so good in bed."

"What's going on?" she asked.

"Cade went out hunting," he said. "We stay alert. Guard the president. Keep the reporters alive. Although I got the impression that's a lower priority."

"You think anyone would miss them?"

He smiled. "Probably not."

They both looked around. The wind seemed to drown their voices. Butler suddenly knew what Cade had meant when he said they were on the Boogeyman's turf now. Somewhere they'd crossed a border. The whole night felt like a conspiracy against them.

"Hey," Alison said. "Get to Sinatra. We've got this covered."

Butler nodded. His place was with the president. Alison knew that. She was a good agent. She'd be fine.

"Keep an eye out. Don't be afraid to yell if you see anything."

"Gary does a great high-pitched squeal," she said.

"Only that time you kneed me in the balls," Fisk said over his shoulder.

Alison tipped her head closer. "And yeah, he's a great shot. But I've got a gun, too. Don't worry."

So she knew. Of course she did. No secrets in the Secret Service.

This was why Alison had handled the revelations about Cade and the Boogeyman better than the others. She was completely pragmatic. She wasn't about to argue that they shouldn't be here or this couldn't be happening. She dealt with the facts on the ground. She was as ready as any of them could be. More ready than he was, in fact.

Butler didn't touch her or say goodbye. He had an urge to brush one strand of her hair from her forehead. Instead, he only nodded and then turned and jogged through the intermittent flakes of snow toward the president's limo.

Later, he told himself. You'll see her later. Right now, his responsibility was the president.

AGENT ALISON DUNN stamped her feet to get the blood going through them again and kept walking the line she'd drawn in her head. She was glad she'd chosen pants over the skirt tonight. Even with her topcoat, the wind was cutting right through her.

She and Fisk had each taken a position; she was mobile, he remained still. They worked well together. Butler's somewhat transparent, somewhat endearing and somewhat chauvinistic attempts to keep her safe by pairing her with the best gunman in the detail had given them lots of chances to learn each other's habits.

Despite that, if she was in charge of the detail, she never would have done it. They were two of the best agents. Putting them together was focusing too much strength in one area. Better to pair each of them with one of the less experienced agents on the detail, to make up for any hesitancy or indecision that might develop there.

But she didn't run the detail. Not yet, anyway. There was plenty of time for that. And she believed in Butler, even before they hooked up. He was very, very good at his job. He didn't need her to question him, because he questioned himself constantly. When the time came for a decision, he made it, but you could be sure he'd considered every angle.

So she was prepared to cut him some slack on this.

She stamped her feet again and turned. The worst part of the cold was the way it took you out of yourself. It was not so much painful as distracting. It demanded its own portion of attention; keeping warm became the body's priority. Her focus narrowed to a tunnel.

The rest of her mind was filled with dread. Dunn was sure she wasn't alone in this. There was a confidence that came from being on the president's detail. Like the others, she knew she was one of the best in the world at what she did. You had to be pretty self-assured to willingly put yourself between assassins and terrorists and the man they wanted to kill.

But she wasn't stupid. She knew none of them would stand a chance against the Boogeyman. Only Cade would. And Cade was scary enough himself. Standing near him, she understood viscerally the shift he represented. His existence informed you that your place in the world was nowhere near as secure as you believed. Now, out here in the night, that feeling of dislocation threatened to overwhelm her. Dunn had the same feeling she got at the top of very tall buildings when she looked down: that some unknown force would cause her to fly over the edge and hurtle toward the ground, as if rationality itself would turn inside out and tear her from safety and toss her into the sky.

She put all that aside as best she could, labeled it in a box in her mind marked DO NOT OPEN.

She flexed her fingers around her gun and flashlight and

swept the roadside with her eyes again. The beam of her light barely penetrated the gloom.

A stray wind carried a noise to her ears. A crunching sound. It could have been a footstep on a stray cornstalk. Or it could have been nothing.

She turned to Fisk. "Gary? You hear that?"

He cocked one hand to his ear. He couldn't hear her, let alone a footstep.

She tried yelling this time. "I said, did you—"

Dunn didn't finish the sentence. From out of nowhere, an ugly, edged weapon flew through the air and stuck Fisk through the throat before splitting the back of his neck and skull.

It was so fast.

Dunn turned and aimed. But she wasn't able to get her finger through the trigger guard quickly enough. The cold had dulled her reflexes just enough.

A dirty-yellow moon came bobbing from the dark at her, resolving in a flash into the latex smiley-face mask of the Boogeyman.

He hit Dunn just as she got the gun pointed in his direction. He was so goddamned fast. She'd been knocked around by much bigger men but never hit harder. Her legs left the ground and she landed on her back a dozen feet away. She tried to reach for her gun, but the wind was knocked out of her and a sharp burst of pain lanced through her from her right arm. Looking at it, she saw it bent completely the wrong way above the elbow. He'd broken bones without even trying.

Then the yellow mask was above her as she gasped for

air. He didn't let her get any. She could almost feel the reluctance in his fingers as he began choking her. If he'd had more time, she bet he would have preferred the blade. That was in his profile. He liked the cutting. The thought came to her in an abstract, detached way. Dunn realized that was bad but couldn't find any strength in her limbs to fight.

He probably would have rather taken his time with her. That was in the profile, too. But she knew that he wouldn't risk her shouting or making any noise. Not if he wanted to get to the president.

Butler, she thought. He was going to be next. The Boogeyman would have to go through Butler to get to Curtis.

No, she thought with sudden anger. Not if she could help it.

Her right arm was dead and useless. But the left still clutched the big Maglite. She swung it like a club.

Without looking, the Boogeyman caught it in one hand. With the other, he kept choking her.

Dunn saw her fingers lose their grip on the Maglite and her arm fall away. Everything was very distant now.

She hoped Butler would be all right.

It would have been nice if her last thought was of him. But it wasn't. It was of Cade.

She wondered why he wasn't there to stop this.

THE BOOGEYMAN WAS DONE throttling the woman. He got off her corpse and walked over to the body of the other agent. He braced one foot against the dead man's chin and yanked his blade free from the bone and meat.

He began walking down the line of buses. Another pair of agents was between him and the president's car. He longed to simply attack, but he needed them to die silently. He could kill every agent here—and he would—but he didn't want to have to do it all at once. The weight of numbers, the guns—it would all be an even greater delay. If he wanted to do this quickly, he had to work quietly. Just for a little bit longer.

The Boogeyman crouched down at the roadside and waited for the agents' attention to turn. Just for a second. That was all it would take.

CADE MOVED LIKE A BULLET. He could smell the Boogeyman—the scent of meat and rot and curdled sweat from all the changes forced on its poor mortal frame. It glowed almost visibly, like a trail in the night.

He was moving faster than ever before. Human blood charged his veins like lightning. He'd never felt so alive in undeath.

The Boogeyman was at the edge of the Secret Service's perimeter, hunched over and waiting. He appeared to be waiting for two agents to turn their backs to him. His jungle cutter was out of its scabbard, resting easily in one hand.

Cade smiled, baring his fangs.

This was going to be easy.

Cade's foot took one glancing step on the earth, barely

seeming to touch as it propelled him along. Cade could see the Boogeyman start to turn his head, the movement as slow as a glacier creeping down a mountain.

Cade was already on him by then, pounding away with both fists, pummeling the face behind the mask.

The Boogeyman was on his back, arms pinned by Cade's weight. The cutter was somewhere in the dirt. The Secret Service finally moved, as if answering a postcard lost for years in the mail. Cade felt like the fight was over already.

Then the idiots shot him.

It didn't hurt—his skin had healed and snapped into its armorlike fibers again—but it did surprise him. He hesitated while the agents sent another volley of heavy-jacketed rounds into both him and the Boogeyman. Cade lifted his head to shout at them, but at the speed he was still moving, it would be nothing more than high-pitched gibberish.

The distraction was enough for the Boogeyman. With a massive burst of strength, he twisted and turned under Cade. Cade went tumbling to one side as the Boogeyman scrambled away from the road, seeking nothing more than escape.

Cade started to go after him, but the Boogeyman ducked down, scooped up his cutter, and, almost casually, flung the blade over his shoulder toward the agents.

It flew like a dart for the head of the one on the left.

Cade knew he had only a split second to save the man's life. It wasn't really a choice. The oath bound him to protect the officers of the president.

So he pivoted on his toes and leaped, flinging himself into the cutter's flight path.

He snatched it from the air, stopping it cold.

Everything seemed to slam to a halt as the handle smacked into his palm. He went back down to human speed. For him, it was like stepping out of an F-14 into quicksand.

The agents stood there gaping, still facing the wrong direction, guns locked open, clips empty. They had caught only the vaguest of shapes and sounds from the high-velocity combat scorching the air around them. To them, it looked like Cade had simply appeared out of nowhere, holding the cutter in one hand.

They began babbling, asking all the usual questions. Cade ignored them. He held the hatchet in his palm. He scanned the darkness but knew it was useless. The Boogeyman was gone.

He should have been angry. He should have felt some guilt at least for snuffing out a human life and for failing to save the lives of Fisk and Dunn. Instead, he found he couldn't stop smiling.

Cade had managed to frighten the Boogeyman.

THEY REGROUPED BY THE BUSES. The media were still snoring away. The engines of every vehicle in the caravan started as if they'd all been freshly tuned. A demented chorus of ringtones sang from every pocket and jacket as cell phones suddenly grabbed signal again. Even the wind stopped spitting ice crystals in their eyes.

Butler walked to the lead bus from the president's limo.

Cade, Zach, Candace and Lanning waited for him. He rubbed his eyes.

"It could have been worse," he said. "We've got a tow truck on the way. We've already got our cover story." He cleared his throat and rubbed his eyes again. "We'll say Dunn and Fisk were in the lead car. The truck is bringing a Crown Vic that's pretty smashed up. We'll take a few photos. No one's going to look too closely."

Butler closed his mouth and clenched his jaw too tight. He seemed to shove whatever he was feeling into a place where it couldn't surface for air. His face was calm again when he continued.

"We were lucky," he said. "No civilian casualties."

"Not exactly," Cade said. They all turned to him.

"Who?" Butler asked.

"Follow me," Cade said.

He began walking off the side of the road. Butler took out a flashlight to follow.

Zach tagged along. No one else would have noticed it. Then again, no one else had spent as much time as he had with Cade. And though he couldn't point to anything specific, he knew something was wrong. Cade was always quiet. He was always contained.

This was different.

MEGAN ROARK'S BODY was not yet cold when they found it. Butler played his flashlight over the corpse and the wound, then quickly pointed it away.

"God damn it," he said. "He practically cut her head off."

Zach only took a short glance at the body. He was too busy struggling with his own unpleasant emotions: relief, mainly. Roark was the biggest pain in the ass of any of the press corps—not because she was the smartest, or even closer to the truth than the others, but because she kept picking at the same scabs over and over. People listened to her, even if it was only because she pitched her voice just below a hysterical shriek. She was the only one Zach worried would question the car accident. He wanted to slap himself for being grateful to the Boogeyman.

Latham, who'd been manning the barricades at the eastern side of the caravan, stumbled down from the road. He stopped suddenly when he saw the body.

"Ah, Christ," he said.

"Well?" Butler snapped at him.

Latham got it under control. "Yeah. She was following us. I stopped her back at the perimeter. She must have gotten out of her car. Or been taken out of it."

"Probably got out," Zach said. "She might have been trying to get closer to the buses."

"Wrong place, wrong time," Butler said. "Shit, shit, shit. Well. Latham, go get the perimeter tape, cordon this area off. We'll need to get a forensics team here. Find out what county we're in, so we can alert the local—"

"Hold it," Lanning said. His chin was down almost to his chest. Zach recognized the look. Lanning was plotting something.

He looked up. They all looked back.

"What's the point?"

Butler struggled to find a response. "Fucking what?"

"We know who killed her," Lanning said. "Same deranged prick who's already killing our people. We're already doing everything we can to stop him. How is it going to make our job any easier if we bring in the local cops on this as well?

Zach didn't like where this was going. "You're not suggesting we leave her here?"

Lanning scowled. "Don't be an asshole, Barrows. All I'm saying is, we don't make things any more complicated. We make this public and the media will start picking away at our story. How did she happen to die at exactly the same time we had a car crash? If there's an autopsy, people are sure as shit going to realize that she wasn't in a wreck. Then we might have to admit, 'Oh hey, Roark was right about there being a killer on the campaign trail after all.' And who knows where that could lead?"

"A lot of unpleasant questions," Zach admitted.

"Exactly," Lanning said.

"Wait a damn minute," Butler said. "It's one thing to lie about what happened to my agents—they signed on for this. But this woman was an innocent bystander."

"No question," Lanning said. "But let's look at this logically. Nobody except Latham saw her catch up with us. She wasn't traveling with the campaign. She was already an unstable person. It makes a lot more sense if she simply disappeared."

"Except that isn't what happened," Cade said. Zach turned to him, surprised. Cade had been too quiet. And frankly, he'd expected Cade to agree with Lanning. Something else was missing, too. He couldn't quite get his head around it. . . .

"I know we've got body bags in the trunk of the limo," Lanning said to Butler. "Have your guys bag her up and get her car out of here. Drive her off a bridge or bury her somewhere. But this didn't happen. Not here. Not tonight."

"You're a piece of shit," Butler said. He looked ready to spit.

Lanning nodded. "I'm worse than that. But I'm going to get Curtis back into the Oval. So do as you're goddamned well told."

Lanning turned back toward the buses. "Barrows, you're with me."

They followed Lanning, slipping in his leather-soled shoes back up the slope to the highway. He muttered curses. Cade followed them both. That's when Zach realized what was missing.

Cade hadn't objected when Butler said "goddamned." Someone had taken the name of the Lord in vain, and Cade let it slide without a word.

He looked at Cade—really looked at him. Despite the beating and the bullet holes, Cade seemed stronger, more alive, than he had in—well, than in the entire time Zach had known him.

Cade noticed Zach staring.

"What?"

"What happened to you out there?" Zach asked Cade quietly. "How did he get past you?"

"I was indisposed," Cade said.

"What exactly is that supposed to mean?"

He showed Zach the syringe that had been stabbed into him. He described his near-death experience.

"It took me a few moments to recover," Cade said.

"Holy crap," Zach said.

"That was more or less my thought," Cade said. "Something like this is black-budget technology. And the compound that it contained had to have been developed in a bioweapons lab."

"Shadow Company," Zach said.

"No. I don't think so. Graves is dead. The Company is still in some disarray."

"Sounds like a good reason for them to try to kill you."

Cade's lip curled in his ghost of a smile. "You would think so. But I find it hard to believe it would work with the Boogeyman. If they wanted a president dead, they'd simply use a high-powered rifle."

"You say that like it's happened before."

Cade didn't reply.

"Okay," Zach said. "Moving on. Who would have access to this kind of equipment and would also know about you, and the Boogeyman, and would be batshit crazy enough to try to cut a deal with him . . ."

Zach finally got where Cade had been for some time.

"Helen Holt," he said. "But she's dead."

"Apparently not as dead as we thought."

Cade seemed a little too sure of his conclusion from too little evidence.

"Cade. If you knew something I didn't, you'd tell me, right?"

"I know a lot of things you don't, Zach. We don't have that kind of time."

Zach realized Cade was hiding something. He wondered what it was. More important, he wondered if he even wanted to know.

CANDACE ELECTED to tell the press—now that they were waking up—what had happened.

Zach went with her. Cade, after getting cleaned up and into a new suit, came along as well.

She delivered the news flatly and without emphasis. It wasn't maudlin or cheap. She simply said that two agents had died. Her manner alone said everything else: that it was pointless and tragic and stupid.

"We'll be on our way just as soon as the trucks clear the road," Candace said. She turned to leave.

But a balding, middle-aged reporter stood up.

"Why should we believe that?" he said, belligerent. "You lied to us before. You said there were no injuries."

Another reporter stood in the aisle as well. "Yeah," he said. "We don't appreciate you playing games with us. We had a right to cover that story. If this is how you're planning on dealing with the press—"

Candace whirled on the reporters. "Excuse me? You really think you were owed a chance to snap photos of two dead people on the road? Tell me where I find that in the First Amendment. Come on. I'm curious."

The reporters didn't speak.

"That's what I thought. For the record, I didn't lie to you. I told you what I was told. But if I had known—then fuck yeah, I still would have lied to you. If you think doing your jobs means getting a close-up of a body in a car wreck, then mine includes making sure their relatives never have to deal with that nightmare on the evening news."

She turned and walked away.

Candace's unspoken message blared out loud and clear to Zach: any day, she might have to see her father's corpse on every front page in the world. There would be no escape from it. He knew she wasn't so naive as to think she could prevent that. But for people whose parents weren't the president, she could try to maintain a little respect for the dead.

Once she was off the bus, one of the reporters found his voice. "Wow. I guess the rumors were true: she really *does* know how to give a tongue-lashing."

Zach's vision went briefly red. His hand clenched into a fist, but Cade stepped in before he could move.

Cade stood a little too close inside the reporters' personal space. The one who'd insulted Candace swallowed audibly.

"I'm sure you gentlemen don't mean to behave in a rude or threatening manner toward Ms. Curtis. I'm sure you would both regret that kind of discourtesy."

Cade's words didn't constitute any kind of threat on their own. But the way he said them left a definite impression.

The men nodded.

"Thank you," Cade said. "Feel free to have a seat."

Both reporters scurried back to their places on the bus.

Zach had to stifle a smile. He immediately felt a pang of guilt as he remembered Dunn and Fisk.

But you had to take your laughs where you could get them. He had a feeling nobody would be smiling much after tonight.

THIRTY

THE SYSTEM—The name given to the loose association of groups and individuals who perform human sacrifice and occult ritual in the United States. Once a splinter group of The Order (SEE: THE SHADOW COMPANY), the System is currently made up of a hard core of individuals "inside the knowledge" and a large group of mostly uniformed followers. It has deep ties within the drug trade as well as fringe elements of some biker groups. (SEE ALSO: BOOGEYMAN.)

—BRIEFING BOOK: CODE NAME: NIGHTMARE PET (Classified)

October 23, 2012, Outside Fargo, North Dakota

The meeting took place on neutral ground, in public. The bikers chose a McDonald's near a rest stop on the highway.

Helen sat under the branches of a fiberglass tree and the watchful eyes of Mayor McCheese with a man who'd killed at least twenty people.

He sucked on the straw of his milk shake. "Fuck's wrong with your face?" he asked.

"I have a condition," Helen said. "What's your excuse?"

He laughed. Actually, Del Collins was quite handsome

under the grime and scuzzy beard. He was muscular and lean. If not for the ring of pentagrams and swastikas tattooed around his neck, he would have cleaned up pretty nicely.

Some of the other men from Satan's Service were here as well. They were even bigger than Collins. They sat at nearby tables. Helen knew she was supposed to be intimidated.

But Helen had seen worse. She'd seen it when the Boogeyman came back after failing to kill Cade and the president.

He'd been furious. At her, at himself. He had done what she'd said, and it didn't work. Cade had survived. He'd deviated from his usual methods, and he'd failed. He blamed her. She'd genuinely feared he would turn on her then.

Fortunately, she always had a backup plan. "We're not done yet," she'd told him. "There's more than one way to rip out the president's heart."

At least three or four, in fact, Helen thought. And these morons were going to help her. They just didn't know it yet.

"Look, Officer," Collins began. He'd been certain Helen was a cop since she made first contact with him. "I don't know what you expect from me. But once again, let me tell you, we are just a law-abiding group of motorcycle enthusiasts. I have no information for you about meth or murder."

Helen rolled one eye. "For the last time, I'm not a cop."

"Your buddy there sure looks like one," Collins said. He nodded at Reyes, who sat nearby, working his way through a tray full of Quarter Pounders. Helen sighed inwardly. Her backup. Good thing she wouldn't need any.

"He used to be. I used to be CIA, as a matter of fact."

"Really? I was U.S. Air Force myself."

He turned his arms, displaying a tattoo.

"I know," Helen said. "I know all about you. You were discharged fifteen years ago after an investigation into a white supremacist cell within your unit. Then you became involved with the occult after joining the Satan's Service biker gang—"

"Club," Collins said. "We're a club."

"—before becoming a major supplier of meth to the Midwestern corridor. Which led to your eventual rise to the leadership of the club. You've sacrificed at least six people I know of, and you've got the bones of one of your rivals ground up and in a jar on the shelf in your house. You snort the powder when you feel the need for more virility."

Collins drained his shake with a loud sucking noise before he responded. "Now, those are some dangerous accusations to be making. A woman might not make it all the way home at night, she goes around saying things like that."

Helen smiled with half her mouth and leaned into him.

"I am telling you all of this because I want you to know that I don't care. I want you to know just how small-time I find the shit you've pulled so far."

Collins laughed again, surprising her. "All right. What would it take to impress you?"

"Funny you should ask. I've got just the thing. You're going to recruit some of your younger and stupider skinheads in the area for a suicide mission. And you're going to supply them with guns and ammo and explosives."

"And what's in it for me?"

Now it was Helen's turn to laugh. "I'm going to introduce you to your god."

COLLINS DID NOT LOOK IMPRESSED.

"I sacrificed blood and souls for this?"

The Boogeyman stood calmly between Helen and Reyes on the sawdust floor of Dewey's Lounge, just outside Minot. It was the bikers' home base. This was where Collins had wanted to meet. But now he appeared to have serious doubts about Helen, despite all she seemed to know about his sick little religion. His eyes rolled up and down the Boogeyman, who stood there, breathing evenly under his rubber mask. But it wasn't the mask that really seemed to bother Collins. It was the poly-blend button-down and the Dockers slacks.

"He looks like a fucking retard," Collins said.

There was no way to know if the Boogeyman registered the insult. Helen did. She was already tired of this. More than that, she was just *tired.* They had been driving nonstop through the night. They were running out of time if this was going to work.

Collins was just bright enough to be paranoid but not paranoid enough to be smart. He could imagine someone coming into his bar to rip him off, but he couldn't believe he'd ever be vulnerable on his home turf.

Still, Helen felt honor-bound to head this off before

anyone would have to change the sawdust on the floor. From the smell, they must have been very attached to it.

"I promise you. This is him," she said. "And he'd like to see you can deliver what you promised."

Collins looked disgusted. "Jay. Pete," he called. Two big men in leathers stood in response. "Get this gimp bitch and her kids out of my sight."

Gimp? *Kids?* Helen thought. Fine. She'd given him a chance.

The big men crossed the floor slowly, working for maximum menace. Reyes flashed a look at Helen, but she shook her head. They both stepped back.

The bikers seemed to take it as a retreat. They flanked the Boogeyman, malicious grins full of white teeth in the gloom. One raised his hand to start with the bully's age-old opening move, the hard shove—

And after the next blur of motion was trying to scream with his own fist jammed in his mouth. His eyes were wide and uncomprehending. His skin mottled to purple quickly as he suffocated, unable to pull his fist free of his shattered palate and jaw.

The other biker stood in mute shock. He might have wanted to help his friend. But at the moment, he was busy watching his entrails drop out from him onto the floor. The Boogeyman's other hand had sliced him so fast and so deep with the hidden knife that it was like he'd been unzipped and all his stuffing had spilled free.

Collins's face was a mix of horror and rapture and fear and joy; a kid who opens his presents on Christmas morning and finds them full of body parts.

The Boogeyman took a languid step toward Collins.

Collins didn't hesitate. He bowed down, knees to the floor now covered in the muck and gore of his two enforcers.

"It's you," Collins breathed. "The Promised One. The Chosen. Forgive me."

The Boogeyman didn't say anything as every other biker in the place kneeled as well.

Helen sighed. "Can we please get on with this?"

Collins took a long, wobbly time standing up. He kept staring at the Boogeyman, mouth open.

But he finally recovered enough to snap his fingers at another couple of bikers.

They brought out several metal cases with military stenciling. Collins's connections with the Air Force apparently hadn't ended when his career did.

The cases were placed with great care on the stage by the stripper's pole. Collins popped them open one by one and stood back.

The Boogeyman couldn't have cared less. But Helen wanted to be sure.

The cases were filled with guns and ammunition. M-16s with thirty-round magazines loaded with NATO cartridges. Standard stuff, available for the right price at any gun show.

But the last case was filled with the real goodies. Twenty pounds of what looked like white wax bricks: C-4.

Helen had a fondness for the stuff. It had nearly killed Cade once before, after all.

"Perfect," she said. "And you've got your boys together?"

Collins nodded. "They're on their way. We'll drive the supplies to them tonight."

"See? All you need is a little faith," Helen said.

"I have faith," Collins said. He could not take his eyes off the Boogeyman, even as the other gang members struggled to collect the bodies of Pete and Jay and stuff them into black garbage bags.

"We have an offering," Collins said to Helen. "It's not much. Not for him. But if he would like, in the back, there are two girls."

The Boogeyman apparently heard this. He swiveled his head, the mask distorting with the movement, and found the rear door. He walked through the crowd of bikers, which parted like the Red Sea for Moses.

The door closed solidly behind him. Helen restrained herself from checking her watch. Looks like they'd be here for a while longer.

Collins's voice was breathy like a schoolgirl's when he spoke to her. "Is he—do you think he's pleased?"

Helen patted him on the cheek. "Of course he is. Just look at that smile."

THIRTY-ONE

President Samuel Curtis' campaign dropped the last of its objections, clearing the way for a last-minute debate against Governor Waverly "Skip" Seabrook. Seabrook's campaign had accused Curtis of dodging "an honest discussion of the issues" for several weeks.

The two will take preselected questions both from the audience and a panel of journalists at Tulane University on Saturday night.

—"Curtis Agrees to Debate Terms at 11th Hour," Associated Press, October 24, 2012

6:19 P.M., OCTOBER 25, 2012, THE ROOSEVELT HOTEL, NEW ORLEANS, LOUISIANA

Cade woke to find that he'd been moved during the day.

He hated when people did that.

He popped open the lid of his travel coffin and found he was in a hotel room. A quick glance around, plus the noise from outside the window, confirmed the campaign had changed its schedule during the sunlit hours.

He was in New Orleans.

He hated New Orleans.

Zach's luggage was in the room. Zach was not.

Cade went to find him. He was tired of playing catch-up. It was now clear the Boogeyman had outside help. Cade had been reacting rather than thinking ahead. It was time to change that.

First he had to get Zach.

CADE KNOCKED ON THE DOOR of Candace's hotel room.

Zach sighed when he opened the door, wearing only the hotel robe.

"Cade. Have I mentioned lately how great your timing is?"

As per usual, Cade ignored his witty banter.

"We've been played for saps since this began. I want to put the heat on for a change," Cade said. "I want you to find something for me."

He told Zach what he wanted. Zach shook his head.

"That's like looking for a needle in a stack of needles. And weren't you the one who said the cult killers didn't know anything about the Boogeyman? That they just followed the rituals blindly?"

"Do you have something better to do?"

"The debate is tomorrow night. We came to terms with Seabrook's people while we were still on the road. So we dragged the whole campaign here, changed the entire schedule. We're scrambling to get our supporters in town. It's all last-minute. I've got FedEx bringing a literal ton of campaign signs and banners and T-shirts. And we still need to get Curtis prepped. Also, if it's not too much trouble, I'd like to finish—"

He hooked a thumb over his shoulder, back toward the bed in the dark.

Cade stared at him. "What's your job, Zach?" he said.

Zach had the decency to look ashamed. "Right. Sorry. What I meant to say was, what do you need?"

"Please tell the pilot of the Gulfstream we'll be at the airport in five minutes. He should be ready to take off."

"You sure that's a good idea? Leaving the president?"

"You said it yourself: the old plan isn't working."

Something in Cade's tone told Zach there was no arguing this time. He took his phone out and dialed. "Where are we going?"

"To get some answers," Cade said.

CADE AND ZACH walked through the crowded streets to get to their car. People were already massing for the debate, and a festival atmosphere—assisted by a river of alcohol—had taken hold.

Cade seemed to glide in and out of the crowds. Zach had stepped in slicks of vomit three times already. The crush of tourists made Hurricane Katrina, the levee failures and the days of flooding all seem like something that had happened only on TV.

"Hard to believe the city was almost wiped from the map," Zach said to Cade.

Just then they passed a group of screaming men beneath

a hotel balcony. "*Eight!* That's eight necklaces we've thrown at you! Now show us your tits, you bitch!"

"Yes," Cade answered. "That would have been a tragedy."

"I'm picking up on some sarcasm there."

"I would be surprised if you missed it."

"I figured you would have loved this place, Cade. Isn't it the vampire capital of the world?"

"You know that's not true."

"Yeah, but the reputation. The books. The movies. The TV shows."

"Reality is thin here," Cade admitted. "The Other Side breaks through easier than it does elsewhere. Ever since Mme. Laveau's time, this city has only had one foot in America. The other is someplace else entirely."

"Yeah, but to be fair, you've never eaten at any of the restaurants."

Cade didn't reply.

"Really, the blackened drum at Prudhomme's? To die for."

THIRTY-TWO

Looking over the historical record, it seems lucky that the United States has lasted as long as it has on the American continent.

Despite its vast resources and abundant flora and fauna, this land has never been an easy place for our species. If the paleontologists are to be believed, it was utterly devoid of human life until the first Cro-Magnon ancestors crossed the land-bridge over the Bering Strait. The cultures that established themselves after that had a bad habit of suddenly going extinct: the archaeological record is littered with the detritus of thriving groups that either collapsed into barbarism or simply vanished altogether. The Anasazi abandoned their city of cave dwellings after descending into cannibalism; the Adena/Hopewell culture maintained a near-empire from the lower portions of what is now Canada to Mexico and Central America before deserting their cities in a great migration; and a few centuries later, as the Fort Ancient peoples began to reclaim some of the skills lost by their ancestors, their population suddenly splintered and dropped back into primitivism. It was almost as if there were some force watching and waiting for these cultures to reach a certain level of advancement. Once they crossed this line, however, that was too far, and it slapped them back to the Stone Age. Without written records, we can't be sure what happened, but there is none of the evidence we've come to expect of wars or disease or famine. Instead, the early

Americans just seem to disappear at the height of their achievements.

These disappearances didn't end when European settlers began their incursion into the Americas, either. The settlers of the first English colony, Roanoke, disappeared with only the cryptic word CROATOAN carved into a tree left behind. Several Spanish outposts were found abandoned by the conquistadors who returned to them after taking their plunder home. And many of the Plains Indian tribes—who curiously, did not claim any relation to the Adena and Hopewell cultures or their massive earthworks or decaying cities—told Old World explorers to avoid great swathes of the new lands or suffer the consequences.

Maybe they knew something we didn't. Maybe when the first human stepped off that land-bridge and onto the half-frozen soil of what we now call Alaska, he was trespassing. And maybe the real owners of America will show up again someday, and serve us all an eviction notice, just like they've done before.

—Journal of Dr. William Kavanagh, Sanction V research group (Classified)

9:40 P.M., OCTOBER 25, 2012, THE WHITE HOUSE, WASHINGTON, D.C.

The campaign's private Gulfstream zipped Cade and Zach back to Andrews in a little over an hour. A car and driver waited for them. Cade's special Secret Service creds got him past the front gate of the White House with a minimum of human contact. Zach stayed in the car, eyes glued to his pad, trying to track down the data Cade had demanded.

It was already late. If they wanted to get back to the campaign before sunrise, he'd have to be quick.

But at the door of the Lincoln Bedroom, he still hesitated.

There were very few things in the world that still frightened Cade.

The Lincoln Bedroom was more than a very expensive overnight hotel for the president's wealthiest donors. It was more than the scene of Zach's humiliation with Candace and the Secret Service.

If you believed the stories, it was haunted.

President Lincoln had participated in séances while in the White House. He dreamed of his own assassination the day it happened. And apparently, his spirit lingered in the White House. When British prime minister Winston Churchill was a guest in the room, he allegedly spoke to the ghost while planning the strategy that won World War II. Eleanor Roosevelt felt Lincoln's presence while using the room as a study. President Gerald Ford's daughter said she would never stay in the room again after seeing the ghost. Countless other staffers had seen the spirit or heard him walking over the floor of the empty room.

Sometimes it was friendly. Other times it filled the witnesses with cold, stark terror.

Cade didn't know what it was. He was all too aware that ghosts existed. He'd fought them. But they were barely nuisances. As he'd told Zach, it took enormous effort to cross over from the Other Side and very few entities could manage it for long. Often the things there would take the shapes and faces of the dead in order to fool the living. They were malevolent and willing to pull any trick to ruin human lives.

So Cade did not entirely trust the thing he knew was inside this room.

But the blood of Lincoln still clung to him through the oath. The fetish that bound him to serve the presidents was wrapped around the bullet pried from Lincoln's skull. Their mingled blood bound Cade to the office and to the men who served it. At times, he could feel the spirit of Lincoln like a great singing note in his veins.

When he had no other options, he came to the bedroom and asked for help. He hated it. He was all too aware that he could be talking to things that only wanted him to fail in his duty. But there were times where the answers he'd received were unmistakably true.

Cade opened the door and walked inside.

As usual, the room felt occupied to him even though no one was there.

He waited. Sometimes that was enough.

Nothing.

"I need your help," he said softly.

There might have been a stirring in the room. It wasn't the heating system. From the corner of Cade's eye, he could see the thermostat. He couldn't feel it, but the temperature had dropped ten degrees since he'd entered.

"I need to know where it is."

Now the thermostat read forty-eight degrees. But Cade didn't hear any response.

"It's killing people. It wants to kill one of your successors. And I"—Cade almost choked on this part—"I don't know where to look."

Now the room had dropped to thirty-eight degrees. But still no words.

"I need a name. A place. Anything," Cade said. "Give me something I can *bite*. You can't let this thing keep killing."

He heard a whisper. It was barely audible even to his ears. Hoarse and strained, it sounded like it was a struggle to form words.

Frost spread crystal fingers over the mirror. The thermostat was stuck at zero.

"My . . ."

My? Or why? Cade couldn't tell.

"Why?" Cade asked. "Why what?"

"Not."

" 'Why not'?" Cade snapped, suddenly enraged. *"Why not?"*

He felt the entity reach out tentatively and touch him—not physically, but inside him, in whatever was left of his soul. It recoiled immediately in horror. It was not fooled by sight as humans were. It could sense the darkness inside Cade, the foul truth of what he was. It knew he had fed on human blood. It knew he had failed the most basic test of morality once again.

The door behind Cade slammed shut as if pushed by

a strong wind. The room's temperature soared back to normal.

Cade scowled and exited.

This was useless. He learned nothing he didn't already know: the room shook him to his core when almost nothing else could. The thought that the Other Side had a presence in the White House and used it to manipulate him was bad enough. But it was worse to imagine that Lincoln's soul was really trapped there, unable to go to its reward, and it shuddered with repugnance every time it was forced to commune with something as unholy as Cade.

CADE GOT INTO THE waiting car. Zach looked up from his screen.

"Take us back to the jet," Cade said.

"What happened to getting the answers?" Zach asked.

"I was wrong. I've left the president unguarded too long. This was a waste of time."

"Wow, somebody woke up on the wrong side of the coffin."

"Zach. Unless you have some new information—"

"That's what I'm trying to tell you. You told me to give you something you could bite. Well, I think I've got something."

Zach tapped his fingers against his pad. "Take a look," he said.

He'd been using his clearance to examine the FBI's National Crime Information Center reports. Ever since the agency had started VICAP, the program made famous for profiling serial killers, it had also collected information on the specific methods used in murders all over the country. True, much of the information was patchwork and depended on the diligence of overworked local cops filling out forms. But certain methods tended to draw attention to themselves, flashing like red lights across the map. They were disturbing or weird enough that they made their way into the database.

He looked for killings that appeared to match the Boogeyman's. Ones that involved hatchets, axes and dismemberment. Ones that involved couples caught in the act of sex. Ones that had weird symbols painted all over them.

Most of them were false leads. Others they already knew about. Some were just mistakenly entered into the database: Zach had no idea why he kept finding reports of cattle mutilations, but they kept coming up.

Still, there was one that seemed to jump out at him: a homeless kid killed near Minot, North Dakota. He was found off the highway, not too far from Minot Air Force Base. The base's name rang bells. He ran another search and it came back to him immediately. The Son of Sam case: David Berkowitz, the shooter, had claimed there was a nationwide network that was responsible for other ritual slayings. One of the people he named was an airman at the base who happened to be the son of one of his neighbors. The airman turned up dead, his brains splattered all over the wall of his apartment. But he had links to another ritual killing at Stanford.

What drew Zach's eye was a single photo, scanned into the database along with the crime report. The body had been badly carved up, but the detective assigned to the case had noted the number 666 scratched onto the kid's hand.

The same number had been scratched into the hand of the airman before he supposedly put a shotgun in his own mouth.

Cade froze. It was like a hunting dog going on point. "Minot?"

"Yeah," Zach said, puzzled. "Minot."

"My. Not." Cade said it again.

"Right. An Air Force base. North Dakota."

"Change of plans," he said. "Call the pilot. Tell him that's where we're going."

Suddenly, Cade was eager to get on the trail again. Zach had never seen mood swings like this before. Vampires, he thought. Go figure.

"It's a pretty slim lead," Zach admitted.

"You don't have to come."

Zach flipped his pad shut. "All right. You talked me into it."

THIRTY-THREE

I'm the Devil, and I'm here to do the Devil's business.

—Charles "Tex" Watson, to his victims at the first Manson Family murder

1:29 A.M., OCTOBER 24, 2012, DEWEY'S LOUNGE, OUTSIDE MINOT, NORTH DAKOTA

The doorman sat against the railing on the porch of Dewey's, next to his bike. Years ago, the line of motorcycles lined up outside would have been enough to warn civilians away from the place. But times change. People who should have been driving Volvos bought Harleys now. Guys who couldn't change a tire or the oil, let alone tune their own engines, wore leathers and bandannas. They took the bikes out of their three-car garages on a weekend and went looking for authentic places where they could drink $1 PBRs and pretend they didn't spend 90 percent of their lives behind a desk. They thought that made them bikers.

They thought they would be welcome in Dewey's.

The doorman was there to disabuse them of that notion. Dewey's was a real biker bar. The kind of place where the titty dancers were meth-skinny and you'd get your ass stomped for wearing the wrong colors. There was serious business done inside the front door. The doorman was there to keep out the tourists.

He was feeling a little twitchy, to be honest. It was a weeknight. Nobody who wasn't in the club had tried to get into the bar, and he was sort of disappointed. Maybe it was this new batch of crystal he was snorting, but he felt the need to flex his muscles.

As if on cue, a four-door sedan pulled off the highway and parked in the lot. The biker smiled as two young men wearing suits and ties got out. They dressed like cops but didn't have the muscle. Lawyers, probably. This was going to be fun.

They walked right up to him. The shorter one was first. He smiled like an idiot. The other one hung back. He made the doorman a little nervous, but the meth rode right over that.

"We're closed," he told the smaller one.

The kid looked at him, then over his shoulder at the neon lighting up the painted-black picture window that was flashing the word OPEN over and over. He put on an exaggerated face of confusion.

"Really?" he said. "Doesn't seem that way."

The sound of whooping and hollering and loud music was barely muffled behind the doorman. "You calling me a liar?" he asked.

"Hey, now, there's no need to get surly. I'm Zach. That's Cade. How ya doing?"

He offered his hand. The doorman stared until he dropped it. He didn't look at all offended. The doorman was a little confused. The other guy, the taller one, just stood behind him, steady as a rock. Neither was reacting at all like he expected.

The one called Zach looked over the bike parked next to the porch with an appraising glance.

"Nice," he said. "Yours?"

The biker nodded, smirking a little. He was used to getting compliments from yuppies about his ride. It didn't get them inside.

"Tell me, do they charge extra for the training wheels?" Zach asked, his face perfectly innocent.

The biker scowled.

"Or does your daddy still hold the seat while you pedal?"

The scowl on the biker's face deepened.

"I know a real car is out of your price range, but here's what I suggest. Next time your sister brings back the fifteen or twenty dollars she makes from blowing guys behind the truck stop—"

That was as far as Zach got before the biker took a swing. Zach could have dodged the punch, but he didn't bother.

The biker's fist was frozen in midair, and the rage on his face melted into bafflement.

Cade held his arm locked in one hand, preventing him from moving an inch.

The biker tried to jerk away.

Cade smiled, showing his teeth.

He tightened his grip. The man's radius and ulna broke instantly, one muffled snap followed by the next, and Cade bent the forearm at a ninety-degree angle, grinding the bones together.

The biker screamed and his legs went out from under him. Cade held him for another second before letting him drop.

Zach looked down at him. "I've got some questions for you."

"Fuck you!" the biker snarled. Zach sighed. He heard the heavy tread of boots on the wooden porch. They weren't going to listen.

When Zach looked up, the first of the reinforcements had arrived. He didn't bother to announce himself. He was even bigger than the doorman, and he was swinging a heavy pipe wrench at Zach's head.

Again, it never reached him. Cade slapped it away and shoved the other biker back. His feet left the porch and he hit hard enough to knock the door off its hinges.

"Someday I want to be the bad cop," Zach said.

"You might have been more persuasive."

"Yeah. Like they were going to cooperate."

Cade didn't reply. He walked through the broken door. Zach followed.

Inside the dim, smoke-filled room, everything but the music had stopped. The man Cade had pushed through the heavy oak door lay on the floor while the other patrons stared. A couple of very skinny, very young women with badly inserted implants stood on the low stage, mouths open. The other men were all one type or another: either elephant-huge with muscle and fat, or whipcord thin with muscle and gristle. Zach saw several more of the tattoos of the Devil and swastikas once his eyes adjusted.

Cade stood a few feet inside the door frame, outlined against the night by the neon of the bar signs.

"Perhaps we can save some time," he said. "Is there any one of you who doesn't want to spend the next six months sipping his meals through a wired jaw?"

As one, a cluster of the bikers hurled themselves at Cade with everything from pool cues to buck knives in their hands.

Zach stepped back out the door. He'd figured Cade could use a light workout. He'd been in a foul mood ever since the attack on the bus caravan. Maybe this would help.

The bikers were tough. They were also only human.

A moment later, the strippers ran out through the space where the front door used to be, fake breasts not bouncing even as they bounded down the stairs. Cade put his head back out the door. "You can come in now," he told Zach.

Broken bodies were all over the floor. Most of the men were unconscious. Some were probably no longer breathing. Zach didn't particularly care. They chose their team. They could take the consequences.

Once they'd made the connection between Minot and the Boogeyman, it hadn't been very difficult to find the most likely suspects. It was right there in their name: Satan's Service. Between their meth deals and antisocial behavior, they generated a lot of business for the local emergency room.

Cade had left one man, one of the biggest, conscious

and on his back by the strippers' platform. His face was gray and sheened with sweat, but Zach still recognized him from the old mug shot his computer had dragged up.

It was Collins, the club's leader. He'd been discharged from the Air Force after being stationed in Minot. He wore leathers and a sleeveless denim jacket covered with patches. He had a ring of swastikas and pentagrams tattooed around his neck. On one bare shoulder was the number 88. On the other was a goatlike devil.

"I think we've got the right guy," Zach said. "What did you do to him?"

There were no visible fractures, but Collins was clenching his teeth in pain. He looked like someone suffering a heart attack.

"I've broken his sternum," Cade said. "And all of his ribs. Along with his collarbone."

That would do it, Zach thought.

"There's most likely damage to his internal organs as well."

Zach kneeled over the gang leader. "Damn, I bet that hurts," he said.

"Fuck you," Collins wheezed.

"You want to keep dazzling me with your witty comebacks? Or should Cade just keep breaking bones until you're faxable?"

Collins spat at him. About the most violent thing he could manage. "Fuckin' worm. You don't know."

Cade kneeled down, looming over Collins. "I know," he said. "I know better than you."

A canny gleam appeared in Collins's eyes. He was not stupid. There was a mean little rat of intelligence running around on the wheels inside his skull.

"You're not . . . what you look like," Collins said.

"No," Cade agreed. "Neither are you."

Collins bared his teeth in an approximation of a grin. "You're like him. The Promised One."

Cade flicked a glance at Zach. The Boogeyman.

"You've seen him?" Cade asked.

"I helped summon him," Collins said proudly. "I have amassed a great harvest of blood in my time. My master has a throne of skulls waiting for me below."

Zach rubbed his eyes. "We don't have a lot of time for heavy-metal lyrics."

"I'll speak," Collins said. "But only to you." Cade. "Only you will understand. And only if you agree to let me go."

"All right," Cade said.

"Cade!" Zach was shocked. Cade's look silenced him.

"Give me your word. I walk," Collins said.

Cade looked into the eyes of the man on the floor. "I swear."

That seemed to satisfy Collins. He smiled again, even as he sucked in air like a bellows and his face went paler. "You won't stop it, anyway. He's already on his way. It was worth it. Fuckin' glorious," Collins said. "Seeing the Promised One in human clothing. It was worth every drop of mongrel and subhuman blood we spilled. Bunch of useless weaklings and faggots and fleas. Their lives were nothing until we turned them into fuel."

"Where?" Cade asked.

"New Orleans."

Zach and Cade locked glances. They both knew what was on the schedule for New Orleans.

The presidential debate.

Cade asked a few more questions, but Collins didn't have many answers. His description of the Boogeyman was useless—a man in a rubber smiley-face mask—and the neo-Nazis following him only a little less so. They had a small arsenal, courtesy of his gang, a stockpile of meth and other chemicals, and Army surplus body armor.

And about thirty pounds of C-4. Enough to take out a small building.

"Not good," Zach said. He pulled out his phone and began dialing Butler. Then he kicked Collins in his broken ribs.

"I think that's all he knows," Cade said.

"Your point being?" Zach said. "Tell me you're not really going to let him go."

"I gave him my word."

"Cade, you can't—"

Before Zach could finish the thought, Cade had lifted Collins from the floor and deposited him on his feet.

Collins's knees buckled. He only stopped himself from hitting the floor by grabbing the nearby stripper pole. He howled in pain as he slid down to the platform.

"As I said. He can walk. In fact, he can even run. All he has to do is make it to the door."

Collins looked stricken as Cade's meaning became clear.

"You said—"

"I wouldn't waste your breath arguing if I were you," Cade said. "The door's right there. Go."

Zach decided to leave after a few minutes. Collins's screams and sobs were making it difficult to talk to Butler. He tried to stumble across the floor, falling every couple of feet. His strength gave out barely halfway across the room. Zach stepped over his prone body on his way out.

"I'll be in the car," he said, pitching his voice over Collins's wails. "The plane is already waiting."

"Don't worry," Cade replied. "This won't take long."

THIRTY-FOUR

The conspiracy nuts have found their latest mystery. (Or lost it. We're not sure how it works, to be honest.) Now, after political blogger and alleged journalist Megan Roark had her second epic career-ending meltdown a few days ago, we wouldn't be surprised if she took a little time off. To regroup. Or possibly fill out some job applications. (We hear Hooters is hiring.)

But no, there are apparently some out there who see a much more sinister cause for her lack of posts or updates. "Isn't it convenient that the Curtis Administration's biggest enemy has gone missing right before Election Day?" wonders the leading light over at something called Real America Today, which we assume is a blog. Another guy, who claims to have an actual Ph.D., says, "Watch what you say. Curtis's goons might disappear you like they did Megan Roark."

I guess if they want to make Mad Megan their martyr—she is *way* hotter than Saint Gundenis, for what it's worth—well, whatever keeps them off the streets. To us, though, it's far more suspicious that anyone actually misses her.

—Mudslinger, a political blog

4:03 A.M., OCTOBER 26, 2012, YMCA INTERNATIONAL HOTEL, ST. THOMAS PLACE, NEW ORLEANS

The Secret Service Counter-Assault Team was flying in from D.C. Backup from the local SWAT team and FBI field office were on the way as well. But until they arrived, it was just Butler and his ten remaining agents.

Butler stood on the street, pulling on his vest from the trunk of his car. Behind him, Latham and Thomason and the others were getting into their tactical gear as well, then putting on jackets that read SECRET SERVICE in big letters on the back.

Butler tried to figure the odds of going in without waiting for help. Sure, the would-be assassins were probably asleep. There was almost no chance they knew anyone was onto them. But every moment Butler and his agents sat here was another moment the skinheads could use to take hostages or barricade themselves inside their rooms. If they moved fast enough, the agents might be able to overwhelm any resistance and short-circuit any chance of a standoff.

The problem was, their intel was spotty at best. The YMCA in New Orleans was a throwback to an earlier time. It still offered cheap rooms for transients and refugees from the streets. Butler and his agents didn't have a clue where the skinheads were inside the crumbling old building. And because of the debate, a lot of young Curtis and Seabrook supporters, mainly college students, were staying inside as well. The Y's old plaster walls would barely stop a sneeze, let alone a stray bullet. One bad ricochet and some rich kid's parents would be spending next year's tuition on funeral services. The press would dance on the victims' graves until Election Day.

In his head, Butler went through the list of weapons that Zach had provided. The skinheads had enough firepower to take on a small Army unit.

There was no good way out of this. No matter what he did, a lot of people would end up dead.

And if the Boogeyman was actually inside the hotel with them, then the number of body bags was going to be higher than he wanted to count.

JERICHO WHITE (formerly Jerome Gayle) picked up his cell phone on the first ring. He was wound tight. Too much was riding on this mission to sleep.

"Hello, Jerome," a voice said. "You should get dressed. You're about to have some visitors from the federal government."

Jericho didn't bother to ask how she knew. He had no intention of squandering the gift he'd just been given.

He hit the number in his contacts file on the phone while he yanked a Kevlar vest and a shotgun from the duffel by the bed.

All over the hotel, other cell phones began to ring.

Despite what people might have thought from the tattoos on his neck or his arrest record, Jericho wasn't an idiot. He'd planned for things to go bad. It was the way most things ended anyway.

But this time he was ready. He pressed an icon on the screen of his cell phone. A conference call opened up among all of the skinheads' phones.

"You all there?" he asked as he placed his headphone and mike into his ear.

Most of the replies were affirmative. A couple guys were still trying to get the phones to work. Jericho would be the first to admit not all of his friends were MENSA candidates.

One in particular.

Drew was still struggling into his pants after finally getting up from the room's other bed. "What's going on? What's going on, Jer?" he kept saying.

Jericho felt bad for what he had to do. But he couldn't wait. The woman had given explicit orders. It was his job to obey.

He raised the rifle and put it against Drew's head.

"See you in Hell, man."

Drew opened his mouth. Jericho pulled the trigger and put his brains all over the wall.

One more thing. The blond woman had given him a yellow latex mask. A smiley face. He scooped up what was left of Drew's head and put the mask over it.

Then he ran out into the hallway, into the stairwell, and smashed open the skinny window looking down on the street.

He saw feds. Their dark jackets and bright yellow letters made perfect targets.

He brought the assault rifle to his cheek, aimed and fired.

THE RAPID *pop-pop-pop* sound told Butler he was out of time. He ducked for cover. Latham was still standing in the open, trying to find the source of the gunshots.

Butler ducked out again and dragged him behind the car just as bullets powdered the curb by his feet.

Latham shook him off and stood, firing at the lobby.

Butler brought him down to the ground again with a hard chop to the backs of his knees.

"Stay the fuck down!" he shouted as the car's windshield exploded under a new barrage from above.

"They're barricading the lobby," Latham screamed back.

We're screwed, Butler thought.

And then a shadow passed overhead. Someone was running toward the lobby. He'd hurdled over their car without slowing down.

Butler knew who it was, but he risked a look anyway.

Cade.

He moved so fast it was like watching someone caught in a strobe light, afterimages of him stretching out against the frozen background of street and buildings.

Butler wasn't sure there was a name for the mixed set of emotions he was feeling. What do you call it when you're actually happy that vampires are real?

CADE DIDN'T SLOW DOWN for the Y's glass doors. He ran through them as if they were no more than gauzy curtains.

Two of the skinheads were in the lobby, still shoving old couches and chairs toward the doors. They ducked from the spray of glass. The furniture skidded across the room as Cade hit it. It slowed him down not at all.

Butler saw Cade rip through the men just as easily. One second they were on their feet, turning their guns toward the door. The next there were two corpses on the tiled floor.

Cade was a disappearing shadow moving up the stairs to the rooms.

"I never get used to that, either," Zach said from Butler's left.

He turned, surprised. Between the gunshots and watching Cade, he hadn't heard the younger man approach.

Butler had to admit it: he had no idea what to do next. "What now?"

"Give him a few minutes," Zach said. "This is what he's for."

CADE WALKED AT A RAPID CLIP through the hallway, knocking each room's door open as he went. Some of the faces were young. Most were old. All were terrified. He told them all the same thing. "Get out," he said. "Down to the lobby and wait there. The men below will tell you when it's safe to leave the building."

Some doors opened on different scenes, however. In one room, a burly young man with the SS symbol inked over his heart struggled with a cell-phone headset and a rifle at the same time. His eyes went wide and the barrel came up. Cade yanked it from his grasp and punched the man right at the spot where he'd had the tattoo. His ribs punctured his heart and he dropped.

"I'VE GOT their communications," Thomason said. He had a portable radio rig from his and Latham's car and was adjusting knobs, scanning for frequencies. "They're using cell phones. Conference call. Strictly amateur stuff."

Thomason listened on his headphones. "The leader seems to be the guy shooting up top. He's yelling for the guys on the first floor."

From above, they heard another crash. They all looked up and saw a man's body hurled through the narrow window of the first-floor stairwell. It looked like toothpaste being squeezed from a tube.

"I think Cade's got the first floor covered," Zach said.

THE SECOND FLOOR was already in chaos. The people there had come out of their rooms in response to the noise.

This gave the man with the gun a wide selection of hostages.

Shaved-headed, wearing a goatee and a leather jacket, Cade turned the corner in time to see him yank a young woman wearing a *Seabrook Stalwart!* sweatshirt and panties into one of the rooms.

Cade headed for the end of the hall.

Another skinhead waited behind a door, watching through a crack, holding a handgun ready. Cade passed.

The skinhead expected more: a whole army of black-helicopter UN commandos. But there was just this one guy.

One dead guy.

He stepped out, pistol head-high, prepared to put a bullet into the back of Cade's skull.

He was unprepared for the speed with which Cade turned, latched onto his wrist and yanked him forward. He hit Cade's other fist with his throat.

Cade left him on the floor to choke to death.

He reached the doorway where the bearded skinhead had dragged the screaming woman. He stopped on one side of the doorjamb and listened.

"Get away!" the skinhead screamed. "You get away from me!" The woman simply wept quietly.

Cade couldn't see through walls. It would have come in handy. He didn't know where the man was pointing his gun.

So he gave him a target.

He stepped in front of the door.

The piggy little eyes above the goatee went wide. The skinhead tried to fire his rifle one-handed. The bullets stitched up the side of the wall, far to the left of Cade.

Cade separated the man from his rifle, his hostage and his life, in that order.

The woman he'd deposited on the bed. He told her about the lobby. She was up and running before he'd finished the sentence.

"HE JUST CLEARED the second floor," Thomason said, still listening. "No response from the phones there."

"We got civilians in the lobby," Latham said.

Butler looked up. There were college kids and transients rapidly filling the small space. They saw the bodies. Panic was going to push them out onto the street any moment. And the guy at the third-floor stairwell was still shooting.

"All right," he yelled at the other agents. "I want suppressive fire. Cover me and Latham. We're bringing them over here two at a time. Someone give me their vest."

Latham got an extra vest as well. Together they sprinted toward the crowd inside. They caught the first two people at the door, draped the vests over them as best they could, and ran back to the line of agents at the cars.

No gunfire from above.

Butler and Latham exchanged puzzled glances. Then Butler figured it out. The shooter was busy with problems of his own.

THE SKINHEADS on the third floor were screaming at each other. Cade found the one guarding the entry door and sent his mangled corpse flying down the hallway. In response, they'd formed a crude firing line, their guns aimed in the direction of the door.

Cade waited. The other guests on this floor seemed to have barricaded themselves inside their rooms. If Cade showed himself, one of them was sure to be hit when the skinheads opened fire.

There was a long moment of silence as the three remaining skinheads in the corridor waited for the corridor door to open again. Their earpieces were all full of Jericho's voice screaming for an update. "What the fuck are you doing in there? Report! Report!"

One of the three, who'd renamed himself Anders because he thought it sounded German, found his voice. "There's—there's something in the hallway."

"No shit," Jericho snarled back, the volume hurting Anders's ear. "It's the feds! Start shooting! Why don't I hear any shooting?"

"I don't think it's the feds," Anders said. "I think—"

Then the ceiling collapsed above him as Cade tore through the cheap acoustic tiling.

He landed on Anders, snapping his spine. The other two put their hands up to surrender. Cade was in no mood. He whipped his hand back and forth, breaking their necks.

He paused to check the rooms. Empty. Nothing there. He caught a familiar scent. It was very faint, and the odors of decades of unwashed residents blotted out almost everything else. He didn't have time to puzzle it out. The skinheads must have forced the other people to move. But why? And where was the Boogeyman?

He moved toward the stairwell door.

Just one left.

JERICHO COULDN'T BELIEVE how fucking frustrating this was.

The assault rifle ran out of ammo as soon as he pulled

the trigger. He'd read that it fired 700 rounds a minute. Why, then, did the magazines carry only forty rounds? And nobody was answering their communications. They should have had the whole building locked down with hostages by now. Where the fuck were those guys?

It all looked so easy when the terrorists did this in *Die Hard*.

When the stairwell door opened, he was almost gleeful for the chance to vent his anger.

Cade moved over the distance between them in the time it took Jericho to blink. Before he knew what was happening, Cade folded him in half as neatly and effortlessly as a piece of paper. There was a muffled pop as his shoes touched the back of his head. He was too stunned to shriek until Cade dropped him on the floor. Then he began making up for lost time.

Cade dragged him inside the hallway. He brought the trembling skinhead up close, staring into his face, their noses almost touching, as if Cade were trying to sniff something out of the man.

"No," Cade said. "Not you, either."

Jericho just kept screaming, even though he couldn't feel anything below his chest. The lack of pain was somehow worse than anything else. He knew he was badly broken. He heard the questions, but all his mind could process was the deadness that filled most of his body.

Cade dropped him again. Useless, Cade thought. He'd been through every floor. Where was the Boogeyman?

He kicked the door to the hallway open and went back inside. He checked every room. No one hiding. Nothing but dirty laundry and mildew. He caught that familiar whiff again. Rot. Corruption. It was almost impossible to separate from all the other human odors. But he knew it now: the Boogeyman had been here.

Cade clicked his teeth in frustration and grabbed the wailing skinhead again. He went down the stairs, dragging the man along behind.

Then, at the second-floor stairwell, he stopped as his mistake occurred to him. He'd checked every floor. But the space between the floors—he'd hidden there. Why couldn't someone else? Why couldn't some*thing* else?

He looked up the ceiling and saw the air vent. He breathed deep. There it was.

Without warning, he leaped, dropping the skinhead and reaching through the ceiling tile in one sudden move.

His fingers caught cheap cotton and skin. As the ceiling collapsed around him, Cade heard a bellow of rage.

The Boogeyman.

BUTLER AND THE OTHER AGENTS got the last of the civilians out. There had been no return fire from the third floor for at least a minute.

"I'm thinking we go in," he said. It wasn't like he was asking Zach's permission, or even his approval of the idea. But he had to admit, he wasn't as confident in his choices as he was a week ago. And he knew that by saying it out loud, he'd hear Zach's opinion. Zach always had an opinion.

"I wouldn't," Zach said.

"No?"

"If the Boogeyman really is in there, you won't help Cade. You'll just get in his way. Trust me. I've been there."

"Yeah," Butler said. He sagged against the hood of his car, coming down off the adrenaline now. Every human instinct he had, all of his training—it all jammed up when he had to operate under the parameters of Cade's world. It had gotten his people killed. He honestly didn't know how Zach dealt with it. *Maybe I didn't watch enough horror movies as a kid,* Butler thought.

"How did you find them?" Zach asked.

"Got a phone tip right after you called. Anonymous. Said there was no time to waste."

Zach found the timing interesting but didn't say anything.

"So what now?" Butler asked.

"I'd go with drunken redneck shoot-out as my cover story," Zach said. He nodded toward the Y guests, standing in a clump on the vacant lot across the street from the building. "You tell them what happened now and that's what they'll repeat over and over. Pretty soon it becomes their story, too."

"You're a little too good at this," Butler said.

"Part of the job."

THEY TORE THROUGH THE YEARS of cheap construction as they fell: particleboard and asbestos tile, cardboard-thin plywood, water-damaged drywall, drop-ceiling frames held by old wire coat hangers.

Cade was grinning. He had his hands around the

Boogeyman's throat, right under the soiled yellow mask, and he was not letting go.

The Boogeyman thrashed wildly as they hit the floor and rolled. His blade bounced away from his hand. He punched, kicked and clawed at Cade. It did no good. Cade's fingers were locked around his neck.

They rolled again, taking down the wall nearest them, scattering the resident's plastic shopping bags filled with clothes and street debris.

The Boogeyman ended up on his back again. He looked around as much as he was able for a weapon. He saw that they had broken the framing of the wall. A broken two-by-four jutted from the floor only a few feet away, still nailed down at the bottom, but with a sharp point sticking straight up in the air.

That should do, he thought.

He put everything he had into rolling Cade to that side.

JERICHO HAD FINALLY stopped screaming. He accepted the cold lack of feeling in his body, as if the numbness had crept up and blanked out his panic as well. He knew that he was probably dying. He'd landed wrong when the vampire went up into the ceiling and he could see blood soaking through several spots on his clothes.

His arms still worked. He reached inside his jacket pocket and found his cigarettes. Only when he got one into his mouth did he realize he'd lost his lighter somewhere along the way. Of course.

For all his belief that nothing ever went as planned, he

realized he still hadn't seen this coming. He somehow believed he'd get out and get away. You can say you're prepared to die, he thought. You can think you're ready to go to Hell. But then Hell comes to you and it's still a surprise.

Ah, fuck it, he thought. Whatever was on the Other Side was probably better than living in a wheelchair and shitting in a bag in a prison hospital.

He reached into his pocket again and came out with his phone. Thankfully, that was still zipped up tight where he'd left it. Jericho activated the screen, scrolled down to the last number under contacts, and hit "Call."

CADE REALIZED the Boogeyman was going to flip him. He saw the broken two-by-four out of the corner of his eye just in time. To avoid being staked, he had to let go of the Boogeyman's throat. He went with the momentum of the roll, flying over the tip of the wood with an inch to spare.

He landed in what was left of another room. The Boogeyman didn't give him a second to get up. A foot kicked into his ribs, sending him crashing into the single bed, knocking it across the room.

Cade saw what was underneath. Stacked in neat chunks, with a wire of primer cord running around it: a block of the stolen C-4. But only one. The cord ran under the wall through a newly drilled hole.

The entire floor was wired to blow.

At that same instant, the sound came to him. Someone hitting a button on a cell phone.

Cade was fast, but not faster than a radio signal.

Everything around him exploded just as he leaped for the window.

ZACH AND BUTLER were interviewing the witnesses and planting the seeds of the cover story when the second floor of the YMCA disappeared in a burst of fire and smoke and noise.

The shock wave knocked them all flat.

Debris was still raining down as Zach's eyes managed to focus. It was oddly familiar. He supposed you could get used to anything, even people trying to blow you up.

What remained of the building collapsed in on itself as he watched. It was all silent. He knew it would be a while before he'd hear anything.

He looked over at Butler and saw the agent already up and moving, checking the civilians and yelling orders his men couldn't hear.

Zach saw movement on the street. One of the larger chunks of debris picked itself off the pavement and stood.

Cade. Smoldering around the edges, battered and bloody. But still on his feet.

Half of the fake tan on his face was gone, wiped away by blood and grime. It made him look half baked, half burnt.

It wasn't that funny. But Zach couldn't stop laughing anyway.

THIRTY-FIVE

There are other Sons out there. God help the world.

—David Berkowitz, the "Son of Sam" killer

7:12 P.M., October 26, 2012, President's Campaign Bus, Outside McAlister Auditorium, Tulane University, New Orleans, Louisiana

The cleanup crews found his blade.

Cade and Zach were not the only people who handled unusual tasks for the government. There was an entire team dedicated to collecting the evidence of things that weren't supposed to exist. Smitty's job description was fairly loose, but if a Roswell crash happened today, Smitty and his cleaning crew would be the ones in the desert throwing the debris into the back of a truck. Contrary to popular belief, however, these men didn't wear black. Zach had a difficult time even picturing Smitty in a suit. Right now, he was covered in brick dust and soot. Along with the rest of his team, he'd spent all day going through the rubble of what they'd told the media was an unfortunate mix of drunken rednecks, bullets, and a leaky gas pipe.

For anyone who didn't buy that, Zach had already planted the counterspin on the Net: he'd posted several angry messages on blogs and message boards calling it an al-Qaeda attack that the government was covering up. The stink of conspiracy theory would scare away any of the mainstream journalists covering the debate. It probably didn't hurt that the story of an alcohol-fueled shoot-out fit right into the prejudices of the reporters. It was the kind of thing they could see happening in a crash pad for bums.

"No chance of getting any DNA off the blade," Smitty said, his Southern drawl turning "DNA" into a five-syllable word. "The metal was heated red-hot by the fire. But it's still pretty sturdy. It's definitely a U.S. Army surplus survival hatchet. More than that, I can't tell you."

They were in the back of Curtis's campaign bus. It was swept for bugs daily and soundproof. It was as secure a spot as they could manage for the president's debriefing before the event. The president sat behind his desk. Butler and his core team of agents were crowded in along with Zach and Cade and Smitty.

"Any identification of the bodies yet?" President Curtis asked.

"Yes, sir, we rushed the fingerprints and dental records where we could find them. Most of the men were known white supremacists with ties to the biker gangs. Arrests for meth, hate crimes, stalking, one conspiracy to commit murder, later dismissed for lack of evidence." Butler read through the charges in a dull monotone. Zach doubted he'd slept in the past three days. "One of the bodies, however, had no prior arrests or convictions. But we were still able to get a partial match on the fingerprints."

"He was a cop," Zach said as it became clear to him. Police officers, like all law-enforcement personnel, were required to give their fingerprints when they were hired.

Butler nodded. "His name was Andrew Nolan. He used to be on the force in Lawrence, Kansas. He was fired—we've been trying to get the personnel records, but we'll need a court order and we can't get that until Monday. However, he went to work as a security guard after that. We checked with his employer. He hadn't shown up for at least a week."

"What do you think? Is it him?" the president asked.

He didn't have to elaborate. They all wanted to know the same thing: was this the Boogeyman?

"Seems pretty obvious to me," Butler said. "What was left of his face was covered in melted latex, just like that mask. And it would explain how the Boogeyman was able to get past security and gain victims' trust. He could have been wearing his old police uniform, or even a security guard outfit. And even before he dropped out of sight, his boss said he'd been really unreliable lately, missing shifts, taking days off without permission, calling in sick. His personal hygiene went to shit. Other security guards didn't want to be in the same patrol car with him."

"Zach?" the president asked.

"It fits," Zach said. "And we didn't find any other bodies, right?"

"Well, parts of them," Smitty said. "But we don't know

yet if they belong to the other bits we've already found. Nobody's counted up all the limbs yet. It's still a bit like a whole bunch of different jigsaw puzzles in the same box right now, only instead of cardboard, the puzzles are made of—"

"Thank you, Smitty, I get the picture," the president said. "Cade. You were closest. You've had the most experience. Was it him?"

All eyes in the room turned to Cade. He had healed completely during his day in his coffin. The new flesh was a pale, stark contrast with the fake tan, which still colored patches of his body in dull brown.

"I can't be certain," Cade said.

There was a ripple of dissatisfaction—even anger—from the others in the room. The Secret Service agents were done. Zach could see it. Their jobs were difficult enough: they were on constant alert against all manner of human enemies of the president. They'd had enough of waiting for an inhuman threat. Zach had felt their relief when they found Nolan's body and the blade; felt the mounting joy as the evidence against him piled up. He fit the profile. He had to be the Boogeyman.

And now Cade was pissing all over that campfire by expressing doubts.

"Cade," the president said patiently. "I'm well aware by now that nothing is ever certain when it comes to . . . this sort of thing. What I want is your opinion of the evidence that's been gathered. Do you think that Nolan was the Boogeyman?"

Cade waited. Zach could feel it, too. Everyone in the room, including the president, wanted this to be over with.

"I would be a cynic to say no," Cade said, "and a fool to say yes."

That didn't satisfy Curtis. "Can you point to any reason—any evidence—that would say otherwise?"

"No, sir. I cannot."

Curtis took a moment to think. It was time he didn't have. The debate started in ninety minutes. He should have been backstage already, doing his final preparation.

"I think we're going to have to say he's gone," the president said. "Cade, I know you wanted to find a permanent solution to this problem. But I don't blame you for how it ended up. The explosion took it out of your hands."

Cade was silent. Zach wondered what was going on behind the mask of his features.

The president stood. "Agent Butler—Cam—all of you. I know this has been unbelievably difficult. I know you have lost friends." He looked at Butler again. "More than friends. If it were possible, I would give you all medals on the White House lawn. But as with so many of your efforts, the public is never going to know about this. I know my thanks will never be enough. But it's all I can offer."

"We'd take some paid vacation time," Latham said.

"Done," Curtis said, grinning. "Let's just get through Election Day first."

Laughter; the tension lifted. Even Butler grinned. The agents formed a cordon and switched their radios back on.

"Sinatra is coming through," Butler said into the mike

under his cuff. They walked the president out of the bus and through the portable plastic tunnel that stretched like an umbilical from the bus to the door of the auditorium.

Cade and Zach did not accompany them. Smitty said something about getting a beer and wandered into the bus's kitchen area to rummage through the fridge.

"Well. I guess we're done," Zach said.

"Not quite. I want you to go to Nolan's home. See what you can find. There was a connection with Holt. I'm not comfortable with the thought that she's still operating."

Zach thought of the basement of a federal building in Los Angeles. He thought of duct tape and a trained dog and scars that had yet to heal and the way his shoulder still hurt if he moved it the wrong way. "Yeah," he said. "You and me both."

"I would go myself, but—"

"Right," Zach said. "You're staying with the president."

"There are still threats out there," Cade said.

Zach still felt slightly unsettled. The president's words had the feeling of a rehearsed speech. He wondered if they were doing the same thing little kids do when faced with the Boogeyman: hide their heads under the blanket and wish it away.

He assumed that was why Cade wanted him to check out Nolan's home. Cade was a big believer in finality. He knew this had to bother him.

"You'll get him next time," Zach offered.

Cade's lip curled. "We'll see," he said.

CANDACE WAITED FOR THEM outside the bus. More specifically, she was waiting for Zach.

"I'm leaving," she said. No preamble. No softening of the blow. "I'm going back to Washington early with my mom and brother tomorrow. We're going to make some appearances for Dad, then I'm going to California."

"Oh" was all Zach could think to say.

Candace turned to Cade. "No offense, but I hope I never see you again."

"None taken," Cade said. To Zach's surprise, he offered her his hand. She only hesitated a little before taking it.

Cade walked toward the staff bus. His box was already open, waiting by the cargo hold.

"So you're leaving?" Zach said.

"I've got to get to my seat. The debate's about to start."

"I meant tomorrow."

"I know. But tonight, I'm going to my hotel," she said. "Hint, hint."

"I'm on my way to the airport," Zach said. "I need to look into this guy Nolan."

"No rest for the hero."

"I don't see any heroes around here."

Candace gave Zach a surprisingly chaste peck on the cheek. "I do," she said.

"I have to go. Seems so anticlimactic somehow. So to speak."

She walked away from him.

Zach felt a sense of loss settle into the pit of his stomach. Sometimes this was just how the work went, he supposed. It finished without the sharp resolution, the slicing of loose ends. Sometimes it was just a pause in the battle and that's what they all had to accept.

He went to find his ride to the airport. He looked over at the buses, but Cade was already gone, coffin and all.

Something nagged at him, but he didn't think much about it. It would only come to him much later.

Cade wasn't carrying anything when he left.

CANDACE HAD NO IDEA how her father did this every day. She was exhausted. She thought she had endurance. After all, out in L.A., she'd regularly stayed up until dawn before hitting the gym and maintaining a 3.75 GPA. But that was nothing compared to the relentless schedule of the campaign trail.

All she wanted to do right now was fall down on the hotel room bed and sleep. She was going home—well, to the White House—tomorrow. She could rest a little. She only hoped she'd be able to get her bra and shoes off before she passed out.

Candace froze. Someone was in the room with her.

In an instant, all the fears she'd managed to keep at bay suddenly piled on her like a pack of wolves. It was the Boogeyman, come to get her. She opened her mouth to scream, knowing it would be useless, that it would probably only draw the Secret Service agents to their death.

Then she realized it was Cade.

"I apologize for startling you," he said.

She went a little weak with—well, not exactly relief.

Cade wasn't a warm and friendly face. But he was better than the alternative.

"You don't believe it," Cade observed.

"What?"

"That the Boogeyman is dead."

"You and Zach said he was."

"No. I didn't. I said that's how it appeared. And that's all that can be proven."

"The building blew up. How was he supposed to walk away from that?"

"I did," Cade said.

Candace shuddered. She realized he was right. She didn't buy it. Never had. Something still felt wrong. Maybe no one else noticed it. Maybe Zach was accustomed to living with it. But she couldn't shake the feeling that her time in the trough of the nightmare wasn't over.

"Why are you here, Cade?" she asked.

"I have to ask you something," he said. "You should probably refuse. But I believe you need to have the choice yourself. I can't justify my actions any other way."

She listened carefully to him. Her anger flared up when she realized what he was asking. But he didn't push. He simply stood quietly while she considered what he said.

"All right," Candace said. "I'll do it."

THIRTY-SIX

Before he was president, Teddy Roosevelt once stopped in a saloon in North Dakota. One of the cowboys took one look at the bespectacled city slicker from the East Coast. He drew his guns and threatened to make Roosevelt dance.

Roosevelt took off his glasses, stood up, and knocked the cowboy out cold.

It's hard to imagine any U.S. President in the last fifty years who'd be able to pull off that kind of bad-assery. Maybe LBJ, but everyone after him? Nixon would hide in the bathroom. Carter might offer some mealy-mouthed words of apology. Bush Senior would have the servants escort the rowdy away. And President Curtis? It's hard to imagine him getting his impeccably pressed shirtcuffs dirty. Fisticuffs somehow seem so beneath the Harvard-trained lawyer, something for the plebeian rabble.

Then again, sometimes there's a hint of something a little more feral when Curtis is at the edge of losing his icy calm. Look at his eyes then, and you'll see someone who's about ready to do more than throw a punch—he looks like he's about to cut a bitch.

Maybe it's a good thing we've never seen President Curtis in a street fight. He might go all Sasquatch on us and then there would be bodies piled up on the floor.

Maybe, like Roosevelt, we should leave the city slicker alone.

—Mudslinger, a political blog

11:12 P.M., October 26, 2012, 37,000 Feet Over Arkansas

Zach didn't sleep. Instead, he watched reruns of the debate on the plane. Despite this little break back in the surface world, he'd received a harsh reminder that his life was belowground now.

But for a moment, he forgot all that and simply watched the big game on the screen. This must be how retired athletes feel, he realized. For a few moments, you could pretend you were still the one making the decisions and reacting to the plays.

Curtis was at his best in situations like this: fluid, eloquent and good at mixing his rehearsed lines with improvisation. Seabrook was not as good but made up for that in points just with his baritone and his solid appearance. Both men had the gift of saying things that sounded very deep and reasonable as long as you didn't start dissecting the actual words coming out of their mouths.

"We live in a world of uncertainty, where there are enemies who want to destroy the American Dream," Seabrook said. "And I'm sorry to say, we are not safer now than we were four years ago. If the president cannot keep his own people safe, then he has failed in the first responsibility of his job."

Oh, son of a bitch. Seabrook went there. Zach could feel the reporters' reaction, as if they'd just watched Seabrook land a body blow on the president.

Of course, maybe half the people watching this would have no idea what Seabrook's carefully veiled reference meant. But the media would tell them, over and over again.

But Zach wasn't worried for his boss. He knew Curtis was waiting for an opening just like this one.

Curtis smiled when it was his time for rebuttal. "I appreciate my opponent's concern for all of our safety," he said, drawing mild laughter. "But the fact is, I don't need anyone to tell me about the dangers of the world. They have come to my front door. And they have not deterred my commitment in the slightest. I am here to tell you that our worst fears can be defeated. I know because I have seen our brave men and women do it with my own eyes. I know the cost of our fight against our enemies. And I know it is not more than we can bear. I know we will win our War on Terror because we as a nation will never surrender to fear."

Despite the moderator's instructions, the auditorium erupted into roof-shaking cheers. Seabrook actually looked stricken. It was a hell of a countershot.

Goddamn, Zach thought. The boss can still bring it.

March 4, 1869
The White House, Washington, D.C.

When the inauguration ceremony was over, Grant went inside the White House. He'd been inside many times, of course. But now it was to be his home. It put every stick of furniture into a strange new light.

He found his predecessor, Andrew Johnson, waiting in the presidential library. The silence stretched between them. Johnson had made no secret of his dislike of Grant. During the war, he'd argued loudly that Grant be removed from command. His dislike turned to hatred when Grant refused to follow his orders during the Reconstruction process in the South. The fact that the nation had chosen Grant to succeed Johnson was a stinging wound in Johnson's inflamed pride. He'd even refused to attend the inaugural ceremony.

Grant, for his part, couldn't have cared less. He was loath to cause anyone offense, but he had no use for Johnson. The man was an abscessed tooth; the sooner he was removed, the better. But now, Johnson seemed to have something to tell him.

He looked uncertain. "I don't know how to say this," he said.

"Plain words might be the best start," Grant said.

But Johnson remained silent. A first for him, Grant assumed. Instead of speaking, Johnson turned to the desk in the center of the office, took a key from an inner pocket and opened a drawer. He came out with two objects.

The first was an old, scarred leather journal. Pages had been added over the years. Grant could see the colors change along the binding from yellow to gray to fresh white. The other was a small leather pouch bound by a cord. Johnson held this in his hand.

Johnson glanced up. Grant's benign amusement seemed to ignite his contempt again. "You wouldn't believe me anyway. Read the book," he said, slapping it to the desk. "It will explain everything." He walked toward the door.

He stopped and offered one last piece of advice. "The key also opens a door in the basement. Do not use it until you've read everything in the book. God be with you, Mr. President. You'll need Him."

With that, the seventeenth President of the United States left his office to the eighteenth. The two men would never exchange a word again.

Grant's curiosity was piqued. He crossed behind the desk and flipped open the book, meaning only to look at the first few pages. It wasn't until Julia came to fetch him for the Inaugural Ball that he realized he'd been standing in place for hours, horrified and fascinated.

He asked Julia to make his apologies. He would be late for the celebration.

GRANT MADE HIS WAY quickly to the White House basement. It was cold and dank. The floor was still dirt in most places.

But in the far corner, far from the rest of the space, a door was locked and bolted on a wall thick enough for an icehouse.

Grant heaved the bolt out and put the key into the lock. His hand did not tremble. There was no hesitation.

He heard something scurry in the dark center of the locked chamber. His boots crushed the skulls and droppings of rats. The stench was nearly as bad as the surgeon's tents in the war.

Grant put a match to the lantern hanging by the door.

The muddy yellow light fell on a gaunt being clothed in rags and dirt. A heavy chain linked a manacle around his neck to a stake pounded deep into the dirt floor.

The creature flinched as Grant entered. Grant held the pouch before him. For the first moment since heading down the stairs, he felt uncertain. Something rose in him that was very like the first time he went into combat.

He saw the creature's fangs first. He'd interrupted a meal. It had caught another rat and was sucking the rodent dry.

Then he saw the creature's eyes and saw the intelligence there.

Just like he did that first time in battle, Grant put aside his fear. He walked closer and showed the creature the pouch.

"You know what this means?"

The creature nodded.

Grant took a deep breath.

"Then let's see what we can do about cleaning you up."

His hands did not shake as he undid the manacle on the creature's neck. Grant knew that if the creature had wished, it could have torn the metal like paper. If it had meant him any harm, he'd be dead a dozen times over by now.

Grant had spent much of his life training horses. Though it seemed absurd, the lessons he'd learned while riding seemed to apply both here and in soldiering. He never understood those who would beat an animal to ensure its loyalty, just as he never understood his fellow officers who held themselves aloof from their men, sending them into death like throwing grain into a thresher. He held himself to a simple standard—those who command must be worthy of it—and that began with how those under his command were treated. This was no animal—indeed, this was nothing natural at all—but it was now indisputably his soldier; he did not see any profit in treating it as if it were nothing more than disposable stock, easily replaced. From what he'd read, it seemed as if the opposite was the case. The future of the fragile, barely healed Union might well depend on the missions this being would carry out in the dark at his order.

"I'm Ulysses S. Grant," he said. He offered his hand.

The creature took it. "Mr. President," he said in a rough voice. "I'm Nathaniel Cade. At your service."

"Yes," Grant said. "I suppose you are."

THIRTY-SEVEN

On the morning of July 2, 1881, Charles Guiteau could no longer resist the demon voices that commanded him to kill President Charles Garfield. The President clung to life through the agony of a long summer before yielding to the assassin's bullet in his back. Guiteau was relieved that he had fulfilled his mission. He went to the gallows confident that the demon he hailed as "Lordy" would take care of him in the afterlife.

—Brad Steiger, *Out of the Dark*

1:14 A.M., OCTOBER 27, 2012,
OUTSIDE LAWRENCE, KANSAS

Zach parked the government car outside the home of Andrew Nolan. It was on the outskirts of the university town where the houses began to give way to fields and pastures. It was small and white and dingy. It looked remarkably normal.

He walked to the front door and knocked. Nobody answered. No surprise there. But he was surprised when the door swung slowly inward in response.

Wouldn't the Boogeyman, of all people, want to keep

his door locked? Suppose the neighbors dropped by for a cup of sugar? Or something like that.

Maybe that's why he moved out here. Old-fashioned American values. You never had to lock your door at night. All that small-town heartland values stuff.

Maybe you should stop stalling and go inside the damned house, Zach, he told himself.

Inside, the place was dull and old but clean. Cheap white paint on the walls. Fairly new carpet on the floor. Not much furniture aside from a TV and an easy chair. It could have been Zach's place.

He went through the living room into the kitchen. There was milk turning to cheese in the fridge. A mostly unfinished twelve-pack of beer. A freezer full of TV dinners and a pantry with nothing but cereal boxes.

There was a door in the kitchen. From his time in many old houses—way too many at this point—he knew where it led.

The basement.

He opened the door. A single bare bulb on a string illuminated a narrow flight of stairs.

Sometimes he hated being right.

THE BASEMENT WAS AS BIG as the entire upper house. It was clear this was where Nolan really lived. A shiny chrome-and-black weight set rested in one corner, next to a top-of-the-line home gym. Nolan kept in shape. A whole gun shop's worth of rifles and pistols were displayed proudly on hooks mounted along the far wall. A workbench included tools for loading cartridges as well as a vise and other hardware. A standing desk had a new computer and printer.

Everything was neatly squared away and organized. His mail was even alphabetized in a standing file.

Zach made a note to come back to those letters and bills, but first he had to check out one last thing.

There was another door.

It was built into the cement foundation and made of steel. It looked solid. It looked like it was built to contain secrets.

Zach really didn't want to open it.

He walked over and put his hand on the knob.

Just as he began to turn it, the door slammed forward and cracked him in the forehead. He went down on his back and something leaped out at him.

SOMEONE WAS ON TOP of him. Someone was hitting him.

He recognized the man beating him. He wasn't sure from where. But he knew they weren't old friends. He was certain because the man was going for a gun in a holster under his jacket.

The pain and blood actually helped Zach focus. He was not, by any stretch of the imagination, a deadly master of kung fu. But he had been trained by Cade to fight for his life. Zach called it "The Way of the File Clerk"—use whatever you can reach, whatever's at hand, however you can, as long as you can stay alive. It doesn't have to be smooth or pretty or dignified. It just has to hurt the other guy. If that means jamming a pencil in someone's eye before he strangles you, so be it.

Zach didn't have a pencil. But he was able to reach a dumbbell on the floor by the weight bench.

While the man wrapped his fingers around his gun, Zach swung fifteen pounds of metal into his ribs.

There was a satisfying crunch and the bigger man fell over, screeching in pain.

Zach got to his knees and brought the dumbbell down again. He missed the man's head but landed solidly on his right forearm. The man grunted and kicked, knocking Zach back into the wall.

Zach didn't wait to catch his breath. He threw the dumbbell as hard as he could. It flew with all the grace of a dead chicken, but it caught the man in the gut, doubling him over.

Zach scrambled on the wall behind him and yanked a pistol away from its hook.

Beretta 9 mm. Dependable, solid weapon. He racked the slide and aimed it with both hands at the other man.

The man froze. He looked right at Zach.

Zach knew him.

Reyes. Augusto Reyes. He'd worked for Helen Holt in Los Angeles. He'd also provided assistance with Zach's beating and torture.

Reyes started giggling, a really unsettling sound in the basement. "Oh, of course it's you. Why not?"

"What are you doing here?"

He sighed. "Waiting to die, *pendejo*," he said. "I don't suppose you brought your friend Cade?"

"He's occupied. Where's Holt?"

Reyes smiled. "I'd hoped he would be the one to finish this."

"My heart bleeds for you."

"You seem pretty sure that thing is loaded," Reyes said.

"You really want to find out?"

"Sure," he said. "Why not?"

He pulled back his jacket, like an Old West gunslinger.

"Reyes. Stop."

"You're going to have to shoot me," he said. "I mean it. I really can't take this anymore. You have no idea what it's like, living with a monster."

"I've got an inkling. Let's talk about it."

"No." Quick as a snake, Reyes had his gun out of its holster and aimed at Zach.

Crap, Zach thought. He pulled the trigger.

The sound of gunfire was deafening in the concrete-walled room.

Zach realized a tight group of three holes had appeared in Reyes's chest.

The blood came a moment later.

Reyes smiled and collapsed on the floor.

Zach crossed the room and took Reyes's gun from his body. He realized the safety was still on. Reyes hadn't even fired.

Then he heard the door slam upstairs.

Someone else was inside.

FOR THE RECORD, Zach hated guns. People used them like they were remote controls, shutting down lives with no more thought than switching off a TV. He hated how cheap they were, how easy they made killing and how they were more likely to be used against the people they were supposed to protect. He hated that most of the things he and Cade faced laughed at them. But most of all, he hated the thrill he got when he held one.

Zach hated guns, but that didn't mean he didn't know how to use them. He was actually pretty good with them. And right now, he was glad to have one as he faced Helen Holt.

He was pretty sure he would hate himself for that, too. But later.

He came up the basement stairs as fast and as quietly as he could, leading with the Beretta. No one was in the kitchen.

He heard something. Footsteps coming back from the rear of the house, where the bedrooms were.

"Reyes!" A woman's voice. Holt. "Did you get the files? I want to get out of here before—"

Zach had the gun almost at her nose as she emerged from the hallway.

"Before what, Helen?" he asked.

"TURN AROUND AND GET on your knees," he ordered her, pointing the gun.

"Oooooh, kinky. I didn't think you had it in you."

Zach fired a bullet into the floor for emphasis. Holt only flinched a little.

"Fine," she said. "Be that way."

Zach noticed how difficult it was for her to kneel. Her body seemed half frozen. She wore a scarf on her neck, not very successfully covering a bandage. And the weird sheen to her skin seemed almost artificial. It was like she'd overdosed on Botox down half her body.

"He's still out there," Holt said in a singsong voice. "You know that, right?"

Zach remained silent. She was still a talker.

"Oh, you didn't know? I'm sure Cade did. I wonder why he wouldn't tell you. I wonder if that means there's a lot he hasn't told you."

Damn, she was good. It's like she had a radar for insecurity. Zach was no slouch in that department, either, however.

"What the hell happened to you, Helen? You used to be hot. Now you're gimping around like you've got a wooden leg."

A long pause. "Careful there, Zach."

"Or what? You'll hobble me to death?"

He could see her shake as she got herself under control. "Nice try," she said. "We could go after each other all day—I haven't even started on your deadbeat degenerate daddy—or we could find a compromise."

"I'm surprised you need me to point this out, but you're not in a very strong bargaining position," Zach said.

"Zach," her tone was scolding. "You should know me

better than that by now. This is all my operation. Everything. I was moving you into place like chess pieces before you knew what a Boogeyman was. I even tipped those little Nazi dirtbags you were onto them. The president would be dead already if that's what I wanted. You should be grateful I didn't have you all killed in your sleep."

"Well, gee. Thanks."

"I know where the Boogeyman is. I know what he's planning to do. You've gotten very attached to the president's daughter lately, haven't you? I had your room bugged. I never would have figured her for a moaner in bed."

Zach tried to keep his voice and his hand from shaking. "What are you saying?"

"I'm saying that there's more than one way to tear out the president's heart and show it to him. There are worse things to lose than an election or even your own life."

She could have been lying. But it fit with Cade's behavior. With the weird, persistent doubt he'd been feeling since the second floor of the Y blew into dust.

The only question was, what would he do about it?

He couldn't torture Holt. She was tougher than he was, trained to resist it, and anyway, he had no idea how. That was Cade's department. He'd only waste time and probably amuse her in the process.

She knew this. She thought he needed her information and he'd be forced to dance to her steps to get it.

Helen Holt was also dangerous. She'd nearly killed Cade—the scariest thing on the planet, as far as Zach was concerned—twice. She'd murdered dozens of people personally and God alone knew how many others with her plans. Zach had no doubt she already had a plan to turn everything to her advantage if he let her get up. If he let her out of this house, her body count would be his fault. Of course, he'd probably be the first victim, so he wouldn't have to suffer the guilt for too long.

Three years ago, he never would have shot an unarmed woman in the back. He would have fought, and maybe even killed, in self-defense as he had with Reyes downstairs. But he would have been incapable of a cold-blooded execution. Holt knew that about him. She depended on it now.

But Zach was not the same person she'd met three years before. The torture he'd undergone at her order was only an introduction to much worse things. He'd survived them all. He had a great deal more faith in his own resources.

And he had a much clearer idea of what would happen if he failed.

"Without me," she said, "you'll never find him."

"I'll take my chances," Zach said, and pulled the trigger twice.

The shots hit her at the base of the skull, right above her scarf, one immediately after the next, sending hair and bone and skin flying.

Helen Holt remained kneeling for a moment. Then her body responded to the abrupt halt in communications from her brain. Her muscles went slack and she pitched forward onto her face.

Zach reached under the gore and hair to check her pulse. He waited a full minute.

Nothing.

Zach had expected to feel something more. He'd expected to feel something, anyway. Maybe tomorrow he'd be curled into a fetal ball and weeping, but at that moment, it was like he'd hung up on an obscene phone call: a slightly soiled feeling that it had taken him as long as it did.

Whatever. He could work that out in therapy sometime. Helen Holt, formerly of the Central Intelligence Agency, Department of Homeland Security and the Shadow Company, was dead.

Right now, he had to figure out what she was talking about, or Candace was dead, too.

THIRTY-EIGHT

In war, you can only be killed once, but in politics, many times.

—Winston Churchill

All right, Zach, he told himself. Time to prove how smart you are.

The problem was, Reyes had had plenty of time to eliminate the clues.

He went back downstairs and booted up Nolan's computer. It was wiped clean, except for a few files that were obviously bait: bookmarks for Satanic websites; photos of the president defaced with cheap drawing software; violent BDSM porn. Everything else was gone. Maybe with the right programs and a couple days, he could find Nolan's real files on the hard drive. But he doubted it. Moot point. He didn't have that kind of time.

He went through the mail neatly stacked on the desk. Nothing useful. Reyes had left just enough to give the impression of an especially tidy single guy who shredded his credit card bills every month.

So no help there, either.

Zach checked his watch. The president's jet was probably leaving right about now. Cade was inside his coffin and dead to the world. Zach was on his own.

From a purely tactical standpoint, it might have been a mistake to unleash his inner badass hit man. The odds of Holt telling him something were surely better when she was breathing.

Then again, she might have something to tell him after all.

BACK UPSTAIRS, Zach searched Holt's pockets until he found her keys and phone. The phone was passcode-locked. He couldn't open any of the apps or see her call history. He was sure she'd probably encrypted her files as well. Again, he didn't have the time to crack them.

But he didn't have to. He took the keys instead.

Outside the house, he pressed the button and unlocked Holt's SUV. It was big and black, with government plates. It dwarfed his little fuel-efficient sedan. Zach wondered why the bad guys always got the cool cars.

On the dashboard, he found exactly what he wanted. A built-in navigation system. Leave it to Helen to include all the bells and whistles on her ride.

Most people don't realize a GPS system keeps a record of its locations even if the owner clears the history from the onboard menu. The information is embedded deep in the machine code of the chipset that regulates the simple timekeeping and synchronization functions that enable the system to pick up seamlessly as the car moves from one satellite area and map grid to another.

Even someone as capable as Helen Holt probably wouldn't think about the data stored in the chips.

But Zach was exactly the sort of geek who did think of those things.

He took out his multitool and had the nav system open and its circuit board out in under five minutes.

It took longer to find the component for his pad that he needed in the chaos of his bag. But he did have the chip reader—it was tangled in an old set of earbuds—and he slotted it into his USB port. Then he clicked in the board.

His universal reader program could decipher everything from languages to codes to lines of software programming. It gave him the GPS coordinates of every one of Holt's destinations and plotted them on a map. Zach figured she wouldn't fly—too many cameras, too many witnesses, and even the laughable TSA security might not let her bring her guns on the plane. It made far more sense for her and Reyes to drive everywhere.

Zach recognized the Mansfield Civic Center's address. She'd been ahead of them from the start.

In fact, aside from the hotels she stayed at, there was only one place Holt had been that Zach and Cade had not.

It was a residential address in Omaha, Nebraska.

Zach wondered what all the antigovernment activists would do if they knew how much data it was possible for someone with the right clearances to gather. Someone like Zach didn't need radio implants or bar code tattoos or whatever the latest paranoid fantasy about the New World Order was. Just by living, people left a Day-Glo trail right up to the places where they kept all their secrets.

The address was in the property tax listings as belonging to a James Kilroy.

The public databases gave him Kilroy's age, driver's license photo, occupation, income and criminal history. He was about as clean as any average citizen could get. Divorced. Running a little behind on his spousal support payments and his other bills, but that was hardly unique in this economy.

It might have been a waste of time, but Zach didn't have anything better. He had to go deeper.

Using an encrypted satellite connection, Zach accessed the National Security Agency's latest version of BASKETBALL, a planet-size net used to sift through every electronic communication floating in the air for key words like "bomb," "terrorist" and "al-Qaeda." A square mile of computing power under the ground at NSA headquarters in Maryland could pluck warning signals from a trillion bits of data from intercepted cell phone calls, e-mails, faxes and text messages.

Zach gave those massive electronic brains an actual name and address. They spat back a response in seconds, almost as if saying the task was insultingly easy for them. The computer-assembled file included a précis of Kilroy's activity on the Internet, his flight patterns as a pilot, his spending habits from his bank accounts and credit cards, and a diagram of his contacts and influences in life.

It was this last chunk of data that drew Zach's attention

first. Software that analyzed human behavior had made enormous leaps and bounds in the past few years, courtesy of billions of taxpayer dollars after 9/11. It was believed that if computers could analyze and diagnose antisocial tendencies, then the authorities could step in before some kid in Modesto decided to play jihad.

The diagram the computers assembled was basically an illustrated version of Kilroy's social life over the past year. Zach didn't need a degree in psychology to see the warning signs.

In the last twelve months, Kilroy's phone calls to friends and family had stopped completely on the outgoing side and dropped to almost nothing on the incoming. His Internet usage went way up, and his spending habits indicated a nearly completely homebound existence: pizza delivery, late-night grocery runs, liquor store purchases. Kilroy had withdrawn from the world except for his job.

Zach didn't like the picture that was emerging from the cloud in his head. The words "loner," "quiet" and "kept to himself" were the greatest hits on the assassin sound track.

Zach clicked on Kilroy's itinerary as a pilot. He worked for one of the regional feeder airlines. His salary was only a little more than he'd make as the manager of a midsize chain restaurant. Zach knew times were tough in the air travel business, but this was brutal.

Then Zach's mouth went very dry as he read the list of cities where Kilroy flew.

The names leaped out at him.

All the sites of the Boogeyman's murders.

Son of a bitch. He wasn't an ex-cop like Nolan. He was a pilot.

The Boogeyman was still alive. He could easily get past any airport security. And at this very moment, the president's family was boarding the presidential jet to fly back to Washington, D.C.

Candace and her brother and her mother. The people closest to the president's heart.

THIRTY-NINE

The demons were protecting me. I had nothing to fear from the police.

—David Berkowitz, the "Son of Sam" killer

Ordinarily, even wearing his uniform, he never would have gotten within a thousand yards of the aircraft. But things just seemed to break his way.

First, one of the security checkpoints at Louis Armstrong International in New Orleans, already clogged and choked due to the presence of the two candidates, shut down completely when a TSA worker was attacked by an irate mother who didn't see why her little girl should be fondled by a male security officer during an enhanced pat-down. Many of the passengers in line sided with the woman. A riot nearly ensued. In the resulting backup, lines stretched all the way to the terminal entrance. In order to get things moving again, pilots and flight attendants were taken through without stopping for the metal detector or an X-ray scanner.

Wearing his uniform, he carried his mask and his weapon in a bag with him right past security.

He took a detour just past the concourse entrance and found a door that had been propped open. It was a pure coincidence. A maintenance worker's electronic ID tag had stopped working that morning. He was due to get a replacement, but it hadn't shown up. Tired of waiting every time he wanted to get through the door, he wedged his janitorial cart inside. It was just for a moment while he went back for more paper towels. But the Boogeyman slipped through unnoticed. A few minutes later, the cleaner came back and closed the door.

Walking with a calm and confident air, he passed luggage handlers and ground crew. Since he looked like he knew where he was going, no one thought anything of it.

He reached the perimeter patrolled by the Secret Service. The hangar that housed Air Force One and its twin, the backup presidential jet, was still on the other side of a runway, across open ground. A counterassault team walked the tarmac. More dangerous were the ones he could not see: the snipers on the roofs of the terminals who could pick off anyone who attempted to make a dash for the hangar.

It was full daylight now. He was weaker than he would have been at night. He might be able to take one or two direct hits from their guns. But they would tear him into hamburger with a barrage of ammunition. Strong as he was, this body couldn't withstand that.

So he stood quietly and waited. Patience was a virtue.

A moment later, every agent on the ground put a hand to his ear. Something was going on. As one, they all sprinted for the doors into the main terminal. He even caught a glimpse of one of the snipers running along the roofline.

His excellent hearing brought him the words from one of the agents' walkie-talkies: "Shots fired! Shots fired!"

It had nothing to do with him. Later, the news would report that a man had packed his hunting rifle, still loaded, into his luggage. A ticket agent had hoisted it up and somehow, when it came down on the luggage belt, caused it to fire.

The 30.06 bullet tore out of the Samsonite, through a particleboard counter and through the thigh of an airport police officer nearby. He pulled out his own weapon and shot back as he fell to the ground, screaming in pain.

Luckily, he missed. But the entire airport was thrown into chaos. The Secret Service was sure it was facing a full-on assault. It pulled all of its agents to the main terminal to repel any attackers.

The Boogeyman, wincing in the sunlight, strolled calmly over to the hangar.

One of the agents, in his haste to get to the shooting, had left the door open.

The Boogeyman smiled. He'd always been lucky like that.

FORTY

Air Force One, the presidential jet, is a near-mythical symbol of US power, shrouded in so much secrecy that even foreign leaders invited on board are forbidden from seeing every corner. But the aircraft just became rather less mysterious after it emerged that detailed plans of its interior and exterior had been made publicly available on the website of an American air force base.

One diagram shows the location of the president's suite, at the very front of the Boeing 747, which is known to include a medical facility, workout room, kitchen and office, as well as a bedroom. Another shows the location of oxygen tanks which could, in theory, be targeted by a terrorist sniper. The information appears to be intended for personnel involved in responding to an emergency on board.

The documents, which had not been removed from the site yesterday, add precise detail to what was already known about the president's plane: that it contains 85 telephones, 19 televisions, facilities for film screenings, flares to repel missiles and shielding to protect onboard electronics from an electromagnetic pulse. They also underline the previously publicized fact that the plane always pulls up at public events with its left side facing people and buildings—protecting the president's quarters on the right side.

—"Security Lapse Reveals Secrets of Air Force One,"
Oliver Burkemann, *The Guardian*, April 11, 2006

Colonel Geoff Martin ran through the preflight check with his copilots and navigator. Since the president wouldn't be on board this run, he wasn't technically the pilot of Air Force One today. Since he had the First Family but not the president, the jet would be called Executive Foxtrot One.

But honestly, nobody paid much attention to that. They called it Air Force One no matter who was on board.

Air Force One is, without question, the safest way to fly. A military version of the 747, the plane is inspected between every mission and given a full maintenance workup before every flight. If so much as a lightbulb is flickering, it's replaced. Fuel for the plane is put in separate, secure holding tanks. Meals on the flight are prepared in advance from food bought by anonymous Air Force stewards wearing civilian clothes. The plane includes electronic countermeasures, overpowered engines, backup fuel, electromagnetic pulse shielding and, thankfully still unknown to the public, an escape pod designed by NASA to eject the president from the plane in case of catastrophic failure. And all of this is guarded on the ground by a Counter Assault Team armed with guns so advanced their model numbers are classified.

Martin took his mission just as seriously as the men with guns. They might have been flying a jumbo passenger jet, but there was as little room for error as if they were dodging rocket fire in Afghanistan. So, no matter how tempting it might be, Martin and his crew never half-assed the checklist or any of their duties. This wasn't the 9 A.M.

commuter shuttle filled with grumpy businessmen. This was the flying White House.

Martin, like every other pilot who'd ever flown the presidential jets, started at the bottom rung of the ladder. Everyone who hoped to get on the flight deck was required to spend their first months in the unit with a chamois cloth in hand, waxing and cleaning the hull of the jets. It humbled even the most arrogant fighter jock and forced him to become familiar with every square inch of the planes.

It had taught Martin patience. He never rushed the details. He was a credit to his uniform. The president was lucky to have him in the pilot's seat.

If life were fair, he'd have spent a long time in the job before a well-earned retirement.

When the door of the lavatory in the flight deck opened, Martin was puzzled. There shouldn't have been anyone else in there.

The other members of the crew turned, just like he did. They were military, but it has to be said they were taken off guard. They were in what was supposed to be one of the most secure locations in the world.

So when the man wearing the smiley-face mask and a pilot's uniform stepped out of the toilet, they didn't react at first. It was just too bizarre. Not one of them reached for an alarm button or even said anything.

Not that it would have helped them.

But Martin deserved a better end. They all did.

FORTY-ONE

Does *everything* connect through the Son of Sam interface? Recall that in 1974 one of Manson's least repentant disciples, Lynette "Squeaky" Fromme, tried to do away with President Gerald Ford. If she'd pulled it off, the presidency would have fallen to none other than Nelson Rockefeller, appointed vice-president by Ford—and whose name is synonymous with the Insider corporate capitalist communist Illuminati occult conspiracy. And Ford himself is a Freemason who sat on the Warren Commission, which covered up the death of one president.

—Jonathan Vankin and John Whalen, *The 80 Greatest Conspiracies of All Time*

Driving one-handed, Zach pulled out his phone to call Cade. He had to tell him. His fingers grasped the phone just as it buzzed with the receipt of a message. He glanced away from the road and checked the screen.

It was from Cade.

But then it hit him, almost as hard as the knowledge about Kilroy. What was missing from his earlier farewell with Cade. Cade was empty-handed. But Cade always took a trophy. Always.

Unless he didn't really believe that Nolan was the

Boogeyman. Unless he knew that his prey was still out there.

Cade had sent him two files, both tagged as urgent. The smaller one, a voice memo, was marked "Listen to This First."

He put the phone to his ear.

"By now you've dealt with Holt," Cade said. "I apologize for acting without you and misleading you. But you'll understand, even if you do not approve, once I tell you what I believe."

Zach listened. He felt rage well up in him, both from Cade's deception and his ability to predict Zach's behavior so perfectly. It was a stark reminder that Cade knew him better than he knew Cade. More insulting was the added realization that Cade knew him better than he knew himself.

Cade explained himself in clipped tones. His even, calm voice did nothing to quell the rising sense of panic Zach felt. He checked his watch, wondered if he could possibly hit the brakes on everything, send Cade's plans to a screeching halt. But it was already too late. It was already happening.

"Believe me when I say this is the only way, Zach. But if it's going to work, I need your help."

Cade outlined what he wanted Zach to do. Zach fumed. He was boxed in. Even if he called the president right now, there was no alternative. He almost hung up the phone. But he forced himself to listen to the end.

"Before you carry any of this out, however, you have a decision to make. Play the video file. You'll understand what I mean."

There was an uncharacteristic pause.

"It's been good working with you," Cade said. Then the message ended.

Zach wondered if Cade was simply emulating the awkward goodbye. Or if he genuinely grappled with his feelings. Either way, Zach had to watch the video to know what to do next. He hit his brakes, causing the drivers behind him to lean on their horns in protest, and skidded to the side of the highway. He suspected this was going to require his full attention.

He tapped the icon for the video. A dark and shaky picture came up on the screen; it looked like a handheld camera in the woods. Then he recognized the voice.

It was Megan Roark.

Zach didn't need to see any more. He knew what the video would show, why Cade wanted him to see it.

But he watched the whole thing anyway. Just to be sure.

August 28, 1872
The White House, Washington, D.C.

After sunset, Cade rose from the coffin on the dirt floor of the White House basement and went to the president's library for his latest set of instructions.

He walked freely through the White House despite the soil on his suit and his unnatural pallor. Over the past few years, Cade had become the White House's ghost. He was seen only at night, occasionally wandering the halls, sometimes on the grounds. Attempts to question the president about him were met with Grant's trademark silence. In that era, that was enough for the staff—and even Grant's family—to know that the topic was not to be broached again.

Washington was quiet. In the summer, the city was a sweat lodge and the population dropped by half as anyone who could afford it abandoned their homes for cooler temperatures.

The First Lady was no exception. Grant's wife, Julia, was away, visiting relatives back in Missouri (and no doubt savoring, at least a little, their discomfort as they were forced to admit that the low-ranking Army reject she'd married had made something of himself).

Cade entered the library and found the president slumped behind his desk.

Grant was drunk.

Cade knew, on some level, this never would have happened if the First Lady or his family were there. Grant had not taken a drink—not even wine, which was served at every meal in the White House—since becoming president.

Grant's eyes were closed. He stank of whiskey. He leaned back so far in his chair that he was almost parallel with the floor.

"Mr. President?"

Grant sat up without any hesitation or clumsiness, his eyes wide open and awake. The reflexes of a drunk and a soldier, combined; the ability to simulate sobriety at a moment's notice. Grant looked at him, seemed to take a moment to place him. Whatever memory came to him left a sour look on his face.

"There are some men who have to die," he said, no preamble. "Quite a few of them, in fact."

He picked up a sheet of paper. Cade crossed the room and took it.

It was a long list.

"You can remember their names?"

Cade nodded.

The president took the paper back, drew a match from his pocket and flicked it to life, then touched it to the paper. He set it in his ashtray to burn as he used the match to light another of his endless supply of cigars.

"You waiting for something?" he asked when he looked up and saw Cade still standing there.

"Yes," Cade said. "Some of those names—they include whole families. Prominent families."

"Yes," Grant said. "Not all humans side with the human race. You'd do well to remember that."

"Women. Sons. Daughters."

"Old enough to know what they've done." Grant's eyes narrowed and glinted with a sudden meanness Cade had never seen in the president before. "You turning parlor soldier on me, Cade?"

"I simply want to know if it's necessary."

There was a brief flare of anger in the president's eyes. Then it subsided and he gave Cade his typical enigmatic smile—it appeared for a fraction of a second as a quirk of the mouth before vanishing. "Because the general is in his cups this evening, you mean."

"My duty is to protect you first."

"Even from myself."

Cade didn't have to reply to that.

Grant opened a drawer of his desk and took out a near-empty bottle. He poured the last of the liquor into a cup and then stood.

"Come with me," he said. "Air's a bit thick in here."

They walked out into the night, which was only cooler than the interior of the White House by a few degrees. The sky was clear. Grant had horses grazing on the South Lawn. It was a moment of absurd peacefulness.

Grant puffed on his cigar for several minutes before he spoke again.

"Why would you question the chance to spill blood?" he asked Cade.

A remnant of pride welled up at the implication. "I am not an animal, sir."

"Of course you are. You're worse than an animal. Because you can think. You know what you are doing. And you do it anyway."

"I have no choice."

"There's always a choice. And like it or not, you choose to survive. You choose to kill. Because the alternatives are worse. I've thought long and hard about every name on that list. Which may explain why I've decided to revisit old habits tonight."

"Who are they?"

"They are the members of a conspiracy dedicated to the end of the United States. They've been active since before the war. Possibly much longer. They had a hand in the assassination of the president, of that I'm certain." Grant may have held the title himself, but in his own speech, only Lincoln was *the* president. "They helped push us into the war. They may have done much worse. But I don't want to see what else they can do. This is my attempt to wipe them out completely. I know that it will mean many deaths. I know a few of them—perhaps more than a few—might not deserve to pay the full price for their actions. But I cannot take the chance that they will carry on. This conspiracy has hidden in the shadows too long already. It cannot survive. And neither can anyone connected to it. I've taken each name onto my conscience. It's my weight to bear."

"If you're wrong, you're asking me to bear the weight as well."

Grant drained his whiskey. "Do you think guilt changes anything?"

"You know my sin."

"Everyone sins, Cade."

"Not like I have," Cade said, surprising himself with his sudden vehemence. "Do you have any idea what it's like to kill your friends? To batten and grow fat on their blood?"

Grant gave him the almost-smile again. "Thousands of them. I killed more men than you ever have. Possibly even more than you ever will, no matter how long you live. I sent boys to die, and worse, I sent them to kill and become killers. And I was celebrated for it. I became a hero. I was given this country's highest honors for that river of blood. You have a long way to go before you can equal the number of bodies I've put in churchyards, Cade."

Cade felt a stirring of something he thought dead inside himself. He felt shame.

"I apologize, Mr. President," he said.

"I don't want your apology. I want you to understand. I take no pride in the deaths I've caused. It was necessary. I did it because I believed the world that would come after the war would be better than the one before. And I hoped, in so doing, I would prevent more death."

"I understand."

"No, I don't think you do," Grant said, still puffing on his foul-smelling cigar. "I am telling you that in this world, we have little control over the circumstances that shape us. We do what we can with what we have. I am telling you that for whatever reason, you and I were given the responsibility and duty of killing to protect others. So I am going to tell you how I decided I must deal with that."

He put the cigar under his boot and then looked directly into Cade's eyes. The drunk was gone; the soldier remained. "When they come and the guns are thundering and the men are falling all around you, there is only one way you will stop it. You are going to have to kill. So you be the best goddamned killer there is."

Cade nodded. Grant gave him that half-smile again.

"Well, then. Get to work," he said.

And Cade disappeared into the night.

FORTY-TWO

Sometimes I feel like a vampire.

—Ted Bundy

Cade woke from a dream of blood. Warm, red rivers of it, pulsing from living wounds into his throat, down into his guts, filling him to the ends of each vessel and nerve.

He shook himself violently. The coffin shifted around him in response.

For a moment, he was consumed by self-loathing. He had not felt such hatred since he'd first woken in a cell one hundred forty-five years earlier with the same realization that he'd fed on a human. Only this time, he had the special sting of knowing he'd discarded all those years of resolve and made them a joke.

Cade did not believe evil could ever be mitigated by good. They were simply incomparable. Any attempt to place them on the same scale was an idiot fumbling to reconcile what could only be justified by God. The sins of a man stretched out from their moment of commission into past and future, and impaled their owner on the spit of eternity. That was the belief of the church he'd been raised in; that was also what hard-earned experience had taught him after he'd stopped being human.

For a split second, he indulged himself in despair. Why did he fight his own nature so hard? Why not simply be what he was and bury himself snout-deep in the blood and entrails of his prey? There was no one to judge him for it. At least, no one who would judge him any more harshly. No president would begrudge him a few meals as long as he fed only on the nation's enemies.

Perhaps it was time to give up the charade and simply be the monster.

It was tempting. But it also stank of cowardice and arrogance, both at the same time.

The world had not changed. Cade was fallen and evil, but he couldn't end himself. Not until he'd ended everything like himself first. Even if he lost, the fight was the only thing that gave the scattered chaos of blood and ruin any meaning. Even if he lost, the ideal was still worth fighting for.

Cade was not human. He was a monster. Nothing would ever change that.

But it didn't mean he could ever stop trying.

He thought of Grant, reclaiming sobriety a day or so after his only bender in the White House. "Just because you slip and fall in the mud doesn't mean you have to live with the swine," he'd told Cade.

Enough, he told himself. You've had your moment of pity.

Now get up. It's time to go to work.

FORTY-THREE

The art of war is simple enough. Find out where your enemy is. Get at him as soon as you can. Strike him as hard as you can, and keep moving on.

—Ulysses S. Grant

Cade entered the main body of the plane through the emergency access panel in the floor of the crew cabin. As he expected, Butler was there. He was scheduled to rotate to another position in fifteen minutes.

"Son of a bitch," Butler said, turning at the sudden sight of Cade. His eyes went wide with recognition and relief at the same instant. "Cade. What are you—"

Cade hit him. Butler crumpled into a heap. He believed he had a fairly good estimate of the man's durability. But he wasn't an anesthesiologist and his precision was less than surgical. It was possible that Butler would never wake up. Cade didn't have much experience with less-than-lethal force.

Still, the Secret Service agent seemed to be breathing well when Cade stuffed him into the storage closet.

If Cade failed, it wouldn't matter. Everyone on board would die anyway.

CADE RISKED FORCING the door to the flight deck. It snapped easily, but the sound could have alerted someone even with the noise of the engines.

He braced himself and pushed inside. He had to be sure.

Sunlight streamed through the windshields. Cade recoiled as if struck, feeling his face and hands burn. Above the clouds, the sky was achingly blue and bright. He forced himself to withstand the glare as he checked each body.

All dead. The flight crew were still strapped in their chairs, heads twisted nearly 180 degrees on their necks. The killer had not wasted any time.

Cade knew he never had a chance to save them. Even if he'd been in the cockpit, the daylight would have left him helpless. The only chance would have been to spread a warning before the flight, and he had decided against that from the start.

He closed the door.

He didn't fool himself. Cade knew he'd taken a risk and these men had died for it. Their lives were on his conscience.

They had plenty of company there.

Then the lights went out.

He felt feverish and weak. He wished he had more time to recover from the sudden, dazzling sunlight. He hoped the sun would weaken his prey as well. Too many people were dead already. But again, he wasn't about to fool himself.

He was headed into a fight where the odds were against him.

It was time for the main event.

Oh, it was all so perfect.

The Boogeyman felt as close as he could come to true joy. So many warm bodies all trapped in a giant steel container with him. It was his own little canned game preserve.

He knew he should have taken more time with them, but he really was anxious to get rid of the Secret Service so he could start on the First Family. The jet's oversized fuel tanks would keep them in the air for seventeen hours. He wanted to use as much of that time as possible on the people closest to the president.

He intended to land the plane himself and leave the bodies for everyone to see. He wanted Cade to know just how badly he'd failed. He wanted to tear out the president's heart without laying a hand on him.

But first things first. Mood lighting.

He found the control panel for the lights on the bulkhead by the crew compartment. He turned them off, then smashed the panel with his fist.

The plane plunged into darkness.

Much better.

In the guest section just behind the staff area, Candace flipped through pages on her iPad, not seeing them at all. All she could focus on was the clock at the top of the screen. She was strung tight enough by the waiting. Her little brother certainly didn't help.

One of Robbie's action figures landed on her screen. Again.

"Robbie, for God's sake, stop throwing your dolls around." She flung it back to him on the couch across the cabin from her.

"It's Rob," he said, puffing his small chest up as much as he could. "And it's not a doll. It's an action figure. And I'll do what I want with it." He went back to watching one of his favorite movies on the huge flat-panel display. She looked up just in time to catch a particularly gruesome disembowelment.

Candace drew a deep breath through her nose and exhaled slowly. It wasn't his fault, she reminded herself. Robbie was born just after her father had been elected to the Senate. Their mother had proudly campaigned until a doctor put her on bed rest; they had lost other pregnancies, and this was their last chance. He came out healthy and perfect. And from the time he'd been six weeks old, he'd been shuttled between D.C. and Illinois. He had more friends on the flight crews than he did at any school. His whole life was spent competing with voters for their parents' attention.

He didn't get any of the time Candace had, before politics became all-consuming, when she and her father would spend a whole afternoon making pizza by hand and then watching old movies. She could still remember going to the mall with her father to buy school clothes without anyone bothering them or even recognizing him.

Robbie didn't get any of that. His life was harder. That had to affect him.

The doll hit her screen again, this time leaving a deep gouge.

When she looked up, he was flipping her off with both hands.

Of course, it was also possible he was just a little shit.

"Robbie . . ." she said.

"I told you: it's Rob," he yelled back.

Their mother, Rachel, poked her head into the cabin from the press area. It was empty this flight, which was why she was doing a phone interview with *People* magazine there. "Honestly, Candace," she said. "You're supposed to be the grown-up."

Candace came very close to saying, *But he started it.*

Then the lights went out.

HE FOUND THE Air Force stewards while they were busy preparing lunch. The two staffers looked annoyed at the loss of light. When they heard him at the threshold of the galley, one turned, already complaining.

"Hey, what the hell is going—"

The words died in the steward's mouth when he saw the Boogeyman. The steward's face went slack and he made little choking noises as he tried to work up the breath to scream. But he couldn't. Horror had robbed him of his voice. He was paralyzed and mute.

Of all the expressions he'd seen displayed by people at their moment of death—rage, fear, grief, agony, resignation—this one was his absolute favorite. It was so perfect, so quintessentially human.

He thrust his blade forward and impaled the steward through his chest, puncturing his lung, robbing him of the ability to speak even if he'd been able to work up the courage. Only then did the other cook turn and see what had happened. She drew a breath to shriek, but he was too fast. He withdrew his blade and stabbed her through the lung as well.

Both were down and bleeding. But not dead yet. He knew he should get moving to the back of the plane.

Still, they were here in the kitchen. And there were so many lovely knives in here: top-of-the-line German steel, all gleaming and surgically sharp.

He could afford to linger for a few minutes, he decided.

After all, who was going to stop him?

"ROBBIE, GET IN the office. Now."

"But—"

"Candace, what's going on?"

Her mother looked annoyed by the failure of the lights, but not scared. She couldn't understand her daughter's urgency.

Latham and Thomason entered the cabin to check on them.

"What's happening?" the First Lady asked.

"Probably just a fuse, ma'am," Latham said. "The plane's fine. We'll get it dealt with."

"The phone went dead as well."

"It's not a fuse," Candace said.

"Ms. Curtis, I know we've all had a very harrowing time," Thomason said. "But that threat is over. We saw it ourselves."

Robbie, of course, picked up on only one word. "Threat? What threat? Are there terrorists?" He sounded way too hopeful.

"Robbie. Mom. Please. Just get in the security office." To the agents, she said, "We need to lock them down."

Another safety feature on board the presidential jet that was kept from the general public: the Secret Service's onboard office could lock itself into a panic room: soundproof, bulletproof and with its own dedicated air supply.

Candace didn't think it would keep the Boogeyman out for long. But it was better than nothing.

"I really don't think there's anything to worry about—" Latham began.

Then they heard a loud crash from the front of the plane.

"You don't understand," Candace said. "He's not dead. He's here."

They were all quiet for a moment. Latham and Thomason looked at each other, then drew their guns.

"Maybe it wouldn't be a bad idea to get inside now, ma'am," Latham said.

THE BOOGEYMAN was a little disappointed in the filleting knife. He'd just managed to strip the skin from the muscle of the female steward and it was already snagging.

He might as well have used a pizza cutter. That at least had been fun as he rolled it over the other steward, cutting triangle-shaped sections from the man's pectorals and abdomen.

Then something hit him. Hard.

There was no warning. None of his usual dry, arrogant humor. He simply attacked the Boogeyman, flying through the cabin and tackling him, slamming him hard into the galley's cupboards.

The executive china and Tiffany stemware shattered around them both in a rain of gold-trimmed porcelain and glass. The Boogeyman was surprised for one split second and then simply enraged.

Cade.

THOMASON PULLED THE First Lady into the secure room while Latham went down the corridor.

"Candace, let's go," Thomason said.

But Robbie lingered in the cabin, looking after Latham.

Candace knew Robbie had a serious man-crush on Agent Latham. Latham was often assigned to Robbie, and they'd grown close. Thomason often commented that this was because they had about the same level of maturity. Latham was always willing to buy the kid ice cream—his mother's health food kick had removed it from the menu in the White House—or play a few mind-numbingly violent video games. To Robbie, Latham was the best pal an eleven-year-old boy could have: cool, funny and packing heat.

Robbie took a few steps farther away from them.

"Robbie, honey, please, get in here," their mother called. She would have grabbed him herself, but Thomason had a firm grip on her arm; he wasn't about to let her leave a safe location.

"Robbie," Candace said. "Come on. We've got to lock up. Now."

He ignored her.

"Candace . . ." Thomason warned. He had his hand on the door, ready to slam and lock it. Candace knew what would happen. In a moment, he was going to close that door whether they were inside or not.

"Rob," she said, using the name her brother preferred. "He'd want you to be safe."

Robbie turned back to her, doing his best to be stoic. He took two steps and was almost over the threshold.

Then they heard the scream.

Candace could practically see the idea form in Robbie's head as he had it.

He hesitated.

"Robbie, no, don't—"

Too late. He was already off and running after Latham.

Their mother screamed. Thomason yanked her back inside. "Candace, get your ass back here!" he yelled. Her mother, she saw, was kicking and scratching him, trying to get after her son.

"I'll get him!" she yelled. "Shut the damn door!"

She heard the door click behind her. No going back now.

CADE DIDN'T WASTE ANY TIME. This was going to be the end. One way or another.

He struck first and didn't let up. He didn't know if the Boogeyman was now stronger than him or faster. He had to press his advantage while he could.

In the wreckage of the galley, rolling among the broken china, Cade found the knives and other kitchen implements on the floor. The Boogeyman had laid a selection of them out, one by one, as if on a surgeon's tray.

Cade wasn't picky. He'd use them all. He grabbed the first one, a long-bladed butcher's knife, and slammed it through the Boogeyman's shoulder. He picked up a thin-bladed fish knife and pounded it like a nail through the Boogeyman's hand. As fast as he could grab them, he picked them up and introduced them to whatever part of the Boogeyman was closest.

He was about to bring down a meat cleaver on the bright yellow mask when the Boogeyman shook him off.

Cade rolled back and gained his feet again.

The Boogeyman was already standing. It slowly, deliberately reached with its right hand and grabbed the handle of the butcher knife, then yanked it out.

The mask's smile seemed mocking now. *That the best you can do?* it seemed to say to Cade.

Cade launched himself again. The butcher knife slashed faster than he thought possible. His biceps was laid open all the way to the bone, and the Boogeyman spun easily out of the way.

Cade slid to a stop. They faced each other again, having changed places.

At the very least, Cade thought, now I know who's stronger in the day.

LATHAM AND THE THREE other agents in the main cabin approached the galley carefully, through the conference room. They heard the slamming and clattering, but no voices. It was an eerie quiet compared to the violence of breaking glass and wood.

Latham nearly lost his footing as the plane hit an air pocket. He wondered what the pilots were doing up front. And where were the stewards? The number of alternatives where this all ended happily were dropping to zero, and he didn't like it.

Suddenly, the wall nearest them cracked and split. Cade's head and shoulders were forced through the paneling, a pair of bloodied hands around his neck.

Ah hell, Latham thought, more resigned than anything else. I'm going to die.

Cade was pinned halfway through the wall, face battered and bloodied. Through the hole his body had made, they could see a man in a pilot's uniform with the now-familiar yellow-and-black smile above his necktie.

The Boogeyman reached up and tore a piece of oak trim from the wall. He lifted it, ready to plunge it into Cade's chest.

Latham remembered the gun in his hand. He fired.

CONTRARY TO WHAT most people believe, a bullet fired on a plane will not result in an explosive loss of cabin pressure if it tears through the skin of the aircraft.

Latham had learned this during his "Flying Armed" class for law-enforcement officers. The worst that could happen, he was told, is that your bullet hits a hydraulic line on its way out. Otherwise, all it does is make a hole.

Still, Latham wasn't anxious to find out his instructors were wrong. He aimed for the Boogeyman's body mass and tried to keep his grouping tight.

It did nothing.

Despite another myth created by movies and TV, gunshots didn't carry enough force to throw a human being back like they were being flung from a catapult. The damage they did was inside the body.

And the Boogeyman—whoever or whatever he was—didn't seem to mind having .357 slugs inside him. All it did was shake him up a little.

He raised the makeshift wooden stake above Cade's chest again.

The other Secret Service agents were putting rounds into the Boogeyman as well. At best they were annoying him. But Latham could see they were about to lose their one chance of saving the First Family when that stake came down.

He aimed carefully. He was no sharpshooter. Even at close range, this was going to be tricky.

Latham fired.

His slug tore through the Boogeyman's upraised wrist,

shattering it. The wooden stake fell from his hand as his fingers went dead.

Then they heard the first sound from the Boogeyman. He howled.

THE BOOGEYMAN WAS SO CLOSE. The grin on his face was almost as wide as the one on his mask. He was finally going to kill Cade.

He'd have to remember to thank Helen Holt before he murdered her, too.

Then there was a slap against his wrist and the piece of wood dropped from his hand and he didn't understand why his fingers wouldn't grab it again.

He looked at the bullet hole and understood. The wound was closing already, but the damage was done.

He let loose a primal cry of frustration and rage. Then his eyes locked onto the agent who had robbed him of his kill.

Oh, he was going to make that fucker pay.

He was so distracted by his fury that he didn't realize Cade had gotten his hands up again. His head snapped back as Cade put a palm strike into the underside of his jaw.

CADE REGAINED HIS FEET. This wasn't going as planned. There was a very real chance the Boogeyman would be able to kill him.

Ours is but to do and die, he reminded himself.

He prepared to hurl himself at the Boogeyman again,

but the Christ-damned thing kept recovering faster than he did. His punch should have snapped its spine, torn its head nearly from its shoulders.

Instead, the still-screeching Boogeyman tackled him and took him through the wall again in a full-body tackle.

He needed his ace in the hole. Where was she? Where was—

"CANDACE!" LATHAM SAID. "Get him the hell out of here!"

Latham had turned at a small sound. He was amazed he'd heard it, but then again, he'd been with the kid for almost three years now, watching his every move, watching him grow up.

So he knew what it sounded like when Robbie Curtis was scared.

He'd looked over his shoulder and seen Robbie crouched in the corner, behind one of the seats. Then he saw Candace trying in vain to pry him out of his hiding spot.

Cade and the Boogeyman tore through the remains of the wall. They collided with two of the other agents. One fell to the floor, screaming, while the other was knocked out cold and strung painfully over two of the seats.

That left Latham and one other agent. They exchanged a quick glance. Latham went for Robbie and Candace. The other agent went to help Cade.

Latham crouched down and got between Candace and her brother. "Hey, buddy, come on. Go with your sister. Get back in the safe room. We've practiced this before, man."

"No," Robbie screamed, reduced by tears and fear to a little kid again, all his straining to be tough erased in a moment. "David, you come, too! You come with us! Right now!"

Ah, God love this kid, Latham thought.

"This is my job, buddy," he said, grabbing the boy and scooping him out of the corner and into his sister's arms. "Keeping you safe."

"Latham," Candace said as she took him. "You could—"

"Don't argue," he snapped at her. "Get him back and get him safe."

He turned and went back toward the staff offices, where the Boogeyman's momentum had carried Cade.

He took one look over his shoulder again to see that they were on their way to the back of the plane.

Robbie had one arm outstretched as his sister hauled him bodily down the aisle, screaming Latham's name. "David!"

It almost broke Latham's heart.

And then the Boogeyman tore it from his chest.

THE BOOGEYMAN WAS GOING to win this time. He knew it.

Unable to hold a weapon in one hand, he pummeled Cade down with his fists, prepared to reduce him to nothing more than a blood pudding quivering on the floor if that's what it took.

But, again, one of the humans kept putting more bullets into him.

By sheer luck, one of the rounds tore out his right eye,

turning that side of the plane into a wet blackness. It would take hours, even with his physiology, to grow a new one.

Clearly, he'd have to deal with this.

He spun and faced the Secret Service agent. The man, a pasty blond, managed to stand his ground and keep firing.

Unfortunately, he didn't realize his clip was almost empty.

His pistol froze up at the same time Cade tried to attack from behind again. The Boogeyman was smarter this time. He yanked up on a window shade and brilliant sunlight streamed into the plane. It hit Cade in the face, blinding and burning him. The Boogeyman took two steps across the compartment and punched a hole right through the agent's face.

It was only one more step from there to the other one, the one who'd robbed him of his earlier victory over Cade. That one was stupidly looking the wrong way. Without breaking stride, he pointed his left hand like a knife and plunged it through the back of the man's rib cage. His fingers hooked and he yanked, bringing as much of the agent's insides out into the light as he could.

CADE WAS FURIOUS with himself. He was too slow, too weak, to do anything to save the agents. One of his eyes was swollen closed from the burns and the beating. He felt bones shift in his chest.

He was barely to his knees when the Boogeyman dispatched Latham.

The Boogeyman turned and faced Cade. He held up the bloody innards like a trophy. The mask's smile seemed to ooze smugness and victory.

Cade's fangs jutted from his mouth, like a parody of a smile in return.

This time, the Boogeyman was going to beg for death.

CANDACE BEGGED. She pounded on the door. She threatened. She pleaded. Then she begged some more.

She'd dragged Robbie, kicking and screaming, away from the fight. He saw Latham's chest explode. He knew his friend was dead. He kept trying to go back.

Finally, Candace got him to the secure section of the plane.

But Thomason would not open up. Not for anyone.

It was protocol. So a terrorist or assassin could not use some family members of the president as hostages or bargaining chips to get at the others.

At first, all Candace heard was the sound of her mother shouting at Thomason. Then she began hitting him. Hard. "Those are my children!" she screamed. "My children!" Candace then heard Thomason shout an obscenity and heard her mother spit.

Good for you, Mom, she thought. Bite him again.

But Thomason was trained for this. There was a brief struggle, a sharp sound of surprise from the First Lady, and then her voice quieted to an indistinct murmur. Candace had always suspected the agents carried drugs to sedate them if they grew uncooperative. Now she knew.

"Thomason," she said, her mouth right up to the seam in the door. "My brother is out here. He's eleven. *Eleven.*"

A long pause.

"I'm sorry, Ms. Curtis. I really am," Thomason said. His voice sounded like something dredged from the bottom of the ocean floor.

He had his job to do.

So did she.

She hugged Robbie tight to her. He must have been scared. He didn't pull away.

Candace looked her brother in the eye. "Robbie. I need to do something. I never meant for you to be out here with me. But now I need your help. I need you to do exactly what I tell you. Can you do that?"

Robbie nodded. His chin trembled a little. But then his mouth set and he looked as fierce as possible for someone too young to shave.

"Let's fuck his shit up," he said.

THEY MET WITH ALL the grace of a car crash.

Cade unleashed a blindingly fast series of punches. The Boogeyman took them all. Then he grabbed Cade and began pushing him, slowly, inexorably, back into the beam of sunlight.

Cade pushed back. But he was already weaker. If he had not taken fresh human blood recently, he never would have lasted this long. The sunlight was the glare of a simple fact, an inarguable truth: he was not made to exist in the day.

He felt the sun on his back. His knees buckled. The

sunlight hit his neck and the flesh began to blister and crack. His power washed out of him like water down a drain.

Then something hit the Boogeyman's mask. Behind the holes, Cade saw one remaining eye blink in confusion.

Another hit. This time Cade saw it land on the floor.

A doll. No, an action figure.

The Boogeyman turned.

Candace and Robbie stood there. He had one more toy in his hand, arm cocked back in an absurd parody of a threat.

"Come on, fucker," she screamed. "Or are you afraid of us?"

Robbie threw the last toy at him. Then they turned and ran for the back of the plane.

The Boogeyman gave Cade a final, contemptuous shove into the window—to Cade it felt like his face was forced into a frying pan—and walked after her.

Cade hit the floor, mercifully out of the sunlight.

Stupid of the Boogeyman to leave without finishing him. But Cade had counted on that. It had taken longer than he thought, but he knew the Boogeyman could not resist the lure of the president's daughter, of a living, breathing and vital young woman. It was why the Boogeyman came on board the plane and not after the president. It was in the creature's nature. It abhorred life. It had to chase the girl.

The boy wasn't part of the plan, however. But no plan survives contact with the enemy. He could save them both.

All Cade had to do was find the strength to stand up.

THE BOOGEYMAN BEGAN walking after the president's children. Then he stopped and reconsidered. No, he decided. This was not right.

He walked back toward the conference area. Then he went past Cade, facedown on the floor. He picked up a meat cleaver from the ruined galley.

Much better, he thought, and turned and went after Candace again.

He would show her. He quivered with the thought of snuffing that juicy wet young life.

As for the boy—well, why not? He'd meant to get to him sooner or later anyway.

He didn't know where they expected to run. But he had to admit it: he loved a good chase.

THEY GOT THE BOOGEYMAN'S ATTENTION. Candace immediately wished she hadn't.

They ran to the place Cade had told her about. But she didn't see it.

She kept looking at the carpet below her feet. Where was it?

"Candace!" Robbie said.

She looked up. The Boogeyman strode toward her, confident, red muck around one eye of the mask, unhurried and unimpressed. In one hand he carried a meat cleaver.

But that wasn't what Robbie was pointing at. He was pointing at the floor a couple of feet back.

Candace realized what had happened. She'd overshot

the access panel. She had to go back a couple feet to open it. Back toward him.

They scrambled. She struggled with the latch. She thought she could feel his footsteps behind her. The skin on her neck crawled, waiting for the touch of his bloody fingers, for the cold metal to dig into her skull.

And then the hatch was open. She threw Robbie in first. Then she slid down into the underbelly of the plane.

The panel wouldn't lock. She didn't waste time trying. She ran as best she could through the cramped space between the cargo hold and the fuel tanks, pushing Robbie ahead of her.

She heard the panel open, heard him actually yank it from its hinges and then drop down into the hold after her.

But she didn't look back. She didn't have time. She could hear his footsteps on the metal floor.

Robbie did too. He looked at her. "What are we going to do?" he said.

CADE WOKE WITH A START. He didn't know how long he'd been out. His senses failed him in the daytime and the sturdy watch Dunn had given him had finally stopped ticking.

The plane was still in the air. Exactly that much was still going to plan. But he had to get up.

He realized he was facedown, very near a pool of the Secret Service agents' blood. It would be so easy to simply lap up a little. Just a little, to do this one job—

No, a stronger voice inside him said. Get up.

He felt the cross burn at the base of his throat. Cade slowly levered himself upward, which seemed to take about as much time as the construction of the Empire State Building.

But he got to his feet.

Now do your goddamned job, he told himself.

THE ESCAPE POD WAS RIGHT where Candace expected to find it. It sat behind the rear auxiliary fuel tank, with the rest of the space given over to cargo and supplies.

The pod was built of high-tensile-strength titanium with reinforced armor plate. Like a space capsule, it would deploy its own chute after ejection to carry the president down to a gentle landing. Despite its heavy shielding, it could float in case of an ocean splashdown. It had freeze-dried food and its own water supply. The existence of the pod was kept from all but the Air Force One crew and the president's immediate staff and family. It was considered the last resort in case an enterprising terrorist managed to put a shoulder-fired missile into one of the jet's engines.

Her half-remembered training session on board Air Force One came flooding back to her, along with relief. Once inside, slamming the door activated the plane's hidden rear door and caused the pod to slide into the air like a bomb being dropped.

She pulled Robbie along with her, practically dragging him by one arm.

The Boogeyman's footsteps echoed behind them. He walked at a leisurely pace. As if they had nowhere to go.

But they did. There was, unfortunately, only room for one inside.

She opened the pod's door.

CADE STOPPED. The Boogeyman had opened all the shades on every window in the back of the plane. Sunlight lanced across the cabin, falling in perfect beams on the carpet. He would have to run a gauntlet of daylight to get to the access panel.

Oh, you sneaky bastard, Cade thought.

He took a few steps back to gain momentum and then ran.

His legs went limp underneath him as soon as he hit the first sunbeam. He landed facedown in the carpet again.

The access panel was still a dozen feet away. It might as well have been a mile.

THE BOOGEYMAN looked at the escape pod. He saw the inviting open door.

Then he turned, scanned the darkness, and found Candace and Robbie with almost no effort whatsoever.

They were wedged to one side of the plane, hiding in the cargo netting that held a small army's worth of survival gear. Candace's arms were wrapped around her brother. His nerve had finally failed him. His face was buried in her neck. She could feel him shaking.

The Boogeyman pointed at the escape pod and wagged a finger at her. Naughty, naughty. Then he shook his head with exaggerated emphasis, causing the mask to wobble back and forth. No, no. Not going to fall for that one, he was telling her.

He took a step toward her. The blade didn't gleam. There wasn't enough light. But it was there, and she could see its dark shadow in his left hand.

He took another step. He seemed to be enjoying her fear as she crammed herself even further back against the plane's hull. There was no place else to run. She was out of room and out of options.

This wasn't how it was supposed to end, she thought.

He was right at the netting now. He very gently, almost fussily, began to pick the straps loose from their hooks. It wasn't easy with one hand mangled and the other holding the cleaver. But he managed.

Candace was shaking harder than she ever had in her life. Robbie whimpered. She wanted to close her eyes, too, but couldn't force herself to look away from the Boogeyman's bloody hand plucking at the hooks.

She couldn't take it anymore.

"Any time now would be good, Cade!" she screamed.

The Boogeyman turned.

Nothing.

He shook his head again and wagged his finger. Naughty, naughty. Then he went back to work on the straps.

Then Cade slammed into him and smashed him viciously into the metal framework of the plane.

THERE WAS NO SUNLIGHT in the hold. Cade felt almost alive again. He tore at the Boogeyman's body with clawed fingers, taking off chunks of flesh, carving it up as it had so many others.

He'd crawled the last few feet to the access panel and then collapsed through the opening. It had taken him several moments to regain his strength once he was out of the light. He had heard Candace shout, but he took another few seconds. He needed them badly. She was still breathing, after all.

The Boogeyman was screaming in full voice now. Music to Cade's ears.

But they were still not evenly matched. With dizzying speed, it brought the cleaver up with its left hand and sunk it into Cade's neck. Cade clamped down on the blade as best he could to keep it from digging deeper and separating his head from his body.

The Boogeyman shoved him and they ended up against the escape pod, Cade pinned by the Boogeyman to the side of the craft.

The Boogeyman still had the handle of the cleaver in one hand and was pushing with all his might. Cade had to use both hands just to keep it from cutting any deeper.

"Anytime now would be good, Candace!" he shouted.

She was trying. Robbie would not let go.

She tried not to get angry. He clung to her with terror and out of some misguided effort at protection. He kept screaming: "No, Candace, no, no, no, no, you stay here! Stay here!"

She had to shove him. Hard. He looked at her as if she'd stabbed him in the heart.

But she couldn't care about that now. She staggered forward from her hiding spot. She swung a leg out as far as she could.

The toe of Candace's shoe connected with the escape pod's door. It slammed shut. A red light began to flash and a deafening siren wailed. She danced back to the cargo netting and hung on for dear life.

The Boogeyman looked over and only at the last second realized what was happening and lunged away from Cade. Cade kept his grip on the Boogeyman's arm.

Then the back of the plane opened and dropped the pod—and both Cade and the Boogeyman—out into the empty air at 37,000 feet.

IT HURT. It hurt worse than he imagined possible. The wind screaming over his skin cooled him not at all as the sun burned Cade and he tumbled through the air. He felt it on his bones.

But he did not let the Boogeyman go. The cleaver had come unstuck and flown away. He was dimly aware of the Boogeyman trying to dig into the exposed muscle of his wound.

The Boogeyman's mask came off in the wind. There was no shock of recognition for Cade. The face was like hundreds, like thousands, he'd seen in crowds gathered everywhere the president went. It was completely ordinary. It could have been anyone.

The Boogeyman thrashed and struggled and screamed.

But Cade would not release him. Even as the sunlight and windburn closed his other eye, Cade pointed his body like a high diver and aimed them both at the ground.

CANDACE HEARD THE KICKING from the closet as soon as she struggled through the access panel. The plane was still wobbling from the sudden departure of the escape pod. She had to crawl over to the door before struggling to her feet.

It popped open immediately when she pulled on the handle and Butler came spilling out.

He had his arm drawn back to throw a punch when he recognized her. He lowered his fist but still seemed pretty angry. "What the fuck is going on?" he shouted. "Where's Cade?"

"Gone," she said. "Cade and the Boogeyman. Both of them."

He put his rage aside for a moment—she could see it, like he was putting a mental bookmark at its precise location—and nodded. He looked at her, then behind her.

Robbie was still as a statue in the chair where she'd left him.

"Your mother?"

"In the secure room. But I think we're still in trouble."

He understood immediately. "The plane" was all he said.

Weaving from wall to wall because of the turbulence, he made his way to the flight deck. Candace followed.

The cockpit door flapped open with each juddering hit of another air pocket. Butler and Candace could see the bodies of the pilots, still in their chairs, heads lolling as the autopilot struggled to compensate for the hole blown in its hatch.

"Son of a bitch," Butler said, almost to himself. "He knew."

"Knew what?" Candace asked.

"Help me," he ordered. He began unstrapping the pilot's body from his seat. She didn't argue. Even though it was hardly the worst thing that she'd seen today, she still trembled like a leaf in the wind as she helped the agent pull the corpse out of the tiny space.

Butler sat at the controls. Then he sat for a long moment.

"Knew what?" Candace asked again, hoping to snap him out of it.

"Secret Service regs," Butler said without looking up from the control panel. "At least one agent on board the transport for the president or any dignitary is required to be flight-trained and certified in case of a need for an emergency landing." He sounded as if he was quoting.

"You can fly?"

"Air Force Academy '95," he said, eyes still on the instruments. "Cade knew. I'm the designated backup pilot."

Candace nearly went to the floor with relief.

"Don't celebrate yet," he said. "It's a big damn plane and I haven't done this in a while."

He strapped himself in, put on the headphones and looked back at her. "You might want to go back there and buckle up now. This is going to be a little bumpy."

CADE FINALLY RELEASED the Boogeyman when he felt something in the air shift around them both. He spun away in free fall. He piled into the earth just a fraction of a second behind and thirty feet away from the spot where the Boogeyman left a crater.

Cade lay there and waited. He couldn't do much else. Fortunately, he didn't have to. His homing beacon on his phone had been activated while he was still in the plane. Provided it really was as durable as the government contractors promised, it should still be working.

Cade listened carefully. He believed his ears might be the only things on his body that weren't broken. For a long moment, nothing. Cade feared the whole ruinous effort had been a waste.

Then he was rewarded with a sweet sound. Sobbing.

The Boogeyman, as broken as he was, was still alive, crying in pain, at the bottom of its crater.

If not for his shattered jaw, Cade might have smiled.

FORTY-FOUR

We are all the president's men.

—Henry Kissinger

Cade couldn't see anything, although he was sure his eyes were open. He felt hands lift him onto a stretcher and into a vehicle. The sun was mercifully cut off as the doors closed.

Zach was there, too, his voice uncharacteristically firm as he gave orders.

"Just run it like you would a regular IV. Open all the way. Both arms."

"How?" another voice shot back. "I can't even find a vein. Christ, look at this mess."

"Just stick the needle anywhere. Go ahead."

Cade felt a slight pressure somewhere beneath one elbow, then the next, as the IVs poked into his parchment-dry flesh.

"I still can't get any— Oh my God, what is that? What is that? It's like—"

"Holy shit," another voice said. Medics, Cade realized.

Zach had brought Army medics for him, too. Cade heard the other man gag.

"Christ almighty, it's like worms—"

"Told you," Zach said. "You don't have to find a vein with him. His veins find you."

Cade felt the life flowing back into him. It was all too familiar to him now. This wasn't the thin gruel of animal blood. It was human.

Cade began to sit up. He wanted to use his rapidly returning strength to tear out the needles and get back to dying.

But Zach stopped him. "Cade, I'm ordering you not to move. Stay perfectly still. You understand?"

Cade didn't have enough power to fight the order or his oath at this moment. He lay back and let the blood do its work.

"Uh, the bags are empty already."

"Plenty more in the cooler," Zach said. "Keep it coming."

Cade heard the medics replace the blood packs. His body began sucking down more. Shapes began to appear in his vision—dim and fuzzy, but definitely light emerging from the darkness.

"Oh my God. Are his eyes growing back?"

"Just keep changing the bags," Zach said.

Cade found he could speak again. The blood was now running through his veins, providing the raw material for his vampire physiology to rebuild itself.

"Did you—" he began.

"He's in the other ambulance," Zach said. "I brought

two. They've got a much larger team in that one. They're doing everything they can. But he's alive right now."

"It," Cade corrected, more out of habit than anything else.

"Oh, get bent, Cade. The only thing that should be coming out of your mouth is 'Thank you.' You know where I had to get the blood? You should be honored. It's his personal stash."

Of course. Air Force One carried a supply of a half-dozen pints of the president's blood, withdrawn and stored at regular intervals, in case he ever needed an emergency transfusion or surgery while traveling.

That meant the plane had probably landed safely and nearby. Cade regretted the deaths of the Secret Service. But he knew that the First Family was safe.

And really, that was all that mattered.

Cade had only one other question.

"Why?"

Zach knew what he meant. Cade wanted to know why Zach would choose to save him even with the evidence that he'd fed on a human being again. There was no way to deny what Cade was now. And Zach was taking some of the blood on his hands.

"You're not done yet," Zach said, voice oddly weary. "Or at least, we're not done with you."

Fair enough, Cade thought. Another pint slid into him. Muscle restrung itself around freshly knit bones. He heard the medics change out the bags once more.

"Oh my God, oh my God," one medic kept saying.

"Hey," Zach said. "Knock it off. He doesn't like anyone taking the name of the Lord in vain."

Cade's lip curled. Then he closed his eyes and fell instantly asleep.

He was safe.

EPILOGUE

Q: Hey, Lanning! What do you think of Seabrook's new ad?

A: The one where he says he's not afraid of America? He might reconsider if he took a walk on Chicago's South Side at night. [LAUGHTER]

BILL O'REILLY: That was Dan Lanning, the president's campaign guru, two days ago with some reporters on the press bus. Only he might not be laughing now. The Curtis campaign is under siege from protesters who say Lanning's comment was racist and inappropriate. Several groups, including the Republican National Committee, have called on Curtis to repudiate Lanning's statement and fire him from the campaign.

We're going to take a look at the fallout from that so-called joke and we're going to ask the hard question: should the president fire his campaign manager for an off-the-cuff remark? Is this a sign of deeper problems inside the Curtis campaign? And finally, can the president get reelected without Dan Lanning? We'll be right back, on the *Factor*, right after this.

—*The O'Reilly Factor,* October 25, 2012

WOLF BLITZER: More bad news for Daniel Lanning today. The Rev. Al Sharpton has called upon President Curtis to fire Lanning to quote—"make an example of him"—end quote for his comments about Chicago and minorities. Sharpton's comments come just a few hours after Jesse Jackson's Operation PUSH threatened to withhold Get

Out the Vote activities on Election Day if Lanning is not fired.

—*The Situation Room,* October 26, 2012

(THIS IS A RUSH TRANSCRIPT, provided for the information and convenience of the press. For questions, contact THE RED-EYE—CNBC2.)

TOM KOEBEL, REPUBLICAN CONSULTANT: I don't think Lanning meant to be racist. I think if you look at his comment in context, you'll see a not very veiled threat against Skip Seabrook. He was basically saying, come to Chicago and our goons will kick your ass.

JANE GARDNER, DEMOCRATIC CONSULTANT: Oh that's ridiculous.

TOM KOEBEL: Try telling that to Al Capone's victims, Jane.

JANE GARDNER: What?

—*The Red-Eye,* October 26, 2012

Daniel Lanning, a consultant to President Samuel Curtis's 2012 reelection effort and the manager of Curtis's previous run for the White House, has resigned after remarks seen by many to be offensive.

Political observers said despite his decisive victory in a debate against Governor Waverly "Skip" Seabrook earlier this week, the controversy threatened to derail Curtis's momentum heading into the last week of the campaign.

Lanning said only he was resigning to spend more time with his family.

—"Under Pressure, Curtis's Longtime Aide Resigns," the *New York Times,* October 27, 2012

October 27, 2012, Shawnee County Morgue, Topeka, Kansas

Helen's eyes snapped open. She blinked the gumminess out of them and realized they'd never been closed. They'd dried out, staring open and empty while she'd been unconscious.

She tried to bring her hand up to wipe the bleariness from her vision, but all her limbs were more reluctant than usual. She realized she was naked, lying on cold metal in a bright room.

She'd been inside enough of them to recognize it immediately: a morgue. She was in a morgue.

It all came back to her in a rush: that little fucker Barrows. He shot her. He'd actually shot her.

With great effort, she raised her head. It wobbled as if attached by a Slinky. Something crunched, something else squished and squirmed. It took everything she had, but she got up and swung her feet to the floor.

A toe tag scraped on the tile with every step she took.

She found a mirror. A good portion of the back of her head had been blown out, along with much of the back of her neck and most of one side of her jaw. In their place, the undying side of her body had spread like scar tissue, growing like a tumor to fill the bloody gutter carved by the bullet.

Her hair was also a mess.

Her head wobbled dangerously again as she began looking around for something to wear. Helen thought she'd have to get a neck brace or C-collar until the new tissue solidified. It was still soft and spongy, but she knew it would harden like bone. For now, she used her good hand to rummage in a drawer of surgeon's scrubs.

She barely noticed that her body was moving much more smoothly by the time she got dressed. Or that any pain she had felt was completely gone.

Helen thought only one thing, over and over, like a mantra:

All right. Now I'm *really* pissed.

OCTOBER 28, 2012, THE RELIQUARY,
WASHINGTON, D.C.

Cade stood at the bottom of the stairwell as Zach entered. He stepped back to allow his handler to pass. Zach walked to his desk and put down his bag as if this were any other night.

Cade waited. Zach would not face him. Zach's head bowed. Cade heard him sigh heavily.

"What do you expect me to say, Cade?"

"I honestly don't know."

Zach gave a short bark of laughter at that. "Yeah. Me either. I went over and over it. And I still don't know how to handle this. I know why you did what you did. I just don't know what it means."

"It means the same thing it always has. I did my job to the best of my ability."

"You used the president's family as bait," Zach said. Cade noticed he'd aged visibly. The lines around his eyes were deeper.

"I knew where the Boogeyman would be. I put myself in the best position to stop him."

"They could have been killed."

"They would have been killed," Cade said, "if I hadn't been here."

"You left the president," Zach pointed out.

"I knew he was in no danger. And if you'll recall, no one ordered me to go with him."

"I know," Zach said. "I told you, I've been thinking about it."

"Then what's got your britches in a bunch?"

Zach didn't even smile at Cade's language. He wasn't going to be distracted. "You played me. I thought we worked together. You could have told me sooner. You should have told me sooner."

"You're wrong," Cade said. "I couldn't tell you. I had no choice. You would have objected. Or you would have insisted on being on the plane. Either way, I could not take the chance."

"I think that's my decision, not yours."

"On the contrary, it is exactly my decision. The president is not the only one I have to protect."

"Putting me in an enclosed space with Helen Holt is your idea of protecting me?"

"She was the lesser of two evils. Quite literally. I thought you could handle it."

"Am I supposed to be flattered?"

"You're supposed to be breathing. That's enough for me."

Zach laughed again. "I never believed it before, but politics is exactly the right field for you. What about Megan Roark?"

"She's dead. The president isn't."

"Is that all that matters?"

"To me? Yes. I gave you the video because I knew your answer might be different. Obviously, it wasn't. If that causes you discomfort, I can't help you. All I can tell you is: I fulfilled my oath."

"That's pretty fucking cold."

"I'm a vampire, Zach. You had your chance to be rid of me. You made your choice."

"Yeah," Zach said. "I hope neither of us lives to regret it."

October 29, 2012, Madigan Medical Center, Fort Latham, Washington

Tom Fowler didn't like working at the Army Medical Center at Fort Latham. He didn't like Washington, didn't enjoy the gloomy weather, never really understood why the locals were always going on about the natural beauty. It all looked like trees to him. He much preferred sunny spots and once held half-assed plans to retire to the desert somewhere. But he didn't have much choice now. This was the only place anyone would still call him "doctor."

To be fair, Fowler was a pretty good surgeon when he had his license. He rarely ever hurt a patient. But he was an addict—drugs, gambling and sex, usually at the same time. (In retrospect, his decision to take a position with a hospital in Las Vegas was probably not the smartest move.) The Nevada medical board was lenient with him for his first half-dozen offenses, but then he began supplying drugs and meth precursors to the local mobsters to pay off his gambling debts. The DEA got involved, and he was stripped of his credentials and forced to testify against his former clients. He was completely screwed: no way to earn a living and a bunch of pissed-off criminals with heavy grudges against him.

One of the feds involved in his case gave him a number. He called it, and within a week he was at Madigan, new ID, crisp new medical license, new job in the trauma department.

Sometimes he thought he might have been better off taking his chances with the mob. Most of the time, he dealt with soldiers and their occupational hazards: bullet wounds, broken limbs, burns—normal, comprehensible problems. But up on the restricted floors, Madigan was home to some deeply weird shit, and he was called in to stitch up the messes.

Those late-night calls, the patients without names, the quarantine rooms, the inexplicable injuries. He'd once been part of a team that operated on two men who were fused together at the waist, like Siamese twins, except these men were not related and they came in screaming and even their uniforms had melded together, the cloth blending seamlessly into one garment where they met. He still had nightmares about that.

And then there was Cade.

Cade showed up a few times every year. He always just appeared on the restricted floors and the military staff there deferred to him. Nobody ever called him anything but "Cade" or "sir," so Fowler had no idea of his rank or agency. Fowler assumed he was with some high-level, off-the-books operation with unlimited funding and a mysterious acronym. But the only thing Fowler knew for sure: Cade scared the hell out of him, and he had no idea why.

Cade stood over the newest patient's hospital bed when Fowler entered the room. Fowler suppressed a shudder.

Cade didn't look up. He watched the patient very closely while checking the restraints that kept him pinned to the bed. He didn't even glance at the TV on the wall, which was more than Fowler could manage. As Cade had ordered, it was set on a constant loop of porno flicks. Nothing too kinky. Fowler had seen a lot worse. Just 24/7 fucking.

Fowler didn't know why that was so important. Or why the heavy-duty straps were on the patient, or why the medical staff could never remove them without armed guards present. After all, the patient had been in a coma since his arrival.

"Mr. Fowler. What's your prognosis?" Cade asked without turning around. He never called Fowler "doctor," and Fowler never insisted on the title with him.

Fowler picked up the chart and checked the latest notations.

When the patient had been brought in, nearly every bone in his body had been shattered. Whole limbs were nothing more than bone splinters and meat. All of his internal organs were damaged, and he teetered on the edge of death. An emergency trauma team had kept him alive, somehow, on a plane from whatever catastrophe had left him in that condition. Fowler and the other surgeons had worked around the clock to save him. Just to get him stable was a feat. If Fowler were allowed to bet by the terms of his agreement or his sponsor, he wouldn't have placed money on the man surviving another twenty-four hours.

Now, miraculously, the patient was healing. Although he still needed a respirator to work his lungs for him, he was improving steadily.

"Amazing," he said to Cade. He still couldn't get over it. "He just keeps getting better. The tears in the cardiac wall are gone. Liver, kidneys, spleen—all functioning again. We're seeing his blood counts rise and EEG response. Even the bones are starting to knit."

"How long before he wakes up?"

"You have to understand, this is all freakishly abnormal. It should be impossible. I can't guarantee he'll continue to recover at this speed."

"Just assume he will."

"That's my point. He won't. Even with this kind of

recovery, his brain was mush. His nerves were severed. You are looking at a slab of meat in pajamas, do you understand? He will never—"

Cade wasn't looking at him. He was looking at the patient's hand.

Fowler followed his gaze.

The patient was moving his index finger. It was only a small twitch.

"That shouldn't be possible," Fowler said.

And yet the patient's finger was definitely twitching, the small bones in the hand visibly moving below the cuff of the restraint at his wrist.

"How long?" Cade asked again.

Fowler looked at him, then back at the patient in his bed. Fowler realized this was another one of those things he would never truly understand. At least, not if he was lucky.

So he did the math as fast as he could in his head, cleared his throat and answered the question. "At this rate, he could be off the respirator in a week. Walking again in six months."

Cade nodded.

"Then I'll be back in five," he said.

Cade leaned over the bed and spoke to the patient. "Better get used to the view. This will be your home for a long, long time."

Then he reached over to the patient's hand, grabbed the twitching finger—and snapped it like a twig.

Fowler jumped as if the muffled crack of bone were a rifle shot.

"I promise," Cade said, and then walked out.

Fowler lingered a moment longer. He was sure his ears were playing tricks. It seemed like the patient, with his jaw wired shut and his lungs pumping only because of the tube forced down his throat, made a noise.

Impossible. But Fowler could have sworn it sounded like a scream.

OCTOBER 30, 2012, COLUMBUS, OHIO

Wyman entered the private office at the back of the president's bus. Curtis looked up and dismissed the Secret Service agents with a nod.

If Butler were here, he would never allow it. Secret Service procedure demanded one agent be in sight of the president at all times when away from the White House. No exceptions. Not even for the bathroom. But Cam Butler was on personal leave in Oregon at the memorial service for one of his agents.

So the agents on the job, after hesitating, nodded to the president and left the small office.

As soon as they left, closing the soundproofed door behind them, Curtis greeted him. "Les," he said.

"Sam," Wyman responded. It was the first time he'd spoken to Wyman directly in months. They had a campaign appearance scheduled for later today. It was inevitable that they would have to talk sometime, but Curtis seemed to be trying to get through the rest of his term with as little of Wyman's presence as possible.

"I wanted to tell you this face-to-face," Curtis said. "We were friends once. I honestly believe that. But I don't trust you anymore, Les. I'm not sure I ever should have."

Wyman nodded. He'd seen this coming. "I suppose you're asking for my resignation."

"No," Curtis said. "It's too close to the election. And you know that. In a couple of months, during the transition, you're going to announce your retirement. I'll be able to appoint a replacement."

"You seem awfully certain that you're going to win," Wyman said. "I've seen the poll numbers. I'm not sure you should make that assumption."

"You haven't seen the latest internal tracking from Ohio," the president said. "Even Seabrook's pollsters are pulling the same results. The bus tour worked. I've got a double-digit lead there now. He can't claw it back; not in two weeks. It's all going to come down to election night, but the race is more or less decided now."

"In that case, you seem awfully certain I'm going to go along with this."

Curtis looked grim. "I don't know for certain what you've been doing behind my back, Les. If I did, we'd be having a different conversation entirely. But I know enough. I know about the encrypted phone in your office. The Secret Service has monitored the transmission bursts from you to numbers that can't be traced. Unfortunately, they only noticed this recently. If you hadn't been with me when those creatures attacked the White House two years ago, I'd suspect you might have even been involved in that. But they nearly killed you, too."

Wyman said nothing. He felt his chest unclench. Curtis still didn't know. He couldn't even suspect all that Wyman had done, because it was too unthinkable that his own judgment would be so flawed as to have an enemy in such a close position to him. Or perhaps the president simply didn't want to believe Wyman would deliberately cause the deaths of so many people. After all, as he said, they had been friends once.

Either way, it was a blind spot that hid Wyman quite nicely once again.

"I don't know if you've been aiding the traitor in our midst or just covering up for him," Curtis went on. "Hell, for all I know, you've just been saying shitty things about me to the press behind my back. But somehow, I suspect it's worse than that. You don't use hardware like that just to leak an anonymous comment to the *Washington Post*. Whatever you're doing, I've allowed it to continue for too long. You have to go."

Wyman shrugged. "I still haven't heard anything that tells me I should just give up," he said. "Even if you really believed what you're saying, you'd never let anyone prosecute me. It would taint your administration forever. You'd go down in history as a dupe and a fool. And if the Republicans hang on to the House, you might even be impeached. Who's going to believe that you didn't know what I was doing? You're either blind or an accomplice."

"You're right. About all of it," Curtis admitted. "I never want this to become public."

"So maybe I'll stay where I am. After all, this is a pretty good job. And there's room for advancement."

Curtis gave him a bitter smile. "And maybe I'll send Cade to visit you after sunset."

"Cade can't touch me. I'm an officer of the United States government."

"Treason is a death penalty offense. Cade doesn't need a judge and jury to pass sentence."

Wyman managed to look hurt. "You'd really have him execute me? Just like that?"

"Let's not find out. There's still a good man inside you somewhere. I know it. Do the right thing, Les. Walk away from all this. Think of it as a second chance."

Wyman was genuinely touched. Even if it was bullshit, Curtis sounded like he believed it. He sounded like he wanted there to be a shot at redemption for his vice president, despite all he'd discovered and all he had to suspect.

And without the Shadow Company at his back, maybe Wyman really did have a chance now.

Wyman nodded. "I guess I have no choice."

"It's for the best. You'll see that."

Wyman held out his hand. "I suppose you're right," he said.

And Curtis, being who he was, stepped forward to take it.

Wyman raised his other hand and sprayed the president in the face with the tiny aerosol can.

"Les, what the hell—?"

He stopped and opened and closed his mouth, as if tasting something foul. Then he looked up, his eyes suddenly wide. Curtis, skin flushed with sweat, fell to his knees.

Wyman, trembling almost as badly as the president,

forced himself to slow down as he carefully peeled the plastic glove from his hand, using it to wrap the small spray can. He'd been sure he was going to get some on himself even as he was terrified it wouldn't work.

He'd received the poison from the Shadow Company years ago but never felt brave or desperate enough to use it. He found it in the back of his safe a few days ago and checked it for an expiration date. Was it possible for something like this to go bad?

Apparently not. Curtis was on his knees, face gray, unable to breathe or move.

The poison was a molecular variant of nicotine. It passed through the skin on contact and flooded into the bloodstream, causing massive constriction of the arteries. At the same time, it triggered a huge release of adrenaline, causing heart rate and respiration to spike.

The result: instant heart attack.

He put the glove and the can inside the hole in the lining of his suit jacket pocket. Only the most thorough searcher would find it there, and he didn't expect to have anyone tear apart his clothing.

Wyman couldn't quite believe he'd really done it. He'd been carrying the toxin around with him for weeks, like a seventh grader with a condom stuffed in his wallet, both anxious for and dreading the opportunity to use it. But when he knew Curtis was about to dump him, there was nothing left to lose.

Now he pushed himself back into action. If this was going to work, it had to look right.

Still shaking like a leaf, he hurried behind the desk,

moving around Curtis's pain-racked form. His hands trembled as he searched inside the desk drawer for the hidden pack of smokes. He took it out, and the smokeless ashtray, and then lit one of the cigs and quickly puffed it to life.

The poison looked no different from the ordinary ingredients of a cigarette on any toxicology screening. President Curtis's one bad habit was about to catch up with him in a very ugly way.

While Wyman fumbled with his props, he wasn't watching Curtis. The president knew he had one last chance. On his knees, clutching the desk like a lifeboat, he focused all his strength on the panic button across the desktop. All he had to do was tap it, and the Secret Service would kick in the door and catch Wyman in the act.

He strained, reaching, reaching

Wyman saw the president's hand just in time. He grabbed Curtis's wrist, holding it like a snotty Kleenex.

Curtis's body went limp then. He had nothing left.

Wyman shoved, and the president rolled gently onto the carpet.

Wyman took a glance at himself in a mirror on the wall. He was covered in flop sweat, face etched with terror. This was how he should look, he decided. Not guilty, but frightened—for his friend, his boss and the nation.

Nobody would question him too closely. He was the Vice President of the United States.

He looked again at Curtis on the floor. Correction: he was now the President of the United States.

Wyman took a deep breath and hit the panic button himself.

A siren blared. "Hurry, hurry," he screeched into the desk intercom. "It's the president— My God, I think he's dead."

ZACH LOOKED at the e-mail again on his pad. He'd tried to drag it to the trash several times. But he always brought it back and clicked it open again. It read:

Zach,

You were right. I don't think I can be in your world.

Love,

C.

THEN HE SWITCHED over to another window: H2OMG!, a new Hollywood gossip blog. The lead item read, "First Daughter Hooks Up with New Boy-Toy." He'd been staring at that one for a while.

Ours is not to reason why. Now he understood why Griff always said that.

"You're reading it again," Cade said from his position across the room, typing at the Reliquary's PC.

Zach sighed. Cade had been back from Madigan for a day. Zach was still pissed, but they were speaking again. He wasn't sure giving Cade the silent treatment was the vampire's idea of punishment, anyway.

"That's annoying, you know?" Zach said. "I don't monitor your Internet usage."

"I'm sure you have better things to do."

"Oh, come on. I'm not supposed to be insulted? This guy isn't even on network TV. She dumped me for someone on basic cable, Cade."

Cade tensed. Zach could feel it: a shift in the vampire's demeanor that charged the air like static. It usually meant violence was imminent.

"No," Cade said.

Then a siren blared. It was earsplitting, like something left over from an air raid in World War II. The lights in the Reliquary dimmed and flashed.

"No," Cade said again.

Zach noticed that the desktop computer was scrolling text down its screen. His own pad had dumped the windows he was looking at and replaced them with the same rolling chunks of information.

He recognized them: Secret Service emergency codes.

SINATRA DOWN . . . SINATRA DOWN . . . EN ROUTE OHIO STATE UNIVERSITY MEDICAL CENTER . . .

Then the newswires broke in as well.

PRESIDENT SAMUEL CURTIS REPORTED DEAD . . .

Zach looked up at Cade, stricken.

Cade was looking at the screen, reading it as fast as the information scrolled down.

"Cade," he said, and realized he couldn't hear his own voice above the wailing siren. "Cade," he said again, yelling this time.

Cade hit a button on the wall. The siren died suddenly.

Cade did not turn around.

"What the hell was that?" Zach asked.

"Alert system. Installed after JFK."

"Not what I meant." Zach realized he was still yelling. He didn't care. "The president—"

"Heart attack."

The words stunned Zach. He realized he was sitting down. On the floor. He'd missed his chair somehow.

For an absurd second he wished the president were here to deliver the news, like he did with Zach's father. Then he felt the chasm open up inside him.

After everything they'd done—everything they'd fought—it didn't seem possible. His mind simply couldn't accept it.

Apparently, neither could Cade.

He finally turned and showed Zach his face. His fangs were fully bared. His eyes were blood-red slits in a mask of fury and pain and hate.

It was the most terrifying thing Zach had ever seen.

"God damn it!" Cade bellowed, and smashed his fists through the computer. He tore the button for the siren off the wall. Something shorted out and the lights flickered and went dead.

Zach couldn't see Cade in the sudden darkness. But he could hear him. Display cases and relics shattered as he plowed through them, leaving broken glass and splintered wood in his wake.

Zach was grateful he didn't have to look at Cade's face. The only light left in the Reliquary came from the screen of his pad, now on the floor next to him.

The last update scrolled past: VICE PRESIDENT WYMAN SWORN INTO OFFICE ABOARD AIR FORCE ONE . . . LESTER WYMAN BECOMES THE 45TH PRESIDENT OF THE UNITED STATES OF AMERICA . . .

Zach and Cade had a new boss.

Judging by the howls of rage, Cade already knew.

ACKNOWLEDGMENTS

I've been the recipient of a great deal of kindness since the first installment of Nathaniel Cade's adventures was published. The names here are only a small sample.

Many thanks to:

My peerless and patient agent, Alexandra Machinist; Rachel Kahan; Ivan Held; Victoria Comella; Tom Colgan; Patrick Fitch; my mother and relentless publicist, Carol Whiteman; Bryon Farnsworth; Amanda Rocque; Philippa Roosevelt; Vin and Emily Rocque; Megan Underwood Beattie; Lisa B. Jenkins; William Heisel; Britt McCombs; Richard Feliciano; the legendary Beau Smith; Beatriz Chantrill Williams; Elizabeth Pontefract; Carrie Hoff; Tom Alfaro; Eric Almendral; Leslie Klinger; John Connolly; Lucas Foster; Gregory Veeser; the College of Idaho; Bridget Butler and her son Camden; and Fountains of Wayne for the clip-on tie and rub-on tan idea.

The map illustration is by Eric Almendral.

Special thanks to Peter Levenda, author of the Sinister Forces trilogy, and Jonathan Vankin and John Whalen, authors of *The 80 Greatest Conspiracies of All Time*, for their gracious permission to quote from their books. For anyone looking for clues as to the real secret history of America, I recommend starting with them.

And as always, thank you to Jean, and Caroline, and Daphne, for being the reason why.

The ultimate secret. The ultimate agent.
Nathaniel Cade returns.

CHRISTOPHER FARNSWORTH

THE PRESIDENT'S VAMPIRE

A Nathaniel Cade Novel

For 140 years, Nathaniel Cade has been the President's Vampire, sworn to protect and serve his country. Cade's existence is the most closely guarded of White House secrets: a superhuman covert agent who is the last line of defense against nightmare scenarios that ordinary citizens only dream of.

When a new outbreak of an ancient evil comes to light—one that he has seen before—Cade and his human handler, Zach Barrows, must track down its source. To "protect and serve" often means settling old scores and confronting new betrayals . . . as only a centuries-old predator can.

facebook.com/AuthorChrisFarnsworth
facebook.com/ProjectParanormalBooks
penguin.com

M1136T0712

The Ultimate Secret. The Ultimate Agent.
The President's Vampire.

From author
CHRISTOPHER FARNSWORTH

BLOOD OATH

Zach Barrows is a cocky, ambitious White House employee—until he's abruptly transferred and partnered with Nathaniel Cade, a secret agent sworn to protect the president. But Cade is no ordinary civil servant. Bound 140 years ago by a special blood oath, Nathaniel Cade is a vampire. On the orders of the president he defends the nation against enemies far stranger—and far more dangerous—than civilians like Zach could ever imagine.

"Inventive." —*The New York Times*

"[An] action-filled debut." —***Publishers Weekly***

facebook.com/AuthorChrisFarnsworth
chrisfarnsworth.com
penguin.com

M993T1011